M.C.

Praise for Laura Renken

Night Shadow

"Hooks you from the beginning. *Night Shadow* has it all: wonderfully warm and complex characters and a page-turning plot. Don't miss this one." —Patricia Potter

"Laura Renken is a master storyteller. *Night Shadow* is a spellbinding combination of spark and sizzle that leaves you breathless and satisfied. A true Platinum read." —*Bridges Romance Magazine*

"This swashbuckling pirate adventure is the real thing. Not since Kathleen Woodiwiss's early work have I been so excited about a novel. Impossible to put down." —*Old Book Barn Gazette*

"Laura Renken has penned another delightful read. *Night Shadow* is a remarkable story of forbidden love. With each family secret revealed Ms. Renken draws you deeper into the lives of her characters, and leaves you eagerly awaiting her next book. Keep an eye out for this author . . . she's amazing." —Addicted2RomanceBooks.com

"Renken's voice is fresh and e̶x̶c̶i̶t̶i̶n̶g̶ ... are three-dimensional a̶ ... making for a read y̶ ... for a swashbuckling ... can empathize with a̶ ... *Night Shadow*. Newc̶ ... ̶nitely an author to watch." —*Scribes WorldReviews*

(Turn the page for more rave reviews . . .)

My Lord Pirate

Golden Heart Finalist for Best Long Historical Romance
2001 Dorothy Parker Reviewer's Choice Award Finalist

"Positively sublime . . . the plot is tight, the action mesmerizing, the characters a blast to witness. Brava!"
—*Romantic Times* (Top Pick)

"The best book I've read all year . . . Ms. Renken weaves a story like no other. Her heroic characters come to life and invite you on an adventure that's so breathtaking it leaves you aching for more. Passion and piracy, loyalty and love, *My Lord Pirate* delivers it all with powerful panache. This one's so much more than just a 'must-read.'"
—*Bridges Romance Magazine*

"Waves of thrills as unpredictable as the battles and storms on the high seas make *My Lord Pirate* a spectacular story. It's sensual, tantalizing, and luscious." —*Rendezvous*

"Ms. Renken's characters come to life and jump off the pages. She's put a new twist or two into the classic pirate story that readers will be sure to enjoy. Don't miss the chance to read her new book." —*Old Book Barn Gazette*

"*My Lord Pirate* [is] a thoroughly entertaining read."
—*Romance Reviews Today*

"A fast-paced seventeenth-century historical romance filled with nonstop action and a sense for the locale that will leave readers feeling sea breezes. Readers will fully welcome Laura Renken, who provides a brisk tale filled with deep and complex characters, into the fold."
—Harriet Klausner

"I was highly impressed with this marvelous pirate novel. I highly recommend this book. It is a must-read."
—Kathy Boswell, *Kathy's Faves and Raves*

Heart of the Condor

Laura Renken

JOVE BOOKS, NEW YORK

HEART OF THE CONDOR

A Jove Book / published by arrangement with
the author

PRINTING HISTORY
Jove edition / July 2002

Visit our website at
www.penguinputnam.com

ISBN: 0-515-13335-3

A JOVE BOOK®
Jove Books are published by The Berkley Publishing Group,
a division of Penguin Putnam Inc.,
375 Hudson Street, New York, New York 10014.
JOVE and the "J" design
are trademarks belonging to Penguin Putnam Inc.

PRINTED IN THE UNITED STATES OF AMERICA

10 9 8 7 6 5 4 3 2 1

This book is dedicated to my wonderful younger brother, John Herring, who refused to allow blindness to become a handicap. You are my inspiration.

Big Sis

Chapter One

West Indies
1692

"*Por favor*, Don Gabriel. You cannot do this," the young ship's master pleaded, his voice barely audible over the surf. He ran along the beach to catch up with Gabriel's long-legged stride. "*Él es peligroso*. There is a price on El Condor's head. They will hang you if you are caught."

Stopping just beyond a pool of moonlight, Gabriel brought his gaze to the sky. The sun had set hours ago. Music floated out to sea and vanished in the darkness behind him. Somewhere life was in full swing. And he stared across the crescent bay toward the mountain that overlooked the island like an almighty godlike sentinel.

Gabriel Cristobel de Espinosa y Ramírez, the former *Almirante* for the New Spain treasure fleet, had never flinched in the face of battle, never lost his courage or run from anything in his life.

Yet he almost did so now.

A wave broke on the sand and raced up the beach, over his boots. "Give me a week to find her," he said to the man standing beside him with a parentlike reluctance to let him go. Behind Gabriel eight battle-hardened men waited at the oars of a longboat. Moonlight sculpted the sandy terrain. He could pick out the path that led up the rocky hill. Frowning, he scanned the length of the beach. Coconut husks littered the sand. If he could see such detail, then others could see him equally well.

"Take the ship to the lee side of this island and wait for seven days." He started walking. His boots slapped the water.

"This is foolish and mad. You can write a letter. Can you not?"

No, he could not.

"Surely your sister can read."

"Dios," Gabriel swore. And he was not prone to blaspheme.

Damp hair lay over his brow. He stopped and awaited Stefan to catch up to him, but his frown faded when all he confronted was concern in the other man's eyes. Gabriel didn't understand his old lieutenant's loyalty, or that of the others who'd remained to serve him when he'd been stripped of his command. He looked at the man who'd become as close to a friend as he'd ever had, and felt his chest tighten.

"She may not want me to find her. But I have to try."

"Can you blame her? You once had her husband and brother-in-law imprisoned. She is probably afraid to let you near them for fear that you will all kill each other."

"¡Santa María . . . !"

"That was not so long ago that anyone here would forget," Stefan persisted. "Even if you have."

"I have forgotten nothing."

Gabriel stood with his feet braced slightly apart as if he rode the bow of his ship. With his black breeches tucked into his boots and beneath a black jerkin, he gripped the hilt of his heavy sword. He dressed more like a dandified pirate than the nobleman he was.

His mouth curled in disgust. He'd spent his life ridding the seas of predators—Englishmen and Frenchmen alike—who combed the Main with a palpable hatred for Spaniards and an unquenchable thirst for gold. *Sí*, he'd once ordered his sister's husband and brother-in-law imprisoned, long before the two had become her family. And he would not hesitate to do his duty again if they raised arms against Spain.

"Let me go in your stead," Stefan argued. "I will find her and bring her to you."

"No." A rare trace of humor laced Gabriel's voice. Like the

other men present and in disguise, Stefan no longer wore the uniform of Gabriel's old command. From the tops of his bare feet, past canvas breeches and a red-and-white-striped shirt, his ship's master looked every inch a cutthroat. "I couldn't risk it," Gabriel said lightly. "Her husband would put you out of your misery at once. I do not have so many friends that I can carelessly throw them away."

When his jest failed to crack his former officer's serious facade, Gabriel felt his grin slide. He turned to look at the town that was nestled just below the mountain. He was never any good at humor and was embarrassed that he'd allowed it to warp his dignity.

Nervousness had made him vulnerable in a way he'd never felt.

But the need to see his sister touched him like the prod of a hot iron, branding him with something he hadn't felt since he'd watched his father die. Emotions were as foreign as tears, and it was ironic that life had brought him full circle back to the boy he once was, where he again questioned the values and goals that forged the very steel of his being. Indeed, what was life worth to a man who had lost his honor?

Next to his daughter, his sister was all that he had left. He needed to mend the rift that separated them, to reclaim something of their past before he went to Spain to fight the charges brought against him by the West Indies tribunal. Whatever the verdict of the impending court-martial, he didn't want to leave this earth never having told her that he loved her.

"Enough discussion. Go now." He edged the shorter man back toward the longboat. "You keep my ship out of the way of pirates and nasty Frenchmen. I would not wish to start a war."

"Sí," Stefan grumbled beneath his breath. He turned away. "Are you not already a thorn in His Catholic Majesty's royal ass?"

Eyes narrowing, Gabriel let the remark pass in the spirit it was given, or perhaps because Stefan was correct. Either way, he'd surely grown soft to allow the insult to slide at all. For he loved Spain, and would not see her insulted by any man.

Leather creaked as he perched one foot against a rotting log. Leaning an elbow against his knee, he watched his men take the longboat out to sea. Watched until the darkness swallowed them, as it swallowed everything, until all that was left was the smell of a tropical night.

The wind chased the moon behind the clouds and brought his gaze to the sky. The salty mist mixed with the smell of rain and cooking fires that drifted on the breeze from town. Straightening to his full height, he looked toward the mountain and the village that clung precariously to its rocky foot. The serrated edginess returned to his mood.

He was past due to arrive in Spain. He had a woman awaiting his return. Someone who would be a mother to his daughter. And he was a thousand leagues away, on a French island that granted asylum to English pirates, looking for a star in a sky filled with darkness.

"Blimey, Lady Sarah. How do ye tell a weed from the real thing?"

Sarah turned her head toward the feminine voice and smiled brightly. Cori rarely picked her brain about anything that had to do with real life. "Smell," she said succinctly, "and sometimes touch. If the leaves are fuzzy, they're definitely weeds."

Cori sniffed. "Seems to me I'm committin' a sin. I'd be thinkin' Father Henri would allow all God's creatures to thrive."

The sun beat down on Sarah's head, and she readjusted the kerchief that bound her long hair. Other than her family and Father Henri, Sarah Drake loved two things in life: a good plot of dirt and singing. As she thrust her hands into the thick rich humus where she grew her treasure of vegetables, she sang the little ditty she'd picked up from Father Henri's newest neophyte. Cordelia Sheldon, or Parrot, as most people called her because of her fiery red hair, had actually served on a real pirate ship. Dressed as a boy, she'd wandered the ranks of deprivation with complete freedom, until Sarah's oldest brother, Talon, had discovered that a girl roamed among his freebooters and at once tossed her into a convent. Cori was so completely naughty and wicked that Sarah had wanted to be her friend at once. She'd become Sarah's source for worldly lore.

Cori had also taken on the role of Sarah's eyes this past year. Sarah was blind, and would never see outside the high stone walls behind which she lived.

Moving down the row of squash, Sarah idly broached what was foremost on her mind. "Father Henri said he caught you kissing Jaime in the stables again."

"Aye." Cori sighed with a dramatic flair. Her skirts rustled as she moved, and Sarah could tell that Cori was wearing her fancy floozy dress. Probably the same one she had worn when Father Henri caught her kissing that morning. "I 'ad to spend the day on my knees in prayer," she said. "And now I 'ave to pull weeds. Tomorrow I'll be moppin' for me penance."

"Someone has to keep the place clean, I suppose." Sarah smiled. "What would we do without all of your indiscretions?"

"Aren't ye wantin' to know what it was like with a man? The kissin' part, I mean?"

Sarah leaned toward Cori. "Of course not!"

"Well, ye pucker yer lips just so—" Two hands shaped Sarah's mouth until she felt like a fish. "Then ye touch yer lips to his."

Sarah breathlessly awaited the next revelation. "Then what?"

"Then nothing. That's it. A kiss."

Her lungs deflated and she went back to the soil. "That hardly sounds worth scrubbing floors for."

"You would know the difference, no doubt?"

She shrugged. "Kissing is obviously overrated."

"And you bein' twenty." Cori sniffed. "'Tis a bloomin' shame you've been so deprived. It's not normal."

Sarah sat back on her heels, miffed by the slight. "I don't feel deprived."

"That's because the only men in yer life are your brothers and Father Henri. And who'd wanna kiss that old geezer?"

"There's Jaime," Sarah pointed out, keeping her voice offhand.

"Aye, he's a fine one, he is," Cori dreamily admitted. "He's seen things, too."

"Like what?"

"Jaime served on the *Dark Fury* beneath yer brother Talon. What pirate worth 'is salt hasn't *seen* things?" she whispered.

Sarah reached the end of the squash row. Sweat dripped in her eyes and she wiped the back of her hand across her brow. "I don't want a man," she boasted, clearly a superior sentiment over Cori's wanton lust.

Cori made a rude noise. The sky grumbled overhead as a late afternoon thundercloud pressed down on the island.

"Besides, even if I did, who would want me?"

She was blind. No one would ever understand that she wasn't helpless.

"If you ever left these walls, ye'd be shocked at the menfolk what would answer that question. You've not seen yerself, Lady Sarah. Yer more beautiful than Madonna herself."

"Shhh," Sarah hissed. "'Tis sacrilege to be so bold."

"Father Henri already told me, I'm going to hell, so I can be as bold as I wish."

Despite her shock, Sarah laughed. "I have no wish to be so bold as you. Nor to see myself. Or ever leave these walls."

"Then why haven't ye taken yer vows?" Cori's voice was suspicious.

Sarah fidgeted with the hem on her smock. "I'll take my vows soon," she whispered, dusting her hands off on her lap. A large plop of rain smacked her nose. "Father Henri keeps me busy enough at the infirmary." She couldn't tell Cori that Father Henri was also the reason her vows remained unspoken.

She'd been devastated by his decision last year, but she knew now that she hadn't worked hard enough and, in time, he would see that she was a valuable asset to the community here.

Dismissing the subject, Sarah climbed to her feet. "'Tis suppertime soon. I'm going to bathe."

"It's unnatural, yer fancy fer washing, milady," Cori complained. "And soap ain't gonna cure what ails you, no matter how hard ye scrub."

Sarah lifted her chin. "Perhaps you should worry about your own soul," she offered. "Mine is safe, and I wish to keep it that way."

"Hah!" Cori laughed, her voice fading as she left the rectory yard. Thunder grumbled overhead. "Nothing is safe," she called. "Yer doomed like the rest of us mortals. Ye just haven't met your pious match, sweet Sarah."

Pious match, indeed!

After Cori left the yard, Sarah sagged. Sometimes Cori required too much patience, even for a saint, which some accused Sarah of being. Working her way over the mounds of soil, Sarah reached the cooling shadow of a tree where she'd set her walking stick. It wasn't there, and she inched forward to the wall.

Cori was wrong when it came to assessing Sarah's life. She wasn't pious. She'd spent the last eleven years working to make the correct choices, trying to inspire admiration in those who chose to shun rather than befriend her. She wanted to be good, not because she was afraid of being bad, but because she had nothing else to offer.

An unwanted sigh left her chest. Laying her palms against the moss that formed in the cracks of the wall, Sarah touched her cheek to the cool stone and welcomed the wall's invisible embrace. She hadn't always been blind. But a part of her mind knew that beasts lived outside the darkness. Her terror of the light isolated her from her peers.

The church bell tolled the supper hour, and Sarah pressed her forehead against the wall to fortify her resolve. Somewhere horses moved as if their hooves were muffled.

The sound caught her unawares.

Sarah knew every noise in this compound. Feeling for a crack in the wall, she laid her ear against the broken stone.

Horses were definitely outside these walls. She smelled rain in the air and something else: the ugly essence of unwashed bodies. Perhaps Father Henri had visitors.

But why would they hide their horses off the main road that led to the rectory? Especially where the animals would be unprotected from the approaching storm. Occasionally her oldest brother, Talon, came in from his plantation and left his horse outside the back gate. But Talon bathed, he had more respect for an animal than to leave it exposed, and neither one of her brothers were on the island.

Sliding her hands along the wall, Sarah took a cautious step.

A twig cracked from somewhere behind her.

She spun. "Cori?" she called after a moment.

Cori liked pranks but she'd never done anything cruel. A shudder passed over Sarah. "Cori, if that's you, this isn't funny."

The nervous wind caressed her face. Dropping to her knees, Sarah crawled over the ground, searching for her walking stick. And her hand contacted human flesh.

"This be no joke, Lady Sarah."

With a gasp, Sarah jerked away from the male voice. "Yer comin' with us, milady."

"Get away from m—" A filthy hand slammed over her mouth, muffling her cries. The stranger had known her name. And he spoke in English. Very few people spoke anything but French on Martinique.

Terror filled her. Fighting wildly, she bucked and flailed her arms. Her fist connected with a jaw. Someone swore— first in Spanish, followed by a rasp in English. A rag was shoved into her mouth and a canvas bag thrown over her head before a man tossed her over his bony shoulder.

Her arms trapped by her captor's grip, she couldn't pound his back. Her hair, upended over her head, caught in the sword slung at his side She tried to kick out. An arm crudely tightened on her backside, and with every jaunt, the breath left her lungs. Her heart pounded frantically. Her breath was harsh in her throat. She couldn't breathe.

Two hands grabbed her beneath the shoulders and lifted her high into the air. Her back scraped the stone wall. They were taking her outside of the walls. Away from Father Henri. Panic infused her limbs. She kicked her legs.

Somehow she spit the gag out of her mouth. But she couldn't scream. Wouldn't scream. A long-ago voice warned her to be silent. Her very life depended on her silence and she wanted to cover her ears.

"Close your eyes, Sarah." Momma's words. *"Don't look. Whatever happens, don't open your eyes."*

The mantra filled her with terror and, for an awful moment, she froze as if time were carved in stone and not something that lived and breathed around her.

A man wrapped an arm around her to pull her over the

wall. His palm fondled her breast, and he spoke in English, whispering crude words in her ear.

With a furious sob, Sarah bit down through the canvas sack. She grabbed on to his upper arm like a wild dog. The bag tasted like garlic, dirt, and the bile of fear. A man's curse penetrated her terror. He jerked away. She was suddenly falling backward off the wall. Something clipped her head. A tree branch splintered beneath her spine. She hit the ground. A burst of colors filled her head. Beautiful colors. Horses stomped and huffed.

And then she heard another voice.

Just at the edge of her consciousness. Different somehow than the men who spewed curses. More ominous for the dangerous tone in his words. But he spoke in Spanish, and the security she'd momentarily felt vanished in the blackness that covered her.

Forcing air into his lungs, Gabriel pulled his gaze from the figure lying beside the stone wall. The girl had taken a nasty fall. Pale limbs showed where her skirt had torn. Feeling rage tighten his body, he held his sword at his side, his dark gaze meeting that of each of the four men who'd whipped around to face him. After two days on this miserable island, a substantial bribe to a local fisherman had brought him to this priory. Though his purpose here was not to rescue maidens, to see one sorely abused sparked him to violence.

A ghost of a smile formed. "The *señorita* doesn't appear interested in your company." He spoke in perfect English.

One man had stringy dark hair, a compatriot who'd clearly strayed. The others were English sea dogs. All had missing teeth. Gabriel recognized the dangerous breed. He'd hunted men like this for most of his life. A grapnel dangled from one man's gloved hand. This was how they'd scaled the high stone wall into the courtyard.

Why would four pirates risk their necks to steal a woman when there were many to be had in town?

The men sliced their gazes to and fro as if expecting an ambush. Gabriel watched for the moment they discovered he was alone and erroneously began to assess their coup. Armament bristled from leather baldrics that crisscrossed their

chests. He'd already made the decision to kill the first man
who reached for a pistol.

The tallest Englishman stepped from behind the others,
only to be stopped by the dark-haired man. A shadow crawled
over the ground as an ugly cloud moved across the sun. "He
will kill you, *amigo*—"

"Pah." The bony Englishman brandished his sword. Canvas breeches reached his dingy calves. "The Spaniard is one
man. We are four."

"Are there four men standing before me?" Gabriel put
himself between the men and the unconscious girl. "I had not
noticed."

The coxswain snorted. "You dare insult us, Spaniard?"

"I expect English pirates to attack women. They are easy
prey." The black hilt of the heavy sword felt comfortable in
his grip. "See what you can do against someone who fights
back."

Two men launched their attack. They were careless and
untrained, displaying pitiful examples of swordsmanship.
Gabriel ducked beneath their attack and on strong legs rose to
meet their assault. He did not intend to engage the barbaric lot
in a long fight. Steel slashed steel. Using their ruthlessness to
his advantage, he parried easily, giving both men little time to
contemplate what remained of their future. His blood
pounded, and he fought now not out of any need to save the
girl but to rid the earth of four putrid cankers. Rain began to
fall. He stepped inside their circle of attack and swung his cutlass, splintering their blades.

Their sudden terror aroused the horses. The hilt of one
sword flew end over end, cracking against the wall. Gabriel
leaped aside as the third man foolishly attacked. With one ri-
poste, he ran the man through with his sword. The dead pirate
collided with the back end of a horse. The panicked mare
reared. In their frenzy to escape, the other horses fought the
tethers that held them to a low tree branch, scattering leaves
and twigs as they broke free. The Spanish pirate took off after
the horses into the sugarcane fields.

Gabriel faced the remaining two cutthroats. Noise from the
other side of the walls began to filter through the heavy silence. A bell tolled an alarm. The pirates turned on their heels

and followed in the wake of their accomplice. Gabriel sneered
at their cowardice.

A rustling movement spun him around.

The girl was on her feet. Her breath coming fast, her fist
gripping a stout branch, she faced him like a vengeful warrior
angel. She was missing one white slipper.

Gabriel's sword lowered. His gaze swept the length of her.
She'd ripped the canvas bag off her head. Alabaster hair
spilled over her pale shoulders to her hips in a tousled mass of
ethereal silk. Dirt streaked a white smock that framed her simple white dress. But there was nothing simple or plain about
her. Her chin was tilted in defiance. Her liquid eyes were a
stark contrast to the black fringe of lashes that only served to
intensify their iridescent silver.

Thunder rolled across the sky and the clouds suddenly
opened. He presented a bow. *"Señorita?"* His voice sounded
harsh, as if someone had laid him across a rack and began to
turn the wheel. Rain spilled over them and plastered her hair
and dress to her body.

He was still staring at the priceless vision when she swung
the branch and hit him square in the head.

Chapter Two

"Is he . . . secured?" Sarah demanded.

Rain had turned the ground to a fleshy bog. Mud sucked at her feet as she stumbled to keep up with the retinue. Jaime would find her other shoe tomorrow. Right now she had other concerns.

She'd take no chances with this outsider. He'd already regained some portion of his wits. Enough to grab her by the hair and threaten to throttle her. It took three stable hands and a screaming Cori to subdue him. Even injured, he'd proved a formidable adversary: a man who had no qualms about defending himself to the death.

Sarah tried to carry his cutlass. Raking the wet hair out of her face, she dragged the distasteful weapon. Jaime had told her that another man lay dead nearby. Skewered by this very blade.

But why?

She didn't understand what was happening, except this Spaniard was a threat. Until Father Henri returned, she would keep him tied.

"Are ye all right, milady?" Jamie took the heavy sword and passed it to someone else.

Sarah leaned her head against his shoulder and let him lead her out of the rain. Their feet slapped in the mud and she lifted the torn hem of her skirt. Other than Father Henri and her brothers, he was the only man she'd ever befriended. But his knobby shoulder was no pillow for her head, and she finally pulled away. "I think I'll live," she said.

"Yer brothers would 'ave my heart if I was to let anything befall you. They told me to watch over you."

"Where have you taken the Spaniard?"

"He's bleedin' somethin' bad."

Sarah leaned a hand against the slippery wall. The thunderous rain could not cleanse the memory of those men's filthy hands on her. Brutal men who would have kidnapped her. Men who knew her by name.

But one had stood apart from the others. One who had spoken flawless English. She closed her eyes and fought to regain her equilibrium. After she'd felled the Spaniard—she should never have allowed herself to touch him.

Sarah pulled her shoulders back. "Take me to him."

"He's not talkin', milady. And he'll most likely wrap 'is hands around yer throat again if ye be gettin' too close."

"I want to know why he tried to kidnap me. I must know."

"Maybe he wasn't the one," Jaime suggested.

"He spoke in Spanish. I heard him speak, Jaime. We don't know who he is for sure. Do we?"

Grumbling, Jaime took her by the elbow and led her into the pebbled courtyard. A creek, now filled with rain, rushed over her feet. Saint Mary's was more than a convent. Christened *sanctuary* by those who entered within these hallowed walls, Father Henri's stone compound reminded her of a castle fortress. The rectory, church, and living quarters for young ladies were all housed within these walls, along with the school and infirmary at the other end of the compound. Surpassing even political boundaries, Father Henri welcomed all who needed care. His vision had built Saint Mary's into a hospice that welcomed men of different creeds and countries. People from other islands often came to seek medical help. She could not turn the Spaniard out.

"Who is with him now?" she asked.

"Cori. He is in the infirmary. You should await Father Henri's return before attending him."

Sarah straightened her spine, determined to face this problem as her brothers would. There was no place for fear in her heart.

"Has anyone identified the dead man?"

"No one has seen him before."

Jaime helped her up the wooden stairs that led to the infirmary. He guided her across the floor to the back storage room. Rain pounded on the roof like tiny pebbles. Water rushed over the ground outside, and Sarah inhaled the scent of wet earth and thatch.

She thought of the Spaniard. She remembered his single spoken word to her. Now that she was able to think clearly, she recognized that his was not the deep voice of a man bent on murder. Or at least it wasn't until she'd cracked him over the head.

"Bring me water and rags," she told Jaime. "Then send a man into town. Find Father Henri."

Sarah walked into the small windowless chamber. Heat from the day had gathered in the damp floorboards and walls. No man deserved this kind of prison. "Jaime—"

The door slammed shut behind her. A hand grabbed her throat, propelling her against the wall. The Spaniard had escaped!

The scrape of a chair sounded. "Ah, *señorita*"—his voice was hot against her wet cheek—"we meet again."

Pounding on the door vibrated the room. He'd shoved a chair beneath the door latch and barricaded her with him inside the room.

"Let . . . me go!"

"Have you sent for the authorities?"

Her fingers tried to dislodge his hold. He was not brutal but neither was he soft, and his strength was not affected by the wound on his head. "I would not wish to mar such flesh, *sí*?" His tone was alarmingly indifferent. "But I will if you fight me."

"Where's Cori?" She clung to his grip. "What have you done to her?"

He leaned against her almost as if he couldn't stand upright. "*Sí*, the red-haired witch. The one with the big mouth." His lips touched her temple. "Perhaps I have killed her."

"I . . . I don't believe you."

"Yet you had me tied like a pig for slaughter."

"Obviously not tied enough."

The press of his body against hers was like honed steel. "But then that is what I do best. Escape. And ravish reckless

women who walk into rooms without looking behind doors."
She could almost hear the half smile behind his words. "What
is this place?"

"Sisters of . . . Saint Mary's," she rasped.

"Un convento." His grip on her throat relaxed. He pulled
back, and she felt his eyes go over her face then dip lower,
down her body. She could barely breathe. He smelled of rain.
"You are *inglesa*."

"And you are Spanish," she shot back, convinced now that
he must be a spy and would probably be hanged if he were
caught here. "Yet . . . you speak English as if you were born
to the tongue."

"I would know my enemy, *señorita*. As should you."

"I *have* no enemies."

His hand traced her collarbone and tilted her chin. "I think
that you have at least three who are still alive."

Doubt made her hesitate. His grip remained dangerous
enough to keep her from fighting. "Who are you?"

The heavy door cracked, splintering the chair.

He slumped against his elbow. "If I ask for sanctuary, will
you grant it?"

She pressed her hands against the hard wall of his chest.
"I . . . no," she said, vexed by his bold request and her sudden
lack of charity. He had no right to wrap his hand around her
throat, tell her that he'd killed Cori, and then request asylum.

His shirt was wet and sticky with blood. With a gasp,
Sarah traced her hands around the firm ridge of his bristled
jaw. Rain matted his hair. A thick forelock hung into his eyes.
She probed his temple and found the wound on his head.

She suddenly felt a fierce ache for what she'd done to him.
"You need help."

"I was told . . . that my sister might be known here." His
voice had grown weaker. The pounding behind her grew
stronger. "She is married to . . . Marcus Drake. She will vouch
for my character."

"Liandra?" Her heart lifted. Marcus's wife was this man's
sister?

Sarah adored Liandra. Her brother had married the Spanish doña last year. But they didn't live on this island as her
eldest brother, Talon, and his wife did.

Suddenly, she realized who stood before her. "You are . . . El Condor?" Horror choked her voice.

Liandra's brother was a feared champion of Spain. A heartless rogue who by all accounts deserved the enormous price the French had placed on his head. "Ah . . . *señorita.*" His voice faded to a cynical rasp. "My life is in your gentle hands."

Then he slid to the floor at her feet.

"Don Gabriel Espinosa! Here! On Martinique!" Spine erect, Sarah sat on the bench nearest the altar. The air smelled of beeswax tapers and the fragrance of sandalwood. Familiar scents that put her trembling thoughts at ease.

As long as Sarah could remember, she'd come to this place in the chapel to seek strength in prayer and to glean understanding from chaos. The stones were cool against her bare feet. Damp hair clung to her torso. It was nearly dawn and she had yet to change.

A familiar mountain of fluff suddenly bumped her leg. Sarah lifted the huge cat, chastising the old tom for invading the church. But she was glad for the company and, rubbing her wet cheek against his fur, quickly found solace in his presence.

Sarah loved this old cat. He'd been crippled as a kitten, much as she'd been when she first arrived here almost twelve years ago. The cat had thrived beneath her care and, through the years, had honored her with his loyalty. On a weekly basis, much to the chagrin of the other residents, he dropped rats and mice at her doorway. Once, he had brought her a snake.

She'd healed people, too. Touched their bodies. And mended their spirits. Father Henri said that her blindness had given her a special gift. But a man's mind held the greatest power to heal. 'Twas not magic that cured, but knowledge of the inner soul.

If only she possessed the power to heal herself.

Movement near the doorway lifted her head. Her grip tightened on the cat. She recognized the warm swish of Father Henri's robes.

"He will live, *chère.*" The words followed the soft tread of his feet. "Though he will be in pain for the crack on his skull."

"He should suffer a little, should he not?" She lifted her chin, angered that her hands shook. "What is a little pain to the man they call the Vulture?"

"He saved your life, Sarah. This I know for a fact."

Her thoughts flew in a wild dance of confusion. She wasn't listening. Don Gabriel was dangerous to her. Her blood hummed with his presence inside the walls of her precious sanctuary. Everything about him unbalanced her.

"He was naught but an innocent bystander," Father Henri said. "He went to Talon's plantation looking for his sister and found her gone. A fisherman directed him here. To you, Sarah."

She nuzzled her cheek against her cat. "I only know that . . . that I should have hit him harder," she whispered.

"It is not our place to judge any man."

His voice told her that he was disappointed in her. But she didn't feel contrite. "It's fortunate for him that Talon and Marcus are gone."

"Your brothers will have to manage their anger someplace else. As will you. As long as he is here, you will treat him with Christian accord."

"Nay. I will not *treat* him at all."

"Your brother's wife deserves more from you. Do not disgrace your family by shunning someone Liandra cares for."

Sarah squirmed. She had an awful feeling this was headed to a place she didn't want to go. Father Henri had a way of turning ill will into the most broad-minded benevolence. Especially under duress.

"I do not have the time to nurse him," he continued. "And after today, I'll not be sending any of the sisters to tend him. He is your brother's family. And you will treat him accordingly."

The cat wiggled. Sarah let him go. The traitor. He was abandoning her, too. "'Tis unseemly." She fidgeted with her smock. "How can I defend myself if he chooses to strangle me?"

"Don Gabriel has seven stitches in his head. I've given him something to make him sleep through today."

"Seven?" Her head suddenly started to ache.

"It will not be safe for him outside of these walls and I don't want him leaving until I know he can walk out of here."

Sarah couldn't understand why Father Henri was making her do this. She rubbed her temples. The men who had tried to take her knew her name. But something else frightened her, too. Father Henri didn't understand her torment. She didn't understand these strange feelings herself. She only knew that a premonition told her to stay away from Gabriel Espinosa.

And Sarah always followed her instinct.

"Don't make me serve him, Father. I cannot."

"Jaime will stand guard at his door should you need help."

"If you're trying to inspire my confidence, you're failing. Gabriel Espinosa has no fondness for the English and for the Drake name in particular."

Father Henri laughed. "Can a hero of Spain who braves the dangers of discovery to seek out his sister be evil? I think not."

Sarah groaned at such inconclusive logic.

"You are like my own child, *chèrie*." He sat beside her. "The only danger to you comes from outside these walls." His voice grew serious. "Those men knew you. No one here could have stopped all four of them. But he did."

"Then you think they will be back?"

His silence frightened her. She clutched his leathery hands, wrinkled with age, almost frail, and brought his fingers to her cheek. "Why, Father? What do they want with me? What have I done?"

Gently disengaging his hand, he stood. "Until I find out more, you stay near Don Gabriel. Do you understand?"

So that was it!

Don Gabriel was to be her shield. Father Henri seemed to think the man capable of leaping the moon.

But Sarah had sudden reservations and, despite her animosity, did not wish to put Liandra's brother in danger. Besides, intuition told her that Gabriel wouldn't appreciate the role of archangel any more than she wanted to be sheltered by him.

"Perhaps someone should ask Don Gabriel first what he thinks."

But Father Henri didn't answer.

The church doors swung open, then closed. A gust of humid air swirled around her calves. He'd left her.

As was her custom, Sarah suffered in silence. She didn't know how to fight the way Cori did. She didn't have her brothers' courage or the bravado of her two sisters-in-law.

She had only herself.

Grabbing her stout walking stick, she tapped her way out of the church, into the empty rectory, and found herself climbing upstairs to the room where they'd taken Don Gabriel. Compelled by reasons she didn't understand, she dismissed the old woman who slept in the chair beside his bed. With the heavy curtains drawn against the sunlight, the room remained cool. Thick stone walls guarded against the island heat.

The covers rustled, and Don Gabriel mumbled in Spanish. Sarah knew that he slept with the restlessness of a man drugged. For a long moment, as she breathed in the scent of freshly washed linens and laudanum, she stood above him, her feet rooted to the cool stone floor. Even in sleep, his presence remained formidable.

And her heart pounded with the chafed rhythm of the wind before a storm. For Sarah believed in fate. Nothing in life happened without a reason. Her path was forever molded by the external events that shaped her world; her choices lain out by a quintessential destiny that constantly surrounded her.

Don Gabriel had stopped an attack on her.

What would fate demand of her life in return?

Without conscious thought, she laid a palm over his heart as she'd done in the infirmary when he'd fallen at her feet. Her breath caught and held.

He wore no shirt now. And the sudden intimacy of her bare hand on his skin startled her. His corded flesh was firm against her palm. The life he led did not lend itself to softness. Or forgiveness. Taking a deep breath, she traced the ridge of muscle to the pulse that beat at his neck.

And her palm found a ragged scar. Barely discernible, it circled part of his neck. Only a noose could mar the flesh in such a way. She jerked back. A hand caught her wrist. Even half dead, this man possessed the strength to crush her wrist.

"I am not . . . so easy to kill, *señorita*."

"How did you survive?" she whispered.

"It happened long ago. They did not live . . . to finish the job."

No man had ever made her feel safe and terrified all at once. A skein of warmth snaked through her veins to where he touched her. "You boast so easily of murder?" she said, frightened by the ease with which he reeled her to him as if she were naught but a fish on a hook. If someone put a rope around his neck, it was probably with good cause. "And you lied to me about harming Cori. Is El Condor a man without any honor, that he would lie and kill with such ease?"

His fingers tightened on her wrist.

Then his hand fell away. And she was alone again with the silence. A silence she suddenly could not endure.

Sarah stepped away from the bed. Father Henri's warning gathered inside her and gave her pause. Curling her fingers into her skirt, she realized the ominous wisdom of staying near the Spaniard's side these next few days. But she didn't have to like it.

Gabriel stirred. A knock sounded on the heavy oaken door, and he realized that the noise had awakened him. *¡Ay yi yi!* His hand went to the bandage that wrapped his head.

Opening his eyes, he stared around the barren room, a mixture of surprise and confusion furrowing his brow. Dark hair hung over the bandage, and he was quick to dispel it from his gaze. He sat up. His hand fell on a nightstand that had been pushed against the narrow wooden bedstead in which he lay. Heavy brown curtains blocked the sunlight. Against the far wall, a wardrobe sat next to a painting of the Virgin Mother. The door clicked open.

A glance beneath the sheet told him he wore nothing.

"Are you awake?" A blond head peeked around the portal. Jesu, it was she!

The uncertain light in the room could not dull the color of her hair and eyes. Or the vague impression that she'd crept out of his dreams. Carrying a tray laden with a bowl of hot soup and bread, the silver imp stepped into the room. With a kick of her heel, she slammed the door shut.

Gabriel flinched. "*Dios,* I am now," he grumbled.

"'Tis good to see you up. The morning is already gone."

He watched uneasily as she set a cane beneath the Virgin Mother. Something else for the little termagant to beat him over the head with should the occasion arise. He hadn't seen her after he'd passed out at her feet. Had he? Someone named Father Henri and a deranged redhead wearing a red satin dockside dress had stitched his wound. Most likely they poisoned his grog with a sleeping potion afterward, which accounted for his near-unconscious state. That and his blasted headache.

"Who are you?" he asked the girl as she approached.

"I am to bring you your meals. As penance," she said contritely, "for bashing you over the head . . . and capturing you." Her smug tone hinted at a boast. He expected to see her limp. But she didn't.

Indeed, she walked tall. The top of her head would not reach his shoulder in height. But then he was taller than most men. Her braided hair lay across her shoulder. Directly into his soup. He frowned.

"Are you *really* a famous hero of Spain?" She breathed the words as if she were an overexcited schoolgirl.

Cautiously, he sat straighter against the knobby headboard. "No," he said.

"Oh, but Father Henri said you are."

Gabriel gritted his teeth. The good father would see him hanged. "Then I think he talks too much."

"He also said you are a noble creature by birth. Perhaps he has forgotten your history of warring on French and English ships."

Gabriel narrowed his eyes on the tilt of her strawberry mouth. She didn't wear the attire of a nun, and her hair was uncovered. It touched him as odd that the exemplary Father Henri would send a maid within arm's distance of the infamous El Condor. Especially one who looked ripe for the plucking. He glanced at the food with suspicion.

"Set the tray down," he said.

She did, and knocked a pewter mug off the stand. The contents spilled in his lap before he could catch either the cup or the tray. Soup sloshed over the rim of the bowl and burned his arm.

Dios, she was a walking disaster.

Snatching the edge of his bedsheet, he began to mop up the damage. She hastily knelt. "I'm so sorry—"

"Por favor . . ." he managed. Her hands probed the bed, and he grabbed her wrist in disbelief before she touched his naked thigh. "I can do this. Forget it."

Dizziness forced him to lay back in the pillows. He closed his eyes. "Perhaps if it wasn't so dark in here you could see better."

She promptly went to the window, and stretching her arms out like Moses parting the Red Sea, she whipped the curtains open. The sun beat into his brain like a mace. He swore an oath in Spanish.

"Is that better?" she sweetly inquired.

Lifting his gaze, he glared beyond her at the church steeple. "No, it's not better. Clo—"

"The view, I understand, is nice from here."

Bending over slightly, she unlatched the window. The plumeria-scented breeze entered, along with the noisy sounds of children playing in the yard below. A distant ship's bell tolled.

Sunlight limned her legs against the white dress she wore. Slowly, Gabriel settled back against the bedstead. His modesty was hardly at stake, and he was just in the mood to wage his own little war. His gaze loped over her backside. "The view will do," he said. "Especially if you continue standing in front of the light."

She jerked around. A blush stained her cheeks. Something dark stirred in his loins, arousing and annoying at once. She was not as aloof as she seemed, or worldly either. She folded her hands. "Father Henri gave you his room," she informed him. "He has never given any guest his room."

Her tone brought his eyes to her face. She was looking at a point over his shoulder.

"You don't approve?" he asked.

"You are El Condor. But you are also Liandra's brother and for that I will tolerate your presence here."

The mention of his sister's name sobered him. But before he could speak, the girl approached the end of the bed. "You will need new sheets."

With a yank, she jerked the top sheet off his body. He

snatched the end just before the breeze whipped over his naked thighs. His patience gone, Gabriel grabbed her busy little hands before she could pull out of his reach. He was not so weak that he couldn't take down a cocky English miss with a pouty mouth that didn't have the sense to stay shut. Her silken braid slapped him in the chin and he tasted chicken soup. She sprawled across the bed, entangled in his sheet and limbs. He hardly cared. Her impudence deserved worse.

"My sister is here?"

"Get off me, you . . . you Spanish lummox!"

He grabbed her hands and locked them above her head. A dark brow lifted. "You have something against Spaniards?"

"I have nothing against the Spanish. My very own mother was half-Spanish."

He looked at her doubtfully. Her petal-soft skin boasted of generations of English blood. Surely, the girl was misinformed.

"It is you that I find disagreeable," she continued. "Which is another reason I am forced to serve you. Father Henri deems my opinion . . . inappropriate."

She smelled of lilacs, and despite himself, he lowered his nose to her hair. "So, you are being punished."

"Very much." Her voice whispered over his cheek. She stared straight ahead like a virginal sacrifice.

Laughing to himself, he let his eyes wander down the length of her before bringing his gaze back to her face. The fearless little fool needn't have worried. He was loyal to another woman and would not stray. "What do you have against El Condor?" he said against her temple. "I have never attacked civilians."

Her chin lifted. "It is no thanks to you and certain others who destroyed our home that my brothers are still considered pirates. Now it seems that you and I are practically family."

Barely suppressing an oath, he pulled back in utter disbelief. "Your brothers are Talon and Marcus Drake?"

"You may call me . . . Lady Sarah," she commanded.

Gabriel raised his eyes to the ceiling. *Ay yi.* But his life was cursed. He lay back and kneaded his head. She shot off the bed like a cannonball. Even as he fought both passion and disgust, he managed some dignity. "Lady of what? The dead and the damned?" This angel was an imperious witch.

"My father was an English earl."

Pulling the sheet around his hips, he closed his eyes. "*Sí*, I know who your father was."

"You do?" She stared in dismay. "How?" When he didn't answer, her expression fluttered, then died. But Gabriel wasn't moved. He didn't intend to talk about her family.

Turning her back on him, she walked to the window. "You've wasted your time coming here," she said. "Your sister doesn't live on Martinique. Marcus is building her a grand home." She ran a finger along the windowsill. "I don't know where exactly. I only know that they are happy together."

Gabriel leaned back into the pillows. Her words took the anvil off his chest. He began to relax. "I did not know for sure."

"Did you know that she is going to have a baby?"

"Liandra? A baby?" A burst of pride filled him.

"Marcus sailed here only a few weeks ago on the *Dark Fury* and made the announcement. Talon left with his wife to help finish their house. That's why no one was at the plantation when you arrived. They are all gone."

"Why didn't you go with them?"

She fidgeted with her skirt. "I couldn't leave."

If he'd known his sister's condition sooner, nothing would have kept him away. Still, there was comfort knowing that Liandra had found peace in her life. He'd wanted to reassure himself that she was happy.

Sarah lowered her eyes and seemed to study her slim hands. "Was it so important to find her?"

Gabriel turned his head away. He suddenly felt tired. "I have been at sea too long. My reasons are of no import now."

"I'm sorry then," the girl said into the empty silence. She turned and made her way to the door. She fumbled for the walking stick. "And I'm sorry for knocking you over the head," she said to the wall. Her spine suddenly stiff, she turned. "I was told . . . I was told that you saved my life."

Gabriel didn't answer. He wanted only to move on now. To get to Spain where a tribunal awaited him.

"I'm sorry you got involved." Her gaze lifted with renewed determination. "But I'm not sorry for disliking what you are."

He'd never deemed such paltry sentiment important. So he'd not expected her words to touch him. "And what am I, *señorita*?"

She stood her ground, her gaze falling somewhere behind him. The tears that glistened in her eyes made her beautiful. "You, sir, are a murderer of dreams."

Chapter Three

A murderer of dreams.

Frowning, Gabriel turned into his pillow. But contact with the fair-haired snip had jarred him from his lethargy. He threw off the sheets. What did a Drake know about dreams anyway? They'd ravaged lives. Did Sarah even know the kind of men she defended?

Restlessness moved Gabriel from the bed to the window. Sunlight framed the church steeple like an absurd golden halo. Beyond the church, the bay glittered. He caught glimpses of ships' tall masts and French soldiers standing in sloppy formation near the beach. His eyes narrowed on the huge stone fortress that guarded the port.

Children's laughter drew his gaze to the courtyard below. A dozen boys and girls of mixed blood splashed in the stream, and for a moment as he watched them play, his thoughts strayed to the laughter of another child.

Pulling the window shut, Gabriel shut the drapes and turned back to the room. His sword lay in a black scabbard near the bed. Finally, he returned to bed and threw an arm over his forehead. His men would not be back to the island for three days.

Somehow, Gabriel slept. When he awakened, the curtains were thrown wide again and the lunch tray removed.

His frown fixed on the room. Fresh linens basked in a lump of fading sunlight at the end of the bed. Wrapped in the sheet, Gabriel sat on the edge of the mattress. As he waited for the dizziness to pass, a young man entered, carrying a tray and a bucket of water. When he saw Gabriel, his eyes widened.

"Yer awake."

Gabriel managed not to roll his eyes. The man's powers of observation were truly remarkable. "Where is the priest?"

The bucket banged against the door as the man stepped into the room. "Father Henri is checkin' about for the family of that man you skewered two nights ago," he cheerfully announced. "The one ye killed used to serve aboard the *Dark Fury* beneath Lady Sarah's brother, Talon. Only a fool what didn't value 'is bloomin' life would harm the Cap's sister. And him bein' gone, too."

"An old enemy?" Dragging the sheet around him, Gabriel moved to the window.

"Most likely a foiled ransom attempt," the man surmised.

Standing to one side of the window, Gabriel looked out. No one stood guard in the empty courtyard below. His gaze lifted to the bay. This place was about as protected as a dove in a nest of spiders.

"Ye can call me Jaime."

Gabriel turned. The lanky man warily watched him. His white shirt was clean. Canvas breeches ended at his knees. Sandals covered his feet. At Gabriel's silence, the boy blew a brown forelock out of his eyes. "I'm to stay outside yer door tonight."

Gabriel lifted a skeptical brow. "Am I to be beset by children carrying stakes while I sleep?"

"Lady Sarah said you could go into convulsions and die. For your sister's sake, if you choose to leave this room, we are to restrain you to your bed. Until Father Henri gets back that is."

His eyebrows slid upward. "Senorita Drake told you this?"

"Aye." Jaime set the tray on the table beside the bed. His sandals hugged the floor. "She said yer demented and will most likely kill us all in our sleep. Head injuries sometimes do that to men."

"Where are my clothes?"

The man looked around. "They're not here."

"*¡Ay de mi!*" Gabriel glared at the youth. Clearly, his intelligence was astounding for an Englishman. "I know they are not here. I want them back."

"Must be getting cleaned," Jaime concluded with a shrug. "They were covered in blood. Lady Sarah cracked yer skull open good."

Gabriel remained ominously silent as he watched the man bend and clean the floor where the soup had spilled earlier. The tawny sky cast an orange pall over the room. Gabriel was curious how an Englishman had found his way to Martinique, to this place.

But not curious enough to ask.

Casually, he strolled to the tray and lifted the silver dome. Steam wafted over his hands and the air filled with the scent of spices. His jaw tightened.

Recognizable only by its swirly tail, a rat, salted and stuffed with apples, basked in the delicious steam.

Jaime sat back on his heels and slopped the rag back into the bucket. "She said if ye be wantin' seconds to just ring the pulley bell at yer bedside. There's lots more where that came from."

Gabriel set the silver dome back on the platter. So the maid would play whilst the good father was away.

He'd eaten rodents before. But somehow the one she'd presented him seemed more symbolic. A gauntlet thrown. A reminder of his past actions against her brothers. Rats were the delicate fare of many a Spanish dungeon.

Fingering the tray, he brought his gaze to the sword. His pulse stopped. The weapon was gone.

He swiveled his head around to search the walls and shadows, his eyes narrowing with his racing thoughts. The twit would make him a prisoner in this stone relic guarded by women and boys barely out of swaddling clothes. The mocking jest was not lost to him. She had surely lost her brain. He stripped the bandage from his head, wincing as he tossed the bloody thing to the bed.

"I . . . know who you are." Jaime was on his feet now. The slop bucket dangled from his fingers.

"*¡Ay yi!*" Gabriel walked around him to the door. "Is there anyone in this godforsaken place who doesn't?"

"I mean, I've seen you before." Jaime drew him around.

His dingy toes curled around the ends of his sandals. "Years ago, when I served in the king's navy, we had the misfortune to meet you near Santo Domingo. You do not fight like other Spaniards."

Gabriel swept his gaze over the gangly man who would have been a child a few years ago. "Because you are still alive?"

"Because you are the best. The British captain was over-confident." He snickered. "We were a brigantine and a sloop. You destroyed the brigantine and set us all on the sloop to sail for Jamaica. England is fortunate that there are not more of you."

Gabriel remembered the skirmish. Seven years ago. A life-time in the career of a Spanish naval captain. His wife had been near to term, and he had been on his way to Hispaniola to share in the birth of their child. As the morning sun touched the sky, he'd come upon the two ships within Spanish waters. He had let them live because he'd been in a good mood that day.

He frowned. The memory pierced him. He'd taken great pains to rid his life of such alluring sentimentality. Lady Sarah deemed to call him a murderer of dreams. At least she'd had dreams. And he'd had his fill of her games.

"In case yer thinkin' about leavin'—"

His patience at an end, Gabriel stopped Jaime with an icy glare. "Where is the elusive Lady Sarah now?"

"She . . . has taken to her bed for the night, milord."

Crossing his arms, he leaned a shoulder against the oaken door. "And is lying not beneath a nun?"

"She is not a nun yet."

"So it is all right to lie?"

"Lady Sarah isn't bad." Jaime stared shamefacedly at his feet but his belligerent expression told Gabriel his loyalty lay staunchly with the girl. "She doesn't like you is all."

"Rest assured, *amigo*. The feeling is mutual." Securing the sheet at his hips, Gabriel turned and swung open the door.

"But yer not dressed!"

"*¡Caramba!*" He praised the rafters. "There is hope for you yet, Englishman."

Not so for a certain lady. The evasive Sarah Drake had much to learn about warfare with the infamous El Condor.

"Lud, you've not seen him, Lady Sarah!" Cori sighed, and Sarah thought the girl would swoon.

"Truly, Cori." Sarah dabbed butter on her bread and bit into the delicacy. The dining room was filled with the clatter of silverware against plates and the quiet rumble of feminine chatter. Father Henri had not returned from town, and Sarah had seized upon his absence as a reprieve. Managing to escape her responsibilities, she'd joined the rest of the sisters for supper. She leaned toward Cori. "Your heart is as fickle as the weather. I thought you were in love with Jaime."

"Jaime is a boy."

"He's older than we are."

"That doesn't make him a man," Cori scoffed.

Sullenly guarding her tongue, Sarah tucked her hair behind her ear. She'd never told Cori that Jaime was a secret fantasy. That during all the hours Cori had sneaked out to the stables for their secret trysts, Sarah had wished that she'd been the one who Jaime wanted.

Pushing her peas around her plate, she suddenly worried over asking him to take Don Gabriel his supper tray. Disobedience was not her forte, nor was cruelty. Yet she'd been heartless to Liandra's brother, and her unkindness troubled her. But everything she'd said to the Spanish don had been the truth.

Admittedly, something inside her had snapped. She'd not fully recovered since those men had tried to kidnap her. She battled a headache, and thinking taxed her mind. Her perfect existence had mutinied into prolific feelings of dissatisfaction. And Gabriel Espinosa's presence embodied her growing discontent.

Gripping her fork, Sarah speared a chunk of fish. "Perhaps if you find the Spaniard so pleasing, you can deliver his meals."

"You've been in a snit all day," Cori said with a sniff. "What's wrong?"

"I don't like being guarded like a prisoner here. I cannot go to the infirmary or the chapel alone."

The room suddenly grew quiet.

Sarah lowered her voice. "And I've been given duties to coddle a man who helped ruin my family."

This last statement seemed to fill the quiet dining room. Tittering followed, and like an ominous cloud, the silence that followed became thick with peril.

Cori spewed her wine. "Bugger all!"

Sarah's head snapped up. A silken thread of danger probed her senses and sent her heart racing.

"Milord." Jaime's voice. "You can't be comin' in here."

"*¡Fuera!* Out!"

Screams erupted. Chairs scraped. A scurry of feminine feet pattered over the floor like a stampede of mice. A door slammed, followed by a click. Someone had thrown the bolt.

Cori had not moved, and as Sarah listened to the approaching footfall, she felt her friend's nervous trepidation.

"We're not leavin' the likes of you alone with her a second time," Jaime declared.

A calloused finger touched her chin and pulled her face around. "Then perhaps the lady would care to return my sword and my clothes."

Feeling a hot blush crawl over her face, Sarah jerked away from his hand. To think that she'd lain with him on his bed that afternoon to the point of physical arousal. She remembered the way his naked body had fit against hers. She'd not touched him, yet his image shaped itself into a powerful dark force in her mind. Did he know she was blind?

"It's all right, Jaime," Sarah said, wishing to avert bloodshed. Despite its unchristian-like sentiment, satisfaction lurked deep inside. El Condor was known for his cool, calculated demeanor in battle. To have ruffled the great vulture's feathers was not an accomplishment that she took lightly.

"Don Gabriel is probably hungry. Jaime, please bring in wine."

"Stay," Gabriel commanded.

"Go, Jaime. And Cori, a clean plate will do for our guest."

"No, *señorita*"—the cool words were hot against her temple—"I do not wish to be poisoned in this place. I want my sword and my clothes back. *Hasta.* At once."

The sudden worry that he might leave riddled her with

doubt. Father Henri had made it clear that Gabriel would not be safe anywhere on the island. He certainly wasn't capable of traveling far with his head injury. She'd already made her point with him that afternoon. She didn't want to be responsible for getting him killed.

Sarah found her glass of wine and fidgeted with the rim. "I don't know where your clo—"

She never finished the words. Gabriel yanked her to her feet, and for the second time in two days, she was tossed over a man's shoulders like a sack of cornmeal. Only these shoulders were different. Stronger. He made the other man a mockery to his species.

Her hands splayed his corded back. She touched bare flesh! "Put me down!" Unlike two days ago, Sarah had no problem screaming. "You can't do this. What are you doing? *Jaime!*"

Coldly impervious to her pounding fists, he kicked open the glass doors at the back of the room. Mosquitoes assaulted her. Her hair dangled like a silken broom to the ground.

Cori laughed. Sarah lifted her head. If she could have gotten her hands on the girl, she'd have yanked Cori's hair out by the roots.

"If you wish to involve everyone else, you do so at their risk," Gabriel warned. He walked down the bank of damp grass. "I am finished playing your games. Where is my cutlass?"

"Are you going to torture all of us?"

The sound of rushing water alerted her. She stopped kicking. The creek coming out of the mountain was still high. What would he do with her? Throw her in the stream?

Water sloshed, and Gabriel tossed her in the stream.

The scream wedged in her throat. Rushing cold water sluiced over her. She came out of the creek disoriented and spitting furiously.

"Where is my cutlass?" the raging Jehovah demanded.

"I don't kno—"

He dunked her. She came up spewing water. "Beneath your . . . bed." Again he dunked her. "What?" she screamed when he let her up for a gulp of air.

"You still haven't told me where my clothes are."

"They're hanging on the line. Cori can show you where."

"My boots?"

She kicked out at him. "What manner of barbarian are you?"

He dunked her again. "A Spaniard," he said succinctly, after pulling her up for air. "A very nasty Spaniard."

Choking, she spit out a mouthful of water. "Your boots . . . are beneath your bed also."

With that he dropped her and she sank into the creek. Water sloshed with the angry stride of his feet.

"Don't leave here."

She heard him turn around. Struggling to gain footage on the slippery bottom, she could feel his eyes on her. The night air shivered over her sodden garments.

"Please . . ." She stopped short of an outright apology.

"Is that an invitation to stay?"

"I did you no harm." Her chin lifted. "I only wanted you to know what it felt like to be helpless."

In two strides, he sloshed back in the water. "I don't need your help to show me that, Señorita Drake."

Unable to keep the sudden tightness from her throat, she realized that short of his abominable reputation on the seas, she didn't really know this man. Except that he'd risked his life to come here and find his sister. He'd saved her life as well, but maybe he wouldn't have been so quick to act had he known who she was. Yet something told her she was wrong. Father Henri was wise indeed when he'd counseled her to caution. *Judge not, lest ye be judged.*

"I'm . . . sorry," she said, and this time she meant it.

He dunked her again. Swallowing a mouthful of water, she came up coughing. "Why did you do that?" her wet voice rasped.

"Suffice to say, *señorita,* you needed it. I would not want you to go soft on me."

His laughter followed him out of the swollen creek. The knave. She could almost see him strut, thinking that he'd bested her. Scraping an angry hand over the water, she dipped back into the creek and let loose a groan. He hadn't even had to torture her at all.

•   •   •

Holding tight to his makeshift attire, Gabriel scattered a gig-gling flock of neophyte nuns as he trudged half-naked back to the dining room and slammed the glass doors behind him. With an indignant Jaime on his tail, he grabbed off the table the pot of fish stew and a bottle of wine, and left to retrieve his clothes.

Once in his room, he threw the bolt on the pirate kid, and after dressing, lounged back in a comfortable chair to eat his meal. He was famished. After devouring the stew, he then proceeded to drink and ignore the pounding on the door. Gabriel wasn't in the mood to indulge the young man in a bout of fisticuffs and would wait out his temper. Meanwhile he gave his attention to the night and a full moon that blanketed the terrain outside with silvery light. It was the kind of night made for poets. A night that wreaked havoc for ships trying to remain hidden.

Impatient, Gabriel stood and walked to the window. His room was dark, which granted no impedance to his nighttime observations. Beyond the church steeple, he glimpsed the village. Lights sputtered with the breeze. A wall of stone encompassed the compound of thatch and rock buildings. Below, a courtyard filled the space that separated the rectory from the church . . . and his gaze fell at once on the girl sitting alone on the cobblestone rim surrounding the circular pool. A stone-carved angel with outstretched wings stood amidst the silvery spring, but it was Lady Sarah Drake who held his attention.

She'd changed her clothes. Her hair was wet, and he watched as she worked a comb through the flaxen tangles. The sudden discovery of her presence seized him as if he'd stepped into the light after a long night, and he found himself pressing closer to the glass, staring like a schoolboy in the throes of newfound lust. Somehow she had touched him, challenged his senses, and he responded if only to touch her effervescence.

He began to consider all the reasons her brothers would put her in a convent on Martinique, a French possession, and came up with no reasonable explanation. Why wasn't she married?

The thought provoked a frown. She was nothing like the

men in her family. He'd known each of them personally and fought them all in battle at one time or another during his life. He'd celebrated her father's death on the gallows and would not bemoan the demise of her brothers if they followed their sire's fate.

Yet even her relationship to them didn't deter his admiration for her spirit. He should not have found anything the least appealing about her. She was an obnoxious rendition of feminine pulchritude compared to her docile Spanish counterparts. He had not ever looked beyond his social caste for a conceivable bedmate much less at a woman who was only a vow short of becoming a nun.

That he actually idled over bedding her shocked him, and abruptly, he set down the wine bottle. He looked toward the door. The pounding had stopped. Gabriel walked over and threw the bolt. As anticipated, he saw Jaime sitting in the grand *sala* that was comfortably appointed with simple furnishing, not boasting of wealth as he'd so oft seen in other vicarages. Jaime sat on a leather chair, his legs outstretched and crossed at the ankles. He came to his feet like a shooting cork.

Crossing his arms, Gabriel leaned a shoulder in the doorway. "What is wrong with her?" he asked before Jaime lapsed into another dither. "Why is she here in a place like this?" Gabriel didn't have to explain who he was talking about.

With an elusive shrug of his shoulders, Jaime decided to settle for conversation over outright war. "Why does anyone come here? Because it's safe. That is until *you* arrived on the island."

Gabriel narrowed his eyes. "Safe from what?"

"She can't return to England or to her home on Jamaica. Her family still has a charge of treason hanging over their heads."

Gabriel shifted his gaze. He was not about to debate such a charge or the English policy that condemned pirates. "That still does not explain her presence here on Martinique."

"This place is recognized for its medicine. I only know that she was brought here as a child. After her parents were killed."

"Then she was injured?" His voice was a whisper.

"Lady Sarah is blind."

Gabriel's arms fell to his sides. He stared in disbelief.

"She was nine when brought here to this island from Jamaica. No one knows what happened to her. She remembers little of the first nine years of her life and nothing of the day the English soldiers raided her house. They say if not for Father Henri, she would have died from her injuries."

Jesu . . . Gabriel's gaze strayed to the window.

"You'll have to talk to Father Henri if you want more information," Jaime said as Gabriel walked to the window. "I only know that Lady Sarah is at home within these walls. She is a healer herself. People come from all over the islands to see her work miracles." He stepped into the room. "And *you're* upsetting her."

Gabriel paid no heed to the accusation. He could not believe that Sarah Drake was blind. He leaned a hand against the glass. Sarah no longer sat at the springs, and he was struck with a strange sense of disappointment, something far more than just being deprived of an admirable adversary.

Gabriel, more than anyone, knew the horror and loss of innocence: the kind that came from such an attack on one's soul. Hadn't he watched pirates kill his own father? Hadn't he endured atrocities at the hands of such barbarians? That Sarah would be such a victim sickened Gabriel to the core.

Closing his eyes, he realized Jaime was talking, and the moment was quickly eclipsed by the incessant ramblings of the Englishman.

". . . then two years ago, the Cap, her brother Talon, married Father Henri's niece. That's why the Cap lives here. That, and to be near his sister. Most of the rest of the crew from the *Dark Fury* stayed as well and live honest lives now."

"Beneath a French flag." Gabriel's lips tightened into a thin line of disgust. Nothing would ever make him fight against his country. The sentiment did not help to improve his black mood or draw his thoughts back from Sarah.

It occurred to him that the former *Almirante* of New Spain's treasure fleet, the famed El Condor, had not only been felled by a girl, but a blind one at that.

And he'd nearly drowned her in the creek.

He raised his gaze to the rafters. *¡Por Dios!* He was an ass.

A knock sounded on the door. Balancing a tray, Sarah entered. Gabriel slowly straightened.

"I hope I'm not intruding." Something about her expression told him she knew very well that she was. "I thought you might be hungry."

For several heartbeats, he stared at her face, a moonlit portrait in the semidarkness of the room. Her slumberous silver eyes were the color of mist. She was incredibly innocent and too provocative not to be dangerous.

And she was blind.

The unexpected kick in his gut pulled him taut.

As if sensing his gaze, she stood without moving. "Cori prepared this tray," she offered into the silence that followed her announcement, "if you're worried about being poisoned."

"He already ate, milady." Jaime's gaze bounced between them.

She shifted uneasily. Gabriel wondered if Cori had really fixed the food tray. Or if Sarah had used the tray as an excuse to visit his room at this inappropriate hour.

Only one thing would bring the abominable Miss Drake within a league of his presence. Suddenly Gabriel didn't want to hear another apology from her.

"Jaime, can you wait in the other room?" she asked.

"And leave the door ajar," Gabriel ordered.

"In case El Condor cries for help. You can save him," she added.

Gabriel lifted a brow. He barely had time to move the bottle of wine before she set the tray on the small round table.

Framed by the window and the picturesque moon sitting over the distant bay, Sarah straightened and seemed to find him in the darkness. "There is something that I came to say."

Without hearing her words, he studied her face. "You are blind."

Her back stiffened as if he'd struck her. "So I've been told."

"Why didn't you say something?"

"Perhaps I didn't wish to give my side the advantage. Where is the fairness in that?" She placed her hands on the high-back chair tucked against the table. "Are you disappointed?"

"I would not wish blindness on an enemy."

"You talk as if you'd rather be dead."

Gabriel didn't answer. He set the wine down beside the tray. Maybe he *would* rather be dead. He couldn't imagine himself utterly helpless in a world that slaughtered the weak. She made him uncomfortable, and he didn't like that.

"You're thinking that I am helpless." Defiance fired her expression. "Ah, yes." Her tone became suspiciously patronizing. "That's why you have seven stitches in your head."

Dios. "I have seven stitches because you *are* blind."

"It is you who does not breathe with your senses," she said. "You are more blind than I." At Gabriel's snort, her chin shot up. "I could tell you what this room looks like by touch, or the time of day by the smell in the air." She stepped in front of him. The top of her head barely reached his shoulder. She smelled of Spanish lilac: the kind that grew on iron trellises at his island home on Hispaniola.

Her palm touched his chest above his heart. Heat radiated from her fingertips. "I can even tell you what you look like."

He laid his hand over hers and pulled away. But did not let her go. The sleeve of her gown had fallen back to her elbow. "I already know what I look like, *chica.*"

"You stand over six feet tall," she said at once, then lowered her voice as if to share a savory secret. "That helps in your profession, I suppose. Intimidation. You probably strike terror in your enemies with your height alone."

Her brass astonished him. He ran his gaze up the length of her arm. His thumb rubbed the fragile bones and tiny veins in her wrist. "You should not be in here." His voice was softer than he intended.

For the first time, he noted the outdated dress she wore. The plain blue gown, too big for her slight frame, was not the garb of a future nun. He might have laughed at her ridiculous appearance but something in her carriage told him that she'd worn the dress for him.

"Clearly, you seem like a man imprisoned by his ideals and opinions," she said. "Are you afraid that I might prove you wrong?"

"You are impertinent," he whispered.

"Yes?" She smiled.

And at once, Gabriel was transformed by something ethereal, almost magical as she gazed up at him. "I have never been told that by anyone," she said, seeming to sober as she realized she'd strayed from the topic at hand. "Will you let me describe you or not?"

He opened his fingers and let her hand go. She stepped nearer. And he almost held his breath in anticipation of her touch.

Placing both her hands on his shoulders, she let her delicate fingers climb to his face. Her palms were soft against his bristled jaw. They moved into his hair, gingerly avoiding his wound.

"Your hair is black . . . like the starless night," she said softly, an evocative invitation to gaze at her lips. She stood on her tiptoes, stretching her torso taut, and Gabriel's eyes slid closed if only for a moment.

"That's not a difficult guess," he managed, unimpressed. Still, he didn't pull away. "Most of my countrymen have black hair."

Her hands stopped their magic. "My mother was blond," she answered, undeterred. "And she was of the finest Spanish blood."

Gabriel rolled his eyes. "Are you only half-blind then to know the difference between blond and black hair or what a starless sky looks like?" He fingered a strand of her hair.

"I have not always been blind." The admission startled him. "When I was a little girl . . . I remember that we lived in a big, white house. I've seen the blue sky. And rainbows in the mist. I used to play on the beach. I remember everything I've ever touched."

He waited for her to tell him more, as if it were of importance to him to know what had happened.

"Your eyes are as black as your hair," she said quietly, continuing with her avid exploration. Her hands touched his face.

"A common trait for a man with black hair."

"Your teeth are white."

"A guess."

"Your breath"—lifting on her toes, she sniffed the air around his mouth—"smells sweet, which tells me that you use a mint brushing stick as a regular habit. Besides, Cori is quite apt to swoon over you. What man with brown teeth is comely?"

Despite himself, he grinned at her ridiculous logic.

"Your hair is groomed, which tells me that you are wealthy enough to afford a chamberlain or whatever you Spanish call such a servant. Your clothes fit you too well not to be made by the finest hand. And yet, you have aged well." She thumped his stomach. "You have not gone soft around the middle."

"I am not so old. And you still haven't told me anything that couldn't have been determined by odds alone."

She lifted her chin. "Your birthday is January ninth, and you are thirty-one years old. You have a little girl named Christina, and you loved her mother very much."

Gabriel felt his jaw drop open.

"Your wife, Felicity, died in childbirth and you have never forgiven yourself that you weren't there. As if you could have saved her. So you have not spent so much time at home in the years since your daughter was born."

She turned away, but Gabriel grabbed her wrist. "How do you know all of this?"

"Do you doubt that I can see into your mind?"

Gabriel felt a skein of alarm climb through him. Then he let her wrist go. "Only my sister would know those things."

Her laughter lacked the appropriate remorse at being snared for a fraud. "Liandra often attended mass when she visited here," she said in a teasing voice. "I know everything about you, Sir Condor."

"Including what I look like."

"No, I guessed that part myself." Her impish finger idled along the chair top. "I was with your sister when she lit a candle for you on your birthday."

"Liandra did that for me?"

"You sound surprised."

Gabriel turned away and looked out the window. For once, he was glad that Sarah couldn't see him. "We did not part on the best of terms when she left with your brother," he finally said. "I came here to this island to make peace with her. With my life . . . before continuing on to Spain."

"And now you will leave without seeing her."

Gabriel drew in his breath. He looked out across the verdant fields of sugarcane bathed silver in the moonlight. Then he lifted his gaze to the velvet dome of sky pockmarked with stars. Bracing his weight on his palms, he leaned his head against the cooling glass. "Perhaps, she is not so far away, after all, *sí*? We look at the same sky."

After a moment, Sarah joined him at the window. Her sudden presence beside him startled him, more so for the warmth that touched his arm even through the sleeves of his fine shirt. "Perhaps not," she said softly. "Your sister worried about you to pray for you often. Are you in trouble?"

"Not so much."

"You're a liar, Don Gabriel."

He found that he could not take his eyes from her face. The wind from the open window stirred her hair. Her presence wrapped around him like fragrant moonlight, and for a moment he forgot who she was.

Suddenly, he was glad to be leaving tonight. He had no desire to explore the strange camaraderie they shared.

"I still don't like you." She sniffed. "Or trust you."

"*Sí*, I know."

"I suppose you will tell Father Henri that I mistreated you?"

Gabriel laughed softly. He could see that it nettled her to come this close to a formal apology. She deserved to suffer a little bit for serving him a rat for dinner. "Would he beat you?"

"I would prefer the strap over the bite of his disappointment."

She was beautiful. Her hair had dried from his earlier dunking and beckoned his touch. His hand curled into a fist. If Sarah Drake possessed any ability at all to read his mind, she would run from him now. He yanked his gaze away from her. Walking to the bed, he tied the scabbard sling around his waist. His sword lay on the rumpled bed. He gripped the cutlass and slid it into the scabbard.

"Then you needn't worry," he said brusquely. "I'm leaving tonight."

"But . . . your wound."

"My surgeon will attend to it once I get back aboard my ship."

"I see." She plucked at a loose thread on her sleeve. He awaited the ragged thing to unravel before his eyes.

"When is Father Henri due back?" he asked, shrugging into his black jerkin.

"Sometimes he goes among the villages for days."

Gabriel went to the window. The night was unusually still. He thought he smelled smoke, but the breeze shifted and all he smelled was Sarah and the summer lilacs in her hair.

"You needn't worry. No one would harm Father Henri," she said. "He is more popular than the governor. But then the governor is not so popular. In fact the man is a rat." She sighed. "I fear that he and Father Henri have butt heads more than once."

"I wasn't thinking about him, *chica.*" It annoyed Gabriel that Father Henri chose this time to venture out on a pilgrimage.

"The roads are usually clear of soldiers. You will not be seen."

He turned to face her. She held out her hand. "If this is to be good-bye, I would not have Liandra's brother leave without a proper farewell. I wish for you to go in peace."

Gabriel lifted her hand to his lips. "Thank you . . . for an entertaining three days, *señorita.* I will think of you the next time I try to blow one of your brothers out of the water."

"Oh!" She snatched her hand away. "Don't do me any favors, Don Gabriel."

He laughed. Twice tonight, she'd made him laugh.

Walking to the door, he watched her haughty march across the front *sala.* The dress looked better from the backside, and with utter debauchery on his mind, Gabriel let his gaze stray over her bottom. "Tell my sister that I miss her," he called.

"I will tell her that you are an oaf, Don Gabriel."

After she left—making him feel almost as if the light had vanished—silence fell upon the room. His gaze found Jaime, who was still staring at the outer door through which she'd disappeared. Slowly the man turned and met Gabriel's unmasked gaze from across the room.

"You look at her like that in front of her brothers and they'll eat your heart for dinner, *sí*?"

The young man's face blanched.

"Follow her and see that she gets to her room safely."

Jaime nodded. Hurrying from the *sala*, he slammed the outer door behind him. Gabriel's mouth tightened. The young pirate was destined for heartbreak. He was in love with the wrong woman.

Cursing at his own ill-fated lust, Gabriel leaned back against the door frame and knocked his head in gentle frustration. Sarah was smart not to like him, or trust him. The man he'd become over the years, the man known as El Condor, was not a benevolent person. The man he'd become, even Gabriel despised.

After a few moments, he stepped back into the room. He would pack the food that Sarah had brought and leave this place forever.

Turning toward the table, he came up short. An orange pall lit the nighttime sky.

Gabriel walked to the window. Outside the high stone walls, down in the sloping valley, he could see field hands filing out of surrounding hovels. The fire came from the other end of the compound, behind the rectory near where they'd imprisoned him the first night. The cobbled courtyard had already begun to fill with panicked women. With an oath, Gabriel lifted his gaze to the horizon where his ship would be waiting. Then clenching his fist, he whirled on his heel. He'd already drawn his sword before he left the room.

Chapter Four

Don Gabriel didn't deserve her kindness! Furious that she'd made one grain of effort to impress the arrogant El Condor, Sarah swept into the rectory. She didn't go back to her room. Instead, she entered the church. With a sigh, she dropped onto the altar steps.

Resting her cheek against her arm, she lay across the top stair. The church was quiet this time of night and she sank into the deep muted silence. But her heart remained restless.

Don Gabriel would leave and she'd never see him again. He belonged to the world outside these walls. Her thoughts wandered. No matter how hard she tried not to think about life outside, tonight she flirted with danger.

Her hand stroked the soft fabric of her dress, and all at once, her chest tightened. She and Cori had made this gown when Talon's little daughter was christened last year in this church. Bunching a handful of her skirt in her fist, she cradled the silly dress to her cheek, wishing desperately that she had not been such a coward. That she had gone with her brothers to be a part of the birth of another niece or nephew.

Outside, bells started ringing. Her heart dropping into her stomach, she sat up.

They were not the church bells, but the warning signal that came when intruders attacked the fortress in town. But she heard no cannons. Still on her knees, she spun around. For the first time, she noticed the smell of smoke.

Fire!

Sarah snatched up her walking stick and stood. Screams outside muted by the stone walls reached into the church. Sarah's room was on the second floor in the adjacent building that housed a dozen women. Women of all ages. Some who had spoken their vows. All who served as healers or teachers for the hospice Father Henri had created. Her first thought was that Cori would be looking for her. She started back to the rectory.

Somewhere a door slammed, followed by a strange man's voice.

Sarah froze.

"I'm tellin' ya, she came this way," a voice said in English. "She ain't in 'er room."

Heart pounding, Sarah flattened herself against the wall. Deep voices rumbled, their harsh whispers echoing off the steeply pitched ceiling. Sarah shifted direction and moved down the wall. Her foot struck something soft and she fell. Her palms smacked against the hard stone floor, sending shards of pain up her arms and into her shoulder blades. Her walking stick clattered to the floor, sliding across the polished surface. Sarah lifted her hands in horror.

Blood.

With a gasp, she twisted on her knees. Long hair tangled in Sarah's feet. A woman! her heart cried out. Probably someone who had seen the intruders.

"I found 'er, mates!" A hand jerked her up by the back of her bodice.

Twisting around, Sarah flung both her fists toward the sound of the voice. Her hands connected with the man's face. Her knuckles grazed his teeth. With a bellow of rage, he fell backward, ripping her beautiful dress straight down the center of the bodice. In a tangle of limbs and weapons, he hit the floor.

"Bitch!"

But Sarah was free, and before he could regain his feet, she'd whirled away.

"Stop her, men!"

"There she is!"

The cry went up.

More voices were to her right.

Sarah could hear their heavy boots loud and obtrusive against the protected sanctuary of these walls. She slid along the wall, then dipped into the stone passageway that led down into the crypts below the church. She knew her way in the damp catacombs.

They did not. She would find a place to hide.

A spark then a hiss sounded, and a pistol exploded. The ball struck the stone wall, sending splinters of rock against her face. She sobbed aloud. Yelling ensued as someone screamed that they needed her alive.

Why? her tortured mind screamed back.

Why would someone do this to her?

She stumbled down the damp stairs and nearly lost her footing.

"Bugger me. This place is fer the dead!" someone cursed from the landing above her.

Desperately trying to still her breath, Sarah listened. But only for the space of a panicked heartbeat.

She tore the lanthorns from the walls as she rushed down the narrow corridor, spilling lard oil and leaving carnage in her wake. Passing every crypt, she flung open the iron gates and let them bang against the walls. The noise echoed through the darkness, a disorienting beacon for those who chased her. She knew every stone, every hiding place in the maze of corridors that laced the caverns beneath the church and rectory. They would be crippled by the darkness. She would not.

She wound around into another corridor. When she stopped to gauge their whereabouts, the intruders were cursing one another. They'd split up.

"We'll get ye, missy." Glass cracked beneath a man's step. "You make it easy and we'll be real nice."

Sarah backtracked and stepped into a crypt, ducking behind a sarcophagus memorial to one of the past commanders of the garrison.

Death surrounded her.

"You know what I'll do to all that hair on yer head if I have to chase ye down . . ." His voice faded, and he hit something. Cursing, he slammed an iron gate against the wall.

She huddled into a little ball and covered her ears.

He moved down the corridor back toward the stairs.

Sarah buried her face against her knees. How long before someone discovered her missing? The fire would keep everyone busy. No one knew where she was.

Voices echoed farther away. Terror kept her frozen. She no longer heard the man nearest to where she was hiding.

She thought of the poor dead woman upstairs. She swallowed hard. And tried not to cry or think beyond the moment.

But her mind rebelled, and she couldn't stop the small whimper that escaped her. She remembered the soldiers. . . .

The vision surrounded her, came at her out of the darkness.

Most wore red coats. Some of them didn't have uniforms at all. They'd come to the house. She'd been playing with her dolls. They'd come to take Papa away. But they'd done more than that. She covered her ears against the screams.

She could not make them stop.

"Don't open your eyes, Sarah. Don't open your eyes!"

"Sarah!"

Gabriel was shaking her. "Get away," she cried, swinging her fists out. "Don't touch me!"

Pulling her to her feet, he took her in his arms, crushing her wet face against his chest. His breath rippled over her temple. "Sarah. It's all right. Shh." One hand held her head; his other still held his heavy cutlass. His strength surrounded her, unrelenting and furious as he kept her safe. "They're not going to touch you." He said the words over and over, a golden mantra. A promise.

He'd found her. Gabriel had found her.

And then she realized that he must have heard her whimper, that she'd somehow given herself away, and the others might find them.

Sarah closed her eyes and let the sound of his heartbeat fill her being and drive away the terror. Voices outside the crypt passed up and down the stone catacombs. She raised her hands to his chest as if to ward off the sound. Her hands curled into fists and she held them tight, unmoving, waiting for the voices to leave.

His whole body hummed beneath her cheek. She sensed his alertness, a soldier's wariness as he faced the gate, ready to fight. An intimate sprinkling of hair touched her nose.

Her senses seemed to awaken. The heat of his skin, his

scent, the coiled hardness of his flesh beneath her hands, all served to lessen the onslaught of danger. One by one her fingers relaxed and opened over the sculpted curve of his shoulders. He wore breeches and boots that stretched the length of his calves. But his jerkin was soft and rich, filled with the smells of him. She turned her face and pressed her nose into the deep slope of his chest above his heart.

Outside the crypt, the voices moved farther away. The men had become increasingly alarmed of discovery. Too much time had passed since they'd set the fire. Two of their men were missing.

A door slammed down the corridor.

Silence filled the narrow chamber, and gradually she sensed the change in Gabriel's breathing. The flat of his palm moved down to the small of her back. Sarah couldn't breathe. She dared not move. Yet she did.

Slowly, she lifted her chin. He was looking down at her face. She could feel his eyes on her, the touch of his breath barely perceptible against her forehead.

"Did they hurt you?" His words brushed her temple. He still held the cutlass clutched in his other hand. "Your dress . . ."

"N-no, I'm all right. Now." Her hands tightened their hold on his jerkin. "I think they've gone."

His palm slipped around the nape of her neck. "It is dark as pitch down here."

"I . . . can see you perfectly."

They were on equal ground down here with only the darkness and the heat from their bodies between them.

"We . . . should go upstairs," he said.

His voice caressed her cheek, and she stood on her toes. "It could be dangerous still."

"Ah, *chica*, not as dangerous for you as it is right now."

His mouth descended on hers. Sarah made a startled sound, perhaps because nothing could have prepared her for the coaxing touch of his lips on hers, the hunger that seemed to grow between them. Her heart catapulted into her throat. And the gasp she made opened her to his tongue. His bristled jaw abraded her tender skin but she didn't care. Sarah leaned into his body. The moan in his chest became a growl as he deepened the kiss, and any misconceptions Sarah had ever had about the glory of merging lips vanished in a hot haze of passion. He tasted like salt and wine and the nighttime breeze that filled her with the lingering memories of freedom. She curled her clumsy fingers over his broad shoulders, sensed strength beneath her palms, and wrapped her arms around his neck, sinking deeper into the sea of wondrous sensations.

His sword arm remained immobile with the weight of the cutlass.

"Gabriel . . . ?" she managed to say unsteadily when he pulled away.

"This is a very bad mistake, *chica*." His voice was breathless, hot against her lips.

"I . . . know," she eagerly said.

He twisted his hand in her hair and seized her lips again. Feasting as if she were a man's last meal. Her blood raced through her veins, his subtle groan pulsing through her mind like a potent aphrodisiac. His mouth trailed down her neck and lingered on her collarbone. Their harsh breath filled the small room. His hand covered her breast, tentative at first, then boldly as she pushed against his palm. She heard herself moaning with strange torment. His hair was soft and silky. Moving his lips back to hers, he plunged his tongue inside her mouth.

Gabriel became her light. The air that she breathed.

She should not want him. Should not be doing this.

But she couldn't stop.

Lost in his kiss, she didn't know at first that he had pulled away. His breathing was harsh against her shoulder as he braced his hand against the wall and leaned with his head down. She thought she heard him swear, but didn't recognize the Spanish word he'd said, only its tone.

"I need to go back," he said. "I have to know what is happening outside."

He'd stepped into her world, inside the walls that surrounded her life, and she couldn't bear to let him out.

"Sarah . . ." he said, as if he sensed her reluctance.

"I'm not afraid. Truly."

"Did you know who those men were?"

"One of them was the man who dropped me off the wall.

Before, in the garden," she explained. "I recognized his voice."

For a long time, he was silent, as if contemplating what he should do with her. Already she had become a little bit afraid of her entangled emotions. She could feel his regret as if he'd slapped the words in her face, as if she were naught but a terrible mistake. She couldn't bear to be his mistake. Not her very first kiss.

That illogical notion in the midst of all this turmoil struck her as selfish and needy, for there could be nothing between them outside of the walls of her home.

Then his hand touched her chin and lifted her face.

"Don't you dare tell me you're sorry for kissing me!" Her knees were shaking now. The aftershock of everything had finally begun to settle over her.

Gabriel straightened. She felt him staring down at her.

The musty scent of aged wood and death hovered in the room. Sarah pressed her face against him. Without a word, he held her close, and she wanted to fuse herself to his courage. His sword scraped the stone walls. They stood together buried in the stone catacombs with only their heartbeats to break the silence.

"My world is not so dark as you think, Don Gabriel," she whispered.

"I don't know how you do it."

Suddenly she didn't know either. She'd lost something tonight. Her innocence perhaps. But she knew it was something more. Something far worse. Her emotional compass.

Somewhere she heard a door thrown wide and the sound of many feet descending the stairwell from the church.

"Light," Gabriel whispered.

She recognized the worried voices and knew the instant Gabriel did, too. He placed her hands on the shredded edges of her dress.

"Your dress, *chica*."

Mutely, she nodded. Her hands started to tremble. Father Henri, Jaime, and Cori would soon find them. There were more people with them. They walked down the corridor. She heard the rattle of a lantern. Gabriel stepped out with her in his arms. Glass crunched as someone shoved away the debris.

"Merciful heavens, *monsieur,* what happened down here?" Movement came to an abrupt halt. "Sarah?" Father Henri demanded.

Gabriel let his arm drop from around her. With a deep sob that came from pent up relief and heartfelt confusion, she fell into Father Henri's arms, eager to hear him tell her that the world had not gone mad, that no one else had died. He was like her father in truth and the events of that night were lost in his embrace. She knew her mind when he was around to guide her.

"There are two dead men upstairs," she heard Father Henri tell Gabriel. "We didn't know what happened."

She could feel Gabriel's eyes on her. "I think you can guess."

"I was detained by the governor. It seems the man you killed the other night was a talent with the sword. The governor demanded to know who had killed him."

"It would be to my welfare that you didn't tell him."

"Would you be standing here if I had? Indeed, you owe me your life for the lies I have told tonight on your behalf!"

Sarah pulled back. The angry tone in his voice startled her, and she fought the sudden strange urge to step back and shield Gabriel.

"Go, *chère.* Cori will take you upstairs. Jaime will stay nearby. He has been distraught because he lost you tonight."

Sarah allowed Father Henri to hand her to Cori. Then she turned. She knew where to find Gabriel in the darkness.

"Thank you," she whispered.

A moment of silence followed. "You are welcome, *chica.*"

Father Henri watched Gabriel Espinosa, the man known to so many as El Condor, push out of the chair and pace the confines of the rectory. Black soot lingered on everything. Henri shut his eyes. He was lucky more people hadn't been killed tonight. The infirmary could be rebuilt again. Lives could not.

And right now Sarah's life was in danger. He couldn't protect her. Didn't even know where to start.

He only knew that he was to blame, and fate had put this man in his hands. "She must be taken off this island," Henri said.

Don Gabriel swore. "She cannot come with me. And I cannot stay. I have to get to Spain."

"Is your haste worth her life, Don Gabriel?"

"Lady Sarah is not my responsibility, and you do her a great disservice by trying to foist her into my care. She has two brothers. Where are they? Find them."

Henri remained standing. The scarlet beads that draped his waist rattled as he walked to the great mahogany desk that sat in a corner of the rectory. How many years had he found himself in this room seeking eternal guidance, strength for his decisions? Liandra's brother was Sarah's only hope.

"It is not that simple." Henri sighed. "That could take weeks."

"Indeed. Tell me something I don't already know. What is going on around here?"

Henri folded his hands. Coming to a decision, he drew in his breath and faced the Spaniard. "Sarah has remained hidden for most of her life here on this island. Until a few years ago, even her brothers thought she was dead. She was safe here. Safe from the people who destroyed her family."

"The Drakes have many enemies," Gabriel scoffed. "Does it not strike you as odd that the attacks on their sister start after they both leave this island? Is it no matter to you the kind of people that have sought amnesty here? You protect pirates, Father. They probably seek to ransom her."

Henri sniffed his disdain. "You are wrong about those who have sought freedom here. As for the coincidence of the attacks, I have already thought of that. But now that the kidnappers have been thwarted twice, the authorities will also know that someone here is capable of protecting her."

Gabriel glared at the rafters. Exasperation crossed the aristocrat's handsome face. And Henri knew the restraint it took him to keep the entire world clamped inside.

"She is a Drake." But Gabriel's voice lacked conviction as he added, "She is no safer with me than if she stayed here."

Henri had seen the look the two of them exchanged in the catacombs. "You care about her."

"She is *inglesa*. She is—"

"Blind? Imperfect?"

"Not a Spaniard," he said darkly. "I am thinking that she should not be taken out of this place. It would hurt her."

Henry crossed the room. His long robes swished on the threadbare rug. "Do you trust in miracles, Don Gabriel?"

His head fell back on his shoulders. His jerkin stretched across shoulders taut with rage. "I am to be *harassed* now? Like an altar boy getting his knuckles rapped?"

"Do you believe?"

"There are no miracles in life."

"You have a daughter. Is she not a miracle of life?"

The Spaniard's eyes narrowed.

"Sarah is blind because she chooses the darkness," Henri voiced. "She chooses not to remember what put her here."

"Maybe that is where she belongs. Where her heart should stay."

"Because the truth is painful?"

"Because . . . it is too hard to live with the truth."

"As it is for you, Don Gabriel?"

Gabriel whirled on his booted heel. "Is this to be a confession, Father? I'm not interested in saving my soul."

"I know what pirates did to you and your family. I know Henry Morgan's raid on your home cost you more than your father's life."

"You don't know anything," Gabriel whispered.

"I know that twenty years is not long enough for you to forget. And you have spent your life hunting the men responsible for—"

"For what they did to me and my mother? *Sí,* I have hunted pirates. And gladly imprisoned them or watched them hang."

"Atrocities have been committed on all sides."

"Pah! I need no history lesson in morality."

"I cannot make the past go away. None of us can. But I can help you see your way into the future."

"Then let Lady Sarah stay where she is."

Father Henri had contended with tall, proud men before when he'd dealt with Sarah's brothers. But the Spaniard would not be so easily healed. His scars ran deep. "You and Sarah are not so different," he finally said into the thickening silence. He tapped his balding head. "You are both trapped by what is here. You are afraid of what you don't see . . . and she is afraid of what she will see. Follow your heart, Don Gabriel, and you will learn what is truth."

Gabriel walked to the door. "I will be gone at first light. Already I'll be late for my rendezvous with my ship."

"Then you'll leave in the morning?"

The Spaniard braced his hand in the doorway. Shoulders stiff, he hesitated on the threshold. "You need to have her guarded until you get her brothers back here. I wish I could help you, Father. But I can't. I have my own problems and must do what I have to do."

And then he was gone.

"*Oui,*" Father Henri said into the naked emptiness. "As do I, *mon fils.* As do I."

Sarah jumped at the sound of Cori's fist banging on the door. Her eyelids were heavy from lack of sleep. Her nerves taut. After dressing that morning, she'd stretched out on the narrow bed and let her cat purr against her cheek. He loved hair, and she'd pinned hers in a braided coronet around her head, where he now nuzzled in sleep. For the first time since she'd arrived at Father Henri's island refuge, Sarah had bolted her door.

"Be patient, Cori," she yelled, standing up to tie a rope of beads around her waist. A long white robe brushed the floor. Sext was in an hour and she would talk to Father Henri first. She'd slept late this morning to avoid confronting Gabriel.

Had he thought about her when he left?

Her hands stilled on the beads. Just the memory of the intimacy they'd shared sent her heart racing in panic. The fear of discovery became all too real after a night's sleep. All she wanted to do was forget Gabriel. Forget what had happened between them last night.

She wanted nothing more to do with the world outside.

The men who'd tried to attack her, who'd murdered that poor girl, reminded her again that her childish fantasies of the world were but beggar illusions of a place that didn't exist. Gabriel belonged to that world outside these walls. Indeed, he thrived amidst the harsh decadence. She did not. She knew that now.

Sarah threw back her shoulders. Last night before going to bed, she'd made up her mind that Father Henri could not deny her wishes anymore. She would take her vows. Tomorrow if possible. Then she would put her life and happiness in God's hands. Surely, she had done nothing wrong—as long as she didn't count that kiss—to deserve His wrath. Faith would see her safe until Talon returned.

Fortified with her newfound strength, Sarah opened the door.

"Lud, milady, I was thinkin' ye drowned in yer crock of water."

"What are you doing up here?"

Cori never ventured to the "virginal hall of sanctum," as she oft called the second floor of the women's residence house. She shared a small room with the cook near the infirmary.

"Jaime is downstairs. He's to take you to the rectory. Father Henri wishes to chat with you."

A chill rushed over Sarah. Her hands went to adjust her cap. "Did he say why?"

"Now, it's not like I'm buds with the old geezer, milady," Cori grumbled. "The only words I hear out of his mouth are to repent."

Despite herself, Sarah laughed. Cori was so dramatic. "He is not that bad and you know it."

Sarah met Jaime downstairs. "Yer lookin' comely, milady."

Her heart eased its frantic pacing as she realized no one could read her mind. Her shoulders relaxed. Her sins would remain hidden and soon forgotten. Placing a hand on Jaime's forearm, she let him walk her across the courtyard. He was familiar and safe. And by the time Sarah reached the rectory, she was nearly her old self again.

God was already working miracles.

"I'll be waitin' outside if ye be needin' anything, Lady Sarah," Jaime said.

Stopped by his strange words, she turned to ask him what he meant when the door shut behind her, leaving her to face the silence.

Something made her hesitate. "Father," she quietly called.

"Come sit down, Sarah."

Forcing her feet to move, she walked to the desk. A chair

had been pulled out and she hit its spindled back. "Father, I wanted to talk to you—"

"I know. But first I have something I must say."

She felt around the back of the chair, and lowering herself, she crossed her hands into her lap. "What is it, Father? What's happened? Were more people hurt last night?"

Movement stirred somewhere behind her. There were others in the room. Her head lifted to confront their presence but Father Henri spoke. "I have prayed on this all night, child. And what I am about to do, you must know I do because I love you." Kneeling in front of her, he took her hands into his. "Your brothers are not here to make this decision for me."

Her first instinct was to pull away, but he held her steadfast in his firm grip. "Please . . . . you're frightening me."

"What happened last night will happen again."

"You're sending me away, aren't you?"

"Sarah—"

"Oh, Father. You cannot. I have done nothing wrong."

"Sarah . . ."

"I would take my vows now. I'll do whatever you tell me to do, except leave this place. I cannot. There is no place anywhe—"

"Listen to me." He gently squeezed her hands. "It's more than that."

Tears welled in her eyes, but she didn't care. She sat huddled on the chair, wanting to crawl into a little ball. To be sent away was worse than death.

"I am not doing this to punish you. You'll not be leaving this place alone. I have arranged a marriage for you."

Her heart stopped. "What?"

His grip on her hands tightened. "You will be wed to Don Gabriel today. He will take you out of here. Off this island."

Sarah heard the words, but she didn't comprehend. "Don Gabriel is gone." Wasn't he? She jerked her head around to the noise she'd heard earlier. "You are mad!" Yanking her hands away from Father Henri, she came to her feet. Her voice sounded weak, choked with shock. "I will not marry Don Gabriel. I will marry no one."

"The papers are already signed."

She shook her head. "I'll take my vows here, Father. I belong in this church. With you."

She knew Gabriel would never agree to this madness. This had to be a trick. She wouldn't do it. She wouldn't!

Dizziness assailed her. "I don't wish to leave."

"In this you have no choice. It's too dangerous for you here. Too dangerous for all of us," he said quietly.

"So I am to be sacrificed to . . . to—"

"Don Gabriel is a proud man, *chère*. You must not say anything you will regret—"

"Nay, Father." Anguish stabbed her.

That Father Henri would do this to her betrayed everything she believed in. He would take it all away. Her love for him, her devotion to the hospital, the children that she'd cared for. None of her twenty years prepared her for the pain. She couldn't breathe.

She was still shaking her head when he touched her shoulders. "Do you think I would endanger your life, child?" he whispered.

"You would hand me over to the man known as the Vulture? He is an enemy of England and France. I would never see you again. I would never see my family." The reality of it struck her with terror. Hysteria was a heartbeat away. She would rather face an army of pirates than the reality of never coming home again. Or of leaving the safety of her paradise. This was her home.

With a sob, Sarah dropped to her knees and clutched his robes. "Father, you cannot mean to do this! Don't make me marry him."

A quiet oath and movement stirred behind her. The creak of fine leather boots followed. "Sarah?"

She snapped her head up. Eyes brimming, she wiped at the hot tears. Gabriel knelt beside her. His presence stole away the darkness. He took her by the shoulders and pulled her up to face him. He smelled of shaving soap and the ocean breeze. He smelled of salvation, and Sarah could not let him go as she spilled her tears against his chest.

"You do not want this either," she said. "You cannot."

Gabriel had stood against the back wall, watching her distress. Cold rage had coursed through his veins as her anger had turned to hysteria. Over Sarah's head, he glared his wrath at Father Henri. With a subtle nod of his head, the priest sent the two men holding boarding pikes at Gabriel's back out of the room.

That the good father would force Sarah to endure this madness was bad enough. To see her fear hit Gabriel full in the chest.

His anger faded in the wake of her obvious terror. The two gossoons who'd roused him from bed this morning had already paid dearly for the disservice with a cracked jaw and a black eye. But there had been enough men to restrain him while Father Henri made his hellish bargain: Gabriel's freedom in exchange for marrying Sarah and taking her off the island. The old priest had dared threaten to turn him over to the French garrison commander for the reward on his head.

If Father Henri weren't a holy man, Gabriel would have killed him. If it had been only his life at stake, Gabriel would have tempted fate. He'd have fought the whole garrison if he'd had to. But Father Henri had threatened the safety of his ship, too. The older man had guessed enough about the rendezvous point that it would not be difficult to set up a trap for Gabriel's men.

For the past few minutes he'd stood braced against the wall with his arms crossed, his eyes fixed on the girl sobbing her eyes out because she thought he was a cold-blooded murderer. Because she preferred death to wedlock with him. Then he had realized it was more than her aversion to him. She was terrified of leaving this place.

Gabriel wrapped his arms around her and let her cry. The tears would end and their vows would be spoken. She would have no say, any more than he did.

"You do me a disservice, *chica*," he whispered into the soft fragrance of her hair. "At least I have a mouthful of white teeth."

She pulled back. With the heel of her hand, she slapped at the wash of tears on her face. "And you mock me, Don Gabriel."

"It is not my want to mock you, *señorita*. Nor do I wish to hurt you. But the deed will be done today as Father Henri deems."

"Then I shall marry Jaime!" She turned to Father Henri. "If it is a man that you wish to foist me off on, then I choose Jaime."

Gabriel dismissed the pull of annoyance.

"Can Jaime offer you his sword? Can he protect your life?" Father Henri demanded, his patience clearly at an end. "Enough of this nonsense, Sarah. I have made my decision. You will obey me."

Silence followed on the heels of the father's final statement. Save for the nervous fidgeting of the rosary around her waist, Sarah didn't move. Gabriel could hear the catch in her breath as she struggled for control. The Sarah he knew was not far behind her determined grip. She lifted her face and her silver eyes found him. Black lashes framed her wet gaze, and he suddenly found himself lost in the depths of those eyes, wondering what it would feel like to know their touch on his body.

To his horror, desire stirred. Gabriel grimaced at the carnal path of his thoughts. He would never know. Nor did he care.

"Very well, I will wed you if I must," she announced as if she were the one doing *him* a great favor. With her holding her chin high like some pagan sacrifice, all he had to do was toss her in the local volcano to complete this farce. "If I have put people here in danger, then I will go." A sniffle briefly eclipsed her bravado. "But I demand that Jaime and Cori be allowed to come with me."

"I'm sure that Don Gabriel will understand," Father Henri said before Gabriel told her she was completely mad. He wasn't going anywhere with that redheaded termagant that passed as her maid.

"Also, I want my personal things," she said, and proceeded to name off a dozen items, including a tub. "And I will *not* leave without my cat."

In the dead silence that followed, Gabriel stared in disbelief.

Narrowing his eyes, he lifted a brow to confront the errant priest. "What makes you think I won't throw her overboard once we get out to sea?"

Chapter Five

S arah felt the vibrations beneath her feet a moment before she felt the danger go through her.

"How often do the soldiers come here, Father?" Gabriel asked.

He'd moved to the large window in the rectory and pulled back the curtains. Sarah felt the late afternoon sun on her face. In her hands, she twisted the leather handle of her portmanteau. She'd filled it with her few possessions. Outside, the guard's bell tolled.

"You can do nothing against the soldiers," Father Henri told the imposing man standing behind her. "They will not harm me. Now go. Cori and Jaime are waiting. There is a horse and a cart filled with supplies ready for you beyond the walls. Sarah will take you out through the crypts."

"But I cannot leave you," Sarah whispered. "Not with the whole of the French garrison descending on the convent."

"Go," Father Henri said. Sarah heard the tremor in his voice. "You are no longer safe here. Nor is your Spaniard. Go."

Don Gabriel was *not* her Spaniard, no matter the holy blessings Father Henri had sprinkled over them a few hours ago. Gabriel hadn't as much as kissed her on the cheek to honor the sacred vows they'd spoken as man and wife.

"Come, *chica.*" Gabriel's arm suddenly pressed her waist. The bag disappeared as he lifted it from her hands. "He is right. There is nothing more to do here."

"Father." She flung herself into Father Henri's arms. "I'll be back again someday. I promise."

"Go, child."

Heart pounding, Sarah reached behind her for the wall and startled when Gabriel's strong fingers wrapped around hers. Chin high, she allowed him to lead her from the rectory. She was leaving her world, her sanctuary, with a man who didn't like her. Who despised her family and her English blood. Who battled his demons with a warrior's passion for combat. Father Henri had surely glimpsed something tender with his eyes that she could not with her heart, for she was more frightened than at any time in her life.

"We best be goin', milady," Cori said when Sarah met her at the back of the church.

Her cat meowed in his cage. Sarah dropped to her knees and laughed. "You found him!"

"I had to wrap his claws to get him in there," Jaime said.

"Oh, thank you." Sarah touched Jaime's arm. "You're truly wonderful."

"Perhaps we should have wine and sardines with our party, *sí*?" Gabriel pulled Sarah to her feet. "Maybe invite the French garrison. Or doesn't it matter to you that you are making too much noise?"

Behind her, the cat meowed again. In the cavernous hall of the church the sound echoed like a blaring trumpet. Conscious of Gabriel's impatience, Sarah kept her mouth closed and let him lead her away. Under the circumstances, who could blame him if he lost his temper completely? They were still in the compound and in danger because she'd stubbornly insisted on finding her cat.

Without another word, Sarah entered the stairwell behind the stone pulpit and began the descent into the crypt. Over the sound of her breathing, she heard faint shouts, and a litany of horrors formed.

The soldiers were here.

Her mind racing, Sarah stopped. She was glad to be standing next to Gabriel if for no other reason than he could see. The fine lawn of his shirt smelled faintly of the soap she'd used to wash the shirt, but mostly it smelled of him.

"Vayase Usted," Gabriel hissed. "Go. Go."

The craggy wall was moist against her palm. Gabriel installed himself in the rear, and already she found that a chill replaced the warmth where his presence had been. For the first time in years, the darkness weighed on her senses. But she knew these catacombs and took them through the narrow hallways and various burial chambers to the second stairway that led beyond the stone walls of the compound.

"Smile, everyone," Cori whispered as they started to ascend the stairs to the topmost levels of the catacombs. "We are leaving the gates of perdition."

Sarah frowned. To Cori, all men went to hell because she lacked faith to care otherwise. For Sarah, it was not any man's place to judge someone else. Ofttimes what condemned someone on the outside masked something very different on the inside. A man's nobility was not measured in words or physical trappings but deeds, and there were many poor men buried here whose greatest deed had merely been to love someone else unconditionally.

Like Father Henri.

A burning sob welled unbidden in her throat. And suddenly she lost her bearings. Cori, who trailed behind her, smacked into her back. Somewhere she heard Jaime trip. Tears choked her words as she struggled to regain her direction.

Gabriel moved beside her. "What happened?" His voice brushed her temples.

"I . . ." She didn't want to be the cause of any further trouble. "I . . . I'm sorry." Trembling, she pressed her nose into his chest. "But he shouldn't be back there alone. He shouldn't. The governor has never liked him, not since Father Henri spoke out against him last year. They had a terrible row. I fear . . . the man will use any excuse to harm him."

"What could be so terrible between them?"

"That murderin' fishmonger, the governor of Jamaica." Cori sniffed. Her voice sounded hollow in the stone passageway. "That's what. Harrison Kendrick came here last year and fairly caused a war."

"Kendrick came here? To this place?"

"That's what the fight was about. The old geezer de-

nounced the governor because he allowed Kendrick on the island. He came here to this mission."

Gabriel had become too quiet. "What did Kendrick want
with Father Henri?"

"He wanted Father Henri's help to capture my brother,"
Sarah said. "To *kill* him, Gabriel, after Talon sought sanctuary
on French soil. The man is evil. And don't tell me that my
family deserves to be hunted down."

"*Sí*, you are a mind reader, Sarah. That is exactly what I
was thinking."

She pulled away and backed against a wall. "And I think
that I don't like you, Don Gabriel."

A hand came up beneath her chin and lifted her face. "Listen to me carefully, *querida*. Go toward your brother's house.
Stay in the cane fields out of sight until you get to the hills on
the other side of the plantation. Await me there."

"Yer leaving us?" Cori choked.

"Are you mad?" Jaime echoed Sarah's sentiment. "They'll
put yer head on a bloody pike."

Gabriel's heart beat against Sarah's palm, and she balled
her fist to keep from clutching his shirt. "It will serve you
right, Don Gabriel, if they do!"

"I am a Spaniard, *querida*, and not so easily killed." Sarah
could hear the Latin arrogance in the deep rasp against her ear.
"I will find you before you can miss me too much. Take her."
Gabriel handed her to Jaime. "Don't let her out of your sight."

Silence fell upon her as Gabriel's movements whispered
back at her, then vanished with the dead. Nobody moved or
breathed a word. The cat meowed.

"Well, don't that just beat all?" Cori said. "Just when I
thought I didn't like him, he shows a sense a humor."

"Maybe someone should have told him that Kendrick is
dead," Jaime offered.

Sarah shivered. Maybe, but that wouldn't explain why a
supposedly noble Spaniard like Gabriel Espinosa would know
an English thief and a murderer like Harrison Kendrick in the
first place. For as sure as she could feel the breath in her body,
she sensed Gabriel's motives for leaving. He wasn't returning
to Father Henri out of any nobleness of character to save the

elder's life; he was returning because Father Henri knew Harrison Kendrick.

". . . me a great deal of money. I know Drake keeps it here."

"Whatever he's paying you, it's not enough, Claude."

Gabriel stopped in the stairwell. The words were muffled in the cavernous church, but he could make out voices. They came from the rectory. He drew his sword, a whisper of steel against leather, as he moved against the wall and approached the rectory. The door hung open. A wedge of light lay over the stone floor.

Slap!

"You always were good at playing the martyr, Jean Henri."

Pressed against the wall, Gabriel tried to control his rage, tried to control the urge to burst into the rectory. But in the face of what he heard, it would take all of his wits to save Father Henri's life and get them both out of here alive. Later, he would demand an explanation from the good father for his subterfuge. He had not told everything about Sarah's past, and Gabriel wanted to know why. Then he would wrap his hands around Father Henri's throat and personally demonstrate the true extent of his benevolence.

The voices grew louder as Gabriel shortened the distance.

". . . the twit is blind. How far could she go outside these walls? Even with help."

"The people . . . won't stand for what you are doing here." Gabriel hardly recognized Father Henri's battered voice.

"What do the people know except what I tell them? You are a traitor, Jean. Harboring Spaniards is a crime. Where has he taken her?"

A fist cracked against flesh.

"Where is the pathetic Spaniard?"

Gabriel leaned to glance into the room. A man stood with his back to the doorway, his hands clasped behind him. Another guard stood near the window casement. Father Henri sat out of sight. Gabriel started to move when the cold steel of a blunderbuss pressed into his head.

Instinctively, he froze.

"Ah, *monsieur*," a papery voice whispered in French.

Silently cursing his carelessness, Gabriel let his gaze fall on the man's elbow.

"The governor said to watch the crypts, and look what worm came up for air."

They would send men into the catacombs to search for Sarah now. His escape route essentially gone, a chill crawled over him. He had a sudden desperation to get back to Sarah. To make sure she'd obeyed him. Gabriel's hand tightened on the sword.

The press of the blunderbuss urged him into the room. *"Mon Dieu,"* Father Henri whispered, and closed his swollen eyes. "You were not supposed to come back, Don Gabriel."

The French governor sat behind Father Henri's large desk, a towering figure in a blue and red satin jerkin. He wore a white periwig with curls aplenty, a ridiculous contradiction to his dark, unshaven jowls. There was a moment of stunned silence while he assessed Gabriel. "Don Gabriel? You are Gabriel Espinosa?"

Feet braced apart, Gabriel tossed his sword on the floor. "Don Gabriel Cristobel de Espinosa y Ramírez." A slow grin lifted the corners of his mouth, and his voice though soft carried across the room. "The *pathetic* Spaniard who is going to kill you."

The man's pig eyes widened. A curt nod to the guard, and Gabriel felt the bite of a man's fist in his gut. Keeling over, he was slammed backward into a chair and held there by two sets of hands. Another man pressed the tip of a cutlass to his chest.

"I have heard of you. Indeed, who has not heard of El Condor?"

Raising his gaze, Gabriel let his eyes fall on the governor: a dead man. The thought gave him some satisfaction. "Who paid you to come after the girl?"

The guard backhanded him, this time a glancing blow to the jaw only because Gabriel saw the fist coming and moved. Even at that, the blow knocked him hard.

Ruffles dangled from the governor's sleeves as he plopped a slice of cheese between his lips. Bread sat next to a glass of red wine. Laying a pistol across his belly, the governor met Gabriel's gaze with indifference. "I don't care if you're God.

When you talk to me, I am *Excellency* to you, Spaniard. Say it."

"Who paid you?" Gabriel rasped, ignoring the order.

The man behind Gabriel dragged a hand through his hair, exposing his throat. His sword lay too far away.

"Excellency," the governor reiterated. His black eyes glittered. "Say it."

The grip on his hair tightened. Gabriel clenched his teeth.

"Say it, Espinosa." The governor sipped at his wine. "If you want answers, say it."

Pride would get him beaten senseless. But some unbidden spark rose within him to fight. He would not plead quarter of any kind, for he would grant none when the time came.

"Allez." The governor finally waved the swordsman off, then took a bite of papaya and looked at Gabriel consideringly. "I don't have the time to break you, Espinosa." The seat protested his weight as he shoved out of the chair. "If you are not here to collect the bounty on the girl, why are you here?"

Gabriel spat blood at his captor's filthy boot.

The governor's eyes narrowed. "Maybe you and I can come to an agreement about the girl. And you can go free. It's well known the way you feel about her family. Mayhap we can strike a bargain. She's worth a great deal of money."

"There is nothing you have that I want."

"What about your life, Espinosa? What about his?" Cradling the pistol, the governor approached Father Henri. "If I don't get her, someone else will." Black pig eyes turned to Father Henri. "Isn't that so, Jean? Tell him how persistent your nephew is. Kendrick will eventually catch her."

Gabriel's attention slowly shifted. Father Henri's stark blue gaze met his in desperate apology.

"Harrison Kendrick secretly came to him a few months ago. Tell him, Jean. We are all friends here. Tell him what a bad boy you've been."

There was an instant of pale silence. *"Mon Dieu,"* Father Henri whispered past his swollen mouth. "I did not know what he was about."

The governor chuckled. "The good father thought that

Kendrick had died from injuries received in a battle with Sarah's brother."

"Oui." Father Henri's watery gaze came back to Gabriel. "He'd suffered terrible wounds. His leg had been amputated. Do you know what that kind of pain does to a man's soul? Harrison came to the island for my help to heal his wounds. He had no one else."

"Kendrick has been here on this island?" Gabriel was incredulous. "And you did not tell anyone?"

"I thought . . . I thought that I could heal his soul as I healed his body. He did not stay here long, as he promised he would not. He kept his word to me to leave. She didn't know that he watched her. Her brother would have probably killed Harrison had he known."

"Keep talking, Jean. Tell him why Kendrick wants her."

A chill crawled down Gabriel's spine. Sarah had been a little girl when she'd been brought to this island. "Jesu . . . You have been hiding her all these years from Kendrick. Does she even know?"

Tearing off a chunk of bread, the governor shoved it in his mouth. He chewed thoughtfully as he probed Gabriel with his eyes. "What is the fun in that, *ami*?"

"I am *not* your friend."

The man's jowls fell. "Unfortunately you are correct." He lifted the pistol. "And I am finished with these games. I have answered your questions; now you can answer mine. Where is Sarah Drake?" In the face of Gabriel's silence, the pistol turned on Father Henri. "If he dies, the people of this island will tear you to pieces, Espinosa."

"God h-have mercy on y-you, Claude," Father Henri whispered through chattering teeth. "But you are the devil."

"No, Harrison Kendrick is the devil." The governor waved the pistol casually. Gabriel held on to Father Henri's gaze. "Or maybe Espinosa over here. But me? I am merely a greedy man." He glanced between Gabriel and Father Henri. "Where is she?" Fury twisted the governor's countenance, but it didn't equal the animal violence inside Gabriel. The gun swung around to Gabriel. "Or maybe I should kill this one, eh, Father?"

Gabriel's legs coiled. "Do it," he hissed. The two men who held him began to lose their grip.

The governor brought the gun back around to Father Henri. "As you wish, Espinosa."

A spark sounded, followed by a flash of gunpowder. The explosion rang in Gabriel's head. Father Henri slammed backward with the force of the shot. His chair toppled.

With a bellow, Gabriel launched upon his three captors. A kick sent one tumbling into the bookcase. Wood cracked with his impact. Ducking beneath the fist of another man, Gabriel leaped to where his sword had fallen. His hand wrapped the hilt. In one furious movement, he pulled his arm back and threw the blade, watching coldly as it speared the governor through the chest. Shock registered on the governor's bloated face. Without waiting for him to fall, Gabriel rushed to Father Henri's side.

"Madre de Dios." Gabriel knelt.

He didn't have to open Father Henri's tunic to know that his wound was fatal. A savagery tore through him. Sarah had loved and believed in this man when he was the one who had brought her to doom. Twice. Once by betraying her to Kendrick, and the second time by marrying her to him.

Outside, the courtyard had erupted. The shot had panicked the people gathered there. The lone French soldier who remained standing fled the room. The governor was still on his feet, his venom-filled eyes half-opened, his hands splayed over the blade of the sword. His knees buckled.

"My men . . . will . . . hunt you down."

Gabriel stalked over to the governor. He wanted to smash the man's face. "What is Sarah to Harrison Kendrick?"

The governor's mouth crawled into a grin. Blood pooled on his lips. "You . . . can't hide her, Espinosa."

Gabriel yanked the sword out of the man's heart and watched him crumple to his face like a rag doll. He stared in disgust at the heap of humanity who would kill a priest, and spat.

"Serpiente. You snake. You got off too easy."

Without emotion, he wiped the blade on the governor's tunic. The chaos outside would give him a few minutes to slip out of the rectory. He could not go back through the crypts.

Sliding the sword into his scabbard, his footsteps inaudible on the dark carpet, he walked past Father Henri, hesitating as he looked at him one last time. Then he shoved through the doors that led outside.

The sun had touched the church steeple in a golden halo that melted into the shadows of an approaching twilight. He heard the uproar as someone saw him. A shot whistled past his head. Without a backward glance, he turned parallel to the gardens. He was running full force when he reached the stone wall.

"Do you think they are all right?" Dusk had brought cooler temperatures and Sarah shivered. "Gabriel should be here by now."

"Probably got 'imself captured," Cori grumbled.

It was no use dwelling on that awful thought. To think of that was to fall into the clutching grip of panic. It was better to believe that they were not running for their lives but on a picnic in the middle of a cane field, in the middle of the night. Her legs were wobbly with exhaustion but the same stillness that surrounded the dying day left her tireless, her senses racing. The way she felt before an electrical storm. In the midst of fear, she was alert. Sarah could hear every sound, including the faraway crack of gunfire. Her heart was too numb to feel what her mind envisioned.

Sarah turned away.

They traveled into the night, staying between the great stalks of sugarcane, stopping often to dislodge the cart from some rut made by heavier wagons during the cane harvest. Once horsemen galloped past not a hundred feet away, going in the same direction, and Sarah huddled with Cori while Jaime kept the horse silent. Insects crawled in her hair. Tucking her knees into her chest, Sarah was glad that she couldn't see if the bugs were poisonous.

"Somethin' has the soldiers in a dither," Cori observed hours later when a third group of riders passed on the road.

"We cannot go to Talon's place," Sarah said, having come to that decision after great thought. Gabriel had told them to go in this direction. Would he find them if they left the fields?

"It's just as well." Jaime broke the brooding silence. "There'll be nothing left anyway. Certainly no place to hide."

Sarah's breath caught on a ragged inhale. In her mind, Talon had built a whole realm immune to destruction, a brick wall of resistance that protected his small world from outside forces. It was a shock to realize that his world here had collapsed as easily as hers, that the same forces that wanted to hurt her would destroy him, as well.

Father Henri had been right to send her away.

Perhaps his methods were less than orthodox, but he'd done what he thought best. For a moment, Sarah gave herself up to the vision of life not just as Gabriel's wife, but life without walls.

The thought had been inconceivable only that morning.

Then she'd laid her hand in Gabriel's and spoken the vows she'd once reserved for her Church.

When next Jaime stopped the cart, Sarah collapsed crosslegged in the grass. She forced down cheese and foul-tasting ale. In the tree branches above, a family of birds scolded them until Jaime threw a pebble and sent them flapping into the night.

Suddenly lifting her face, Sarah could feel the velvet sky above; she could feel the morass of a thousand stars, an infinite abyss of shadows broken by the strange sense of growing freedom. A dozen times during the past few hours, she'd stopped to listen to the wind and reveled in the moist caress of salty air on her face, her fear of capture momentarily obliterated by her sense of longing, of touching something just beyond her reach. That feeling struck her as odd since she'd always been content with her working with Father Henri. Until now, she'd longed for nothing.

Above her, leaves stirred and shivered as if awakened by the same divine portent that stirred in Sarah, and she knew the instant Gabriel had walked into the clearing.

Sarah felt his presence even before she'd heard Jaime's exclamation or Gabriel's answering voice. She'd felt the touch of his eyes because in the sudden stillness, her body hummed with a tumult that she could not name and didn't entirely understand; yet it filled her with awe.

And in that moment, she knew what it must be like to see.

Chapter Six

Abruptly, Gabriel lowered the glass. A dust cloud grew like a plume of volcanic ash as soldiers drove their horses through the lower cane fields. He felt the weight of his cutlass on his hip as he looked toward the distant town. "The soldiers are headed south. Away from here."

"We should go back for him, Don Gabriel," Jaime said. Wind filled the treetops.

Gabriel was crouched beside Jaime. Three leagues of grassy terrain and bright green cane fields lay between them and the coastal town. Sarah and Cori awaited them a half mile ahead. All afternoon Gabriel had remained surly, saying little in answer to anyone's questions except that Father Henri had chosen not to leave the mission.

Tamping down a vague twist of dread, Gabriel returned his attention to the far away steeple and listened to the bells toll. No self-respecting Spaniard would have run from French soldiers to hide in the grass. Not while the same men who had beaten and murdered a priest might attack women and children.

With a snort of disgust, Gabriel took in the sky and measured the hours before nightfall. A distant storm made the sky purple. He stood and, without waiting for Jaime, began his descent down the steep hill back to where Sarah waited with the cart. Twigs and dried leaves crackled beneath his boots. They needed a good rain to wash away the tracks.

"I've been thinkin' about how we might get Father Henri—"

"Thinking is dangerous, Englishman. Particularly when there is nothing more we can do there. Father Henri would not leave that mission even if he could."

Jaime fell into step beside him. He was running to keep up with Gabriel's angry stride. "What are we going to do?"

"Pray that Stefan knows how to keep an appointment, *sí*?"

Gabriel found Cori and Sarah sitting in the shade. No one spoke. The heat of the day was already bearing down on them. By midday, Gabriel finally turned north toward the hills. Sarah kept to herself in the cart. She soothed her frightened cat. It was hungry and thirsty, and Gabriel watched her quiet suffering as she tried to feed the thing cheese.

Near sunset, they reached the rendezvous point with his ship only to find that Stefan had not anchored the frigate anywhere in sight. Leaving Jaime to make camp, Gabriel walked the length of the horseshoe cove. A stone escarpment rose on either side of the deep blue sea. Turtles bobbed in the gentle surge. Placing his hands on his hips, Gabriel stared out at the empty horizon.

"Where are you, Stefan, *mi amigo*?" he asked the night.

The first hint of exhaustion pulled at him. Yesterday, he'd slept little. Today not at all. Father Henri was dead, and Gabriel didn't know how to tell Sarah, or even if he should.

He paced the secluded cove, the urge for action drumming against him like a maddened fist. Finally, he settled against a huge boulder washed smooth by centuries of pounding surf and drew his legs into his chest. Resting one arm across his knees, he stared at the endless horizon. Even at night, light reflected off everything. The sand, the cliffs, the flawless black sky, the huge moon that eventually rose and hung suspended in the sky like some taunting testimonial to immortality.

Jesu, he felt small. His turmoil insignificant.

Gabriel dragged his hands through his hair, flinching when he scraped his stitches. "Don Gabriel." Jaime's voice pulled him around.

A knot of annoyance tightened Gabriel's chest. At once, his gaze lifted to the small grove of trees where he'd left everyone. "I found a freshwater stream and set camp," Jaime said, handing Gabriel a wooden plate when he stood. "Milady wanted me to give you this."

Noting the lump of cheese and bread, Gabriel accepted the proffered plate with a simple, awkward nod.

"Your ship is not here," Jaime observed.

"Clearly, you possess the eyes of a hawk to be so observant."

Jamie's head snapped around. "You don't like us much, do you?"

Shadows darkened the Englishman's eyes. Gabriel placed his age at most at four and twenty. Not much older than Sarah. He carried on as if they were comrades in arms, as if Gabriel hadn't hunted down men of his creed for piracy every day of his life. Still, the Englishman had held up with little sleep and even less food. They all had.

Including Sarah.

"My acquaintance with you is . . . unexpected," Gabriel answered neutrally. "That's all."

Jaime looked at the sand. A crab skittered across the toe of his ragged boot to disappear in a pile of driftwood. "None of us expected this. . . . If Cap'n Drake thought she was in any danger, he wouldn't have left me in charge of her welfare. Are ye really wedded to her?"

Gabriel didn't miss the look in the young man's eyes before he dropped his gaze and studied the tear on his sleeve.

"I didn't think she would ever marry." The Englishman kept talking. "Not that she isn't beautiful. Lud, but she has eyes of the fanciest silver sterling. You should see her without her robe. . . ."

When Gabriel still didn't reply, Jaime raised his gaze. Something in Gabriel's eyes must have made him pale. "Not that I've ever seen her nak— . . . undressed," he croaked out. "I merely meant that she has sometimes worn other clothes." Shifting uneasily, he cleared his throat. "Father Henri seems to trust you with her life."

Without answering, Gabriel pulled his gaze back to the empty sea. "It will be a long way to Hispaniola," he said half to himself.

"That is your home?"

Gabriel had homes in Spain, Puerto Bello, and Havana.

Hispaniola was merely the most isolated and protected. The home he'd built for his late wife: the mother of his child. The place he loved most.

Looking down at the plate in his hand, he studied the cheese. Having rarely eaten with his fingers, he took a careful bite. *"¡Ay yi!"* Spitting out the stuff, he glared at Jaime. "What is this?"

"Goat cheese. We make it at the mission."

Gabriel stared at the plate in horror. No wonder Sarah's crusty feline preferred to starve to death. "Is this all we have to eat?"

"That and the bread ye ate today. Two days' worth only. Maybe less. We finished the fruit this afternoon."

Later, after he was relieved from watch, Gabriel plumbed the cart to check the supplies. Father Henri had packed dishes, rope, a Bible, a holy cross, and an exemplary amount of hideous goat cheese. It occurred to him then that their food supply wasn't all that was in doubt. They had no weapons save the cutlass Gabriel wore on his hip.

Casting his gaze to the sky, Gabriel stopped short of committing outright blasphemy. Something snatched at his sleeve. From behind the bars of its bamboo cage, Sarah's cat swatted his arm. Gabriel scratched its ears and frowned. "Leave it to a priest to throw his trust in God, eh, *amigo*?"

When Sarah awoke, someone had put a blanket over her. Fingering the soft material, she sat up. The cloth belonged to no blanket but to Gabriel. He'd folded his jerkin and placed it over her while she'd slept. The musky scent of him filled her senses, and she pressed the coat to her face while she tried to discern his whereabouts.

"He's at the stream." Tucking a mango into Sarah's hand, Cori plopped on the grass. "He came back an hour ago with some fruit. Jaime took the horse. He's on watch. The ship still isn't here."

"Is he . . . all right?"

"Yer Spaniard?" Cori sniffed. "He's a bloomin' rock, 'bout as sociable as a turd if ye ask me. But he seems to care about you, milady. Wanted to know what yer cat ate."

Her poor cat would probably eat Cori at this point. Sarah

bit into the mango and edged the peel away with her teeth. "He's not used to being caged," she said quietly.

"You talkin' about yer new husband or that ornery cat?"

Cori's words brought Sarah's chin up. She had not thought about Gabriel as her husband or that she was a burden to him. But she must be. He was far safer without her along. Yet he had stayed with her when he could have sought his own refuge.

Lapping juice off her chin, she said, "I'm talking about my cat, Cori."

"Well, in that case, you needn't worry. Don Gabriel fashioned a harness for him, so he couldn't wander off. Jaime filled a bowl with water. If all goes well, a plump mongoose will waddle by."

"Gabriel did that?" A fierce sense of gratitude filled her. "He doesn't even like my cat."

"He's a strange one, milady." Cori yawned. "Practically has Jaime bowing at his royal boot tips doing his bidding. If Jaime bows at anyone's boots, it should be mine." She made a rude sound. "I don't trust that Spaniard."

"You don't trust anyone, Cori."

"That's not true," she grudgingly disavowed. "I trust the Cap, yer brother. And Lady Regan has always been fair-minded."

Lady Regan was Talon's wife, and Sarah adored her as she did Marcus's wife, Liandra. Both were content with fate, although their lives had not gone as they'd originally planned. What they'd found instead had been better.

Sarah drew in a breath and settled into the idea of having her old dreams circumvented. Of suddenly belonging to a family of her own. Of having children.

Her pulse beat a little faster at these thoughts. That Gabriel Espinosa was really her husband began to take a greater share of her thoughts. That he should belong to her filled her with pride.

Hastily, Sarah tossed that sentiment aside. Father Henri spent an abundance of time preaching against the sins of pride, which he'd always claimed was a worse form of blindness than what ailed her.

Still . . . Sarah nibbled on the fleshy part of the mango and let her thoughts travel down this new road. She was drawn to Gabriel as if he were a beam of sunlight on her face.

Sarah could discern no explanation for this except her heart was following a course her mind had always envisioned. A course that Father Henri had long seen as her fate even if she had not: the reason why he had not allowed her to take her vows.

And at once, without consciously willing it to happen, Sarah knew that her vows to Gabriel were a tangible mark of certitude that bound her to a life she suddenly wanted above all else.

But what of Gabriel? What had Father Henri seen in Gabriel's heart that he would bind *her* to him? Bind them to each other forever?

"Where is he?" Sarah asked.

Cori lay down, taking Gabriel's jerkin with her. "If yer meanin' that husband of yers, he's down the hill." Cori turned over in the grass. "Blessedly bare-assed as the day he was born," she added. "Or at least he was a few minutes ago. He's bathing in the creek."

"You watched?"

"Of course, I watched. What else is a girl to do around here?"

"So why aren't you still down there gawking?"

"Because he's yer husband, milady. And I *do* have my principles."

"Oh . . ." Sarah let that thought sink in. Part of her wanted Cori to tell her everything that she saw, while the other ached to hit her friend senseless for daring to trespass on ground that didn't belong to her.

"Besides," Cori sighed, "he's been in a temper since he got back from the mission. Keeps that nasty sword nearby, so don't be approachin' him too quietlike or yer likely to get skewered. Not in the way I imagine that would please you either."

"Really, Cori." Sarah tossed the mango away and wiped her hands on the damp ground.

"Don't tell me ye've not thought about it, milady. Lying with him, and enjoyin' it, too. And don't think I don't know that yer wantin' me to tell ye what he looks like either."

Sarah stood and brushed the grit off her robe. Sometimes Cori seemed to relish shocking Sarah with her observations. It was Cori's favorite pastime, Sarah was sure. But Cori had come with her when she didn't have to, and Sarah would not forget that.

As for Cori's commentary, Sarah had thought about what it would be like to lie with Gabriel since he'd kissed her in the crypt.

The illicit memory sent wanton shivers over her entire being. She was not nearly afraid of such a carnal presence between husband and wife as she thought she should be. Indeed, the butterflies that fluttered in her belly did so out of nervous anticipation. Not fear.

Though God had closed the door behind one part of her life, he had given her a roomful of windows to choose from. Her palms now braced one of those wooden casements and she pressed her nose to the crystal panes as she envisioned this new world offered her. All she had to do was break the glass and breathe.

Following the splashing sounds, Sarah carefully made her way down the grassy bank. Her slippered feet touched sand, and when she rounded a pair of prickly bushes that caught at the hem of her robe, she heard the sea not so far away. Gulls circled in the sky, their cries joining with the smell of salt spray that assailed her senses. Taking another dozen steps, she stepped into water. Gabriel was not so far away that he hadn't heard her gasp of surprise. The splashing stopped, and silence filled the distance separating them. He was looking at her. Perhaps even testing her. Most likely, he just wanted her to go away. After all, he had not spoken to her since he'd walked into the clearing two days ago. He'd gone to a great deal of trouble to avoid her since.

"Your ship didn't make your rendezvous point," she ventured.

For an instant, Sarah thought he wouldn't answer. "They weren't there," he said. The splashing resumed, and she wondered if he was naked as Cori said he was. She remembered the fit of his clothes. She'd touched him at the mission, too. He was the type of man who took great care of his physique.

A breeze stirred her hair. "Do you think something happened?"

The splashing came closer. Clearly, he'd given up the hope that she would go away. "These are French waters," he said. "Tell me something that *wouldn't* happen to a Spanish ship. If there was danger, they would have sailed away."

"Oh . . ." He seemed bothered by the abandonment, but the fear didn't appear to be for himself. He was worried for his ship. He had stopped a few feet in front of her. She took a step backward out of the water. "Will they leave you here?"

"No, *chica*. Not if they can help it."

"Are you concerned about the French soldiers?"

"At the moment, I would rather not be caught," he answered in an evasive manner that brought to mind another conversation that they'd had in the crypts before he went back for Father Henri.

"Do you know Harrison Kendrick?" she asked.

She could feel his eyes on her as if the question surprised him. "I know him," he answered.

"I see."

"Do you, *chica*? What exactly do you see?"

The sand was soft beneath her slippers. She shifted uneasily, sensing that there was something behind his stare, behind the tone in his voice that was just beyond her grasp. "Are you sure Father Henri is all right? He and the governor do not get along. Did you ask him about Harrison Kendrick?"

"Sarah . . ." He sloshed out of the water and sat down on the log that she'd nearly tripped over a moment ago. Movement told her that he was getting dressed. "I am very tired," he said.

"Have I done something wrong, Gabriel? Because . . ." She plowed ahead. "I have something I wish to say before you leave here."

She could feel his impatience but he didn't stop her from speaking. Perhaps he could see how important it was for her to say what was on her mind. She had noticed that about him. His patience with her seemed boundless. And his mind didn't seem to wander in a thousand directions when she spoke. He paid attention.

She tucked her hands into the folds of her robes. "I have

thought about what it will be like leaving this island," she quietly began, but her voice picked up strength as her new convictions filled her heart. This was no longer about being afraid. Fear was something that she would have to manage on her own. She didn't want Gabriel to think that she was weak. "You see . . . my whole life . . . at least most of what I remember, I've spent here. I don't know any place else. So if I acted poorly a few days ago, it's only that I don't take shock well. But if I have to leave, I'm glad it's with you."

She heard his exhale and sensed his quiet frustration with her words. Confused by his reaction, she rushed on. "Thank you for allowing me to bring my cat. Dog has been with me for years—"

"Dog?" he queried.

"My cat. His name is Dog."

"Dog?" he said again, as if he hadn't believed her the first time.

Then he laughed. Actually laughed. The sound was quiet and barely discernible above the running brook, but it was there all the same and she felt a little proud that she had been able to make the celebrated El Condor laugh. Even if he laughed at her.

"You see, when I was a child, I wanted a dog." She sidled closer. "I prayed that one would drop out of the sky. I thought a dog would make a good companion. But Father Henri would not allow dogs into our rooms. Then one day I found this kitten curled up on the steps of the church. He'd been injured. And I healed him. I am a healer." She stirred the sand with her toe. "At least people believe I am, and Father Henri always said that believing in something is half the battle won."

"That is good, *chica*." He stood and slapped a boot on the log as he pulled it on. "Because I need these stitches taken out of my head before they grow into my scalp."

"I can do that. Gabriel . . ." Her voice grew in nervous excitement. "I want to make the best of this marriage between us."

"Sarah . . ."

Another step and she drew beside him. "I've thought about this all night. I've thought about the kind of man you are."

"And what kind is that? You don't even know me."

"You are brave."

He snorted as if he thought her observation the most ridiculous thing in the entire world.

She tucked a strand of her hair behind her ears. "You have also seen much of the world, which makes you worldly. I wish to be worldly, too. And you came back for us when you could have left," she said, "which makes you honorable as well. I don't know anything about being a wife or that much about being a woman either, but I have learned to read the hearts of those around me."

She touched his chest and was shocked to feel that he wore no shirt. His flesh was warm against her palm. So different from the soft contour of her own body. His heartbeat was strong. All of this she felt in the seconds before he pulled her hand away.

"Sarah, there is much about me that you do not know."

"There is nothing about you that will change what I know in my heart. I wish to be your wife in truth."

"Ay yi. You've been through a lot, Sarah. You're confused."

"Don't you understand? For the first time in my life, I'm *not* confused."

"Two days ago you were distraught over leaving the mission."

Her hands fumbled with the rosary at her waist. "Everything was different then."

"Now you are suddenly ready to toss away the veil and sail the seas with me. I am not your walls, *chica.*"

That he would know her fears as well as she stunned her speechless. Her stomach dropped like rock.

"I am not your knight. You think that you are in love with me. You are young, Sarah. Impressionable. When your head clears, you will think differently."

"I know my heart, Gabriel."

"It won't work between us." His voice was gentle, almost as if he spoke to a child. Only she was no child. "I am not for you, *querida.* I'm sorry."

"But . . . I can learn to be a wife."

"It isn't that."

"Then what?"

"I have a little girl. She needs a mother."

"Truly it would not be that hard to love your child."

"Can you teach her the ways of her class? Can you teach her to be a lady and mingle among royalty? Can you follow her to court and be a part of our life there? A part of mine?"

"Is that so important to you? To mingle among royalty?"

He took both of her hands. "I think that you are more beautiful than moonlight on golden sand. I could even find pleasure in your body. Jesu . . . what man could not? But I cannot give you what you need as a husband."

"I need only you," she whispered past the stricture in her throat.

Dropping her hands, he walked away and, by the measurement of his movements, shrugged into his shirt. "I have a life, Sarah." Growing frustration was evident in his voice. It had not been her plan to make him angry with her. "Or what's left of it that I'm trying to salvage. Now I will have to delay returning to Spain."

His shoulders blocked the sunlight, for the warmth had vanished, and she hugged her arms to her chest. "I don't wish to be the cause of your delay."

"I made a vow to Father Henri to protect you. On my life, no one will harm you while you are in my care. That vow protects you from me, too. I must find a way to get you to your brothers."

The shock of his words froze her. "No." She scraped her hand through her hair. "If I go back, I will only be a burden to them. They have their own families."

"And I have mine, Sarah."

Which didn't include her.

She hadn't truly considered that he would not want her at all.

Her chest felt heavy, as if an anvil had been tied to her heart. She had never been in love before. She didn't believe Gabriel's comments that shock had made her vulnerable to his protective presence. Perhaps she had been originally drawn to his strength. But now it was more than that, for it hurt too much inside.

He was correct about her in some ways, but not all. It was

true that she didn't know anything about Spanish *señoritas,* or how to be a proper lady. She'd never learned the basics of proper table manners, or where to place a fork, or on which side of a plate one set a glass of wine. She knew nothing of fashion or hairstyles; those things that might matter to him. None of that was important to her. But she knew more about survival than any ten women because her lack of sight made her stronger in ways that they could not begin to comprehend.

Sarah could learn the other things.

"Come, *chica.*" An arm came around her shoulder. "We will talk no more of this, *sí*?"

She relented on a sigh. "Very well, Gabriel." They walked back to their small camp. "But I will ask one thing of you."

"Anything."

He was kind to her. How could he not care about her? Even a little?

"I ask . . . I ask that you not shame me before the others. At least pretend that I am your wife in truth until we can resolve the matter of our marriage. It will be bad enough that people will feel sorry for you. I could not bear it that you were shamed by me as well. Is that so much to require?" she asked when he didn't reply.

"I will not shame you, Sarah."

The answer was more than she hoped for. She also sensed that she was not all that undesirable to him just as he had told her. "And I will ask one more thing," she ventured.

"Could I stop you if I tried?"

She ignored his sarcasm. "I would have you kiss me."

He pulled away. *"¡Ay caramba!"* She could feel his appalled glare. "What do they put in that goat cheese, *señorita*?"

"You didn't kiss me when I spoke my vows to you. I wish to have that kiss now. Only because I will never wed again." And because she knew Cori was watching. Cori, who had kissed twenty men and bragged shamelessly about each one. But more than because of any rivalry with Cori, Sarah wanted Gabriel to claim her. Even if his affection didn't transcend into the bedroom, she would exact what she could.

"A real kiss, too—"

"I'm not going to kiss you, Sarah."

He stood in front of her, looking down at her face. She

could feel his annoyance and reveled in his dilemma. Her heartbeat picked up pace. "I had heard that Spaniards are a passionate lot," she said breezily. "That one kiss could curl the toes of an English prude."

He made a choking sound. "Where did you hear that?"

"Cori told me." She lifted her shoulders in a shrug. "I cannot honestly report back to her that she was correct."

Something in his demeanor changed. "So this is about showing your carping orange-headed *amiga* that you are a woman, too?"

It was really starting to annoy her, this ability of his to read her so clearly. But he wasn't entirely correct. This was about kissing him. About pressing her lips to his and maybe even touching his tongue again. Lust pure and simple with an added shake of curiosity that would not let go of his naked image.

Lifting the hem of her sodden robe, she swept past him, brushing his arm. "I am beginning to think that you are the prude, Gabriel."

The heat of his presence suddenly covered her like a cloak, until only inches separated them. "You play a dangerous game, *chica*."

The warning in his voice gave her pause an instant before his mouth touched hers. Despite the chasteness of his lips, languid heat softened her bones, and she sighed silkily, like a schoolgirl content to discover this wicked bit of wantonness. With a broken breath, she opened her mouth. After all, what did she know of physical intimacy, except what he had shown her in the crypt? He jerked away.

But he didn't go far.

She could hear his staggered breathing. She grabbed for air. Then his hands scraped through her hair and he lifted her face. A whisper of heat grew between them, gathering like the tidal forces of the distant waves that pounded the sand at her feet. "Is this what you want?" The growl in those words froze her. He backed her up until she hit against a tree. "Do you want me to lift your robes and bury myself in your body? So you can say you are no longer a virgin? Is that what you want to share with the world?"

Sarah willed herself not to faint.

"Don't play games with me, *chica*. You don't know the rules."

His tongue slid between her lips, searing her mouth, the power of his touch shattering control as he began to plunder her senses in earnest. Even the scratch of his stubble burned like an erotic pulse through her veins. What had started as a test to measure his feelings quickly spiraled into a lesson out of control as the sensuous current swept her along.

Suddenly panicked that she had waded in waters too deep to swim, she groaned. Her fists pressed against his chest, slowly opening like a flower in full bloom. Her fingertips braised his muscled shoulders where the sun had warmed his back. He wore a wet shirt opened to the island breeze. She trailed her palms across the velvet texture of the fine cloth to finally curl her fingers into his wet hair. She was conscious of nothing but the heat of his mouth, the taste of his breath, the pulse of his heartbeat that hammered against her chest. He pulled back just a whisper. Stunned by the chaotic flurry of her emotions, she dropped her arms, but the tree at her back kept her spine erect. Their breaths mingled.

"Don't make me test my honor, Sarah."

Her heart crashed.

When he pulled away, the world seemed to go with him, and she was left with naught but the wind in her hair where his fingers had been. It hurt to breathe. Her knees were wobbly.

"Gabriel . . ."

"When I deliver you to your brothers, you *will* be chaste."

His words more than anything else brought her back to her senses. She gathered her bearings and managed to call Gabriel's name before he'd walked a dozen furious steps back to their camp. "That was very nice, Gabriel. But the kiss wasn't nearly as perfect as the one before." She finally had his attention. Then, because some vampish creature had taken hold of her body, she added, "And maybe I don't wish to be a virgin any longer."

He marched back down the hill. Alarmed, she took a step back. In a moment, he lifted her in his arms. "What are you doing?"

Water sloshed as he entered the freshwater spring.

"Put me down. Gabriel!" She kicked her legs and bucked, but fighting his strength was like trying to wriggle out of an iron vise.

"You have a naughty mind, *chica.*" He dropped her in the water. She came up gasping as cold sluiced over her body, clothes and all. "I'll have Cori bring you soap to cleanse those impure thoughts."

"Have her bring *you* soap first. And a razor! Your face is scratchy, Don Gabriel."

Murmuring something rude in Spanish, he turned away. She scrambled through her repertoire of curses for one shocking enough to throw at him, but the sounds of the waves on the distant beach claimed his footsteps. With a sigh, she lifted her face and listened to the caw of blackbirds overhead. She would have to ask Cori to refresh her vocabulary. Lying back in the cooling current, she decided the water felt delicious. Besides—she rubbed her tender face—yelling would accomplish nothing. She didn't want to be the cause of bringing a garrison of French soldiers down on them.

After all, Gabriel had kissed her. And she hadn't thought he would.

Chapter Seven

Mango.

Gabriel still tasted mango: a freshly plucked from the tree, sun ripened sweetness kind of mango he hadn't tasted since he'd raided his mother's forbidden fruit garden when he was five.

Adjusting the looking glass, he was able to see the cart over his right shoulder. Absently, he rubbed a hand across his bristly jaw. The mirror was cracked, the silvering warped. Gabriel was a cold-blooded pragmatist, but unlike everything that had its proper place in his life, fantasy had begun to unveil weakness in the order of his existence. He found Sarah in the mirror. She sat on the back of the cart. Beneath a lock of his dark hair, he watched as she combed the white silky length of hers.

She wore his black-and-silver jerkin. It swallowed her, but she didn't seem to mind. Not as long as her robe hung on the nearby bushes to dry. Her leg curved slightly as she bent her head to further assess the tangles. In the fading daylight, her skin shone like warm ewe's milk.

He snapped up his shaving cup and began frothing the soap. Father Henri had wedded him to an unrefined coquette with legs up to her breasts and hair the color of bleached sand. At what point in her life had she *ever* thought that becoming a nun would ever be enough!

The brush whipped faster in the cup. He was not some untutored adolescent in the throes of budding manhood. Even if he *had* enjoyed dumping Sarah in that creek.

A slow grin eased some of the tightness from his shoulders. The vision of her suddenly fresh in his mind, he lifted his gaze back to the mirror . . . and looked directly into Cori's eyes.

"Shaving can be dangerous, Spaniard." She took the cracked wedge of glass that he'd managed to balance on the tree trunk and held it up for him. Gabriel's reflection glared back at him. "All that gawking and ye might cut yer throat. Perhaps ye need help."

Gabriel snatched the mirror. Waggling the razor, Cori plopped on the edge of the log where he'd set his shaving cup. "I'm good with a knife. Comes from time spent in prison." Clearly her favorite subject, she cheerfully amplified, "The deepest dungeon in Port Royal. For stealing, murder . . . you name it, Spaniard, I was guilty of doing it."

Gabriel caught her hand. "Lying?" Easing the razor from her grip, he stood and repositioned the mirror on a higher tree branch out of her reach. "I can shave myself, Señorita Sheldon."

Spreading her skirts, she made herself comfortable on the log he'd just vacated. "Most men I know don't bother to shave."

"Perhaps you are not acquainted with men, *si*?"

"Certainly none so ancient as you."

Gabriel soaped his face. He readjusted the mirror. Sarah was no longer at the cart, and he turned to scan the clearing. He'd learned yesterday the significance of the rope Father Henri had given them. Jaime had rigged around the camp and to the stream a line that Sarah now used to guide her steps. She'd stopped to pick up her cat lounging in the only pool of sunlight left in camp.

Cori studied her nails. "I suppose blue-blooded dons are never seen with a bristly face."

Jesu, the redhead needed someone to stuff a rag in her mouth.

She sighed. "Too bad," she persevered beneath his scowl. "Put a silver earring in yer ear and you could pass fer a needy pirate."

Gabriel found her in the glass. "Do you know why pirates wear one silver earring, hmm, *niña?*" He slapped more froth over his jaw. "So that when a Spaniard kills him that silver will pay for a burial. The only proper investment a pirate ever makes in his life."

"Blimey," she murmured, impressed. "Is that how you made yer riches? Robbin' them poor souls of all that silver? Or are you called the Vulture because you just kill 'em?"

Gabriel scraped the razor up his jawline. "I just kill them, *señorita,*" he said flatly. "But I *have* cut out an occasional tongue first if it suited."

She sniffed. "The only real Spaniards I ever saw were the ones I looked at across the bow of the Cap's ship. Just before the *Dark Fury* blew 'em out of the water." She fluffed her skirts. "Except yer sister," Cori said. "She was a decent sort, and pretty, too."

With a frown, Gabriel wiped shaving soap off his blade. Cori's idolization of Sarah's oldest brother surprised him. But not as much as Sarah's strange friendship with this guttersnipe. He studied Cori in the glass. She wore her ridiculous red satin dress, an unkempt complement to her ill manners and obscene mouth. Father Henri had told him that she'd played at being a boy for sixteen years. The dress was the only one of its kind that she'd ever deigned to wear. She was the antithesis of Sarah. Everything bold and forbidden. The bright red apple in Sarah's Eden.

"How is it that you speak English so well?" Cori flicked a beetle off her arm. "I thought Spaniards snubbed everything English."

Turning, he grabbed the linen rag from the branch. He wiped the soap from his face and neck. "Don't you have someplace better to be?"

"The Cap always says that to destroy an enemy, you have to know him first. Is that why ye speak so fluently? To know yer enemy?"

Gabriel raised a brow.

"Why do you hate the Drakes?"

"I don't."

"You imprisoned them. They were innocent of their crimes."

"They were innocent of nothing, *señorita*." He tossed down the rag and turned. "They were convicted in their own courts."

"Pah! By Harrison Kendrick's cronies. Are ye going to imprison Sarah in yer island fortress?"

"No." Bracing his palms on the branch, he said quietly, "She is free to do as she pleases."

Cori's stiff skirt crinkled as she moved behind him. "I don't want to see her hurt."

Gabriel turned. Earnest blue eyes searched his face. She barely reached his chest. "Neither do I, *querida*."

She nodded, and a quiet understanding passed between them. Then she sniffed. "I'm very particular about my friends."

"You needn't worry, *señorita*. I am more particular about mine."

That settled between them, her lips smiled. The bond they'd formed didn't mean they had to like each other to care for Sarah's welfare. "The Cap, he never wore an earring," she said brightly. "Reckon he never planned on being buried at sea by you, Spaniard."

Despite himself, the corners of his mouth lifted before he remembered himself and frowned. "Reckon not," he mimicked the brazen twit as she sashayed away. Drying his hands on the rag, he wadded it up and tossed it next to his cutlass.

Later, carrying a makeshift fishing pole, Cori took Sarah and walked to the beach. Gabriel had lain down on his pallet to grab some sleep before he relieved Jaime at watch, but unable to doze, he sat up when he heard them leave. Sarah still wore his jacket, and a dull pounding slapped against his ribs. He would never look at that black jerkin again without seeing it wrapped around her body like a well-cooked tortilla.

Bracing an elbow on his knee, he watched Cori's slow progress down the hill to the beach. Her absolute devotion to Sarah puzzled him. Sarah suddenly danced from foot to foot as her toes squished in the cooler sand. The warm breeze carried her yelp of laughter.

A part of him resented her peace with a world that exacted a high price just for living, while the other side of him envied the innocence that came with the loss of part of her childhood memories.

Which was why he hadn't asked her about Harrison Kendrick or pressed her about any association that she might have had with the former Jamaican governor. Gabriel would seek out Kendrick.

If he lived long enough to get off this French prison.

Gabriel leaned his head back on his shoulders. Distant lightning flashed above the trees.

He should not have kissed her.

Twice.

Or put his tongue in her mouth and sampled just how good mango could taste.

Sarah didn't follow Cori into the waves but remained standing at the edge of the sea. It was a few baby steps farther than he'd seen her take last night when Jaime had brought her down to touch the sand.

Listening to the melodic rhythm of her voice and the wash of waves on the sand, Gabriel lay down. With his fingers laced beneath his head, he stared at the sky, a glittering dome of stars. A mint in childhood dreams lay buried in that celestial plateau.

She was slowly healing.

Gabriel knew the process and recognized the signs. Including her hero adoration of him.

"He ain't come back," Cori said.

Sarah yanked the belt tighter around her robe. Cori had begun to slip more and more into the cockney brogue she had once been so familiar with. Father Henri had worked a year to teach her correct English as well as a smattering of French.

But they were all scared, and it showed. Like in the way Jaime groused at her that morning when she'd tried to help him fish. Or the way Cori refused her help in camp. Gabriel . . . she didn't know what he felt except he hadn't allowed her near him earlier to remove his stitches. Turning away, Sarah hadn't cared at that moment if Cori scalped him. They all deserved one another.

"He's been gone for hours." Cori's pacing rustled the leaves.

Sarah sat and pulled her cat into her lap. "Instead of fretting, we need to cook a decent meal."

"I heard 'im tell Jaime that the soldiers came within a mile of here last night. Oi've never seen the buggers so focused. Pirates could attack the garrison and find it empty for the lot that are out hunting us. What did ye do? Kill someone?"

Again, everything was somehow her fault. After Cori left the camp, Sarah sat alone in the grass, listening to the trees whisper. The sea joined the quiet music. Her cat nuzzled her chin, and Sarah found solace in his purrs. Everything around her sang with life.

Sarah set her mind on gathering sticks. She made a pile, then lit it with the flint. Jaime had brought back island yams that morning. If Cori caught any fish or a turtle, they would all eat a much-needed meal. No sooner did she bend over the sticks to work the flames when someone grabbed the back of her robe and hoisted her up.

"Jesu, Sarah!" Gabriel's voice was harsh. "Are you trying to burn yourself?"

Sarah wavered like an insignificant blade of grass before him. "Do you expect me to do nothing?" she snapped. "Everyone is treating me like an *enfant*. Have I not proven myself capable for eleven years? See"—she worked her lungs in demonstration—"I am still breathing."

His silence touched her, and she felt his dark eyes roaming her. She knew without a doubt that those eyes were dark as coal dust. He smelled of the sea and all things bold.

"You have very protective friends, *chica*."

"And you have no idea what it feels like to be a constant burden to everyone."

Gabriel surprised her by taking her arm and leading her to a log. "Sit," he commanded. "Where is your *cepillo*, your hairbrush?"

Sarah had no notion what he was about or what strange ailment had suddenly felled his reasoning. But she was game to learn.

After she pointed in the direction of her portmanteau, he returned. "When you work with fire, keep your hair tied."

The brush picked the tangles out of her hair. So unprepared for this action from him, she almost sighed before pulling herself back to a dignified pose. As if his actions granted her permission to talk, she moved toward the thought uppermost in her mind.

"How is your head?"

His grunt boded ill for the condition of his scalp.

She smiled. "Usually Cori leaves her victims gutted and gasping for air after one of her medical procedures. You survived well enough."

He bent nearer to her ear. "Maybe you've softened her."

"And maybe she likes you. If she doesn't slit your throat in the next week, you'll know for sure."

A breath of amusement came out with his words. "All of you make me ache, *chica*."

"That's good, Don Gabriel," she said in all earnestness. "I was beginning to think that you didn't like us."

His fingers felt beautiful in her hair. Her body hummed the same contralto melody her mind was wont to sing aloud. She closed her eyes, unable to imagine this man's hands performing a woman's toilette. Frowning, she wondered if he did this often. He was certainly skilled enough. "You know how to weave hair?" she questioned when his fingers skimmed the dip between her shoulder blades.

"I have on occasion braided my daughter's hair. She is forever running about with wild hair. Since my sister left, I fear that her *dueña* cannot control her, and sometimes I am called to help. Of course, she is far younger and less cooperative than you."

"How old is she?" Sarah wanted to know so much about him.

"She just turned seven," he quietly replied. "She is very beautiful . . . like her mamma was." And Sarah read the reverence in that one simple response. The man known to the world as El Condor hid a heart beneath the armorlike reputation.

She lowered her chin. Nobody had ever loved her that much.

Who was the woman who had been his wife before her?

"Gabriel—"

"Finished," he said, and stood.

Cori returned with fish, and again Cori's efficiency relegated Sarah back to helpless ornament. With a sigh, she gave up trying to help or tend the fire or cook the yams. Several hours passed with little more said between anyone. After the sparse meal, Sarah found her cat and lay down in the soft spongy mound of sea grass near the cart. But the movement of an insect alerted Dog, and he bounded away, leaving her to commune alone. She woke up later when Gabriel laid his jerkin over her.

Remaining on her side with her hands folded beneath her head, she listened to his footsteps walk away. Sarah tried to grasp what was happening to her. Until she'd met Gabriel, she never felt resentment for her blindness. His dark presence had tainted her world with light.

Perhaps until now, she'd been naïve. But she'd never allowed her blindness to become a hated thing within her before. Self-worthlessness too often followed self-pity. But outside the walls of Saint Mary's, she began to feel the first bite of inadequacy. Worse, she could blame no one for treating her as an invalid.

Only herself for her shame.

An unwelcome shiver enveloped her when she recalled the feel of Gabriel's strong hands in her hair, the deference in his voice when he spoke of his dead wife. Sarah wanted to be the woman who commanded that kind of reverence. The woman who spoke to his heart: the one who could teach his soul to sing again.

But more than her inability to see separated her from Gabriel. The past as well as cultural differences had shaped their worlds with irreconcilable differences. Differences that only weeks ago had forged a frightening impression of him in her mind. But Father Henri had believed in Gabriel's inherent goodness. And she believed, too.

Sarah buried her nose in Gabriel's jerkin. If Father Henri were here, he would take her in his gentle arms and reassure her that the world had not suddenly crashed into the sea, that her silly heart was not drowning.

"Holy *horseshit!*"

Cori's raspy expletive brought Sarah straight out of a deep sleep. She had no idea of the time, for the night was empty of all sounds. She smelled faint tendrils of smoke and wondered if someone had forgotten to bank the fire. "Cori? What's the matter?"

"The sky is red, milady. Red as gore, it is."

"How can you do nothing?" Jaime paced the clearing behind Gabriel. "We can't just stay here and hide."

Gabriel lowered the glass. Hunkered outside the circle of ancient trees at the uppermost point above the beach, he didn't move. The horizon glowed. Even from this distance, the stench of burning cane seared the back of his throat. "If you choose to go back, do so." He braced an elbow on his knee. "I don't have the liberty to leave."

"But the soldiers are burning the mission," Jaime said, his voice taking on the same desperation that haunted Gabriel.

"They are not burning the mission, only the outlying fields."

"And everything in their way. What could be so important to them that they'd be burnin' their fields?"

"Burning cane fields is common," Gabriel said tonelessly. "It does not destroy the cane. But it does rid the fields of vipers and poisonous insects."

"And us," Jaime spat. "They are hunting us like criminals."

By tomorrow, everything alive would have fled the fields and run north away from the fire. The French soldiers would turn their search toward the inhospitable terrain that bordered the rocky cliffs.

"You and Señorita Sheldon are free to go," Gabriel said into the silence that followed. "It is not you they are after."

His gaze fell on a violet orchid that had twined around a dead branch at his feet. The blossom stretched languidly into the darkness, peaceful and out of place in the clutter of his mind. He reached to touch the flower when Jaime's boot landed firmly on the bloom. Gabriel's mind went momentarily black.

"How can you do nothing?" Jaime demanded.

As Gabriel stood, the rage barely contained surfaced. "Have I not already done enough? What can two men do against five hundred?"

"We can go back for Father Henri."

"That will do no good. Do you understand?"

"What kind of heartless bastard are you?"

Gabriel grabbed him by the loose scruff of his shirtfront and slammed him against a tree. "I am El Condor, Englishman. My soul is already black. Killing you will make it no less filthy."

"Did . . . you murder him?" Jaime rasped in sudden dawning. "Is that why we shouldn't go back? Are those soldiers hunting *you?*"

A muscle worked in Gabriel's cheek. "You're very fortunate that you are her friend, Englishman."

Gabriel let his grip loosen. Jaime crumpled to the ground. Grasping the hilt of his cutlass, Gabriel stepped back and turned.

Sarah and Cori stood like white granite facing him. Nothing prepared him for the shock. Sarah's presence was as unexpected in this brimstone setting as that orchid had been.

With her hands grasped in front of her, she seemed to be looking directly at him. But he knew she could not see him.

"He's dead, isn't he?" Jaime whispered from behind him.

His eyes on Sarah's pale face, Gabriel didn't reply. The man was intelligent enough to figure out the truth.

"Ye didn't tell us. Why?" Then, at Gabriel's silence, Jaime's gaze traveled past him and found Sarah in the trees. Understanding and horror dawned. "Mother Mary and Joseph. I'm so sorry, Sarah."

"How?" Sarah's voice was flat, emotionless.

"The governor shot him."

Gabriel stared down at Sarah's ashen face, dueling with the logic of offering his hand to this angel woman who knew nothing of Gabriel's mind or how his silence inadvertently protected a man who in his stupidity had betrayed her. Nor did he tell her that without hesitation, he'd skewered Father Henri's murderer through the heart. Somehow, thinking the thought while looking at Sarah Drake made him feel foul.

Gabriel folded his fingers into his palm. Turning, he pulled Jaime to his feet. "We'll leave here at daybreak."

"Where will ye be takin' us?"

"*¡Ay de mi!* You tell me," Gabriel snapped. "This is your

paradise. Not mine." He turned, only to stop. "And Englishman—" His voice took on the chill of ice. "Do not question
my honor again."

Gabriel swept past Sarah, his boots leaving deep wounds
in the tender soil at her feet. He didn't go back to camp. The
loss of Father Henri was hers, not his. He felt nothing!

Not for any of them.

Running the length of the secluded cove, he reached the
rocks until he could run no more. In a fit of rage, he snatched
up a piece of driftwood and hurled it into the surf. Drawing
breath into his lungs, he bent and braced his hands on his
thighs. Did his ship lie at the bottom of the sea, shot to splinters by some French brigantine? For nothing short of outright
destruction would have kept Stefan away this long. Gabriel's
reasons for coming to this island paled against the price his
men might have paid for his foolish sentiment.

Jesu . . . will I never learn?

The reality that he might never see his daughter again and
that he would die and leave his name in a state of disgrace
weighed like an anchor in his heart. He dropped onto a damp
log and kicked at a crab that had skittered out from beneath.
Dawn had yet to burn the night away but the sky glowed.
He'd seen that kind of ethereal orange once during a night
battle when a full broadside by an English frigate had sent one
of his countrymen's ships to the seafloor. The ship had burned
for hours, her crackling timbers devoured by flame before finally surrendering to the sea. The struggle had been valiant
but in the end useless.

His jerkin suddenly fell over him. Sarah stood beside him.
His startled gaze went over her oval face, her rosebud mouth,
her silver eyes wet with tears that she'd shed before she faced
him. With her long pale hair, her white robe, she looked like
a moonbeam.

"It's cold," she quietly pronounced. "You should not be
down here without your coat."

Waves broke over the beach, a gentle lull that grabbed at
Gabriel. "How do you do that? How do you find me the way
you do?"

"I am blind, Gabriel, not deaf." A sniffle escaped. "You

have been pacing the beach. Besides, Jaime brought me down here."

Gabriel glanced around her legs but saw only the glitter of silver bubbles on the wet sand. The wind actively courted the foliage and trees. His eyes burned from fatigue.

Sarah lifted her chin and looked away. "I know why you didn't tell me. I also know that you didn't ask for any of this."

Gabriel shifted but still didn't reply.

Her throat wobbled. "I think that you don't want anyone to know that you're afraid," she said, "so you hide."

"Is that what you came down here to tell me? That it's all right to hide and nurse my wounds?"

"Are you wounded, Gabriel? I thought perhaps you might be worried for the welfare of your ship."

At once, he felt like an ass, and he scraped his hands through his hair in quiet frustration. "What about you, *chica*?"

Sarah fidgeted with the folds of her robe. He noted that the bones of her hands were delicate like the finest porcelain, her fingers long and capable despite the fact that they were curled protectively against her chest as if whatever was inside, she was determined to keep there. The contrast between fragility and strength brought back the image of those hands in his hair. Unbidden, he raised his gaze to her face, and he was suddenly remembering more.

"Come." Gabriel pulled her down beside him so they could share the jerkin. "It is too cold for both of us."

She didn't move close enough to share the jerkin. Her spine stiff as ice, she merely sat with her hands folded tightly in her lap. "I am not so weak, Don Gabriel. Don't coddle me. Does someone coddle you?" she challenged.

"That is different. I am a man."

She snorted, the tremble in her bottom lip nearly eclipsing her bravado. "I don't need you to feel sorry for me. Father Henri's legacy will not die with him. My sadness is selfish, for in my heart I know . . . I know that he is in a better place."

Gabriel didn't reply.

"You are a man of honor," she continued. "I release you from your promise to Father Henri. Jaime, Cori, and I will return to the mission."

"No, *chica*. You are my responsibility."

She stood. "I do not choose to be anyone's responsibility."

"You are still my wife."

"Then I divorce you."

"You cannot divorce me. Our annulment will be granted through the Church, and then I will see you safely delivered to your brothers. When I find them," he muttered in after thought.

His words seemed to take the life out of her and she slumped down on the log. "Why can't we stay married, Gabriel?" she whispered.

Gabriel lifted her onto his lap, and she laid her cheek against his shoulder as if it was the most natural place to rest her head. She trembled from more than early morning chill.

"We have already gone over this." He stroked the hair from her face and pulled her chin around. "Besides, by to-morrow you may be a widow and the matter settled."

"That is a horrible thing to say!"

"But true."

Tears filled her eyes. After a shivery exhale, she said, "Tell me about your daughter."

"*Ay, chica.* Her name is Christina María. She has climbed an occasional tree. She is very bright. . . . *Sí,* I miss her."

"You loved her mother very much, didn't you?"

"She was my life."

Desperation seemed to unmask her expression. "I loved him, too, Don Gabriel. I truly did. He was like my father. He . . . he had no right to . . . to get himself killed."

Her fingers fretted with the open collar of his shirt. He pulled the jerkin to shield them both from the sea-chilled breeze.

"Is your father still alive?" she asked.

Hesitation crawled through him. "He's been dead for many years."

"How?"

"He was . . . killed by pirates. I was ten," he said without emotion. "Henry Morgan attacked Puerto Bello. My father was killed along with hundreds of others."

"My father sailed with Henry Morgan," she said after a moment. "Is that why you despise my family?"

"Sarah, this is not a topic—"

"I wish to understand you, Don Gabriel. Father Henri married me to you and I want to know why. He never did anything without a reason. There *is* a reason."

"He asked me to take you away from here."

"No . . ." She suddenly buried her face into his shirt. Warmth bled from her silent tears. "He should not have sent me away. Father Henri was wrong to do that."

"You didn't kill him, Sarah."

"I . . . wish to understand." She wiped her face with the back of her hand. Her voice hiccuped slightly, then as her body surrendered the fight, her shoulders racked with sobs. He wrapped his arms around her, shielding her as much as he could, knowing it would never be enough. She babbled about her life at the convent and the mission school. She spoke of her brothers, her dreams, friends come and gone: a whole world apart from his.

"I left sanctuary last year," she admitted, "when Talon's daughter was born. I'd never left before. I didn't stay outside the walls for long. I'm ashamed of my cowardice. If I'd been braver, I would have gone with Talon to be with everyone. It's because of me that Father Henri is dead and you are stranded on this island."

"Have you ever raised your hand against anyone, *chica*?" He splayed the bend of her narrow waist.

"What does that matter? Something inside me is very wrong. It's ugly. And it makes me afraid of everything. Sometimes . . . I hear screams. I think . . . I think the screams are mine."

Her unseeing eyes, bright with tears, flicked over his face. "I don't want to be afraid anymore. But I am. I thought that if I stayed inside Saint Mary's forever, I would be safe."

Gabriel touched his mouth to her temple. Her hair was damp from the tears. "There is no place that safe in the world, *chica*."

"But don't you see?" She wiped her wet nose with the heel of her hand. "Father Henri knew that, too. That's why he didn't let me take my vows as an escape. Only when I am healed of heart will I be healed of mind. Only . . . only you are my heart, Don Gabriel."

"No, *chica*," he whispered against the corner of her brow. "I am nobody's heart."

She tasted salty, like the open sea that he loved. Jesu, he was one afflicted *bastardo* to want to lay her on the beach and lick her all over, she tasted that good. He had no strength to quit the inner tumult. No guardian to expel the impulse to kiss away her suffering as if he had the power of God to heal anything. She was bleeding her hurt out to him, and he wanted to love her in the sand. He wanted to bury himself in all that innocence.

"Do you believe in angels?" she suddenly asked. He barely heard the words. "Because I hear . . . bells, Don Gabriel."

His head lifted. Above the sound of his beating heart, he heard it, too. A ship's bell.

The distant change of the night watch.

He twisted to gaze out across the sea. Silhouetted against the silken coral sky, a square-rigged frigate drifted languidly into the sunrise.

Chapter Eight

"**S**he is close-hauled and still weathering on us, *Capitán.*"
    Stefan's voice barely penetrated the haze in Gabriel's head. It felt good to think in Spanish again. He didn't have to inspect his every word. Or think of to whom he was speaking.

A spur of naked land jutted out from the east just at the tip of the horizon. "We are too close to landfall. Take the soundings. I have no desire to find this ship impaled upon a reef."

"It is not like you to run from a fight," Stefan said for the third time in as many hours since he'd dragged Gabriel from bed.

"The *Felicity* is not prepared to fight."

Unshaved and uncombed, Gabriel had barely slept since his ship had returned and plucked him off Martinique. Nor had he seen Sarah. Displacing his loyal ship's master, she rarely ventured from the small cabin she shared with Cori. A storm passing to the south had made the seas rougher than normal these past five days, but it was the English warship that followed in his wake that concerned him most. The same ship had been the cause for Stefan's delay. Gabriel suspected who might be on board, but the *Felicity* sailed in open waters frequented by all nations and he could not be sure.

Lowering the glass, he lifted his gaze to the topgallant sails. Bathed crimson in the sunset, the canvas spread out in the wind. A westerly breeze drove them easily through the sea.

Gabriel had captured this ship from English pirates only

two years before off Cartagena and converted her to a prof-
itable merchantman. Riding high in the water, she was
equipped for speed, not for war. But still, the *Felicity* could
defend herself better than most Englishmen could fight.

"When it is dark, put the ship on a starboard tack. Keep her
as near the wind as she'll lie, *sí*?"

"Then you intend them to catch us?"

"No. I intend to *lose* them. We are not at war with England
this month, *sí*? Maybe they are pirates. Who is to say? But we
are going to San Martín for supplies." The sea spray had
dampened his white shirt, and it clung to his chest and shoulders. He handed Stefan the glass. "If you wake me before daybreak, I will throw you to the sharks."

"But what about the white-haired girl?" Stefan stopped
him from leaving the quarterdeck.

Gabriel's patience snapped. The wind caught his hair and
pulled at his sleeves. "Is she eating? And breathing?"

"The Englishman, he is caring for her and her redheaded
maid. They were up here last night after you went below."

"Then there is no problem."

"She is asking for you every day, Don Gabriel."

"I cannot help that."

Stefan blocked the stairs. "*Capitán* . . . I have no wish to
question you. But should we not be on a tack for Spain?"

With an oath, Gabriel looked away. "I should, but I'm
not," he finally said at length.

"You will miss your court inquisition," Stefan informed
him unnecessarily. "I wish to understand what it is you are
thinking. And what this woman is to you."

"Stefan, *mi amigo,* you would not understand if I told
you." His eyes narrowed. "Do you find something amusing?"

"It is just . . . that you have never called me your friend."

Gabriel raised his gaze to the sky. "*¡Santa María!* You and
most of this crew have served me for more than seven years.
I am godfather to your son. Why should it be strange that I
call you friend?"

"Then I will tell you, as your friend, that the men whisper
among themselves. They say you are changed. You would
never have the *ingleses* on board this ship. Not even as
hostages."

"As I said before, the lady is under my protection," he answered. "That is all I'm prepared to say."

If his men discovered that she was a Drake, they'd crucify her. They'd certainly never understand that he'd married her, even if that marriage may not be legal under Spanish law. Either way, he wasn't prepared to explain his logic to Stefan, not when he still waded through the quagmire himself.

"And, Stefan, I pay the men well enough not to question my orders. We sail for Santo Domingo."

Gabriel's cabin stretched across the stern and gave him plenty of light. The presence of a twelve pounder brought home to him that despite the luxury of the ship and these quarters in particular, they were still in dangerous waters and he could take nothing for granted.

Stripping off his wet shirt, he threw himself onto his bunk. His eyes were gritty. He laid an elbow across his forehead and stared at the sand-colored walls bathed crimson by the reddening sunset. Above him, bare timbers braced the deck. Cherry-wood cabinets lined the walls. A desk in the corner near the windows added luxury to the room while an elegant Turkish rug lent comfort. A lifetime collection of miniature art shared the shelves with two priceless silver chalices and a half dozen dolls. Even in his absence, Stefan had seen the room kept free of mold and dirt. The dolls belonged to his daughter. He'd left them on board during her last trip to Havana.

One of the silver chalices held an emerald. Upon his return from Seville, he'd planned to make a ring for the woman who had been his daughter's caretaker for more than a year. Doña Betina had been his wife's closest friend, and through the years since Felicity's death, she'd been a stable figure not only in his daughter's life, but his. She was connected at court: a widow with a pragmatic perception of the marriage bed and marriage as a contract. He'd chosen this emerald for her eyes, and his gesture was more romantic than he'd ever been since he'd lost his wife.

Yet it was not emeralds that captured his thoughts now, but silver likened to the finest diamonds.

Movement turned his head and he spotted the gray-and-white cat leaping onto the narrow shelf below the window. Sarah's cat kept him awake at night, twined incessantly through his legs, and was generally a pain in the ass during meals. He should have tossed the thing overboard along with his three other problems.

At San Martín, a small Spanish garrison where the *flota* made first landfall after their arduous trip from Spain, Gabriel planned to take on enough fresh supplies to allow them to reach Santo Domingo. He'd also scratched out a letter to the Catholic tribunal in Vera Cruz requesting an annulment from Sarah Drake, including the circumstances of the marriage. Because of the haste of the ceremony and lack of royal decree required for him to wed, there was the possibility the marriage wasn't legal. Stefan would post the letter to go out on the next military packet headed to New Spain.

In the meantime, Sarah was safest away from him.

"Did ye know he's rich?" Cori said. "He is a marquis. The Marqués de Villena or some such place. Jaime told me this morning."

Sarah lay on her side in her narrow bunk. All around her, the ship breathed as if alive. The walls were bones that creaked with the ship's rise and fall on the sea. The heartbeat, centered somewhere deep within the bowels of this hull, yielded nothing to her touch, her insignificance amplified by the sound of engorged sails and the wash of waves as the wind bore her farther from her world on Martinique. Splaying her palm across the cool planking moist with the essence of salt, she could imagine nature's awesome power, equaled only by the man who sailed this ship.

The way Father Henri had navigated forces of a different kind to save her.

She still could not believe that Father Henri was dead. That his essence had vanished from this earth.

"That would make you a Missus Marquis to be sure." Cori tried to sound cheerful—poor Cori, who had been so sick for days.

"Did Jaime find Dog?" Sarah asked, tracing circles on the wall.

"Jaime said that 'e's probably in the hold fat and 'appy with an endless supply of rats. Yer not to worry. Milady."

Cori's wispy voice turned Sarah in her bunk. "Oi think I'm going to be sick again."

Sarah pulled her legs over the side of the bunk and bent to find the slop bucket. Cori found it first. Water sloshed in the wooden bowl Jaime had set on the narrow table attached to the wall between the bunks. Sarah dipped a rag inside and then covered Cori's brow with it.

"Lord lay me in the bog to die a painless death . . . Oi hate ships, milady. They suck the livin' life right out of ye."

The rise and fall of the deck beneath Sarah's feet made her queasy as well, though her continued lethargy grew from something worse. Something more fetid.

"You survived Talon's ship, didn't you?" Sarah gently replied.

"Better than yer surviving Father Henri's death, milady. Ye ain't hardly spoken in five days. You just lie there and stare at the ceiling. Maybe ye should be cryin' or somethin'."

"Has it been that long? Five days?"

"Ye never sleep. Ye've eaten like a bird. Me an' Jaime . . . we don't know what we should do, milady."

Sarah felt responsible for the misery Jaime and Cori suffered on her behalf. The realization that she'd allowed herself to sink so low in so short of a time laid starch down Sarah's spine. She brushed her hands across the soiled skirt of her robe. The cabin reeked of sickness and an unemptied chamber pot. Cori needed fresh air.

Forcing herself to stand, Sarah felt her way around the bunk and opened the door to the gangway. Blindness did not incapacitate her sense of smell. Indeed, the smell of a room more than anything told not only who was present, but what had happened in that room. Jaime was not on guard outside her door. The man who stood before her now had eaten chicken for dinner and topped the meal off with grog. She wondered if she smelled half as bad as he did.

"I wish to speak to your captain." She aimed her voice at the nameless pair of legs that stopped pacing when she'd opened the door.

The man's breathing seemed to quicken. His lack of response alarmed her. A moment later she felt a hand touch her hair. She yanked back and hit her head on the door. People always touched her when they first met her, as if they had some inalienable right to paw her like she was someone's pet monkey. She wasn't at the mission anymore. No one on this ship had the right to touch her. Slapping his hand away, she braced herself against the ship's movements.

"I said that I wished to see your captain."

"Un momento, señorita," the voice uttered, and his hand pulled her into the corridor. "I have waited for you."

Sarah stumbled. But she wasn't stupid and knew that he took her in the opposite direction of Gabriel's cabin. His palm was moist against her arm, and she detected a tremble. Perhaps he was taking her on deck, but she would not chance it. Intuition brought her feet to an abrupt halt before he'd taken a dozen steps.

"Where are you taking me?"

"The *capitán,* he does not wish to talk to anyone. But there are many who wish to see you, *sí*? We have watched you at night on deck."

"Milady?" Cori called from behind her.

The grip on her upper arm was not cruel, but Sarah was frightened when he handed her down a length of stairs. "You will follow me."

Heart pounding, Sarah tried to twist her arm away, but the man was insistent. She felt the bulkhead scrape her shoulder. The ceiling seemed lower, pressing down on her. Her throat tightened.

Then suddenly he stopped, and his hand dropped away. She massaged where he had tightened his grip. The ship canted, and underfoot she felt the planking groan. Male voices surrounded her. They spoke in Spanish, harsh, uneasy. She understood the words *white hair* and something silly about angels. No one approached but she felt their stares. They were a superstitious lot no different than most people when they saw her for the first time.

"I wish for you to pray for my brother," her kidnapper said. "You can make him better, *sí*?"

Sarah felt a sinking reluctance when the man laid her hand on a boy's brow. People often came to the mission specifically seeking her out as if she possessed some God-given capability to cure the lame and diseased with merely the touch of her hands. The boy's body was cool beneath her touch.

"Is he sick?" she asked.

"No, *señorita*. It is . . . it is only that he was born wrong. His foot is twisted and he cannot walk without pain. He is my only family. I wish you to help him."

"I . . . if he is not ill—"

"*Sí, senorita*. He has a bellyache to end all bellyaches. Do you not, Juan?"

Sarah heard a faint mumble of agreement.

But Sarah had no more gifts to offer this boy than she had to offer herself. Father Henri had believed in something inside her that wasn't there. She was no angel or savior to work miracles, and she was too angry with God to think He'd care to listen to anything she might want to ask of him. Any God who let Father Henri die was surely not all-powerful. Any God who made her blind was cruel!

She pulled her hands away.

"I would feed him fresh rainwater and boiled rice," she said. "It is the only food he should eat. Take him abovedeck where he can get sunlight and air." She didn't know if he understood her but she didn't care .

"Will you not pray, *por favor*?" The man pressed a crucifix into her palm.

Sarah wanted to shout at them all that she was no angel, not even a real nun, though she wore the attire of one, but the hope in the man's voice silenced her retort.

After she finished a prayer, Sarah could not back away as another man knelt before her and asked for her prayers. She realized in horror that men had lined up to receive her touch.

"Please," she said in growing panic.

Shouts behind her drew the man up. She felt him shrivel. Voices filled the room, followed by a furious scuffle as Jaime barreled into the man. Another man yelled, his tongue-lashing cowering even her.

"Stop!" Sarah finally cried. "Nothing has happened to me!"

Jaime was suddenly beside her. Breathing hard as if he'd just ascended from a fight, he took her arm. "Cori said that someone had taken you. Are you all right?"

"Yes . . . yes. I'm fine." She wasn't though. She was suffocating within these walls. Her chest tightened. Her breathing grew shallow. "This boy needs to be taken on deck. Please."

"You have my most profound apologies, *senorita.*" A man spoke in English. He took her hands but she was quick to yank them away. "My name is Stefan," he said, "and the *capitán* has put you in my charge. If any of these men have harmed you . . ."

So Gabriel had not even told his men that she was his wife. He'd stuffed her away in an airless cabin out of sight the moment they'd boarded his ship and told everyone that she was a *señorita,* not a *señora* or even a doña. He'd been that quick to rid himself of her presence. That quick to forget that they'd been friends, at least a little bit. He'd struck a bargain that he would not shame her, and now chose not to honor his word.

"The only person who has injured me is your esteemed *capitán,*" she said in rising hysteria, feeling more distraught with each passing moment she stayed in this airless coffin. "My maid needs help to come on deck. I cannot carry her. This boy is ill and should not be down here between decks." She allowed Jaime to wrap her in his arm but only until they reached the deck, and then she didn't want even his touch. "And I can't find my cat!" Wind buffeted her robes and hair. "You can tell my . . . Don Gabriel that rats and roaches are accorded more hospitality aboard this ship than he's granted me! Perhaps it would make him happy if my poor blind self fell overboard, and he can explain to my brothers how his prisoner expired in his care."

"But he has assured me that you are no prisoner, *señorita*—"

"Drake." Tears filled her eyes and threatened to ruin her tirade. She didn't care who knew her identity. The world was bound to find out anyway when Gabriel was forced to house her. "D-R-A-K-E, in case you do not understand my pronunciation. I am a vicious half-English pirate," she flaunted with relish, horrified by this awful version of herself that had taken hold. "And you tell Don Gabriel that he can drop me off at the nearest port and I will find my own way to my brothers. This ship is not big enough for the both of us."

"*Señorita* . . . let me take you back to your room."

Bottom lip trembling, Sarah stepped out of his reach. If he touched her, she was sure to strike him with her fist. "The only way that you will return me to my cabin is by deadly force, sir."

The banging of spars and blocks filled the shocked silence that followed. Canvas flapped as the ship pitched in a roller, and all the while Sarah remained balanced on her feet as if she belonged to the sea. No one breathed a word. And as if the melodrama wasn't enough, thunder grumbled overhead. A sudden electrical surge filled the air.

"Blimey, milady," Cori whispered when the first drop of rain plopped on the deck. "You went and cooked the goose now."

"Feed it to Don Gabriel," she told Señor Stefan.

Lifting her face into the rain, she stretched out her hand for Jaime to take her to the ship's prow. Men parted ranks to let her pass. If they'd given her special powers by virtue of her appearance, then surely conjuring up a rainstorm bore home the wrath of Jehovah.

Sarah grasped the ship's taffrail and would not be pried loose. The deck rose and fell as the ship sliced through the powerful waves. Rain battered her face. Wind caressed and melded her senses to the storm. Surrounded by a thundering symphony of sounds, Sarah opened her mouth to taste the sea. Her hair whipped around her like a banshee's scream in the night. But she didn't care. Nor did she know how long her hands and feet held her captive. Time was as endless as the darkness, as deep as the anger that burned hot inside her.

Sarah didn't know what was happening to her. She recognized nothing familiar about herself. Her wants and needs were as alien as her emotions, and suffocated her. She needed to breathe, to feel the salty air against her face. To fly!

Jaime and Cori had long since abandoned their efforts to pull her off the rail, so she stood like a figurehead, relishing the storm's fury. When she felt a presence move beside her, she thought Jaime had returned with a blanket, only because he had never left her this long before.

A hand fell over both of hers attached to the taffrail. Alarm skittered down her spine. *"Chica?"* Gabriel's voice was dangerous, more powerful than the storm.

Sarah's heart stopped. "Go away, Gabriel." She pressed against the rail as far as she could to escape his presence.

"What are you doing? I have to be pulled out of bed because no one else will approach you," he said over the wind. "Look at you."

Sarah's grip on the wet rail tightened.

Closing her senses against him, she lifted her face to the wind. "I have done this before, Gabriel. I can feel it in my heart."

"Come—"

"No!"

He pulled her easily around into the circle of his arms. "You are chilled. I don't want you out here."

"I won't go back inside." Her arms stiff at her sides, she turned her chin away. "Besides, I am not your wife, which makes me free to do as I please as long as I'm not hurting anyone else." The wind pulled at her words. "Am I hurting anyone else?"

"You are angry, *chica*," he said judiciously. "I apologize for the actions of some of my crew. No one will bother you again."

Sarah's response became tangled with confusion. Her chest tightened. His men had not harmed her. He didn't understand that her turmoil had naught to do with his crew.

Her fists clenched. "Leave me alone, Gabriel."

He lifted her into his arms. His shirt was unbuttoned as if it had been haphazardly thrown on. He was wet to the bone, as was she. Without moving her arms or fighting his, she turned her face away and resisted in stiff silence. He would take her to the cabin, and unless he locked her in the room, she would merely leave again.

She could feel the stares of his men. He spoke to Stefan in Spanish. Then a door slammed behind her and Gabriel was descending into the gangway. He walked past her cabin and into another.

At once Sarah recognized his distinctive male scent in the room. She could feel the space surrounding her. This cabin belonged to him. He set her down. Her feet touched carpet.

Still, she didn't move. She stood with her chin held high, staring into oblivion. Her body, which had been fine in the cold before now, began to shake.

"Remove your clothes, Sarah." She heard the snap of a metal latch. When he threw open the lid of her trunk, she heard his quiet oath. *"¡Ay yi!* This thing is filled with nothing but junk and an old Bible. Don't you have anything else besides that robe to wear, *chica?"*

Tilting her chin away, she would not answer his sarcasm. When she'd packed, she'd been stubbornly resistant to the idea of leaving the mission. She'd taken few clothes. Besides, he would not understand that these *things* were all that she had left of her family. The Bible belonged to Talon. Sarah had not understood why Father Henri had made her take it, but she was glad now that he had.

Shaking in earnest, she heard another trunk open and the *whish* of cloth as he delegated her something to wear from his own wardrobe. When he stood before her and saw that she had removed nothing and instead dripped water over his floor, he reached down and yanked the robe up over her head.

"You are soaked. Is it your wish to die of lung fever?"

She still wore her chemise and soggy stays. His hands worked the laces below her breasts. With an oath, he finally cut the laces.

"A-are you as w-wealthy as they say you a-are?" She shivered. "Because s-stays are expensive and l-laces are not easy to come by."

"Ah, my fey wife speaks," he mocked. A towel briskly rubbed her hair dry. "I will hire a dressmaker to make you ten more if you wish." His anger at her had become a palpable thing that began to stir the air between them.

"W-wife is it now? Does anyone else know?" she inquired with equal ire. Her voice was muffled. "Or do they merely add *puta* to their opinions of me."

The towel stopped. He stood within a sigh of her touch. "Everyone knows," he said after a moment. He resumed the rubdown. "I cannot have my crew accosting you to perform some miracle every time you step outside this door, now can I?"

"They didn't hurt me—"

A finger tilted her chin. "If they'd hurt you they would be dead."

"Surely . . . you have not punished them?"

"Punished?" His incredulous tone made her flinch. "I have more than a hundred men on this ship. They *will* obey my orders or find themselves flogged to within an inch of their lives. The man who took you below is in chains and will be removed from this ship at our next stop."

Sarah's fingers curled into her palms. This was a part of Gabriel she had only briefly glimpsed.

Finally, her chemise followed the way of her robe, and Sarah stood in Gabriel's room naked as the day she was born. Her heart banged against her ribs. The chill rose bumps on her skin. She could not breathe for the torment that settled between her legs.

Sarah didn't understand the physical anomalies that occurred in her body when she was in Gabriel's presence, but she felt his eyes on her now, and it was hard to understand how he could remain so unaffected. Well, so could she. Turning her chin away, she made to dismiss him. Her teeth had not quit their chatter.

A whisper of cloth fell over her head and down her torso. Gabriel's tangy scent fluttered over her skin. She breathed in his redolence. He shoved her arms into the sleeves of his shirt and yanked the laces tight. The shirt hung nearly to her knees.

"I'm g-glad you're rich," she finally said, ignoring his ministrations.

He stood back. "Why is that, *chica*? Hmm? Do you wish me to buy you jewels? Perhaps build you a house in the clouds?"

"C-could you?" she asked in sudden disbelief. "I mean build a house in the clouds?"

"Is that what you want?"

Sarah blinked, unable to comprehend if he was joking. Or if he really possessed such wealth at his disposal. "I w-want a dress," she said at length. "A red dress like C-Cori's. With fancy lace. I want to f-feel the rustle against my legs when I walk."

This time it was his turn for shock or disbelief, Sarah couldn't tell which. Then a blanket fell around her shoulders.

"I would not give you a dress like Cori's if you were my worst enemy, *chica*."

She lifted her nose. "I want to dance the minuet in a red dress. Do you dance, Gabriel? D-do you?" she asked when he didn't answer.

"Not in many years."

"But you've attended balls where beautiful women wearing velvet dresses were all fluttery just for a dance with you." She wobbled a hand over her breasts. "I imagine you leave the ladies breathless. Liandra said that everyone takes notice when you walk into a room."

Irritation crept into his silence.

She sobered, her determination rising to quash his stillness. "I've never danced. I've never learned to swim in the waves. Nor caught turtles like the other children did. I've never ridden a horse. Or climbed a tree."

She'd never loved with her body as she did with her soul. There were too many nevers to count. The invisible walls that had been her security for eleven years were now her prison.

And she would no longer be confined.

"I wish to be like Cori." She thrust out her chin. "She has lived life and known the grandest adventures." The ship lurched and she stumbled slightly. Gabriel caught her shoulders.

"You wish to be like Cori?" His voice was flat.

"I want to be worldly. To experience all things." She was suddenly cold again, and pulled the blanket around her shoulders.

Gabriel spun her around. Her feet moved in double time as he directed her to a chair. Wood creaked beneath her weight. Two glasses rattled on the table. He wrapped her fingers around one, and the sound of sloshing liquid followed. She wrinkled her nose at the horrid smell.

"Black rum," he confirmed. "My plantation on Hispaniola grows the sugarcane that makes this rum. It will take the chill out of your blood. Have you ever tasted rum?"

She shook her head. Gabriel finished his glass and poured a second. "Go on," he encouraged. "You wish to experience all that life has to offer. Life starts here, Sarah Drake."

He mocked her, she could tell. But she was not such a

coward as he thought. Nor would she allow his cynicism to come between her new self and the old Sarah that was afraid of everything. What did he know, anyway, of the terrors that came with the light? His life was a golden rainbow filled with all the treasures she suddenly wanted.

Sarah tipped the glass and drank. Fire burned down her throat and exploded in her belly. Gasping, she sucked in enormous gulps of air. To her credit, she didn't spew the vile stuff all over Gabriel.

She heard him toss back the second glass. "Was that good?"

All she could manage was a weak shake of her head and a rasp.

His rum-warmed breath fluttered against her cheek. "Life is like that, *chica*," he gently warned. "You may not find any of it to your liking. It is wise to understand what you want before you indulge your fantasies."

Still choking, Sarah let Gabriel lead her to the bed. After he'd tucked the blankets around her, she could talk a little better. Warmth spread languidly through her stiff muscles. "That wasn't nice, Gabriel."

His voice fell over her. "Who said I was nice, *chica*?"

Chapter Nine

"I'll probably be roastin' in hell come Sunday, but I refuse to take part in another mass." The door slammed. Cori's voice was breathless as if she'd been running. "These Spaniards repent with more pomp than Father Henri ever had!"

Sarah went back to her morning meal of black beans and bread.

"I'm sorry, milady." Cori's footsteps hurried over the carpet. "I didn't mean to insult the ol' geezer."

"I know." Sarah's voice was flat.

She wiped her mouth with the back of her hand. At daybreak, the ship's priest led the Te Deum. Mass for the crew began with the sunrise. In the evening, they sang the Salve Regina and ended with the rosary. But Sarah refrained from voicing her discord. By now God was surely privy to the anger in her heart. If she went to hell with Cori, so be it.

Sarah picked up her cat.

"Lud, ye found 'im, milady," Cori exclaimed.

"He's been in here all week." Snuggling her nose against his neck, she plopped him on the table and let him finish her meal. She walked to the bunk. Bed ropes creaked as she dropped onto her back. "He hates me, Cori."

"Your cat?"

"Don Gabriel. I'm not allowed on deck anymore. That man Stefan . . . he guards Gabriel as if I am a spider." Her shoulders rose and fell with her breath. "I'm *really* beginning to dislike that man."

"Don Gabriel?"

"Stefan!"

Sarah smoothed the shirt over her legs. She'd taken to sleeping in Gabriel's clothes, and had yet to change. They'd spent the last two days at San Martín, a Spanish fortress, loading supplies, and another long day languishing in the sea without wind. This morning, Gabriel had been called out of the cabin before dawn.

Cori plopped on the bed next to Sarah. "Jaime said ye ate with the ship's officers last night."

Sarah groaned in her hands. "They eat with forks and knives and so many spoons I lost count." Sitting up, she demonstrated on her lap. "Everything was set just so."

"Who needs a fork, anyway, when fingers do just as well?" Cori said with a sniff.

"There is wine served in crystal glasses. Soup in fine porcelain bowls. Fruit and bread over here." Patting her bare knee, Sarah scoffed, "And by the weight of the spoons, fine sterling for each plate and platter."

"They have too much time on their hands to eat so much."

"Gabriel could feed all the children in Martinique for the price of the silver and food he had on his table last night!"

"Snobs fer bloody sure, milady," Cori confirmed.

Sarah growled her exasperation. "I'm blind, Cori. How do they expect me to eat? I *touch* my food."

"Blimey, milady. What's wrong with that?"

Sarah shoved off the bunk and walked to the cabinets built into the bulkhead. She flattened her hands against the smooth surface. Expensive treasures sat innocuously behind the cabinets' brass bars. "Because I *felt* their horror. I was sorry for Gabriel."

"Are ye upset, milady?"

With barely a shrug, Sarah moved down the case, but no matter her attempt at nonchalance, she could not hide her pain. Gabriel had been sharp with her for days. Nothing she did pleased him anyway; last night's disaster may have confirmed her lack of breeding but it did not make her less of a human being.

She ran a finger over frothy lace and ruffles. "He collects dolls for his daughter." Sarah lifted one fluffy doll to her nose.

Cori came to stand beside Sarah. "Maybe ye better not be touchin' her."

The silken hair smelled faintly of beeswax. The dolls had never been played with. So much of Gabriel's cabin was filled with expensive, untouched trinkets. It seemed as if his whole life and existence lacked for nothing but simple human touch.

Sarah pressed the doll against her cheek. "I would never let anything of mine sit on a shelf."

"You are awake again early this morning, Don Gabriel." Stefan's brows rose with an unspoken query. "Perhaps you should retrieve your hammock and join me out here on deck."

Gabriel restrained from snapping at Stefan. The sea was rougher today but the sunrise, a disk of orange fire, was so bright Gabriel's eyes hurt. He was in no mood for Stefan's humor. He hadn't had a decent night's rest since he'd installed Sarah in his cabin. She slept in his bed: a bed no other woman had ever shared . . . and him, one of the wealthiest men in all of Spain, delegated by his conscience to a cold hammock in the corner of the room. Saying nothing to Stefan's comment, Gabriel continued to study the distant ship in his sights.

"That ship is edging us too near the Virgin Gorda Straits," he said over the brisk gust that sent the *Felicity* thrashing through the waves. He handed his ship's master the glass. "Have Berto do an accounting of our munitions."

Stefan trained the glass on the distant sails. "It's definitely the same *inglés* bastard from before." Wind whipped Stefan's black hair. He wore the faded blue-and-gold jacket of his old rank, now stripped of its epaulettes. "She is trying to let us catch her? Or is she trying to help us onto the rocks and capture us?"

"You tell me." Gabriel pointed behind them. Another ship was clearly visible on the golden horizon. "A British man-of-war," he said. "Berto spotted him an hour ago and pounded on my door."

Stefan seemed to absorb this news with placid acceptance. "Then they mean to snare us between them near the Straits.

"If we veer, we will overrun San Juan and be at the mercy of that man-of-war." Gabriel's gaze ran aloft the full length of the *Felicity*'s main mast. Every inch of canvas was spread.

Just below the flag of Spain, his banner whipped like a red-and-gold beacon visible to anyone within two leagues.

His cold calm yielded to anger. Whoever was on that ship ahead of him knew who he was. They had guessed his heading easily enough, which was why Gabriel had not been able to lose them when he'd stopped at San Martín.

"By allowing the ship to get in front of us, I sailed right into their trap."

Stefan's silence echoed Gabriel's self-reproach. A man didn't make mistakes in this life and expect to survive long enough to learn from his errors.

"Why do I get the feeling this has to do with your guests? More precisely, your new *inglesa* wife." Stefan's dark mustache curled with cynicism. "Or should I rephrase that to 'your wife in name only'? To quote your exact words."

Raising the glass back to his eye, Gabriel ignored him. "You are too bold with your comments, Stefan," he said at length. "I owe you no explanation for my decisions."

"Me?" Stefan snorted. "I follow you as do most of these men because you have fought Spain's enemies and proven yourself to be a man of honor. But the crown will not be as forgiving of her great hero's decision to take the sister of a notorious pirate for his wife or understand why he has chosen to ignore the charges the *Capitán-General* of the Spanish fleet has brought against him." Stefan's voice lowered. "Nor will you be able to explain your new wife to Doña Betina or to your daughter, who are both awaiting you in Hispaniola for your glorious return from Seville."

Gabriel lowered the glass and faced Stefan. "Why would Christina be in Hispaniola? And not in Havana, where I left her protected?"

"It was to be a surprise upon your return from Spain." Stefan shifted his feet. "Doña Betina knew that you would go to Hispaniola first and wanted to be waiting with Christina to greet you."

Heart pounding, all Gabriel could conceive was that he had somehow put his daughter in danger. If he did take the *Felicity* farther north to bypass San Juan, no one could stop that British frigate from sailing on to Hispaniola. "Why didn't you tell me this sooner?"

"I didn't know that we would have the British navy down our throats. Or that you had wed. I would have told you the moment you came aboard had you been more forthcoming, Don Gabriel."

"Mierda." Gabriel snapped the glass shut.

Stefan moved to block Gabriel's exit. Dark eyes narrowed on Gabriel's face. But they were not as furious as Gabriel's. "You are not thinking straight," Stefan rasped. "Would you shield Sarah Drake at the cost of everything else in your life?"

"Get out of my way."

"Listen to me." Stefan grabbed Gabriel's arm.

Gabriel's eyes dropped with deadly intent to the man's gloved hand. If Stefan weren't as close to being the only family Gabriel had, he would have clapped the man in chains for the insult.

Stefan dropped his hand. "Have you considered that whoever is chasing us might want only the girl? She is *inglesa*; they are *ingleses.* What is their fight to us, *amigo*?"

The door to Gabriel's cabin crashed open.

Sarah spun. Gabriel's presence filled the room like a black storm cloud. She stood with the silver urn clutched in her hands. Still wearing his shirt and nothing else, she was hardly presentable.

The door slammed shut. "What are you doing, Sarah?"

"Gabriel . . . I—" Fumbling with the precious piece in her hands, she tried to replace it back on the shelves.

Cori made her excuses and abandoned Sarah.

"I have told you not to touch anything in this cabin."

"Nothing is broken," she said in defense of herself. Her thick hair, still tangled from sleep, fell in disarray to her hips. She shoved it out of her face. "They are merely things, Gabri—"

"They are *my* things."

She crossed her arms.

A ball of fur brushed against her calf. She bent and scooped the cat into her arms. The cat was plucked from her. "Sarah—" Irritation crept into Gabriel's voice. He took her elbow. "We have to talk."

He smelled of the sea and wind: the kind of morning

zephyr that chased clouds across the sky. She'd wanted to tell him that last night she'd seen clouds in her dreams. That she'd dreamed in colors as if she'd opened her eyes and looked outside a window. For as long as she could remember, Sarah had never seen such colors.

She allowed him to lead her to the table. The Bible she'd pulled from her leather chest sat in front of her, and she folded her hands atop its leather casing.

Gabriel pressed both hands on the table and leaned toward her. "Tell me about Harrison Kendrick. How do you know him?"

The vision of clouds vanished. Her mind went blank. "Harrison Kendrick is dead." Her laced fingers tightened. "Talon said so."

"Your brother's assessment of the man's demise was premature." His hand gripped her chin and pulled her face around. He was kneeling beside her now. "Why would it matter to you that Kendrick is dead?"

"I . . . it mattered to Talon that I know."

"I need you to tell me everything that you remember about the man. Do you understand?"

"No, I don't understand." She jerked away. "Harrison Kendrick means nothing."

"Then why does he want you so badly, *chica*?" He cupped the sides of her head with his palms and forced her to face him.

She pulled at his hands. "I don't know. Why would that horrible man want me for anything? I've done nothing to him."

"Then you know him?"

The ship plunged through a wave, and she felt the deck beneath her feet cant slightly. "He came to Martinique over a year ago. That was the first time I'd ever met him." A shiver suddenly crawled down her spine. "He never hurt me. He . . . was kinder to me than he was to anyone else. But there was something about him. I found out later that he had come there to kill Talon. After he left, I was told that he'd died of the injuries received in a battle against my brother."

"You said that you have not always been blind. Could you have known him before Martinique?"

"Gabriel—"

His fingers gave up their painful hold and spread into her hair. "I know that he was one of the men who destroyed your family."

"How . . . do you know this?"

"Jesu," he whispered, "who does not know?"

Sarah's hands fell away from his.

"What did you see, Sarah? What happened to you?"

She squeezed her eyes shut. Images prevailed that challenged the darkness. Sunlight. The touch of waves against her body.

Tears welled. "Gabriel . . . I don't know what it is you want. Why are you doing this?"

"You put me in a very bad predicament, *chica*." He slowly exhaled. "My ship is sitting between an English naval frigate and a man-of-war. They have been following us since we left Martinique."

"And you think Harrison Kendrick is aboard one of those ships?"

"Your Father Henri as much as told me that Kendrick was responsible for the attempts to kidnap you."

Shock clenched her hands. "Why didn't you tell me this before?"

"I wouldn't have told you now, except when a man risks war with Spain, I would know the stakes. These are not pirates I face."

She shook her head. "Now I'm the one who doesn't understand."

"England and Spain are not at war. There has been great initiative to bring peace between our countries."

"Then"—she dragged the words across her throat—"are you going to hand me over to him?"

Shamed by the fear that he would, Sarah tried to turn her head away. If she had one noble bone in her body, she would volunteer to go willingly. But since she met Gabriel, she'd found that she wanted very much to stay alive.

Gabriel's palm fanned her cheek. He wore no gloves. His flesh was warm against hers. For all his wealth and blue-blooded aristocracy, the calloused hand hinted at vulnerability.

"Perhaps this is merely a vendetta against your family, *sí*?" his voice whispered. "But if he wanted you dead, you would already be so."

Her heart beating wildly, she twined her fingers in her lap.

He stood. Sarah heard him walk to his desk and riffle the shelves. She didn't know how to repair everything that had come between them since they'd left Martinique. Her courage had faded with the dread that he would hand her over to the English ship if it came down to a fight.

Drawing a deep breath, she stood. Feeling along the wooden ledge, she reached the door that lead to the balcony outside the cabin. The stern gallery opened to the sea. Sarah had discovered the balcony yesterday. But she didn't dare step out. Below her, the sea churned like boiling liquid inside a cauldron. This wasn't like standing on the main deck. She could feel no rails on the balcony, no sense of an enclosure that safely fenced her in. Though a part of her was drawn inexplicably to the waves, as far as she could tell, one step out was one giant leap into the sea.

She had leaped before.

The memory slammed her heart against her ribs.

Bracing her hands against the wooden door frame, she let the wind slide over her and tried to remember if her flight into the sea had been a dream. If only she could recall something of her life that would be useful to Gabriel.

Gabriel was suddenly behind her, his hands pressed just above hers. "Did you know that once long ago people believed the world was flat?" His voice touched her hair. His body was a solid wall at her back, part comfort, part malice. "When the sun left the sky, they thought it fell off the edge of the earth. People were afraid to sail the seas for fear of dropping into the same emptiness, and for centuries they languished and did nothing but wonder and dream. Their lack of courage set men back hundreds of years."

Sarah's stomach clenched in raw panic. "I . . ." Her grip tightened on the door. How had he guessed her fear of the sea?

She wanted to take a step back into the safety of the cabin. Her shirt flapped against her hips. "This from someone who would have me choke on rum?"

"The lessons are the same. But there is a difference between foolish rebellion and fear of the unknown." Gabriel's heartbeat was strong beneath her head. "You won't fall. There is a sturdy rail three steps out."

Her tongue slid out to moisten her lips. "I have been nothing but a problem to you, haven't I?" she asked.

"*Sí.* You are a lot of trouble, *chica.*"

She stood in the doorway and didn't move. The ocean smells, and Gabriel's presence seemed to ease some of the fear.

"Where *does* the sun go when it disappears?"

His body seemed to smile with his response. "To another place in the world not unlike here, except for the people who live there."

"You've been there?"

He leaned into his hands. "I have seen coasts alive with volcanoes. I've seen mountains that touch the sky, and forests in the clouds. Places, like here, where the sun is a red disk that drops into the sea."

She longed for so much more than the touch of those words against her ears. Remembering the words he'd spoken to Jaime the night she'd learned that Father Henri died, she smiled back. "The black-hearted vulture is a poet."

"Didn't you know?" His whisper caressed her cheek. "I have framed the words for many a man's epitaph."

Sarah jerked away. But no matter how hard she tried to behave with dignity around him, it never quite stopped her from flirting with danger. She turned. "Do you want to know what I see?" He caught her hands before she could touch him. "You are not without light, Gabriel. Black is merely the color of your eyes." Grinning, she leaned into him with impish delight. The salt spray had dampened his shirt. "Your hair, too."

He pressed her against the door frame. "*Dios . . .* you have a simple mind, Sarah."

"I know that the mind is everything." She shoved against his hold on her wrists. "But it is not more powerful than the heart."

Still holding her hands, he took them behind her back and pulled her against the hard frame of body. His mouth slanted over hers, barely touching, compelling her to her toes. "Perhaps you don't remember what made you," he said, "but I remember what made me."

Her heart beat at her ribs. "A man can change."

There was only a whisper between his silence and her anticipation. Then he was kissing her deeply, melding his mouth to hers as if it were the perfect fit, the perfect shape. Her senses exploded, then soared. Her tongue edged between his lips, and she felt a wealth of sensations in his indrawn breath. Shock. Anger. Need.

"You do care for me," she whispered when he broke the kiss to trail his lips down the slim column of her neck. "You do. You do."

"*¿Como no?* Why not, Sarah?" His words burned her mouth in a kiss deeper than the first. He ruthlessly drank in her moan and stole her breath. Beneath the shirt, his fingers opened over her ribs, moving to cup her breasts, then down the length of her spine. Pleasure erupted through her. That and a terrible fear traveling over nerve endings that centered in her loins. She swallowed and felt suddenly like a small bird in a cat's sharp teeth.

"Because I enjoy this very much, *chica*?" His mouth nibbled at the throbbing pulse in her throat. He made her knees tremble, and her hands splayed the muscled curve of his shoulders, pushing now. "Because you dress in my shirts? Did you know that you are blond, Sarah? Everywhere?"

The liquid words were like a splash of cold reality.

"What man wouldn't take what you are offering?"

She tried to pull away. Hadn't he warned her not to tempt fate? "Let . . . go of me!"

His laugh was filled with more than self-disgust. Enmity laced his words even as his calloused thumb lightly grazed her cheek. "I purge the sea of pirates, Sarah. Men like your brothers . . . and the man your father was. I hunt them down and hang them or imprison them and let the Inquisition tear out their souls. They call me the Vulture because I am very good at my job, *chica*. Don't make me break your spirit as well. Nothing will ever change me."

Sarah listened to his furious footsteps take him to the door. "I am not afraid of you, Don Gabriel!"

Her words stopped him in his tracks. The weight of his

gaze raked over her. She could feel his amusement at her boast. Because he *knew*! He knew he had frightened her as he'd intended.

"You won't be going on deck again, Sarah. Stay below."

She fought back tears, the last thing she would ever allow him to see. It was enough to know that Harrison Kendrick hunted her without also being afraid of Gabriel.

He turned away. The door opened and shut behind him. And in that instant, Sarah felt many things inside.

He *was* everything that he claimed. He had conquered worlds with force and little mercy. He was restless and arrogant, ever patient with her silliness because he thought her simple and docile, like one of those shelved dolls he never allowed anyone to touch. Her hands fisted. His lack of respect for her was more than her pride could endure.

Turning, she walked out the stern gallery door that remained open. One. Two. Three steps to the rail.

Her hands grasped the smooth, wet wood. Heart pounding like thunder against her ribs, she felt suspended above the sea. The wind roared over her. The sensation was dizzying . . . and triumphant.

If only a little bit.

"I am not afraid of you, Don Gabriel. I'm not."

Stubbornness set her back straight, and she repeated the words aloud.

It didn't matter that Gabriel had gotten her out here when nothing else could. "*Sí,* Spaniard." She lifted her arms. "I can fight the same as you."

"The English ship will probably be sitting here as we pass the straits," Stefan said. His finger traced a path along the chart Gabriel had slapped over his desk.

The heat in the cabin had risen with the sun's zenith hours ago. A bead of moisture gathered at his collar. In annoyance, Gabriel looked down at the gray cat twining around his ankles.

"To sail between the straits and the other ship will put us in range of cannon fire until we pass," Stefan said.

"They would be mad to fire on us." Berto snorted. "We are a ship of Spain."

Without looking up, Gabriel splayed his hand flat on the chart to keep the parchment from rolling. His second in command was still a young idealist, and Gabriel let the comment pass. His eyes continued to study the shoals recorded by countless ships' pilots, including his own when he'd sailed with the Spanish *flota*.

"Sailing too near the Virgin Gorda Straits is always dangerous," the *Felicity*'s pilot concurred. "I would not attempt to do this deed at night."

Gabriel's gaze lifted to assess the remaining daylight, and stopped on Sarah across the room. Attempting seclusion as much from him as from his men, she sat in the alcove in front of the stern gallery windows.

His thoughts toppled to the floor like a hundred-year oak gone soft in the roots. Framed in a halo of sunlight, her pale hair falling over her face, she was bent over a tear in one of his shirts. Small white teeth tugged at her lower lip as she worked the needle through the expensive fabric. One bare foot fidgeted beneath the ragged hem of her white robe. His mouth flattened.

She'd pilfered every chest in the cabin in her quest to stay busy or to annoy him—he didn't know which for sure, since she now refused to speak to him. Normally he would not have allowed her such servile work, but he was beginning to realize that beneath Sarah's demeanor, she had a will of iron that defied his every effort to dismiss her. Her busy hands had violated his world. An orderly domain that he liked the way it was. Worse, she could *not* sew.

Rolling the kink from between his shoulder blades, Gabriel dropped his attention back to the chart. When he got to Hispaniola he would have to replace every single one of his shirts.

Silence had fallen around him. Gabriel raised his gaze inquiringly. Stefan's dark brow lifted. But it was Berto who made the mistake. "Perhaps her skills with the needle are better than her table manners, *sí*, Don Gabriel?"

Chuckling at the jest, Berto turned to Gabriel. The cocksure smirk vanished. Shifting his gaze to Stefan, Gabriel said, "Put men on the mizzen course sails. I want the *Felicity* running before the wind when we reach the straits." He rolled the chart. "Night or no, we stay on this tack or face that man-of-war come dawn. Set the bell watch.

"Berto." Gabriel stopped that one from leaving. And all three men turned. "Perhaps I have failed to make clear my feelings toward Sarah Drake, and for that I will not have you keelhauled for your ignorance. But the lady, no matter who she is, is still my wife."

Beneath his trimmed goatee, Berto paled. Stefan stayed behind as the other two officers turned away. Whatever it was he'd started to say remained unspoken. "I will see you on deck," he said instead.

Sarah looked up when the cabin door clicked shut. Her cat leaped onto her lap and nearly upset her mending. With a sigh, she set aside Gabriel's shirt. "So you want a rub, you bad cat." She nuzzled his neck, then set him on the ledge behind her. Her head fell back against the sun-warmed glass.

Crossing his arms, Gabriel leaned against the door to admire the curve of her neck. A hard knot of desire twisted inside him.

Men made her nervous. He'd seen it the other night at dinner. In addition, Gabriel's rapid-fire words excluded her from listening to all of their conversation. But she had been a topic, and he wondered if she remembered enough of the Spanish that had been her mother's birth language to understand what had been said.

"Are you hungry?" he asked.

She snapped straight and pricked her hand with the needle she'd set in his shirt. She'd thought he'd left.

That surprised him. Usually she was more astute.

"I . . . I ate with Cori and Jaime a few hours ago. We had fish and mangoes," she offered into the silence. "Your cook is very good. You must thank him for me."

Gabriel didn't move. Her comeliness was made more alluring by the profile presented him, but he wanted to pull her chin around so he could see her silver eyes. "You're a liar, Sarah. We have no mangoes on board." He shrugged off the door and walked to the desk. "And my cook is a gunner who just happens to know more about the backside of a fish than anyone else on board. But I will relay your words, if it will make you happy."

Clearly, Sarah was contemplating using her sewing needle someplace other than on his shirts.

"I will send Cori and Jaime in here later with your dinner."

Turning away, she gave her attention to her cat "I think Stefan and Berto are *bastardos, sí, mi marido*? My husband." She shocked him by speaking in Spanish. "Perhaps a blindfold would test their true mettle. I would see how well they survive the day."

As always she surpassed his expectations and surprised him. "Perhaps that would be a fitting punishment. I'm sorry that they said those things."

She spun around on the seat. The robe framed her breasts. "You are not without guilt yourself, Gabriel."

"Ah, but I have never claimed to be, *chica*."

It was as if they chatted amicably from across the room.

"No, you are the Vulture. Where is the innocence in that, *sí*?" Again, she gave him her profile and stroked her cat. "Will you attack the English ship because of me?"

Agitation stirred inside him as she pandered to that worthless feline. With a slight jerk, he strapped his cutlass around his waist. A whisper of steel sounded as he contemplated the shiny blade. What he did now with the English, he did for himself. "Do you worry for the English onboard her?"

"I worry for you, Gabriel."

He cursed viciously and silently at his letting her feelings for him touch him. She was so vulnerable that he regretted his cruelty to her. But it was the only way he knew to separate himself from the difficulty of her presence. She had to be made to see the danger in this predicament between them—for her *and* for him. There could be no future together for them.

Her hands clenched to the bench where she sat; her gaze seemed to find him. "What do you plan to do?"

He shoved the cutlass back in its leather sheath. "I plan to sail down Kendrick's throat, *chica*. Teach him a lesson in Spanish diplomacy, *sí*?"

"Gabriel . . ." She stood.

He was lost in her struggle to be brave. "Cori and Jaime will be here in a few moments." His voice was sharp. "They will take you to the hold until this is over."

Gabriel left her standing in the middle of the cabin. Heat bounced off the main deck of his ship. He was on the quarter-deck for less than an hour when he spotted his quarry.

"There she is." Stefan pointed to a place off the *Felicity*'s starboard bow. "Right where you said she'd be." The sound of cannon fire broke his words.

Cutlass in hand, Gabriel did not seek cover. A mass of verdant land stretched like fingers, converging on the blue waters of the channel. He studied the frigate bobbing like an innocent gull bracketing him against the inlet. There was little room to maneuver through the shoals. And he could not tack around the English ship without overshooting his bearing to San Juan.

Another cannon fired, out of sequence to the plume of smoke that sputtered from the English ship's deck. An iron ball hissed across the *Felicity*'s prow. "That was a warning," Stefan chuckled. "He is signaling for us to heave to."

"How does one signal back to go to hell? Hmm?"

"A full broadside?"

Gabriel gripped the ratlines and turned to survey the deck below. His gunners stood ready. Kneeling behind the bulwarks, his crew watched expectantly. Gabriel read fear in most of their young faces. No man would be normal if he weren't a little afraid. The first broadside was always the worst.

If it came to that.

The deck hummed beneath his feet as the sails grabbed the wind. "Stay on this tack," he told Stefan.

The English ship's deck swarmed with sudden activity as their captain realized Gabriel had no intention of stopping. Men clamored like frightened puppies on the deck. Cannon ports creaked open, but the *Felicity* had the wind full in her sails. She canted slightly. Spray dampened his shirt. His face for lack of shaving bore the hint of a beard. The Spanish aristocrat had become El Condor, and his blood pumped through his veins in wont of a fight. The emotion steadied him.

Earlier that day, he'd made the decision not to change course. In any case, he was capable of outsailing but not outgunning the English frigate.

"Stand ready." His eyes remained on the disorder across the water.

Stefan relayed the orders down the line. "They are not rigged to move out of our way." His tone conveyed uneasiness. "You are sailing close."

Wind rippled Gabriel's white shirt and caught in his sleeves. One booted foot rested on a coil of line. Smoke bellowed from the English ship. Cannon fire exploded over the stern. A ragged hole appeared in the sail above Gabriel. His furious gaze locked onto the damage above him. *Jesu.* Farther up the mast two of his men scrambled to repair severed leech lines.

"She's opening fire," Stefan rasped in disbelief.

One did not waste the first broadside at this distance. Narrowing his eyes, Gabriel ordered the helm to port, then lifted his gaze to Stefan. "At my command, fire chain shot into their rigging. Let them give chase with half their masts gone. *¡Bastardos!*"

Wind whipped around him. "Stand by," Stefan shouted, and the order fired down the line in rapid Spanish.

Gabriel lifted his eyes to the topmasts to gauge the wind as the *Felicity* plunged headlong into gun range. But some inner warning flagged his actions. Perhaps it was the ease in which he'd been baited, or the fact that he'd already been led into one trap. He'd been stripped of his military commission and held no letter of reprisal. Then his gaze took his attention to the man-of-war not a league behind him. They mocked Spain, but for all their foolish conceit to ensnare his ship, ensnare him they would, if he stopped or changed course.

Cannon fire from the other ship no longer fell short of the *Felicity*'s bow but struck his foremast. Wind scattered the smoke and brought the shouts of the English crew as they fought to bring the ship on line.

In minutes, they were passing within fifty yards of the English frigate. "*Capitán . . .*" Stefan's voice relayed urgency.

Gabriel's hand fisted in the ratlines. But whatever Gabriel was inside, he played no games with the devil.

"Fire!"

In a rolling crash of guns, chain shot spewed through the

English frigate's masts. Wood splintered and tangled in the leech lines as the mizzenmast gave way in a billowy fluff of white canvas. Rigging collapsed over the deck and fell like writhing snakes into the sea.

The Felicity met the other ship bow to bow. His men ready at the sheets and braces, Gabriel gave the order to tack away, making it a close thing with the shoals nearby.

"Perhaps we should wave, *sí*?" Stefan yelled. "Or blow kisses."

Relief underscored Stefan's words, and Gabriel turned. His gaze moved past his ship's master to his eager crew. The corner of his mouth lifted. "Give them many kisses to remember us by."

His crew erupted with glee.

Whooping and hollering, they waved their hats and gestured rudely to their English counterparts. The undignified raucousness received a bawdy retort from the other crew. But the moment for battle had passed, and the *Felicity*, with the wind full in her sails, swept past the English frigate toward San Juan.

Hours later, as the sun crept across the ship's bow to drop into the sea, Gabriel remained topside to oversee the caulking where cannon shot had damaged the deck. He remained long after Berto had brought him his meal. Long after the moon had appeared among a thousand glittering stars. Sarah would be waiting for word of what had occurred here today.

But he didn't go below, and soon a streak of orange hinted at the distant sunrise.

"You are going after him?" Stefan asked from behind him.

Gabriel drew in a breath. His gaze touched Stefan, who understood him better than most. "I have no choice."

"Does she know of your association with Harrison Kendrick?"

Gabriel looked back across the sea. "I have waited too long to sever my ties with the English madman, *sí*?"

"Harrison Kendrick is a dangerous man to have as an enemy." Stefan suddenly chuckled. "But then so are you." He stepped to the rail. "They say that she has unearthly powers. That she has put a spell on you. The men are afraid of her."

That one white-haired woman could cower his crew

chafed Gabriel, but a part of him recognized the danger for Sarah of such superstition. He leaned a hip against the rail. "And what do you think?" His arms crossed. "Have I been hexed by a simple blind girl?"

"*Sí.*" Stefan regarded Gabriel with the somber visage of a priest giving him his last rites. "You are in love with her. And where the heart leads, logic does not follow. She has succeeded where all the navies of England and France have failed. She has brought El Condor to his foolish knees."

Gabriel shoved open the door to his quarters. No lanthorn burned away the predawn shadows. A downy pattern of light scattered the darkness but did not ease the tight knot in his gut. He let his eyes go around the room. Sarah was asleep, her gray cat rolled in a ball beside her. He closed the door.

Tearing at the buttons on his shirt, Gabriel yanked the garment over his head. The muscles in his shoulders bunched and stretched with the violent movement. Dropping the shirt on the floor, he removed the rum bottle from the cabinet.

Stefan understood nothing!

Gabriel leaned a fist against the wooden door and drank. *Madre de Dios,* who truly understood anything? Especially a man's past?

A soft murmur came from the shadows. He walked over to his bed and gazed at his fey wife sleeping contentedly in his shirt, beneath his blanket, and in his bed, innocent to the night. Her white hair spilled over her face and shoulder like a ribbon of light that he blindly followed. He touched the strands, his mind drifting as Sarah's presence became something greater in his thoughts, something he did not comprehend. All the fetid ails that had blackened his soul were not enough to shield him from her magic.

Eleven years ago, Sarah had lost her home and family.

Eleven years ago, with no regret, Gabriel had bargained with Harrison Kendrick to put her brothers in a Spanish prison to die. She'd been a child, as he'd been when her father had devastated his life.

Now he had sworn to protect that child who had become a woman.

The child he'd helped destroy.

Gabriel tossed back a swallow of burning rum and went to stand in the stern gallery. Dawn glittered on the oily sea, purging his thoughts. He closed his eyes and let what remained of the night fill his veins.

He was past the straits and nearly into the warm waters of the Caribbean.

In two days, Gabriel would be home.

Chapter Ten

"Has Don Gabriel already returned to the ship?"

"He left last night, milady," Jaime said through a mouthful of hot bread. He stood on the verandah steps near a pond of noisy frogs. China clattered as Cori finished breakfast.

Sarah set down her spoon. Gabriel hadn't even said goodbye. He was probably now trying to find Talon and Marcus.

Three days ago she'd arrived on Hispaniola. Gabriel had introduced her to his daughter and the woman, Doña Betina deSalvo y Gonzáles, who had been caring for Christina. He'd handled Sarah with an ever-so-polite deportment that made it clear to all the servants that she was to be treated with deference. But he never touched her, except her elbow slightly when he'd guided her to a chair, and he never remained alone with her. Not like he did with Doña Betina, whom he seemed to admire. On more than one occasion Sarah had heard them walking on the verandah late into the night, even after Christina had fallen asleep against his shoulder and had been put to bed.

Sarah had been given spacious room's at the opposite end of the sprawling plantation house, away from the rooms Gabriel had shared with his first wife. Away from Doña Betina's suite of rooms. But near Christina's nursery, which the child shared with her *dueña*.

The enormous maze of rooms twisting from one end of the house to the other would take weeks to learn. Already she'd

tipped and shattered an expensive vase, a case of crystal fig-
urines, and a dozen wall ornaments. She felt like an *enfant*
learning to walk again, and resented that Doña Betina had
claimed Gabriel's last hours here. Clearly, they were friends,
and probably more so, considering he'd entrusted his daughter into the woman's care for the past year. Considering they
shared the same end of the house.

"I suppose"—Sarah traced a finger around the rim of her
glass—"Don Gabriel knows how to take care of himself."

"And he's left ye well-protected," Jaime said. "Stefan's
family lives on this island. Don Gabriel put him in charge of
yer welfare. I won't be leavin' ye either, milady."

"Besides"—Cori pushed her plate away—"where would
we go? Till the Cap finds us, we're at the Spaniard's mercy."

"I didn't hear you complainin' none when those dressmak-
ers were takin' yer measurements yesterday."

"Maybe it's because he went and threw my dress away.
Have ye thought of that, mister Jaime? What do you suppose
I should be wearin' if the governor decides to drop in fer tea?"

Fidgeting with the folds of her robe, Sarah smiled. "I suppose clothes make the lady."

"Aye, milady." Cori nudged her. "Ye should 'ave gotten
the most expensive clothes ye could. It's only fitting of yer
station."

"I wouldn't know what an expensive dress is, Cori."

Sarah had only cared that she would be a true lady when
next Gabriel saw her. Doña Betina underestimated Sarah if
she thought Sarah wouldn't fight for Gabriel.

A breath of sea-scented wind snaked across the verandah
and set wind chimes to music. Up and down the length of the
terrace, music swayed in tune to the welcome breeze.

"They seem rather quaint for this fortress," Cori observed.

"They belonged to his sister, María Liandra," Doña Betina
said from the dining room doorway. Her contralto voice
sounded kind and welcoming to the casual listener.

Sarah was no casual listener. "They make beautiful
music."

Doña Betina's movements rustled like the many silken
ferns that lined the floor next to the balustrade and hung in
baskets from the ceiling. The scent of gardenias filled the air.

"Don Gabriel's sister spent much of her time with the street children at various missions in Santo Domingo," Doña Betina elaborated. "They made the chimes for her from shells or glass. Christina made two or three. That is why Don Gabriel allows the chimes to remain at all."

Cori sniffed over a grumble. "How fortunate for Christina."

Doña Betina's voice tightened. "He does have his standards, but he is soft when it comes to dealing with matters of his heart. He allows Christina anything she wants. If she wanted no wind chimes"—a snap of her fingers sounded—"there would be no wind chimes, *sí*?"

Sarah frowned. As for little Christina, Cori had summed up Gabriel's daughter in two words the moment the little girl had yanked Dog's tail and sent the cat screeching into the nearest ceiba tree.

Rotten brat.

Caressing the strange feather that had been left on her pillow this morning, Sarah guessed the child was merely starved for affection. Yesterday the gift had been a frayed rope doll.

"You have known Don Gabriel for a long time?" Sarah set the feather beside her plate.

"I was Felicity's dearest friend. This was her home. He imported every stone of it from Spain to build her this house."

"Blimey." Cori's voice was filled with awe. "Every stone?"

"*Sí*, their romance was the talk of Spain." Wood creaked where Doña Betina leaned against the balustrade. "Felicity was the daughter of a duke, and Don Gabriel an untitled Creole from New Spain. Already he was a naval hero knighted at court, and Felicity, once she set her eyes on him there, would have no one else. When Don Gabriel married her in Valencia, he was given his title and a dowry that rivaled Spain's wealth. *Ay yi,* they were a beautiful pair. Felicity died a year after their marriage, giving birth to his only daughter."

Sarah flushed, the heat in her neck rising to her cheeks. She was aware of Cori's silence and Jaime's interest in the tale, which Sarah suspected had been embellished. Already she disliked Felicity.

The woman had been enshrined. Nay, entombed in golden

memories. No wonder Gabriel could never move on with his life. He wasn't allowed to. And what of Christina? How could a little girl live up to that kind of legacy? Especially if her birth had killed her mother?

Doña Betina stretched her arm across Sarah's shoulder to lift a cube of cheese from the breakfast tray. "My own husband died two years ago, and while I was in Havana, Don Gabriel came to me to ask if I would care for Christina. You see," she sighed, "his sister had married an English pirate."

Setting her teeth, Sarah clasped her hands in her lap. The movement helped check her temper, which she was beginning to discover seemed to live just at the surface of every waking thought lately. "He and Marcus have made their peace," she said.

"Pah! The peace he made with your brother cost him his ships, his command, and his crew. He left his post because he thought his sister needed help, and his ships sailed to Spain without him. He allowed personal business to interfere with his duty to Spain."

"But he has done much for Spain's interest—"

"*Sí*, his popularity would make it difficult to convict him. But now? Who is to say? He did not return to appear before the tribunal. Perhaps the council will think that he considers himself too important to face the charges."

Betina swished back to the balustrade. "His return here was to be one of celebration. I had everything planned."

"And here he's returned with a wife—"

"Cori!" Sarah hissed.

"'Tis true!" Cori wrapped an arm through Sarah's. "Someone has to champion you, milady. Yer not doin' a very good job of it yerself."

"Perhaps you would care to take a walk over the grounds, Lady Sarah? Alone?"

Beside Sarah, Cori stiffened like a board. "Not on yer bloomin'—"

"It's all right, Cori." Fumbling for the walking stick Jaime had made for her the day before, Sarah stood. She tapped her way off the verandah, then hesitated as she turned back to Jaime, who had started down the stairs to follow her. The earth was spongy beneath her slippers, as if it had rained. "I will go only as far as the trees." The trees began two hundred paces past the veranda. The distance was not so far to walk alone with this woman.

"Perhaps you would care to take my arm," Doña Betina offered into the silence that followed their departure from breakfast.

Overhead, a blackbird's caw mixed with the sound of gulls. Twenty paces past the trees a person entered the gardens where a path snaked down the steep hill to the secluded beach. Sarah had discovered the cove yesterday.

"What is it that you wish to tell me?" Sarah asked after they'd walked awhile. The Spanish woman's sleeves flared over Sarah's wrist. Doña Betina was not much taller than Sarah, but she carried her small stature with a regal bearing that bespoke authority.

"I wish to talk of your . . . marriage, *sí*?"

Sunlight broke over the open grounds, and Sarah felt the warmth more acutely on her face. "Surely you must have heard the gossip that he was forced to marry me. Everyone seems to accept that Spain's hero did the noble thing in bringing me here, considering my relationship to his sister's husband," she said evenly. "I'm no threat to anyone."

"Pah." Doña Betina's skirts swished in agitation. "Don Gabriel cannot be forced to do anything against his will. Perhaps in the beginning he married you to protect his name and yours. It is true that an annulment is far simpler to manage with the Church than an accusation of fornication."

Sarah's face burned. She knew that Betina spoke the truth. Father Henri had implied as much. But to hear the reminder so blatantly spoken hurt. Especially when Gabriel had not really touched her; not the way she'd wanted to be touched by him.

"Then why say anything?" Sarah pulled her arm away.

Doña Betina stopped walking. "In the beginning that might have been true, but no matter what he may feel now, you are fighting for something that cannot happen and in the end will only cause pain for everyone." Her clipped voice took on a conciliatory tone. "What can you give Don Gabriel that I cannot give him thrice over?"

Her quiet entreaty drew Sarah around. Heart pounding, she

stood motionless as Doña Betina spoke. "I am a full-blooded Spaniard, not a Creole, a citizen of Spain who is born here in the New World—"

"I know what a Creole is," Sarah whispered.

"Then you also know that I can offer Christina a secure place in proper society. Don Gabriel will seek his annulment from you if not for anything but to secure Christina's future. He will never allow Felicity's beautiful daughter to be an outcast as he once was."

Sarah turned her face away. Her unbound hair fell over her profile and shielded her from Betina's gaze.

"So you see, Lady Sarah"—Doña Betina gently enfolded Sarah's hands—"I'm sure that you will make someone a good wife, but not Don Gabriel."

Sarah listened to the wind shake the foliage outside. Somewhere in her dreams, a little girl had laughed . . . and she'd awakened with a start. Her breath stilled by her racing heart, she lay on her back, cloaked in darkness trying to put a face and a time to the memory. Outside, the chimes on the verandah banged against her wall in a whispering cadence, knocking harder as thunder rolled across the sky. She finally sat up.

She had no idea of the time when she'd dressed and left the heat of her bedroom. With her walking stick in hand, she followed the serpentine path that led to the cove. The restless wind lifted her hair and stirred the trees. She no longer wore her robe, but a simple blouse and skirt that she tucked in her waistband so she could walk.

Sarah stepped into the water. Often, in the middle of the night, drawn by some inexplicable need, she came to the cove. That same girl in her dreams played in waves like these and knew how to swim like a fish.

The girl inside her feared nothing.

Lifting her face to the sky, Sarah let the scent of the sea fill her senses.

Gabriel still had not returned. In the weeks that had followed his departure, the widow Betina had ingratiated herself into the role of Sarah's benefactor. With an efficiency that bespoke her station, she ran the household and all of its many

servants, who acquiesced to Sarah only at Doña Betina's dic-
tate.

Perhaps this was what Gabriel wanted. In truth, she could
not have run the massive household. She was only beginning
to relearn and think in her mother's tongue. But no one outside the stone walls of this house ever spoke to her. Most people thought her blindness was punishment for past sins. The
village priest wouldn't let her near the children in the parish.
Everyone seemed to tolerate her presence only because she
was no threat to the status quo.

Though Sarah was shunned, Gabriel's rank in society had
offered her an opportunity to learn, which she hadn't squan-
dered on self-pity, no matter what the future held for her.

Cori, through much spying on the various Spanish en-
tourages that came to visit Betina, had learned the proper way
of setting a fancy table, and bent that knowledge on Sarah.
Spoons, forks, and knives all had their functions in her head
now, alongside the plates, bowls, and platters they escorted.
Sarah knew the names of each course, and the difference between port and Madeira.

A wave washed over her knees, startling her.

"Señorita Drake?"

Stefan's voice whirled Sarah around. Her hand went to her
breast to still her pounding heart.

"I am sorry to have frightened you, but you didn't answer
when I called your name."

He spoke in English, and she could tell that he had just
been awakened. When he wasn't with his family in the village, he lived in the guard house. "I have told you not to come
down here in the middle of the night, *señorita,*" he said. "It is
too dangerous in the dark."

"And I have told you that I am not Señorita Drake."

"You are to Don Gabriel."

Resisting Stefan's efforts to return her to the house, Sarah
backed a step. More than anything she hated that he seemed
to feel sorry for her. "I thought Don Gabriel's yards were protected. That I am not to be a prisoner."

"It is true, this cove is protected by shoals. No ship can
land within a hundred meters. But to walk around in the middle of the night . . . it is unseemly, Lady Sarah." His voice was

filled with firmness. "You make no effort to protect your character. Everyone here thinks . . . they think you are touched in the head."

She snatched away from his hand. "Can't I have any privacy, Stefan? I am relegated to my rooms at the house. The darkness means nothing to me. If I awaken and wish to go for a walk, what is the harm? Why must I be judged for everything that I do?"

"I have come to escort you back to the house," he said evenly.

Again he took her elbow.

Sarah allowed him to walk her back up the trail. The rain stopped by the time they reached the yard. A chorus of ill-tuned frogs sang in the wet air. "I haven't spoken to you in nearly a week, Stefan," she finally said to break the stilted silence between them. "Where have you been? Have you heard anything from Don Gabriel?"

"I don't expect to hear from him until his ship returns."

Sarah lowered her head. Her wet skirts slapped against her legs.

"My son is ill, *señorita*." Stefan walked her through the long grass. "I am needed at home. But I have not left you unprotected. I want your word that you'll not leave the house anymore tonight."

She gripped the hem of her wet skirt to keep Stefan's pace. "I didn't even know that you had a son. What is his name?"

"David," he said after a moment.

"David is a strong name. It was borne by the man who slew Goliath."

"*Sí*, it was." Pride infused his quiet words, and he slowed his gait. "He celebrated his sixth birthday yesterday."

"Then he's just a little younger than Christina."

"They were born a year apart. You have met Christina?" he asked carefully. "No spiders in your bed or molasses in your shoes yet?"

"I certainly hope not!"

"She has been known to be a terror. Most of the servants are afraid of her and leave her alone to do as she pleases."

"Then they are fools."

It was a morning and evening ritual for Gabriel's daughter

to sneak into Sarah's bedroom, as if Sarah didn't know she was there. So Sarah ignored her, ofttimes peeling an orange, or unwrapping small disks of chocolate, and leaving them like bread crumbs, drawing Christina deeper and deeper into the room. The chocolate was especially worthy bait since Doña Betina didn't allow Christina any sweets. Come morn, the offerings were always gone.

"She does not speak to me yet," Sarah declared. "But she will."

An exhale sounded. "You are so sure that Christina will accept you, as you are so sure of everything, *señorita*."

Stefan's resentment of her did not surprise her, but the animosity behind his words did. "Yes," she said simply.

"Why is that?" Incredulity underscored his tone. "Where do you get your faith when you have been handed such misfortune?"

Sarah lifted her face and tried to decipher this sudden assault.

"You trust people you should not trust, including me. You smile when people turn away from you. You love when there is no hope that it will be returned. You have peculiar taste in friends, and think nothing of setting a cat on the table to share your meal. You are strange to me, Lady Sarah."

"Is that why you don't like me? Because I am strange?"

They had reached the edge of the verandah. Wind chimes rattled in the wind. Stefan didn't answer, and by his rigid stance beside her, Sarah didn't think he would. "I don't like you because Don Gabriel should be in Spain," he quietly said. "Because I don't want to see him hurt. I have no understanding of someone like you. Probably no more than Don Gabriel, yet he is willing to lay down his life for you. Pah! I don't understand him either. You are both mad."

Sarah remained speechless. Stefan knew Gabriel well enough to know that he would lay down his life for anyone he'd sworn to protect. And Stefan had read her all wrong to think that she had faith in *anything*.

Before he turned away, she touched his arm. "Can I help your son in any way? I know much of medicine."

Stefan backed a step. "He will be fine in the doctor's hands."

He waited for her bedroom door to close. With her ear pressed to the glass, Sarah listened to his steps fade on the verandah tiles. Finally, she turned and sighed. Movement in the nearby chair alerted her. The sound was no more than a whisper, but Sarah had heard it.

Christina was in the room.

Sarah straightened and went to the closet to remove her wet clothes. Once encased in dry attire, she sat on the bed and started to comb the wretched tangles from her hair.

Outside, the rain had started again and pebbled against the tile roof. Thunder exploded, and Christina gasped.

"Would you care to share this bed?" Sarah asked, ready to end their silent standoff. She spoke in rusty Spanish, which wasn't so different than French. Clearly Christina was terrified of the storm.

Without awaiting an answer, Sarah plaited her wet hair and crawled beneath her sheet. Her braid smelled of vanilla and coconuts, a product of the oil she used to help with her tangles.

"It seems rather foolish to remain cold and frightened. Don't you think?" she said.

"Are you really my stepmama?" the tiny voice asked.

The question startled Sarah. She had not considered this aspect of her marriage to Gabriel. Sarah drew her knees to her chest. *"Sí,"* she was unsure how much to say. She didn't want to develop a deep relationship with this child, only to be thrown out of her life. Nor did she know what Gabriel might have told her. "I suppose you can say that I am."

A burst of thunder brought Christina to the bottom of the bed. "Are you going to punish me?"

"Why would I do that, *niña?*"

"Rosa said that you will turn me into a frog, a *muy grande rana,* if I am bad to you anymore. Is that true?"

"Rosa is your *dueña?*"

"Rosa said all English are barbarians and eat with their fingers. You don't look like a barbarian."

"If eating with my fingers means I'm a barbarian, then I suppose Rosa is correct. How have you been bad to me?"

Bed ropes creaked. The girl edged closer. "I gave you ugly

presents because . . . I wanted to know if you were really blind."

Sarah hid her smile. "Hmm. That could be very serious."

"The feathers are from crows," Christina confessed. "No one likes crows because they eat the seeds out of the garden."

"I love crows. All birds eat the seeds."

"That doll . . . Papa hates that rope doll because . . . it looks like a rope. It isn't pretty or useful for anything."

Sarah tucked a stray length of hair behind one ear. This time she did smile. "My brother made me rope dolls when I was little."

"He did?" Christina's voice filled with sudden cama-raderie.

The childhood memory, as bright and vivid as a rainbow, went through Sarah. Excitement filled her. Marcus had made her a rope doll every time he'd cut his dark hair.

"My brother was very creative," she said. "He would give the dolls whiskers and hairy chests. And lots of bushy hair."

Christina giggled. "*Sí,* like my doll."

Fragmented imagery came in bursts of color and sound as Sarah suddenly remembered more. Her house had been grand with pillars that lined the front and back verandah. Inside the foyer, a crystal chandelier had twinkled in the breeze. Like the wind chimes.

"I loved those dolls." Sarah straightened her back. "We shall have to make you a doll with a hairy chest. That will really make your papa cringe."

The next bolt of thunder rattled the house. Christina scurried up the bed. "Do you really know how to turn people into frogs?"

Pulling the sheet over them both, Sarah turned on her side and faced Christina. "I might," she answered neutrally.

"Could you teach me?"

"Who do you want to turn into a frog?"

"Papa," she whispered. "Then no one would want him but me."

Chapter Eleven

Standing just inside the doorway that looked out on the muddy dockside street, Gabriel peered around the dimly lit taproom. Outside, thunder cracked across the sky. His hand easing to the hilt of his cutlass, he never felt more out of his element.

Dressed in black breeches and a black jerkin threaded with silver, he wore a fancy plumed hat over a black scarf. A heavy cutlass hung from his hip, a stiletto braced his calf, and two pistols, hanging from a leather baldric, draped his chest. He had not shaved in over a month.

The noise inside was deafening. Glass and pewter clinked freely. The room smelled of hashish, unwashed bodies, and the stench of fornication: a pirate watering hole on an obscure island barely two hours south of Santo Domingo.

"'Ey, lovey." A black-haired whore twined her finger around the ruffle at his collar. Her long hair was uncombed. "Son of the devil hisself." She lifted on her toes to kiss him. "Oi likes 'im mean."

Gabriel stopped her hand from dipping into his pants. He looked down into the woman's once-pretty face and pity stirred with disgust as he moved her aside. Pouty lips pulled at her expression before a beefy hand reached over and thrust a hand up her skirt. Squealing, she turned her attentions to the other table.

Gabriel's gaze stopped on the man sitting in the farthest corner of the crowded room.

Harrison Kendrick wore a muddy-colored periwig. Sipping ale, he was casually watching Gabriel. A black patch covered one eye on the same side of his body where he'd lost his leg a year before.

A slow glance around the room told Gabriel that a dozen or so of Kendrick's men were in attendance. But then Gabriel had known the man wouldn't keep his side of the bargain.

Someone started to sing an obscene ballad recounting in vivid detail the romantic interlude between an English sailor and a mermaid. Gabriel was forced to walk through the boisterous revelers.

"Like old times, Espinosa," Kendrick said over the noise as Gabriel settled into a flimsy chair against the wall.

Kendrick turned his head. A flick of his gloved hand brought a pretty barmaid running to the table. After he ordered two ales, Gabriel flipped the barefooted girl two gold coins.

"A clean mug, *sí*?"

The girl's expression brightened. Smiling at Gabriel, she dipped and skittered away.

Kendrick shifted his brown eye to Gabriel. "You flash that kind of gold in here, you'll be robbed before you reach the door."

"*Sí,* they can try." Gabriel's smile was a deliberate act of arrogance. "But I will still have a clean mug."

"I suppose I won't start out this meeting by offering you money. You already have more than the world's share."

"Don't get the impression that I'm here because I like you, Kendrick." Gabriel doffed his gloves. "I should have made pig slop out of your double-dealing tongue years ago."

"I never dealt with you except in honest matters. Besides"—Kendrick studied the hem of his royal velvet jerkin—"it is I who should be angry. You fired on my ship."

"Did you think I wouldn't?"

A fight started somewhere across the room. Men, dressed in the tattered remains of once fine clothes, jumped in front of Gabriel to view the raucousness. Relaxing an elbow against the table, Gabriel gave Kendrick his full attention. "I had no idea you commanded a ship in the English navy. I thought you were Jamaica's esteemed lieutenant governor not so long ago."

Kendrick flicked a roach off the table. "I'm no longer governor because I chose not to be. Too confining. Even for a man with one leg. The king was very sympathetic to my cause."

"Which is?"

"Eradicate the seas of any man who might be a threat to England. Including you, Espinosa." The chair squeaked as he leaned back and crossed his arms. Expensive lace dangled over his wrists. "I've been given a royal commission to hunt down pirates. The king's decree offering amnesty to those who sail without a letter of marque . . . has been revoked. I have three ships under my command. I serve on the vice-admiralty board in Jamaica now. A far more lucrative position."

Kendrick examined one gloved hand. "And I have a few old marks to settle, *sí, mi amigo*? The first one is with a particular family named Drake." Patting his wooden stub, he tightened his mouth. "You are familiar with vengeance, El Condor?"

The serving girl appeared with two pewter mugs in hand. "I cleaned the mug myself, *monsieur*. As you asked," she offered with a shaky smile. Her eyes held Gabriel's.

She gasped as Kendrick shoved a gloved hand up her skirt. "Get rid of the stench between her legs and she might be pleasing," Kendrick chuckled. "Wouldn't you agree, Espinosa?"

Gabriel shifted his gaze, wiping the smirk off Kendrick's face.

Dipping her head, the girl scurried away.

"Where is your sense of adventure, Espinosa?" Kendrick bent forward, his finger tracing the gouges in the table. "Or do your tastes run in a different direction? Heard tell you were a boy when Henry Morgan's men raided your home. That you and your mother . . ." Kendrick brushed his palm along Gabriel's wrist. "How shall I say this?" His eyes met Gabriel's. "Some say that once a man—"

Gabriel slid the tip of his stiletto beneath Kendrick's offending hand. "I *will* have no problem severing this part of your anatomy, *old friend,* if you do not remove it from my arm."

Kendrick sprawled back, the chair creaking beneath his meager weight. "I merely seek to remind you that the past can never be forgotten. It makes the man. It made you, and it's made me. I want Sarah Drake. Among other things, she has an old warrant over her head. I have a legal right to her."

"*Mierda.* For what?" Gabriel jammed the stiletto blade into the soft wood of the table. "Anything her family did, it was when she was a child and not responsible."

Kendrick sipped his ale consideringly. "You can't hide someone like her for long. If she's not on Hispaniola, then I will eventually find out where she is anyway. Without your help."

Gabriel fingered the leather hilt of the stiletto. "What is the real reason you want her?" He swigged the ale, and barely restrained himself from spitting the brew back into the mug. Like everything else in this place, the ale had probably been fermented in the local privvy. He slid the pewter mug aside. "And don't tell me it's over an obscure warrant issued more than eleven years ago."

"You and I go a long way back." Kendrick smiled. "I give a little. You give a little back. We have always had a partnership."

"*Sí.*" Gabriel's smile was thin. "We are saints."

Kendrick set the mug down with a *thunk.* "Last year when you captured the *Dark Fury,* the ship was headed to England with a captain of His Majesty's navy on board, a Captain Quentin Roth. It seems that Talon Drake was cashing in his hopes and banking on a pardon in return for certain proof that his family had been wrongly accused of treason twelve years ago."

"And were they?"

"Does it matter?" Kendrick continued, "Thanks to you, the information Roth carried never reached the king. I'm assuming it was destroyed along with the crew."

"The crew wasn't destroyed. They were handed over to the English government in Port Royal."

"Still, the information Roth carried hasn't resurfaced.

There is only one left alive who can bear witness against me for what I call my past indiscretions—"

Gabriel's hand fisted around the mug. "So you wish to begin a new life," he said behind a casual grin. "Start all over. Fresh as the day you were born. Except for one problem. What did Sarah Drake see?"

"Sarah is so much more than a witness of past crimes," Kendrick whispered, suddenly humbled by something that Gabriel could not see. "She is my salvation."

Gabriel's eyes narrowed. "She is only a woman."

"I don't expect you to understand." Kendrick studied his ale, seemingly oblivious to the noise around them or to Gabriel's question. The fiddlers had stopped but not the dancing.

Lifting his face, he confronted Gabriel's frown. "I'd never seen her until that day the soldiers came to her house. She . . . she was the most beautiful child. There was something about her."

"What did you do to her, Kendrick?"

"Her mother escaped from the house as the soldiers came." His voice hardened. "She'd hidden Sarah in the rocks above the cliffs. But I didn't know this when I'd caught up to that Spanish bitch. Mary Francis—I think that was the mother's name. The woman was a Drake, a Spanish whore, too good for the likes of me." Gabriel watched as Kendrick opened his hands and stared into his empty palms.

Madre de Dios. Gabriel had heard enough to guess what Sarah had seen that day. "So she saw you rape her mother. And kill her, too?"

"I hadn't even finished with the mother . . . and I looked up into Sarah's eyes wide with horror. That was the one time in my life that I had ever regretted something that I'd done. Then she plunged a dagger into my shoulder. Mary Francis started fighting me . . . as if I would have hurt Sarah. I took the dagger . . ."

"Jesu . . . that must have been a proud moment for an officer of the English crown to share with a child."

A look of disgust fell over Kendrick's flaccid features. "You've grown soft, Espinosa," he snapped in fury. "Your hands are no less bloody than mine for the killing you've done."

Gabriel stood. "Maybe, Kendrick. But I did mine under a flag of war. I did not rape and murder women and children."

"Sarah is alive."

"As sure as there is sunlight, Sarah Drake died that day."

Kendrick's jaw clenched. "Not so long ago you had your mind set on ridding the seas of pirates. Now you protect the daughter of a man who took part in the attack on your family? Many years ago, I handed over the sons of the man who killed your father. You were very grateful then for my cooperation. You owe me, Espinosa. Where is your bloody honor?"

"Even if I could, I would not give her to you." Gabriel put a booted foot on the chair and leaned an elbow on his knee. "You see, Lady Sarah is now my wife. And I will never hand her over to a savage like you. Be grateful I don't kill you where you sit."

Shock filled the silence between them. "You would never marry a Drake. Not willingly . . . So the rumors on Martinique were true."

Kendrick's expression cleared and his gaze focused on Gabriel. "You won't kill me." He snorted. "We came here under a flag of truce. That would mean you'd break your word. However, I suffer no such handicap." He raised his hand as if to give an awaited signal.

Gabriel's cutlass went to his throat. "Before you call your dogs on me, consider this, Kendrick." He smiled icily. "Mine are the men without the whores on their laps."

Kendrick stilled as the wisdom of Gabriel's advice penetrated. "All I have to do is yell your name in this room," Kendrick rasped.

This time Gabriel laughed. The room wobbled slightly, and he straightened. His vision blurred. "Would your reception here be any warmer, Kendrick?" He sheathed his sword because it had suddenly grown too heavy in his hand. "I'll let you live as long as you remain in here. Outside? Our truce is off."

Gabriel stumbled and reached his hand back to catch himself on the wall. Kendrick's smug grin came into focus. "Anything you wish, Don Gabriel, O trusted partner of mine."

Gabriel's gaze swung across the room to the bar. Eyes wide, the dark-haired serving girl watched him, turning away when the man behind the bar cuffed her shoulder. She hastily placed pewter mugs on her tray.

"It's unfortunate you didn't drink more." Kendrick relaxed in the chair. "As it is, you may still be alive when my men find you."

Gabriel backed a step.

Kendrick raised his glass of ale in toast. "I do so enjoy the chase, Espinosa."

"*¡Hijodeputa!* Son of a bitch *inglés*," Gabriel swore. Bracing one hand against the rough side of a building, he waited for the dizziness to pass. "I should have known. . . ."

"Can you make it to the ship?" Wind whipped the feather on Berto's hat.

Gabriel made it as far as the end of the street before he emptied the contents of his stomach. An evening storm had cleared the muddy streets of most people, and he welcomed the pounding rain on his back. The alley smelled of a cesspool. Wiping the back of his hand across his mouth, he looked up. Movement at the end of the street warned him that Kendrick's men were now on the prowl.

"Order the men to split up and return to the ship any way they can," Gabriel told Berto. "They are not looking for you."

"*Señor.*" A woman's desperate voice pulled him around.

The dark-haired woman who'd served Gabriel ale stood a few feet away. His look behind her revealed only darkness. Rain battered her face. She wore a mantilla lace wrap over her head and shoulders. "*Por favor.* I heard the Englishman say that they are waiting for you and your men at both ends of the town."

Gabriel's fist tightened, but it was Berto whose hands whipped out and pinned her against the side of the building.

"What did you give him?" Berto gripped her throat. "Tell me or I will crush your neck."

Wide-eyed with terror, she twisted toward Gabriel. "I tried . . . the Englishman paid my brother to see that you drank the ale. They are looking for your ship," she cried, clawing at the hand. "The Englishman said that a ship cannot stay hidden here on this small island for long. I came to help."

Rain slashed through the darkness. Gabriel peered down at the terrified girl. Light from a nearby window pooled in her eyes. "Why?"

She held his gaze. "Because you were kind to me when you didn't have to be. No man is kind to me. I do not wish you to die at my hand."

She wore a faded blue skirt and blouse. Mud spattered her ankles, which told him that she'd run from the tavern to reach him. Gabriel lifted his gaze and fixed his eyes on her wide blue ones. She was probably no older than fourteen.

"Release her, Berto," Gabriel rasped, his eyes never leaving her face. "Do you know what was in the ale?"

"Oui." She scraped the heel of her hand across her cheek. "Belladonna."

Berto snapped a horrified gaze back to Gabriel's face.

"Nightshade," she whispered. "It was a powder."

Gabriel knew what belladonna was without the added explanation. Other than arsenic and cyanide, no stronger poison existed. But why was he feeling the effects now? It usually took hours; then death came swiftly.

"My ship is a league south of here," he said to the girl. "The other side of the wooded cay. You know another way out of town?"

"There is a path through the swamps. I will take you."

Gabriel stopped her with a hand on her shoulder. "They will know that you are gone from the tavern."

"Let them." Her chin lifted in a way that reminded him of Sarah, and suddenly he had enormous respect for her courage. "The owner is my father. I make him much money. He will not beat me, or that will hurt his profits."

Gabriel nodded to Berto. *"Vete.* We will follow her."

Two hours later, the girl led them out onto a moonlit beach. The rain had stopped, but not for long, as the wind still swayed the treetops. No longer able to stand without help, Gabriel walked between two of his men. The moon was an empty skull in the sky.

"Will you come . . . with us, *señorita?"* His voice was a harsh rasp.

Her shadowed eyes were filled with fear when she shook her head and told him that she had a daughter and that she couldn't leave.

"*Sí, vete, vete . . .* go to her."

Despite his throbbing temples, the sentiment was one that Gabriel understood, an emotion that quickened his heart, an instant before he dropped to his knees.

Aided by another man, Berto helped take his arms. For an hour . . . or for days, they ran and ran. Gabriel didn't know how much time passed before they finally reached the cove where his ship lay anchored. The sky had turned a bloody red. Crabs crawled over the sand and nipped his boots. No one else seemed to notice them. He could hear the rhythmic clicking of their claws as they raced up the wet sand and over fallen tree stumps and mossy rocks. Thousands of crabs. The noise grew louder. "Get me out of here, Berto," he whispered as Berto loaded the men into boats. He spoke in Spanish or French. He could decipher no language in his head. "*¡Dios!*" He tried to back away. But his arms were suddenly pinned to his side. "Don't let them get me!"

He kicked out. Then he began to fight in earnest. For the first time since he was a child and a horde of English refuse had crawled over his land and into his home, he had not been so terrified of being caught. His clothes were drenched with his sweat. His heart pounded against his ribs.

His breath wouldn't come . . . and when he finally screamed, he didn't know if the sound had been his or from a hapless boy whom the crabs consumed.

Sarah came awake with a startled cry.

The storm had abated hours ago. She sat up. Her braid, still damp from the rain, draped her shoulder. The wind chimes outside gently swayed in the breeze. Beside her, Christina slept.

Yet Sarah's heart raced with a sense of urgency.

Someone had screamed.

From the other end of the house, she suddenly heard yelling. Sarah twisted around. Without throwing on a wrapper, she grabbed her walking stick and left the room. Weeping could be heard among the whispers of terrified servants.

Down the corridor, near Gabriel's room, Doña Betina's voice was buried beneath a man's furious bellow.

Something shattered against the wall, followed by a flurry of shoving and shouting that sounded like a fight.

"Oh, *señorita, señorita*." A hand clutched her nightdress. Sarah recognized the terrified voice of Rosa, Christina's *dueña*. The old woman sank to her knees before Sarah. "You must help him. You must."

Sarah knelt beside the hysterical woman. "What has happened?"

"He is mad!" Rosa wailed. "Berto has had to tie him to the bed. They say he will die."

Sarah shook the woman. "What are you talking about? Who will die? What has happened?"

"Don Gabriel," she sobbed. "He has been poisoned."

Sarah's heart stopped. She stood.

"The physician is here but Don Gabriel, he fights him. They've had to restrain him."

Hands trembling, Sarah snatched up her stick. "You go to Christina. Whatever you do, don't let her see her papa like this. Stay with her in my room. Be strict. Do not let her out."

Her hand fumbled in the air until it came up against the wall. She walked as fast as darkness allowed, moving around paintings she knew to be hanging in the corridor. Voices grew as she approached Gabriel's room.

Hands grabbed her. "You cannot go in there, *señorita.*" Berto spun her around. "The doctor is with him."

"What poison?" she demanded. "Tell me."

"Get her out of here, Berto," Doña Betina shouted.

Fear burst through her in mindless panic. She jerked her arm away, and with a savage oath, Berto stumbled as he attempted to subdue her. "Answer me! What poison?" she demanded.

"Belladonna." His raspy voice bespoke the prognosis of such a toxin. "He drank the poison in his ale. He has been having terrible hallucinations. I don't know how he has survived this long."

"How long?" Her fingers hooked around the hand on her arm. "How long has he been this way?"

"Almost six hours." Berto pulled her down the corridor.

"We left Cay Island, a few hours south of here, and sailed home at once. It took me longer. I am no *capitán*. I do not know all of the shoals."

The symptoms confused her. "Wait! Berto—" She dug her heels into the carpet. He'd dragged her into the dining room. "How long after he drank the ale did the poison hit?"

"Fifteen minutes, a half hour . . . I do not know." He jerked her forward. She was too stunned to fight. "And I don't have time for this, *señorita*."

"Please . . . I am Don Gabriel's wife, Berto."

"Haven't you already done enough harm?" He forcibly sat her in one of the sixteen chairs that encircled the dining table. "If you care about him you will stay away and let the physician do his job. He is bleeding Don Gabriel to get the poisons out. There is nothing more any of us can do except pray."

"Bleeding him! You will kill him for sure!"

"No, *señorita*. You have killed him. Don Gabriel met with Harrison Kendrick last night because of you."

The words struck Sarah. But before the reality of the situation galvanized her to speak, Berto was gone, his bootsteps sounding loud and furious on the wooden floor of the corridor.

She lowered her face into her hands. Gabriel had met with Harrison Kendrick.

But Gabriel's life now was all that mattered.

Sarah fumbled for her walking stick and left the house to go to the servants' quarters.

"Cori!" She shook Cori awake. "You must wake up now. Wake up."

How Cori could have slept through all the screaming and shouting over the grounds, Sarah didn't know.

Rustling sounded. "What is it, milady?" Cori's sleepy voice was muffled by the blanket. Beneath her weight, the bed ropes creaked.

"Go fetch Stefan. I know that his son is ill, but you must find him and bring him here. Tell him . . . tell him that it is a matter of life and death. On your way, tell Jaime to find me in the garden next to the herbal. I need his help."

"Milady," Cori whispered, "but you are not dressed."

"Go, I said. Get Stefan here now."

Sarah didn't wait for Cori to leave. She found her walking stick and stepped outside Cori's door into the yard. The servants' quarters consisted of a long row of apartments next to the main house. Shaded by tall trees, the earth had not yet dried from last night's soak. A wind gust whipped her nightdress around her knees. Sarah had come here often enough with Cori to know the way back to the house, but as she stood in the damp air, warmed now by morning light, she found that she was suddenly lost. Her hands trembled.

Lifting her face, she pictured the yard, the trees and gardens, where she wanted to go. She finally set her bearings.

Jaime found her pacing in front of the wooden door that led to the herbal below, which was much like a food cellar. Gabriel's sister had known about medicinal plants and the various herbs used to aid the sick. Sarah only hoped the herbal had been maintained and that she'd find what she needed. Jaime would be her eyes.

But he would not be her hands. Or her defender this day.

For she was finished taking orders from everyone.

Chapter Twelve

"Let me in the room, Berto. Now!"

No sound emitted from behind Gabriel's door when Sarah next stood before Berto. She'd cleaned her hands of dirt and loam. A small straw basket dangled from her wrist. Jaime had taken the herbs she'd found to the kitchen, where they would be steeped in water. Gabriel's sister had also kept a supply of bitters and vinegar on hand. Sarah would kiss her personally when she saw Liandra next.

People no longer blocked her path. Most had stepped aside at her approach. But Berto remained steadfast in front of the door. "Doña Betina has forbidden anyone to enter," he quietly informed her.

Without hesitation, Sarah stepped around Berto to open the door, and found her hand seized. "I am sorry, *señorita*."

She did not relinquish her hold on the latch. It was cold beneath her hand. "Are you ready to hit me, Berto?"

"*Dios,* Berto." Stefan's frayed voice suddenly filled the corridor. "What has happened?"

Cori had found Stefan!

The hallway erupted in chatter as a dozen voices leaped to detail the events that had transpired.

"His son is ill, milady." Cori joined her at the door. "But he came when I told him of Don Gabriel."

"Thank you, Cori. Jaime is in the kitchen. Go to him. He will tell you what needs to be done."

Sarah opened the door, but stopped when Berto snatched her hand. Doña Betina was inside sobbing.

"Dios." Stefan pushed past Berto.

"He is convulsing, Stefan. We cannot stop it."

"Let me go to him!" Sarah twisted and shoved against Berto.

"Let her go," Stefan said.

Berto released her. Stefan guided her toward the bed.

Kneeling over Gabriel, Sarah set her basket down. Blood caked his wrist where he'd pulled at his restraints. His powerful body lurched and bucked in the bed. "I want him untied."

The physician protested. "It has taken four men to tie his arms down."

"Do it," Stefan said.

"Take his arms," she cried when Stefan cut the restraints.

Stefan and Berto held Gabriel's shoulders. He shouted about bloodred skies. He cursed at them all. Awful language she had never heard from him.

"Hold him!"

Doña Betina helped Sarah still his head while Sarah ground the leather knife strap between his clenched mouth to prevent him from biting off his tongue. She spoke quietly, soothingly. Never had she been so strong as she was that night to keep him in her lap.

"He thinks the room is filled with crabs," Berto said. "He is fighting us all."

"He's been like this since Berto brought him home," Betina cried. "We've tried to bleed him."

Sarah held the leather strap wedged between his teeth with every ounce of her strength. "You cannot—"

"A man must be bled." The physician's voice wobbled. "The humors—"

When Gabriel finally went limp with exhaustion, Sarah cradled his head. Betina collapsed to her knees in tears.

"You bled him?" Stefan's bootsteps came around the bed. "Jesu. You know he would never allow this to be done to him."

His face damp, Gabriel continued to mumble incoherently. Tears welling, Sarah splayed her palms on his rigid chest. His heartbeat had slowed to a *thump . . . thump.* He was cold to the touch.

"What have you given him?" she asked.

"Laudanum." Doña Betina's voice was watery with tears. "He has been in such pain."

Sarah's hands whispered over Gabriel's restless mouth. He had not shaved in weeks. The sheets were drenched with his sweat. "He needs to flush out the poison. Not sleep with it festering in his organs. You cannot give him any more opium."

"Do you know what to do, *señorita?*" Stefan asked.

Her chin lifted. "I know that whatever has poisoned him is not belladonna."

"How could she know that?" Berto stood behind Stefan. "She is blind. What does she know about anything?"

"Because I know what belladonna poisoning is. It is true that he has many of the symptoms, but the poison takes hours to act on the body. You said the symptoms struck almost at once."

The room grew deathly quiet.

"Can you help him?" Stefan touched her shoulder.

"What can she do?" the physician demanded.

Sarah laid her palm over Stefan's hand. "I know that your son is ill and needs you. But please. Gabriel needs you, too. I will be in your debt and will do all I can to help your son when this is over."

A skirt rustled. "Stefan—"

"Stay out of this, Doña Betina. I want to know why the girl has been kept away."

"She practices magic," the physician said. "I have heard of the mission where she is from. Sorcerers, all of them."

"Berto, get him out of here."

The physician jerked around when Berto grabbed him. "You do not want my wrath, Stefan Delgato!"

After Berto escorted the physician out, Stefan returned to Sarah. "*Señorita,* I pray for both our sakes that Don Gabriel is still alive when this is over."

"Milady." Jaime entered. "I have brought the tea."

Sarah rolled up her sleeves. "The tea is an astringent, similar to bitters," she told Stefan. "We must keep liquids inside him."

Throughout the afternoon, Sarah fed Gabriel chamomile, milk, and egg whites. Her arm stiffened with her effort to keep him nourished. In the early morning hours of the next day, he had another seizure. As the second day passed, Sarah knew that she was powerless to save him from the pain he endured. That whatever Harrison Kendnick had given him was beyond any antidote.

She also knew that he would not die.

But she knew nothing of how to save his mind.

Her breath broke on a sob.

She had done this to him. He'd come to the mission on Martinique in search of his sister and brought away a wife he didn't want with a deadly threat that loomed over her. Father Henri had misjudged everything. He'd had no right to condemn Gabriel in this way.

The floor creaked as someone laid a shawl over her shoulders. "You are chilled," Stefan said. "You need to eat and sleep. You have gone too long without both."

Sarah knelt beside the bed, resting her cheek on her forearm, her hand in contact with Gabriel's chest. Berto and Jaime had fallen asleep on the floor. Doña Betina slept in the chair at the end of the bed. Cori was in the kitchen, brewing more tea.

"I have heard tales of hallucinogenic poisons," Sarah said. "The Indians in the jungles of Panama use such potions to commune with their gods. The drug is made from mushrooms."

Gabriel mumbled and tossed his head, and Sarah put pressure on his chest. Stefan waited for Gabriel to calm before he sat on the floor next to Sarah and propped his back against the bed. "Do you think he was given these mushrooms?" He sounded haggard.

"It's possible that the fungi were ground into a fine powder and disguised in the foam on his ale. Maybe mixed with something else." Her eyes closed. "What happened to him, Stefan? When he was a boy."

"No one really knows." Stefan folded his knees to his chest and dropped his head forward. His words were muffled. "His mother died a few months ago. She was the only one alive who knew the truth. She'd been with him during Henry Morgan's raid on their home in Puerto Bello. He was a boy."

"My father sailed with Morgan." She turned her cheek into the crook of her elbow. "I'd always heard the raid was such a proud victory for England. You never think about the other side, do you?"

"No, *señorita*. No one ever does, I suppose. But no country is truly innocent, I think, including Spain."

Sarah wiped at her face. "How is it that Don Gabriel could consent to meet with Harrison Kendrick?"

"They are not strangers to each other."

She paused. "Will you tell me how they know each other?"

He expelled a slow breath. "Many years ago Harrison Kendrick came to Don Gabriel with information about a ship that carried two English prisoners being transported from Port Royal and bound for a hearing in London. Don Gabriel took that ship . . . and took your brothers. They spent five years under the Inquisition."

A knife edge of pain sliced through her. But Gabriel had never lied to her about knowing Kendrick. He just hadn't told her the whole truth. Now she knew why. The wounds between their families went far beneath the surface.

"Talon has always claimed innocence for what the English courts in Port Royal did to our family," she said.

"It didn't matter to El Condor, *señorita*. It will never matter."

Her heart would not cease its rapid pounding. "Why . . . why are you telling me this?"

"Because Don Gabriel Cristobel de Espinosa y Ramírez is El Condor. And you are English. One is night, and one is day."

Stefan's voice faded. "I respect you, Sarah Drake. I didn't think I would, but I do, and I don't wish to see you hurt. Don Gabriel is not that boy who was once innocent. He hasn't been in more than twenty years."

Tears choked her throat. This was not a world she understood. Nor did she think that she could survive the kind of violence that robbed a child's soul of life. The kind that Gabriel had survived.

Gabriel had not only endured but risen above the ugly horror. He'd built wealth and rank like the stone walls of this house to protect him. He'd filled his world with beautiful things, including a beautiful wife named Felicity who gave him a daughter.

Sarah had been such a selfish fool to think that she could give him anything that he needed. It only took meeting her for him to lose it all.

The windows had been opened. Lifting her head, Sarah heard the faint chatter of birds. A hand scraped through the thickness of her hair. Her breath caught.

Gabriel's fingers splayed the back of her head. Even weak as he was, he had the strength to pull her nearer. *"Te amo, chica."* His rasp touched her temple. "Do not weep, *por favor*. You make me worried."

"Gabriel—"

Her hands, wet with tears, went to his beard-roughened face and touched his lips. His breath was warm and faint against her fingers. She knew he was not lucid, but more than anything in the world, Sarah wanted, at that moment, to see into his eyes.

"I love you, too, Gabriel Espinosa." She lowered her brow to his lips, where his mouth seemed to savor the touch. "*Sí . . .* you will be all right now. You have an angel watching over you, I think." She thought she felt him smile.

Then his hand fell away.

In minutes, his even breath came to her. For the first time in days, he was sleeping soundly.

Gabriel stirred. The scent of mint-sprigged sheets cleared his senses. His pillow smelled like the kind of paste he usually used to clean his teeth. Every muscle in his body ached.

His eyes slowly came open.

He stared at the cornices in the ceiling overhead, blinking twice before he recognized where he was. His hand went out, searching . . . searching for what?

Turning his head, his gaze fell unexpectedly on Doña Betina in a bright red chair beside the bed. His movement startled her. "You are awake." She fumbled to shove her needlepoint into a basket beside her leg, and rushed to his side. She placed a cool palm on his forehead. "Do you recognize where you are?"

Gardenia brushed his senses. A frown furrowed his brow. He could not recall why he was here in this bed. He'd had dreams . . .

"Where's Sarah?" His voice scraped his throat.

"Lady Sarah is with Señor Delgado." Straightening, she rang the bell beside the bed. The tiny jingle hurt his head. "His son is ill with a fever and Sarah has gone to help with his care."

Gabriel digested this information. He remembered very little from the instant that Berto had taken him to the ship. The lapse of memory annoyed him. Lifting his gaze, he found hers solidly fastened on him with concern. He studied Betina's face and tried to remember something. With her hair pulled atop her head and covered with black mantilla lace, she was strangely ethereal, bathed in morning sunlight.

"Have you been here the whole time?" he asked.

"*Sí,* Don Gabriel." Betina turned and a brought around a cup filled with dark liquid. Her taffeta dress rustled. "I have not left your side. How do you feel?"

Evading the liquid, Gabriel struggled to sit and suffered a spell of dizziness. He closed his eyes.

The mattress sagged as Betina sat next to him and took his hand. "It may take a few days for your body to recover from the poison."

"How long have I been here . . . in bed? Where is Christina?"

"So many questions." She laughed in delight. "You are weak. You need to eat more than the soup and tea we have been feeding you."

He tightened his grip on her hand. "How long?"

"Four days." Her voice lowered. "We thought that you might die."

"*¡Ay yi!*" He rubbed his temples. "I will kill Kendrick."

"Not today." Betina brushed the hair from his brow, her green eyes earnest. "Today, I will send someone in to shave you, and you will bathe. It will take some time for you to regain your strength."

His brows drew together. "What is wrong with Stefan's son?" He closed his eyes. Too weak to sit straight, he laid his head back.

The door suddenly swung open, and Christina burst into the bedroom, breathless. Her arms were wrapped around Sarah's huge cat.

"Papa!" she cried.

Rosa bustled into the doorway. Her face was flushed. "I am sorry, Don Gabriel. She has been too excitable, especially since Lady Sarah left. She heard the bell. . . ."

Betina caught his daughter as she ran past. "What have I told you about being a lady? Your father has been ill."

Christina's wide blue eyes fell on him with so much tragedy, Gabriel frowned at Betina for making his daughter sad.

"*Sí,* Doña Betina," Christina said contritely. "You said a lady never runs in the house or climbs trees." She dipped and let the cat go free. "And to leave the kitty alone."

"It's all right," he told Betina. Gabriel held out a hand to his daughter.

With a sniffle, Christina climbed into his arms as he tried to straighten against the headboard. He wore no shirt but he did wear drawers, and the sheets wrapped him securely. He felt clumsy. Perhaps it was uncouth to allow his daughter to see him so unrefined, but at the moment he didn't care.

"I have missed you, *ratón.*"

"*Sí,* Papa." She cupped his bearded jaw and giggled. "You look like a pirate." Christina leaned her cheek against his chest. "You are not going to die?"

"No, *ratón,* little mouse. I am not going to die."

His daughter smelled of grown-up things like lilacs and coconut hair cream, as if she'd played with Sarah's personal effects.

A white-clad house servant entered carrying a food tray.

"Come." Betina clapped her hands. "Your papa needs to eat."

"She is fine," Gabriel said quietly. "Send Berto in here." Gazing over his daughter's dark curls, he queried Rosa. "Did Lady Sarah say how long she would be gone?"

"No." Rosa dipped into a brief curtsey. "Only that she would not return until Stefan's son was well."

•   •   •

"I'll not be returning to my quarters here at the house for another few days," Stefan said as he helped Sarah from the carriage. His hands wrapped around her waist and lifted her out. "Berto will be in charge of your security."

Sarah leaned into his arm. He wore a military uniform jacket, perhaps the blue-and-white colors of Gabriel's guard. Cori had told her what the jackets looked like. The sleeve was rough beneath her hand. "Your son will be fine," she reassured him. "He is to keep sipping the hot water and ginger no matter how much he complains, until his cough is gone."

Her legs were stiff from the bumpy ride back to Gabriel's fortress. That's what she called Gabriel's house of stone. Rock walls as high as seven feet encased the grounds. The entrance to the main yard led beneath a gate where sentries with muskets stood guard over the grounds. She'd been told that Gabriel's men had watched over Stefan's small cottage while she was there.

Stefan took her hand and walked her along a wooded path. Their steps were silent. Behind her, in a rattle of harness chains, the carriage returned to the special dwelling that housed Gabriel's coachmen. A single horse remained behind, where Stefan had tied him to a hitching post. "In another day, Don Gabriel would have come for you himself," Stefan said. "He has been out of bed for days."

Sarah stiffened. "Cori has not been remiss in keeping me informed. I can assure you that I've not been needed here."

"My wife and I are in your debt, Lady Sarah," he said quietly. "And I thank you." He stopped. "But I think it is best for both of us that I summon someone else to take you back to the house."

"That won't be necessary." Gabriel's voice sounded.

Sarah's heart hit her rib cage. Her husband's unexpected appearance startled her. But though Gabriel loomed before her like a powerful shadow, she also wanted to throw herself into his strong arms. She was not prepared to face him quite yet while her own feelings were too tender to protect.

Gabriel moved beside her. The tension surrounding both men, alerted Sarah. "You're son is well?" he asked Stefan.

"*Sí,* Don Gabriel. He is out of bed now."

"I understand that your wife is expecting your second child. My congratulations on your news."

"We have been blessed. Sometime in August."

Tension arced between the two men in a way that Sarah didn't understand. Her blindness hindered her from reading the situation, but something was dreadfully wrong. She was suddenly afraid for Stefan.

Turning, she tipped on her toes and kissed Stefan's bearded cheek. "I've enjoyed staying with your family. Please thank your wife for her kindness. I will visit again soon, under circumstances more pleasant. David will be all right. He merely needs rest and good food now."

"Good night, Stefan." Gabriel dismissed him.

Stefan's bootsteps sounded harsh on the rocky path. A moment later a horse rode away down the drive.

"You were very rude, Gabriel," Sarah admonished when they were finally alone. "I'm surprised. He's your friend."

She'd felt Gabriel's eyes on her, and now they seemed to go through her like shards of thin ice. But his hand was gentle when he took her elbow. "It has taken all of my restraint not to go after you this week, *chica*."

Sarah pulled away. Contact with him hindered her resolve to keep distance between them. She didn't want him touching her. "Why should you, Gabriel? You left me in his charge for over a month. Now you rant because I choose to spend time with his family?"

"I am not ranting."

She walked three steps and hit the low branch of a tree.

"Dios," Gabriel mumbled beneath his breath. He brushed the leaves from her hair. "Is it so hard to endure my touch? You cannot walk out here alone."

Sarah didn't have her walking stick and was forced to accept Gabriel's guidance as he led her to the back of the house. The air smelled of crushed pine. She focused on her steps, but all she could hear were his. In moments, he slowed as they reached the verandah.

"We need to talk," he said quietly.

Sarah pulled away. "Yes." Her hand found purchase against the wall of the house. "There is something I wish to discuss with you as well." Folding her hands in front of her, she lifted her chin. "I've thought hard about this and decided to approach you at once when I returned. Now is as good a time as any to speak."

She'd resolved that she would be useful during the time that she had left here on this island. "You have many families who oversee the running of this plantation. Who man the crew on your ship."

"Excuse me?"

Wetting her lips, Sarah forged on. "They have children who are in need of a school. In addition"—Sarah paced—"Christina is seven. It is time that someone teach her to read and write her letters. She has run free for too long. And she misses you, Don Gabriel."

"You have decided all of this in the short time that you have been here?"

Sarah stopped in front of him. "You may buy her the world, and it will not substitute for your presence in her life."

"Anything else?"

"Yes." She started to pace again. "I also want someone to help me rebuild the herbal. It has been left to rot since your sister left. I don't know about your other homes or how you run your households, but this one is in need of repair."

"I see."

"Do you?" Her voice became hopeful.

"You wish to run my household here."

Taken aback, she lifted her chin. "No. I haven't the slightest idea how to run a household. Doña Betina is quite adept at that job. But I do know how to care for people."

"*Sí* . . . very well," he conceded. "My sister always dealt with those things. But I will talk to Stefan."

"I already have," she said excitedly. "He is looking for a teacher now. We have only to find a place to build the school."

"I will not send Christina to a school. You can tutor her."

"Me?" She laughed. "I know nothing about letters. Gabriel, she needs to play with other children her age. She is lonely."

"Sarah . . ." Gabriel planted his arm against the pillar. He stopped her pacing. "I have missed you."

The words startled her, but not as much as his proximity or the lemony scent of his shirt. Her pulse picked up pace.

"Gabriel, we both know that ours is a marriage made under less than ideal circumstances. It is not real." She lowered her chin. "You will seek your annulment now that you are here. Or maybe my brothers will find me before too long and take me . . . they will take me . . ." It occurred to Sarah that Talon's home on Martinique had been destroyed. She had no idea where she'd be living. In frustration, she straightened. "Tell me I don't speak the truth."

When Gabriel failed to reply, anger swelled. Did she not rate an answer? His arrogance was too much. She shoved away from him. "And one more thing I would ask. Nay, I demand. You will stay away from Harrison Kendrick. His fight is with *my* family."

Gabriel laughed. "Not anymore, *chica*. When I find him, I will do your brothers a favor and cut his throat."

She gasped. " 'Tis true!" A hand went to her heart. "You have *not* changed if you can speak of cutting a man's throat as if it were no more than a simple brisket to be sliced."

"Kendrick is not a man."

Her breathing came too fast for her to gather her thoughts. "Isn't it enough that Kendrick has nearly killed you? He is evil and cannot die. I don't want you anywhere near him. I am afraid, Gabriel. Truly afraid . . . Please, you cannot—"

"Shh." He grasped both her hands in his. "Nothing will happen to me. Or to you. I promise."

"I think . . . that he is the devil. I have seen his face, Don Gabriel. The devil's face."

Gabriel wrapped her to him. His hand brushed the length of her braid. "He is not the devil, *chica*. He is merely an evil man."

She buried her nose in the cleft in Gabriel's chest. His heartbeat pounded solidly against her forehead. "I don't want anything else to happen to you."

"I don't want anything to happen to me either." His voice hinted at amusement. He moved his mouth over her temple. "I was an idiot."

"I could not bear it a second time," Sarah whispered. He wore a silken robe over his shirt and breeches. She slid her foot toward his toes and felt his leather slippers. "You are not dressed, Gabriel." She cupped his face and found his jaw smooth. He had shaved. "What will the servants think?"

His hand boldly traced the curve in her spine. "They will think that I have been concerned for you."

"Why?" Her lips found solace against his jaw.

"Because I have missed you."

"I have missed you, too."

"What should we do about this, *chica*? Hmm?"

"Do?" The single word sounded drugged. "I . . ."

She pulled away. She would *do* nothing. He must surely still be deranged to even suggest . . . "I have been awake a long time, Gabriel. I fear I'm not thinking straight. And neither are you."

His arm barred her exit yet again. "Berto is bringing the ship in tomorrow to Santo Domingo. Perhaps you would like to go there and see the sights. Or . . . I could tell you what the city is like. Christina is coming as well. I will need someone to be with her."

Panicked by the sudden intimacy, Sarah ducked beneath his arm. Her head brushed against a chime and set it to music. "Doña Betina is better suited for such a job," she pointed out. "If Christina should get away from me, I would never find her in such a place as Santo Domingo. The place is too . . . it's too big. I won't go."

"I will have men with me."

She backed farther and hit the table. At least she knew where she was now. Her hand reached out and touched a pillar. "Why would you wish to be seen in public with me, Gabriel? Everyone thinks that you will soon marry Doña Betina."

"Sarah—"

"Isn't that true?"

"Sí," he said after a moment. "It has been assumed for some time that we would wed."

"And nothing has changed."

Gabriel waited for Sarah to close the door to her bedroom before finally turning away. He stood for a long time, half-expecting to see her light a lamp.

He wanted her.

Jesu, he ached for her everywhere.

Sí, he was deranged. The fever had smoothed the hard edge of his temper as much as it had his brains.

With a quiet oath, he returned to his room and dressed. He'd recovered most of his strength this past week but not all, and he felt the weakness in his arms when he latched his cutlass sling to his hips. He went to the stables. After the groom saddled his horse, Gabriel mounted and found Berto at the sentinel gate.

"You will stay behind tomorrow." Reining in the horse, Gabriel brought the spirited stallion under control. "I will have Stefan bring in the ship."

"*Sí,* Don Gabriel."

"I'll be gone for a week in Santo Domingo with my daughter. Keep the men at the cove's entrance. I don't trust Kendrick."

With that, the horse turned in a circle, leaping forward as Gabriel nudged his sides. He should reach Stefan before the man got home.

Chapter Thirteen

"Put them over here," Sarah instructed. Her knees were damp from kneeling in the garden beside the verandah.

"Shouldn't ye at least send a note?" Cori muttered in reproach. "Maybe join him for lunch?"

Sarah measured out dirt for the various pots lined up beside her. She'd spent the past week cleaning the herbal. Gabriel had surprised her when he'd assigned a bevy of servants to help with the task while he was gone. He'd even presented her with a batch of rare chamomile seeds and ginger root upon his return from Santo Domingo. But his thoughtfulness wasn't enough to bend her resolution to avoid him, no matter the nights in bed she spent fantasizing about him.

"I'm not attending supper, lunch, or any other meal with him, and that's final, Cori."

"He's trying to be nice, milady," Cori bleated with all the subtlety of a lovesick lamb. "This is the second invitation he's given you since he's been back. Glory be. The rest of the island wants his favor. This is *your* chance to impress him."

"Cori?" Sitting back on her calves, Sarah finally heaved a sigh. "What is it like? I mean, for a woman to be with a man."

Sarah sensed Cori's glare. "He was gone a week with that—that Betina!" Cori slapped a clay pot down beside Sarah. "You could have been with him and found out yerself. But no. Instead, ye remain here playing nursemaid to every servant's child who has a sniffle. You let that scheming witch have him!"

"She's not a witch." Sarah shoved aside one pot and pulled another near. "Not entirely anyway. She worked as hard as anyone else to save Gabriel's life."

"Why wouldn't she? If he died, you would still be his wife."

Sarah grabbed a fistful of loam and flung it into the small pot. "I thought you didn't even like him." Abruptly, she stood. "I finally choose a course that is best for everyone, and now you argue my every decision? I won't tolerate it. Do you understand?"

Cori's speechlessness gaped between them for a long moment.

"Blimey, milady. You've gone an' gotten yerself a temper." Her voice said she was impressed. "At least that's a start."

"Oh!" Sarah tossed up her hands. Specks of dirt flew everywhere. "Do *not* play Cupid with me."

She briskly scrubbed a damp towel over her hands and forearms. "Give me my walking stick."

"Are you going to bash that Betina over the head?"

"I have to talk to Don Gabriel about another matter. Is he back yet from the stables?"

"He and Christina came in an hour after you got back from the village this mornin'. He's in the library," Cori casually said, "probably mulling over how best to spend his next million ducats now that he's going to be home for a while."

Sarah snatched up her walking stick and found her way back to the house. Gabriel had returned from Santo Domingo two days ago. Not that she'd counted the hours since she'd seen him last, but her once-peaceful coexistence with this household had somehow been upended.

Rumor also abounded that he'd brought back a schoolteacher handpicked by Doña Betina herself, the famed taskmaster, miracle worker, and lady of many talents. Sarah's fists clenched the stick.

If it weren't for the fact that the woman loved Christina, Sarah would hate her to the core of her being. But there was nothing about her to hate, unless one counted competence as something less than a virtue. Doña Betina was everything Sarah wanted to be.

The low mumble of voices in the library told Sarah that

Gabriel had a visitor. Standing away from the door, she didn't have to wait long for the man to leave. Heart pounding, Sarah drew herself up.

A tap on the library door brought no answer. Sarah knocked harder. "*Sí.* What is it?" Gabriel called out sharply.

Clearly, his mood was not conducive to another visit. Since his return, she'd noticed that through a steady stream of appointments and by invitations for soirees that arrived daily, people ceaselessly demanded his attention. Sarah had never truly appreciated his enormous popularity and what it must be like for him to constantly be in the public's eye. She wouldn't like that at all.

Before Sarah changed her mind, she entered. Papers rustled at the desk across the room as if Gabriel had just looked up and seen her. "Sarah . . ." Whatever he'd been reading went back to the desk.

"What have you done with Stefan?" She felt Gabriel's penetrating gaze in the silence that followed, and held her stick against her. "I went to see his son this morning. Stefan was gone. His wife told me that you two had argued."

Leather creaked. She sensed Gabriel's approach before she smelled the familiar lemony soap he used to bathe with. The scent framed him like sunlight. "Stefan is in Santo Domingo with my ship while it's being refitted."

"You had no right to send him away. His family needs him."

"He's my second in command. His job is with the *Felicity* until she's ready to sail again."

"And when will that be?"

Gabriel leaned against the chair that sat nearest to the door. Wood squeaked. "A month, maybe less. She was damaged in the storm when Berto brought her back here. She needed new canvas anyway."

"I see," Sarah said, remembering that awful night with clarity.

"Every ship must be refitted once or twice a year, Sarah. This is not punishment for some perceived crime."

Sarah clutched her stick. Knowing little of ships and the mechanics of sailing, she could not argue the point and suddenly felt the fool for overstepping her bounds. She knew

Gabriel planned to hunt down Harrison Kendrick. Clearly, he wanted no impediment to that onerous task. Of course, once he completed the job, his ship would be ready for his eventual return to Spain, and he'd be leaving here.

Outside, wind chimes whispered in the breeze.

"Is there something else you wanted, *chica*?"

Sí. She wanted him to put his tongue in her mouth and end this insane want of him.

Scarcely breathing, Sarah turned to flee, but her fingers froze on the brass latch. "Have you tried to find my brothers yet?"

A hand went over her shoulder and pressed against the door. "Are you tired of my hospitality already?"

Gabriel stood so close behind her, the heat from his body bled into her clothes. Her head reached his shoulder. He wore costly breeches and an airy silk shirt tucked into his waistband. All of this she sensed in the seconds that his body made contact with hers.

Wrapping her arms around herself, she turned, but could squeeze no farther from him than the bookcase beside the door allowed. He'd been acting differently toward her since he'd awakened from the drug Harrison Kendrick had fed him. The change frightened her. He was acting contrary to expectations. He confused her.

"I find no fault in your hospitality," she said to his chest.

Gabriel tilted her chin with his forefinger. "Then what?"

"I miss my family. Besides—" Her voice ended on a whisper. "I don't belong here."

He dropped his hand from her chin, and the breath eased from her lungs. His steps went to the cabinet stretching the back wall. "Your brothers might be on New Providence. It is a British possession north of here." The clink of a crystal dropper sounded, followed by a slosh of liquid in a glass.

"Will it take long to travel there?"

"Long enough from Martinique. Your family probably has no idea what's happened to you yet."

"Then will you send someone to tell them? So that they may come get me?"

"They will find me in time, I think." She heard him drink from the glass. "But my sister is with them and it will be good to know where Marcus Drake has set up housekeeping. I have already sent someone to check the rumors."

Folding her hands in front of her, Sarah lowered her chin. "I should have gone with my brothers."

"But you didn't"—she felt his eyes slowly go over her—"and now you are here with me."

Her stomach fluttered. Terribly unsure of herself, Sarah fumbled behind her back for the door latch. "I still demand that you allow Stefan to return to his family," she said firmly, amazed that her voice held such iron. She swung open the door. "You are being unreasonable about everything."

The library door slammed, and Gabriel flinched.

Unreasonable!

Gabriel tossed back the drink.

Sí, he was unreasonable like the leopard that hunts for food. If Stefan wishes to nibble, he can do so in someone else's jungle. "He is lucky I let him live, *chica,*" he said to the door.

Christina's voice cried out from outside the window. "Doña Sarah!" His daughter sounded as if she were running across the yard. "I have looked all over for you," she squealed. "Come! I have something to show you."

"*¿Dónde?* Where?" Gabriel heard Sarah answer in Spanish.

His wife was very well versed in the language, he realized with more annoyance than he had a right to feel.

Gabriel walked to the window and pulled back the pale fabric that did little to block the sunlight. The room was hot. At least his servants knew to open the window when he was home.

"Hurry!" His daughter giggled.

Gabriel watched his daughter take Sarah's outstretched hand. His fey wife was not as helpless as she looked. Indeed, for a blind woman, she was very independent, coming and going as she pleased. The guard he'd set to protect her could hardly keep up as she flitted about the countryside unchaperoned like some mercy-driven sprite.

As was her custom, Sarah wore her pale hair uncovered. Her braid swung with her hurried gait, and Gabriel's thoughts shifted as he leaned an elbow against the wall and watched his daughter pull Sarah down the hill. He liked the way her simple red skirt flared over her hips and emphasized her small waist.

But he liked her better naked.

Did she know about the mole just inside her left thigh . . . ?

Movement turned his head. Betina stood at the edge of the trimmed hedge to his right, her long emerald dress fluttering in the breeze. Gabriel glimpsed a shapely ankle before he slowly lifted his gaze and found her watching him.

Betina deSalvo y Gonzáles was the epitome of Spanish beauty. Dark haired and petite, she knew fashion and wore her clothes to appeal to the baser instincts of a man.

Gabriel had bedded few women since Felicity's death. And not any that he could remember with clarity. He'd been discriminating to the point of indifference. Doña Betina had always held herself back from him, perhaps because their relationship had meant more than a single night's pleasure, or perhaps because she knew that she would never see him again had she'd ever responded to his subtle overtures.

Betina had been wise to deny him. But her green eyes told him today as they had in Santo Domingo, that she would deny him nothing now if he asked her.

He thought about it, thought about backing her against the wall outside and taking her up on the invitation this very moment. He was a man, after all, who had gone a long time without intimate relations. Her body would offer him relief.

If that were all he wanted.

Gabriel dropped the curtain edge and leaned his head back against the wall. "*¡Ay yi!*" He glared at the ceiling. Betina had been compassionate to him for more years than he could count.

Now he didn't know how to find the words that would send her back to Havana. Not when she was the better woman for his wife.

But Gabriel had not petitioned the tribunal in Vera Cruz for an annulment from Sarah. The papers remained in the desk on his ship.

Closing his eyes, he attempted to summon the warrior inside him. The antagonist. The survivor. Gabriel had spent his life building power on a reputation for action. Every move he'd ever made had been calculated to give him the best advantage, whether it be in battle or the marriage bed. But he was trapped by something deep inside, something he had only just begun to understand when he'd faced Kendrick across the table, knowing that he might die before he could get back to Sarah, afraid because he'd failed her and the whole damn world. His heart jumped furiously. But no matter what he'd done to demonstrate his feelings since his return, he'd done it wrong.

Starting with Stefan.

Shoving away from the wall, Gabriel found solace back at the cabinet. He sloshed rum into his glass.

Next to Liandra, Stefan knew Gabriel better than anyone alive. He'd been the one to hold Felicity's hand when she'd died. He'd been the one who'd buried her because Gabriel had not returned in time to see his daughter born.

Gabriel was godfather to Stefan's son. Yet, a week ago, he rode to Stefan's house ready to skewer him in front of his family.

Gabriel studied the amber liquid in his glass. He was not unreasonable.

He was in love.

"I have a *sorpresa*, Doña Sarah," Christina squealed. "Papa bought me a pony. Hurry! She only just arrived."

Trees hindered the long winding walk down the hill as Christina led Sarah to the stables. Her progress was too slow for Christina, who could barely contain her enthusiasm enough to keep hold of Sarah's hand. When they finally reached the stables, Christina was dragging Sarah behind. "She's gray with blue eyes and a white mane."

Christina took Sarah's hand and stuck it through the stall door. "She's soft. Feel." The horse whinnied and backed away.

Sarah withdrew her hand. "Is she safe?"

"Papa said that horses were like beautiful women." Christina climbed on the stall door. "They are willful, but if trained properly, they will eat out of his hand in no time."

"Your papa said that?"

"*Sí*"—she giggled—"to the man in the city who sold him the horses. I heard them talking."

"You are very bright to remember such a conversation."

"Come—" Christina jumped off and grabbed her hand again, dragging her past stalls. "This is the one Papa bought for you. She's a girl, too. A mamma horse."

Sarah's heart stopped. Oblivious to the harsh wood against her palms, she leaned into the stall door. "He bought a horse? For me?"

"*Sí*." Christina laughed. "Tell her, Papa."

Startled, Sarah stepped back into Gabriel. She had not heard him enter the stable. "I'm sorry—"

"Come, *chica*." The hard curve of his biceps pressed against her as he reached over her shoulder to open the stall door.

"But I don't know anything about horses."

He caught her against him and prevented her from backing away. "Then you can learn, *sí*?"

Gabriel walked her inside. Rather than tussle with him in front of Christina, Sarah let him win. His body framed her smaller one as he placed her hands on the mare's neck. "She is gentle."

The pungent scent of straw and horseflesh filled her senses. That and the citrusy essence of Gabriel Espinosa. He'd stepped imperceptibly closer, just enough that every single sense screamed with awareness. His heartbeat was strong against her back.

"It is not so hard to learn to ride, *chica*."

"But I didn't expect that you would purchase a horse," she whispered. Some of her panic had subsided, if only a little.

Leaning slightly, she placed an ear against the horse's body. Sarah's head rose and fell slightly with every intake of its breath.

"She's an Andalusian. The cleverest and most beautiful of all horse breeds. She comes from Spain, naturally."

"Hah." The mare continued to breathe against her ear. "Every horse here on the island comes from Spain."

"But this one moves with a dancer's grace," he said into her hair. "She also comes to me when I whistle."

Sarah's snort said she was unmoved. "Clearly, she is too easy."

"Do you like her?" His voice was offhand, but something in his unstudied tone told her it mattered.

"She's truly magnificent, Gabriel. Thank you." Sarah straightened. "Do you ride well enough, then, to teach me?"

She sensed the sudden smile in his eyes as he bent his mouth to her cheek. "I've had no complaints, yet . . . *chica*."

Her breath stuck in her throat. She wanted to elbow him in the ribs. "And do all Spaniards boast with such ease?"

"There is nothing that I cannot do, *mi esposa*."

For a breathless instant, his words hung between them, begging to be explored like some spectacular meteor shower that filled the skies. . . . Gabriel had called her his wife.

Christina's voice shattered the strained stillness. "Can I ride now, Papa? *Por favor?* Can I?"

Gabriel held Sarah longer than considered proper before dropping his hands. "No, *ratón*," he told Christina, finally turning away. Drawing in her breath, Sarah reached out for the stall door.

"The horses have come a long way today. Get to know your pony first. Perhaps in a few days."

"But I wish to ride, Papa."

"Not today."

A foot stomped. "I want to ride *now*!" Christina started to cry. "*Por favor.* You said that she was mine. I want to ride her."

Sarah felt Gabriel vacillating, acquiescing ever so slowly in the wake of his daughter's cries. Sarah straightened in disbelief. Beneath all that masculine swaggering, the great Condor was naught but mashed yams in the girl's small hands. He had no sense when it came to dealing with spoiled girls, and Sarah suddenly felt warm all over with the want to plant her lips against Gabriel's beautifully shaped mouth. Sometimes being one's best meant not trying so hard.

Sarah stepped between Gabriel and Christina. "Your papa said no. Would you wish to hurt your pony because you are impatient?"

"I want to ride." Christina pouted.

"Come." Without arguing, Sarah took the girl's small hand and left the stall. She found her walking stick. "You were going to teach me how to fish when you returned from Santo Domingo. Are you not a young lady of your word?"

"I don't *want* to fish."

"Then perhaps you would rather take a nap, *sí*?"

"I don't wish to take a nap either."

"You had best not let Dog see you acting this way, Christina."

Sarah knew that Gabriel's daughter prized that cat's affection, and at once, Christina stopped whining. "He has missed you," Sarah said, "but will not wish to sleep in your room tonight if he sees that you are misbehaving."

"*Sí*, Doña Sarah. Tomorrow can I ride my pony?"

"Tomorrow you will get to know her as your papa said. In the meantime you can think of a name to give her."

Their voices faded.

Gabriel had walked outside the stables. Hands on his hips, he remained atop the hill. Berto came to stand beside him. His boots crunched the dead leaves that had fallen during the last wind storm, and together they watched Sarah and Christina disappear hand in hand into the trees.

"I owe her my apology," he told Gabriel.

Gabriel turned. Berto wore the uniform of his guard. Some of his youthful arrogance had faded. "How so?"

"When you were ill"—Berto straightened his back—"the physician was with you, and I am ashamed that I didn't know what to do. But *she* knew. The lady, your wife, fought to get to your side; then she fought like a warrior to keep you alive. She did not leave your side for three days, and only then because she'd promised Stefan that she would go to his son the moment you were out of danger."

Gabriel's dark gaze went back to the woods.

"I have not been kind to her, Don Gabriel. And for that I owe her my apology."

A slow smile touched Gabriel's mouth and spread through his body. He had not dreamed of the silver-haired angel after all.

She had been real.

"Shall I put it with the other gifts?" Cori said, unimpressed.

Smiling to herself, Sarah sprawled naked across her bed; a

murmur of shells sounded. An early storm had filled the rain barrels, providing a wonderful bath. With her chin propped on her hand, she traced a finger over the bracelet. Cori had discovered the velvet box atop Sarah's dresser upon their return from the village.

Unlike the jewels that had preceded this gift, inside the velvet box had been a simple shell bracelet that whispered like the music of the sea. "No." Sarah ran a finger over the shells. Sand and time had smoothed the sharp edges. Much like her strange relationship with Gabriel. She abruptly straightened.

"This I'll wear."

Cori scrubbed the towel over Sarah's wet hair. "Rosa said that Don Gabriel asked you to attend the governor's social tomorrow night. And that you told him no."

"I don't belong in a place like that, Cori."

"Now he isn't going. Betina is quite fit to be tied."

Cori's words stilled Sarah. "When did Rosa hear this?"

She sensed Cori's casual shrug. In frustration, Sarah grabbed the busy towel from Cori's hands.

"Last night at dinner. He didn't give a reason, milady. But he is allowing Christina to attend with her friend María." Cori snatched back the towel and finished scrubbing Sarah's hair. "So I suppose it will just be you and Don Gabriel here for the next few days."

Sarah lifted her face toward the sunlight spilling through her windows and surrendered to the spark that sent her heart racing.

"I visited Stefan's son this morning," Sarah cheerfully announced, interrupting Gabriel's late breakfast.

Holding a hot cup of *café*, Gabriel's hand froze halfway to his mouth. Sarah's presence in the dining room shocked him, especially since she'd never ventured here before. Sunlight filtering through the beveled glass at his back traced the golden threads in her gown.

"He and his mother received the food that you sent over."

"I'm glad you approve, *chica*."

"Felicity was very generous with the people here," Doña Betina offered. "Don Gabriel would do no less."

Gabriel bit back an edge of annoyance, but Sarah didn't seem put off. Clearly aware of Betina's eyes on her, she turned away, the shells on her ankle whispering with her provocative movement. "Feeding Stefan's son is good." She smiled impishly from the doorway. "I'd say that's an excellent start, *mi esposo*."

His pulse checked at the sound of those words. Leaning slightly, he watched her disappear around the corner. A smile curved his lips.

Since the day at the stables, it had become a game of cat and mouse between them as she spurned his efforts to openly court her. Gabriel had soon found himself in a quandary. He knew he held appeal to women. The looks he'd received told him in more than words that he was pleasing in face and body. But how did he impress a woman who could not see his appearance? Who neither needed nor wanted any part of his wealth? He'd never met anyone so completely oblivious to everything that he had to offer.

She hadn't accepted the jewels he'd given her. So he'd begun to leave other gifts in her room. An ivory hairbrush, jars to mix her oils in, and finally a simple ankle bracelet made of seashells.

He heard the bracelet move in tune to her walk. Turning back to his meal, he lifted his gaze, and felt his smile flatten.

"She does not cover her hair." Betina sipped from her cup. "I have tried to properly instruct her. But she does not listen to anything I have to say."

"Is it really so important? Who is to see?"

"She is younger than Felicity," Betina said after a moment.

Gabriel set down his spoon.

"What do you suppose Christina's grandparents would think of Sarah Drake's presence here? Now that Stefan is gone, who watches her when she leaves the house for her midnight walks?" She acknowledged his startled look. "I see you didn't know."

"Enough!" Gabriel tossed down the cloth napkin. "Felicity has been dead for seven years. It is time to move on, Betina."

"I don't understand you, Don Gabriel." She pushed away from the table. "You have an army of men to watch over this woman. Why?"

"This is my home. If you don't like how I run it, you're welcome to leave."

Tears welled in her eyes. "Is that what you want?"

Gabriel didn't know what the hell he wanted anymore. Seeing Sarah today only reminded him that he'd spent too long wanting her and not enough time understanding anything else.

"Don Gabriel." Betina lowered her head. "It was never my intent to upset you. We have known each other for many years."

"Go to the island social tonight," he said. "Have fun. We will talk of this later, *sí*?"

"How long has she been coming here?" Gabriel asked.

"Since she first set foot on the island." With legs outstretched, Jaime leaned against an outcropping of rock. "Stefan put the guard farther out on the point. We take the shift here."

Gabriel frowned.

"She comes to hear the sound of the waves." Jaime crossed his arms. "She stays down there for about an hour. Since yer being back here and all, I thought ye might have known."

A gust of wind traveling through the treetops whipped at Gabriel's sleeves and hair. He stood at the top of the cliff, looking down on the moonlit beach.

Sarah walked its length, her long white hair unbound to her hips. She wore only a shift that reached just below her knees. The moonlight surrounded her like a beacon in a storm. It was no wonder his men thought her otherworldly. The stirring vision of his wife only added to the uncertainty in Gabriel's mind. He could either lock Sarah up or keep his men permanently away from this place.

Hands on his hips, Gabriel looked at Jaime. Maybe the drug Kendrick had given him had boiled part of his brain. The part that held logical reasoning and an unfailing command of emotions and that could stand up to a full broadside. But something was happening to him.

"Has she said anything? About why she comes here?" Gabriel made himself ask.

"No one knows, except maybe the bastards who hurt her."

"Go." Gabriel's eyes fastened on Sarah's pale silhouette. "This watch is mine from now on."

Taking a step nearer to the cliff edge, he didn't hear Jaime leave.

Conflict raged within him. He was a *bastardo* for what was on his mind, for wanting Sarah when he may not even be legally married to her but knowing he was about to go down to the beach tonight.

Consequences be damned.

The carnal thoughts filling his mind only liberated what was left of his conscience. But twice when Gabriel started down the pathway, he stopped each time, plagued by an unfamiliar nervousness.

Since he'd awakened in his bed, he'd done naught but think of her naked beneath him and wonder what it would be like to feel those soft hands of hers soothe more than his fevered soul: musings that led into deeper waters where a man could drown and never regret that he'd let himself stop swimming. He'd rather look down the cannon of another ship than face the uncertainty of her rejection.

Gabriel's boots made little sound on the soft earth as he picked his way down the narrow path to the beach. At the bottom of the trail, waves rushed over the sand, then left in gentle retreat. Silver bubbles glistened. Gabriel turned in a slow circle and swept his gaze over the beach, finding Sarah nowhere. Unease crept up his spine.

Setting off at a jog, he started down the beach. She could not have gotten past him. A glimpse of white sent him nearer to the woods. But he discovered only an outcrop of rocks and bleached wood washed up on shore from some aged shipwreck.

"Gabriel," Sarah called, stopping him midstride.

He turned abruptly. The tilt of her luminous face challenged him as she took a step out of the concealment of the trees. Before he could respond, his glance over her shoulder stopped him.

A yellow blanket was spread against the sand. A bottle of his finest Madeira weighted a corner against the scented breeze.

"Sarah . . . ?"

As if following the sound of his stunned voice, her hands slid over his chest. "I thought you would never get here."

The jolt of her warm lips as they pressed against his went through him like fire. Madeira filled his senses, tantalizingly sweet, hotter than life itself.

His arms, hanging rigidly at his side, went around her, as if he were suddenly awakening from a long sleep. He heard her small sigh, the sound dying against her mouth as she leaned into him, holding him tightly. He'd been numb inside for so long that the startling rush of his emotions nearly felled him. His hands slipped beneath the silken cloud of her hair and down the slender curve of her back. A faint mewl wafted over him, and he thrust his tongue into her mouth, yielding forevermore to the madness that possessed him.

A low, hungry growl rose from his throat, and he dragged his mouth from hers. His hands curved around her waist. "*Dios,* Sarah."

"This will be our secret. Promise me." Her voice trembled.

Bound by his honor to protect her, he closed his eyes and barely allowed himself to breathe. His very existence since he'd met her had been a stead of torture, and his torment was no less now.

"Jaime knew about this tonight?"

"With everyone gone, I'd hoped that you would finally come out here tonight."

"Why?" he asked against her lips. "Why are you doing this now?"

She slid her mouth to the unsteady pulse on his neck, over the scar that lay imbedded there and the memory of a past he begged to forget. "Because you called me your wife," she whispered, seeking the heated rasp of his words. "Because no matter what, I'll love no man but you. I wish to know you as a wife knows her husband. To treasure what we have now. I don't want anything to ruin our time together."

His urge to protect her had never surged so hard as it did now. Gabriel pulled her chin up. He looked into her luminous silver eyes and felt a moment's regret that he might never know the touch of her silver gaze. But if seeing meant remembering her childhood, he would shield her forever.

Mistaking his silence, she stretched against him. "People

will talk, Gabriel. They will think you are bewitched." She stood on her toes, their whispers melding. "Let this moment be just ours, please."

Gabriel lowered his head and brushed his lips across hers. His tongue moved into her mouth. She met his thrusts, and they shared a long, hungry kiss. "*Sí.*" His hands spread over her ribs, then fanned into the tangle of her hair, and for the first time in his life, he threw responsibility to the wind and took what he knew he should not. "This moment will be only ours."

He tasted her, drowning inside her as he sank with her to his knees. Sarah made love with her mouth as she lived— without convention—and Gabriel, who had lived by the strictest rules, liberated himself in her carnal innocence. His palms moved over her bottom and lower still as he gathered the cloth of her shift. He pulled the fabric over her head, and it trembled to the sand.

"Tell me you want me, Gabriel." Sarah wanted to hear the words.

His muscles coiled as he bent and dragged the shirt over his head, sending it the way of her shift. "*Sí, mi amor,* you have to ask?" He lowered her to the blanket. "You are beautiful, *chica.*"

Sarah's palms roamed the rippling strength of his arms as he held himself above her. His lips slid down the slim curve of her neck. He closed his mouth over one breast and then the other. A cry broke from her lips. She clung fast to his sureness, consumed by his possession of her. He slid his palm down her stomach, to the juncture between her thighs, parting her to his touch.

Her breath gasped against his lips. "Don't . . . stop."

And he didn't.

The blood pounded through her veins, racing faster and faster, as his fingers did wonderful and powerful things to her body. His mouth suckled her breasts. Holding on to the pleasure, she wrapped a leg around his waist, dragging a low growl from deep in his chest just before he pulled away. Her voice caught on his name.

Dazed, Sarah sat up, only to find his hand firmly planted on her shoulder, easing her back into the blanket.

"I am not leaving you, Sarah."

Then he was easing her thighs apart, and never more vulnerable, her heart fluttered as she felt his slow gaze burn over her body, all of her that was exposed to him. Leaning over her, he pressed a hand between her legs, opening her with his fingers. The first hot probe of him seared her.

"Jesu . . . Sarah."

Hands braced on either side of her, Gabriel eased past her resistance, filling her until he was part of her being.

Sarah clung to him, wanting him, even if it hurt.

Forging her name in the damp strands of her hair, his ragged breath touched her mouth then fell over her ear; then he was rocking against her, moving slowly at first as if savoring every inch, until her body finally accepted all of him. Until all that remained of her innocence was the pounding surf and the answering drumbeat of his heart against hers. His breath mingling with hers, she dug her fingers into the rippling flesh of his back and met his thrusts with a burning all her own. She threw her head back, crying out as the first hot wave hit. His hands clenched in her hair. Always so controlled, he wasn't now as he pushed deep inside her.

When he lay heavily on her, Sarah let her sated arms fall to the blanket. "Am I truly your wife, Gabriel?"

"*Sí.*" His husky voice touched her ear. "You are mine."

Chapter Fourteen

Gabriel reached the top of the path before Sarah stirred in his arms. The first blush of dawn had spread over the flawless sky by the time he walked beneath the canopy of trees that edged his yard. Wrapped in the blanket, Sarah snuggled deeper in his arms. Her head lay against his shoulder. He looked down at her, so fragile in the pale daylight.

She had been a virgin.

The knowledge still shook him. Gabriel hadn't known if she'd been spared that part of Kendrick's brutality until last night, and then it had registered too late. But the fact that Kendrick had refrained from one indecent act didn't change the truth that the man was still a murderer. Gabriel would still ferret out the bastard.

But right now, an inexplicable lightness filled him.

Sarah's arm rose to encircle his neck, and looking down into her smile, he bent and kissed her temple, tasting the soft dew of her skin. "Tell me about the scar on your neck," she said quietly.

"No." The emotion in his voice surprised him. A small stream appeared before him and his boots slapped through the water. He remedied his tone. "It's not important." It was not something he cared to talk about. Not when the night still clung to his thoughts.

"Do you swim?" She sat straighter. "Take me into the water."

Her hair lay like a silken web over his arm. He adjusted her weight, bouncing her lightly. "Now you sound like Christina."

"Tonight then? After the world goes to sleep," she whispered.

"How do you feel?"

"Hmm." Her legs dangled prettily over his arms. "How am I supposed to feel besides sated?"

"I didn't know if you might be . . . tender."

She laughed and nuzzled his neck. "Truly, I can hardly walk. I never felt better."

He set her down on the verandah in front of her door and kissed her long and slow, a languorous remnant of the night they'd shared. "Good night," he said against her mouth. "Or good morning."

Still wrapped in her blanket, she continued to remain where he'd left her standing, as if she were listening to his jaunty steps fade on the stone. His clothes were in disrepair. His jerkin hung open. His rumpled cambric shirt lay unbuttoned to his waist. Scraping a hand across a day's growth of beard, he turned again to look behind him. She was no longer standing beside the lilac trellis, and her doors were closed.

"This is my most best one," Christina said. "She has yellow hair. Mostly yellow." She giggled. "But it is turning purple."

Sarah stood on a chair beside Christina. Little fingers guided hers over a collection of numerous leather and wooden dolls. Most had never been touched, outside a brief caress, as they were placed on a high shelf. "Papa brings them home for me."

"Then why don't you play with them?"

Her shoulder shrugged. "I don't want to make them ugly."

"They will get ugly just gathering dust. You shouldn't waste so much time staring at them when you can enjoy their company more."

Sarah gathered them all up in her arms. Carefully edging off the chair, she tossed them upon the bed.

"But Papa will be angry."

"What do papas know about little girls and dolls anyway?"

"Not a lot, obviously," a voice said from the doorway, and

sent Sarah's pulse racing. Gabriel's casual presence filled the room.

Sarah turned to the door, and despite her want to act composed, she felt her whole body blush beneath his regard. "If papas played more with their daughters, they would understand," she said.

"When do I have time to play, *sí?*" His voice told her that he wasn't very happy that she'd just destroyed Christina's doll display. But neither was he all that angry. His eyes warmed her.

And Sarah breathed in his wonderful essence. Her skin felt tight and heated. She'd been with him so little since that night on the beach. If it looked like she was staring, she couldn't help herself.

"We can play *now*, Papa!" Christina jumped on her bed, laughing, and that was enough to break the spell. "Can we? *Por favor?*"

Sarah could hear all that Latin masculinity squirming beneath his daughter's excitement. With her stick in hand used to negotiate the toy-strewn passageway, she walked to the door. She and Christina had effectively turned the room inside out in their quest to reexamine the proper face of childhood.

"I think playing dolls is a wonderful idea," Sarah said. "I'll leave the two of you alone."

An arm blocked her exit. He smelled of wind-baked leather, as if he'd been riding and only just arrived at the house.

"Your daughter wants to be with you," she whispered.

His other hand tenderly cupped her cheek. He still wore his riding gloves. "What about you, Sarah?"

"You've hardly been around in days to see her."

He pulled her outside in the hallway; then he was plowing his hands through her hair, and his lips covered hers.

"Gabriel . . ." she finally breathed, "you promised to keep our life private. This house is filled with servants."

"They are *my* servants. If they wish to stay here they will remain discreet."

"And guests," she added before his mouth could touch hers again. "Why just this morning—"

"They can wait."

Sarah fidgeted with the small pearl buttons on his vest. The leather was warm beneath her touch, the full sleeves of his shirt soft. "I don't even begin to know what to say to these people."

His face pulled away. She could feel him staring at her.

"Doña Betina sat for an hour chatting with your neighbor and his little daughter, María, while they waited for you. Your life is very busy, Gabriel."

"Not on purpose, *chica*. If they frighten you, stay away."

"I didn't say they frightened me, exactly." She frowned. She only knew that somehow, in their small paradise away from the horrors surrounding them, they had found something that was theirs alone. He belonged to her.

She toyed with the soft edge of his hair just above the nape of his neck. "I suppose your notoriety goes with who you are."

He released her and leaned a shoulder against the wall. "And who am I, *chica*?" he quietly asked.

"I . . ." She brushed the toe of her slipper over his boot. "I don't really know, Gabriel."

"Papa!" Christina was bouncing on the bed, bed ropes protesting the abuse. "Hurry!"

For a moment, they stood in silence. She tapped him on the cleft of his chin. "Methinks the warrior needs to know that he has a family, or I will be forced to turn him into a frog."

He surprised her when he grabbed her elbow as she turned away. "Don't talk like that, Sarah. People believe it."

Sarah's heart gave a start. "Do you?"

He touched her cheek. "No, *chica*. I don't, but—"

"Good." She stood on her toes, melding her whisper to his. "Because you're the only one who matters."

"Sarah." He stopped her again with his hand. Then his thumb brushed over her mouth as if whatever he was about to say was no longer of import. "There will be a small gathering here tomorrow. Make an appearance. Come to the stables at least. *Por favor*."

He'd said please so nicely, she felt her heart melt. But these weren't servants he spoke about. These people were his peers.

"You don't need to be afraid, Sarah. Let them see us to-gether."

Her chin lifted to denounce the apprehension he'd read so easily in her face. Sarah reached behind her for the wall, afraid to commit to a single yea or nay. But he deserved more than her panic.

"I'll be there," she said quietly, then fled.

"Papa, *mira*. Look at me!"

Christina pranced her pony across the yard, her dark curls bouncing brightly. Riding sidesaddle, every inch a young lady, she wore an emerald green riding habit and little black boots to protect her feet from the stirrup bars.

Gabriel was inside the riding ring with Christina when his glance found Berto leading Sarah up the path from the house. His gaze froze midturn. Everything inside him twisted, and didn't loosen until he breathed. It had been like this with him since the night at the beach—no less now, as pride found its way into an unfamiliar grin.

She wore a black lace headrail over her beautiful hair. He saw her rub her hands self-consciously down her simple red skirts. She'd probably not realized the riding yard would be so crowded. People lined the fence. Sarah said something to Berto, which brought their faces together, and Gabriel's smile vanished.

His hand clenched the riding quirt. A man yelled out some-thing about the pony. Gabriel turned and answered. His pulse picked up when in the side of his vision he saw Sarah wriggle into the crowd next to the fence instead of leaving with Berto. He knew that strangers made her uncomfortable. And these people were friendly to him, Spanish to their very core, their memories loyal to Felicity.

It annoyed him that they could not move past the memory of his first wife. Or that he could go nowhere without being recognized or whispered about, which precluded him taking Sarah outside these grounds. He supposed a man accredited with two national celebrations in honor of his naval victories should show some appreciation, but things that had never bothered him before rankled him now.

He was not a man prone to restraint. Still, he knew Sarah's

prudence bore wisdom. He would introduce her into society slowly: diplomacy meant proper strategy.

So for the next hour Gabriel socialized with his fellow compatriots, most of whom owned the neighboring plantations and had come to see the Andalusian mare that had cost El Condor a king's stipend to attain. Many Betina had invited in reparation for the score of social invitations that he'd turned down this past month.

Then he was talking to Christina, calling out encouragement to his daughter, his pride obvious as Christina continued to remain in the saddle her first week out. "I am good, *sí*, Papa?" she laughed when Gabriel finally brought the pony to a halt.

"You are good." He leaned into the saddle. "But not so good that you cannot fall off if you get careless, *ratón*. This is only your fifth time out. And now you must let your pony rest."

"Will I be able to jump logs soon?"

"Not until you get a bigger horse."

"When will I get a bigger horse, Papa?"

He laughed and scooped her off the saddle. "When you grow, *ratón*. Don't tell me you are already tired of your pony."

"But María has a bigger horse. Her papa brags that he is rich."

Gabriel's gaze found little María perched against the fence next to her father, a big man wearing a black full-bottomed wig beneath a hat trimmed with colorful ribbons. A gold brocade jerkin caught the sunlight with enough flash to spook Christina's pony. He was as overdressed in this heat as he was a fool for giving his daughter a horse that would probably see her killed. Doña Betina leaned next to him, chatting more than amiably.

Gabriel tapped the quirt lightly against his thigh. After handing Christina off to Rosa, Gabriel ordered the Andalusian saddled.

He found Sarah easily, and felt his eyes harden. She stood alone against the fence, abandoned by his countrymen as if she were a leper. At once, everything inside came crashing down.

To hell with them all!

"Come, *chica*." Boldly approaching his wife, he startled her when he lifted her over the fence. "It is your turn to ride, *sí*?"

Sarah's gasp ended on a choking sound. "Surely you jest."

"Spaniards never jest." He leaned his mouth to her hair and inhaled her deeply. "We are a passionate lot. Remember?"

"Gabriel." He watched her blush. "I've never been on a horse. Shouldn't I wait a little longer?"

His groomsman brought the mare into the yard. Stepping a tall boot into the stirrup, Gabriel mounted. Despite Sarah's trepidation, he could tell that she was excited by the prospect of riding a horse.

"Don't worry, *chica*." He plucked her off the ground and set her across his lap. "I don't intend to share this lesson with anyone."

His arm tightened around her waist as his other hand gripped the reins. The horse pranced in a circle. A nudge from his knees sent the mare over the fence, and in a heartbeat, the wind hit his face as they were flying over the wooded path toward the house. Sarah was laughing. In moments, he reached the house. Pulling on the reins, Gabriel turned the horse in an indecisive circle, before he urged her to climb the steps of the verandah. *Click, click* on stone. Servants rushed outside as he trotted the horse past windows on his way to the back. Then he was galloping the mare beyond the gardens and down the backside of the cliff to the beach.

When he'd slowed the mare to a walk, Sarah was laughing and clinging to him. "You are disgraceful, Gabriel."

Turning away, she stretched her hands through the mare's black mane. "The mare is so soft. I love her. I really do."

The surf rolled languidly over the shore.

Gabriel tightened his arm around her. "I wanted to say hello in private." His hand flaring over her stomach, he brushed a thumb over her breast. "You came to the stables."

"I am trying, Gabriel." She snuggled against him but only briefly before her back straightened and she tilted her chin away.

"Don't turn away from me, Sarah."

She removed his hand and forced a laugh. "I'm not a horse to be eating out of your hands, Mister El Condor."

"That's very fortunate for me, *chica*." He bent his head forward to kiss her. "Since I would prefer to ride *you* instead."

"Oh!" She squirmed, pushing him away again. "You are impossible, Gabriel. And you confuse me to no end."

Gabriel sat back, his mouth flattened into a line. "Why?"

"What happened to keeping our private life away from the public eye? You are impossible to think that you are any safer from censure than I. You make me afraid . . . therefore I'm confused."

He turned his head away and stared out over the whitecaps on the sea. "Perhaps it's you who listens to too much gossip."

Halfway down the beach, he finally slid from the horse and sank to his ankles in the spongy sand.

"What are you doing?"

"The mare can't take my weight and yours, Sarah."

"You won't let go of the reins?"

"No, Sarah. Relax." He readjusted the stirrups to her feet and tucked her skirts beneath her legs.

"I want to thank you for what you did for Stefan's family," she offered into the abrupt silence. "Cori said that you moved them to your apartments in Santo Domingo until your ship is ready to sail."

"Despite what you might have thought, I am not an ogre, Sarah."

"I didn't say that you were." Her voice smiled. "I said that you were being unreasonable. There *is* a difference."

"*¿Sí?* How so?" With a hand on his hip, he straightened. The wind caught in Sarah's hair.

"An ogre is an ass who steps all over those who are weaker than he is. Unreasonable is a form of confusion derived from misinterpreting the facts. You had no cause to be jealous of Stefan."

Gabriel rolled his eyes at her lack of logic.

Then he was watching her coo and pet the mare as if he'd given her a treasure of gold instead of a simple horse. As if no other care in the world existed. He cupped her soft cheek in his hand, a contrast of light and dark that mirrored her presence in his life.

"I am jealous of any man who spends time with you."

"Then you are jealous of yourself," she whispered against his palm. "Don't be angry with me, please."

"*Dios,* I don't even know who I am when I'm with you."

She laid her palm over his heart. "You're the man I love."

Quietly exploring her beautiful face with his eyes, he wanted to reach inside her and find that elusive flame he glimpsed every so often in her eyes. He wanted to make love to her again on the beach. More than anything he wanted to understand himself when he was around her.

Gabriel plowed his fingers through his hair.

Somewhere between his meeting with Kendrick and now, he'd stopped thinking rationally.

Jesu, he'd stopped thinking. Period.

Suddenly, she bounced in the stirrups and laughed. "Do I get to ride, Gabriel? Or are we going to sit here all day?"

A glance over her shoulder pulled his attention. High on the bank above him, people had already begun to gather to watch his frolic on the beach. Taking the reins, he began to walk, and wondered when life had stopped being fun.

The stall door slammed, upsetting the Andalusian mare. The currycomb in Gabriel's hand stopped. He'd long since sent the stable hands to bed. Rising off the three-legged stool, he looked over the mare's back and met Betina's furious glare.

"How dare you humiliate me in front of everyone!"

His eyes narrowed. She reeked of rum. "Unless you want to get hurt, let yourself out of this stall. It's dangerous in here."

"But not for you, of course." A hand plopped on her hip. Her cerulean skirts flared with the movement. "Where else can I go to find the imperious El Condor alone, not pawing that English slut?"

Setting aside the comb, Gabriel walked around the mare to escort Betina out. "Go back to the house. You're drunk."

She yanked from his grip and staggered backward out of the stall. "Christina cried because she could not attend María's birthday celebration this evening."

Gabriel latched the gate. "If you want to visit that pompous ass father of hers, you can walk. You're not taking my carriage or my daughter anywhere as a cover for your tryst."

Slap.

"You are a *bastardo*, Don Gabriel!" Betina's shriek carried through the rafters. "You've made a fool of me in front of your neighbors. All day they are laughing behind my back! And yours!"

"Betina . . ." Raising the back of his gloved hand to his lip, Gabriel brought his eyes back around to her. "I have erred in not being more forthright in my intentions. But if you make me strike you, so help me, it will be a moment we both regret."

Her eyes widened before she dropped her chin away. "You have injured me too much, Don Gabriel."

"It's no one's business how I choose to spend time with my wife. Not even yours.

"Wife! Is that what you call her now? What do you suppose Christina's grandfather will think of your afflicted English *wife*?"

"Sí," he countered her smug voice. "I know that she goes to the cove at night. I know that she stands in the rain and likes to sing for no reason at all—"

"And digs holes in the herbal. She builds mounds of nothing!"

"So she likes dirt. What the devil does it matter?"

Betina twisted her hands. "Some say that she has bewitched you. That she saved your life and that of Señor Delgato's son by laying her hands on you, and that she can call up thunder when she is angry. She is . . . not normal, Don Gabriel. People have been talking. They say that she is a danger to Christina. Felicity would never have—"

"Enough!" He shoved away from the stall door, his long strides carrying him over straw to the main door. "This is my home. Christina is my daughter. And her grandparents will have to accept how I choose to live my life, as will everyone else in this damn world!"

"Do you intend to keep your indisposed bride hidden away here forever while you attend to your life in Spain?" She followed on his heels. "Encased in glass like one of Christina's dolls? Another trophy of conquest for Spain's conquering hero?"

Gabriel raised his fists to the rafters. *"¡Ay yi!* So help me, Doña Betina—" He spun on his heel.

She nearly collided with him. Black hair had fallen from her coif.

"These last few months, you have purchased enough clothes and jewels to attire every woman in Madrid." He stalked her, forcing her backward. "I have paid your dead husband's debts in Havana and Seville, and will settle another sum on you tonight just to get you out of my life. Consider us even for the care you have given my daughter."

Huge tears wet her eyes. "Don Gabriel—"

"Until I get you back to Havana or to Spain, you are welcome to move into my apartments in Santo Domingo, or wherever you wish to go. I don't care what you do." His voice was low and dangerous. "Except you *will* leave this house tonight."

Betina's hands flew to her face. "No matter who you think you are or what power you might wield, she does not understand our world. She will *never* be able to handle her duties as your wife!" With a loud sob, Betina fled the stable, a faint essence of gardenia chasing behind her.

Gabriel glared at the rafters. Her words lying like an iron mantle over his chest, he closed his eyes.

"Has Don Gabriel returned yet?"

Sarah stood at the edge of the wooded path as Berto appeared and greeted her. She could smell rain in the late evening air.

"No, Doña Sarah."

"I found these in the garden." She dangled the carrots in her hand, aware that her skirts bore stains from her digging. "I thought perhaps I could await his return at the stables. Do you know where he went at this late hour?"

Berto walked her down the wooded path. "He went to the village to see Father Antonio. I expect he'll return late."

"I see." A knot tightened her stomach. The pain was so unexpected, Sarah brought her palm to her heart. "I imagine Don Gabriel didn't go to Father Antonio to attend confession." Sarah forced a laugh. She lowered her head, embarrassed because Berto had surely read her sudden fear.

"I don't know why he went," he said quietly.

In the back of her mind, she'd never forgotten that Gabriel had once promised to annul their marriage.

Her heart didn't believe he would. But her heart could not convince her brain.

Berto seemed unaware of her turmoil, for he chatted contentedly about Christina's riding lessons, leaving out Gabriel's unorthodox behavior that afternoon when he'd galloped off with her across his yard to the beach. Or the fight Gabriel had had with Betina.

Everyone was talking about the argument. When the woman had left a few hours before, Cori had practically danced, as if Betina had died and gone to hell. Thank Providence Christina had been asleep.

Sarah only felt sick to her stomach.

Somehow, despite everything, she'd hurt Gabriel. Thanks to his protective efforts, he'd made her feel safe and alive and wanton in ways she'd never envisioned from her once-sheltered world. She'd wanted to cling to her heart, selfishly guard what they had. Yet she could not seem to do or say anything right of late. Her efforts had only come between them and not protected him at all.

Berto led her into the stables. "I will be outside when you are ready," he said.

Sarah stood in front of the mare's stall. For a long time, she didn't move as her senses absorbed the pungent smells of the stable. Oiled harnesses lined the outer stall. She ran her fingers over the smooth leather. Like everything else in Gabriel's ordered life, only the finest of all things found their way within these walls.

The mare butted against her arm. Sarah laughed as the horse ate out of her hand. Heavy jaws crunched and consumed the offered carrots. "Aren't you the hungry one?" The words echoed in her thoughts, strangely familiar. Except they weren't hers.

Tracing the wood of the stall, she found the latch.

Gabriel would not like her entering the stall alone. In fact, he would be infuriated. A tame horse could still be dangerous in close quarters. But drawn by something inside her, Sarah stepped into the stall, and stretching out her hands, she

touched the mare with her palms. The horse settled at the
sound of her voice. The mare's sleek coat trembled beneath
her palms.

Close your eyes, Sarah.

And she did.

Outside, thunder grumbled across the sky.

She'd dreamed last night of riding a white horse; then
she'd dreamed she was running in sunlight. Warmth filled her
senses. Familiarity underscored her actions, and she laid her
head gently over the mare's shoulder. The heartbeat in her ear
grew stronger and stronger, melding into Gabriel's voice.

Sarah snapped straight. Gabriel's muffled voice came from
the riding yard outside. Her hand flew to her chest. He spoke
again, his Spanish too fast for her to catch. The big door
squeaked opened, and the groomsman entered, leading
Gabriel's big stallion.

"Berto said she was in here," Sarah heard Gabriel say.

Squeezing her eyes shut, she pressed against the back wall
and didn't catch the mumbled reply. He would never allow
her here again if he caught her alone in this stall.

A few minutes later she heard the groom working in the
stall next to hers. Barely breathing, she waited for him to
leave. Her legs were numb from standing by the time the stable finally grew quiet. Sarah listened to the stallion slurp
water from the trough, and quietly she slipped out of the
mare's stall.

Berto wasn't outside. She paced, waiting for someone to
approach, when thunder shattered the sky. Rain trickled, then
turned into a downpour. Sarah stumbled along the muddy
pathway back toward the house. She fell flat and lost her stick
down the hill. She tried to find it in the mud. But the rain
made it impossible to separate the path from the hillside.

She'd never been this disoriented before. Her heart hammered.

Once, she thought she heard her name. But she was shiv-
ering too hard to hear anything but the lightning.

Drawing her knees to her chest, she hunkered to the
ground while the wind and rain beat her back. Then as the
thunder moved farther away, she heard voices crawling over
the woods. In moments, someone called out that he had found

her. Sarah groaned. All she could think about was that Gabriel would surly kill her ten times over.

Berto reached her first, his voice breathless as if he'd been running. "You have had us all worried." He took her elbow. Her knees were weak when she tried to stand. Her sodden skirts clung to her thighs. "Don Gabriel is frantic. Forgive me, Doña Sarah. But I thought that you had returned to the house with him."

"*Por favor*, please, Berto—"

He was so frenzied; Sarah wanted to shake sense into him.

"The Andalusian escaped her stall. Don Gabriel thought maybe someone had been here and . . . He's out looking for you now."

Sarah knew an instant of panic. *Oh, Lord.* She'd not properly latched the stall! A knife couldn't have sliced her deeper.

She'd carelessly neglected precaution, and because of her, the frightened mare had escaped. In the dark, Gabriel's prize horse could break her leg or go over a cliff.

"Señorita Sheldon is waiting for you at your room. Come."

"No." She jerked away. "Take me back to the stable."

Berto had to carry her fighting him all the way to the house. Cori forced her to change into dry clothes. Servants brought a tray of warm broth and linens to dry her hair. An hour later, Sarah was standing outside on the verandah when she heard the furious pounding of horse's hooves. She knew the instant Gabriel appeared. A skein of alarm passed over her as she felt the men around her fall away.

"Take him back to the stable." She heard Gabriel slide off his horse. "Rub him down."

Her heart ticked away in the silence before he finally spoke again. "*Vayanse!* All of you."

His furious heat fell over her. She needed him to hold her. She needed him to tell her that he loved her.

"Did you find the mare?" She touched his cheek.

"No." He pulled away. "We will look again at first light."

"You're bleeding."

"*Sí*, it is dark, Sarah. Some of us aren't as adept as others at night. Trees have nasty branches."

"Gabriel. Truly—"

"*¡Ay caramba!*" His rage made her flinch. "Are you *loco*,

Sarah? You get lost in a storm, when you should not even be out! You let the Andalusian escape. *¡Por Dios!* I should put a guard on your door. Lock you away. Is that what you want from now on? I can't even trust you to take care of your own life."

Desperately unsure, she pulled herself to him. His shirt was sodden beneath her palms, alive with the heat of his flesh.

"Jesu." His hands closed around her head, stretching around her skull as if he would tear the thoughts out of her head. Rip them asunder. "My beautiful fey wife, the elusive Sarah Drake, the ghost in the mist." His breath touched her ear. "What am I to do with you?"

"Stop . . ." she pleaded against his mouth. "Don't be angry, please. I cannot bear it." She tried to kiss him.

"Why?" He held himself stiffly away from her. "Because I'm not allowed to get angry? Because you've attached some virtuous aura around me that gives off the delusion that I am somehow different from other men? Or from the man I've always been?"

"Oh, yes. I forgot." She wrapped her hands in the folds of her skirt. "You are very feared by much of the world. Your accolades reach far and wide, even behind the walls of Saint Mary's. My brother Talon certainly holds a high opinion of your character. Marcus is more forgiving, but being married to your sister has probably helped dampen his aggression."

"Do I detect a hint of sarcasm, *mi esposa?*" He moved his hands to her waist, pulling her against his body; and even through the layers of their clothes, she felt him hard against her. "You give yourself to me on the beach, then take it all away as if I must win some play-nice contest to have you again. I don't know who you are, Sarah. You scare the hell out of me. And I don't like it."

Her hands curled into fists. "Then what do you want? An annulment? Is that why you visited Father Antonio tonight?"

She felt the sudden fury in his eyes. "Do you believe that?"

"I don't know what to believe," she whispered. "I should never . . . we should never have . . . I made a terrible mistake."

Reaching behind her to trap her between his arms, he pushed her against the cool stone surface of the wall, bracing her with his knee. "It's a little late for regrets, hmm, Sarah? Especially when you enjoyed it so much."

Sarah turned her head away. Her hair fell over her face. "I want to go home. Back to my brothers where I belong."

A finger on her chin forced her around. "This *is* your home, and you'd better get used to it because you're stuck here forever."

His voice was so controlled, when hers had risen in hysteria; she suddenly hated his restraint, his indifference in the face of her need. He was a rock: a soulless object without depth. What did El Condor know of defeat? Or of sitting stranded in a storm, terrified? All he cared about was the horse. She kicked him.

Then she was fighting in earnest, pounding her fists against Gabriel's chest. There was no strength behind her blows, only a sad echo of pent-up failure. Arms like iron bands wrapped her to him. Her fists clenched the soft fabric of his sodden shirt. All she'd done was hurt him. "I want to go home. I hate this stone house. I hate this island. I hate everything here."

"Everything, *chica*?" His heart was a harsh drumbeat against her forehead. "Including me?"

Her hands splayed his chest to push him away. But she couldn't.

"That's right. Touch me, and tell me that you hate me. That you want to go away." He brushed his lips over hers. "Or do you wish me to play with more dolls, or dance in the rain? Sing sonnets to the moon? Have I not done enough for you yet?"

He took possession of her mouth and kissed her hard. His chin scratched her face. He made her tight and wet in secret places. Made her groan. She no longer resisted his hold. No longer cared so long as he went on kissing her like this forever.

Her hands slid over the ridges of his stomach to his hips. He wore his cutlass. He'd been that afraid for her tonight, and her heart squeezed against the pain she'd caused him.

Gabriel lifted her into his arms. He didn't speak to her. His violence was a palpable thing, filling with darkness. The air smelled sweet, and Sarah knew they'd passed the lilac-draped trellises outside her room. Gabriel had not ever been in her room. Shoving with his shoulder, he sent the glass doors crashing against the walls.

Then he tossed her on her bed.

Breathing hard, she sat up, her hair a tousled mess in her face as she gasped to reclaim her senses.

"When you make up your mind about us, let me know, *chica*."

With one last expression of fury, Gabriel slammed the doors upon his exit . . . and the glass shattered.

Sarah's jaw dropped open.

Silence joined the strains of shock, as she listened to the last piece of glass topple to the floor with a final *ting*.

"*¡Ay yi yi!*" Glass crunched beneath a boot. "*Shit!*"

Chapter Fifteen

Acquiring a skilled glassmaker had proven difficult even with Gabriel's resources. It took three men and a carpenter as many days to repair Sarah's door as it had for God to create the world. Considering the investment in time and money, he should have sealed the wall with gilded bars.

Finding the Andalusian took two days longer. Gabriel's overseer discovered her happily romping in a neighbor's pasture a league away, and after having the mare examined, Gabriel was told that she'd likely be breeding now.

"Don't know who the proud papa is, Don Gabriel," his groomsman said. "But she doesn't seem the worse for her adventure, *sí*? We can only hope it wasn't a donkey that did the deed."

Thoroughly disgusted, Gabriel left the stable.

When he finished his morning business with Berto of working on the ship's manifest, he found Sarah in the herbal. He'd intended all day to tell her that the mare was safe. She'd been worried that the horse had come to harm. Folding his arms, he leaned against the back wall and closed his eyes. He was still angry over the debacle. He didn't know why he was so furious, perhaps because Sarah had been so oblivious to danger. Or because he found himself doing things he'd never intended, like carrying her on his horse across the manicured grounds of his house as if he were in the throes of newfound adolescence. Or shouting at Betina.

"You!" Sarah's warm laughter opened his eyes.

Discovering her cat rolled up in one of her newly potted vats, she hugged the pudgy fur ball. "Go catch spiders." She shooed him away, then bent to repair the damage.

She'd wrapped a red cloth over her head to keep her hair out of the dirt. He watched her hands follow the bench along the wall to the barrel, where she scooped water into a bucket. She'd been content to stay away from him. And that annoyed him more than anything.

In a world apart from his, she was perfectly at peace with her solitude, unpredictable in her behavior, and so damn vulnerable that she scared the hell out of him. Sarah struggled with dragons that he couldn't slay. He didn't want to hide her behind walls. He wanted to understand her.

His eyes went over the herbal, taking note that the walls had been throughly cleaned. He'd visited here only once since his sister had built the place. Mostly it was a dank cellar with green moss dangling from the ceiling. Across the narrow room, stairs led up to a heavy dome-shaped glass structure: the only source of light for the cellar.

He'd learned from Cori yesterday that a special routine went with gardening. Building mounds kept the small seedlings from drowning during irrigation. Those mounds of *nothing* that Betina had described sprouted green fuzz in every bin.

Sarah had brought the whole place to life.

And at once, a surge of emotion weighted his heart.

No one visited her with their ailments anymore; but then no one had called upon her since rumors had put her in his bed.

He wasn't surprised. No matter how hard she'd tried to fit in here, most people didn't talk to her. She didn't wear fancy clothes or pretend to be a Spanish doña. She'd accepted that she was different, that people snickered behind her back, but Gabriel knew that she hurt for him.

For all her beautiful simplicity, Sarah had been under no delusions when it came to society's strictures and the weight public censure carried, especially for him. He was a son of Spain, expected to conduct himself according to the mores of a society that she surprisingly understood only too well. Elevated to a national symbol by the very virtues bestowed on him, he was as imprisoned by his persona as she was by her blindness.

She didn't belong here. Not to this stone house.

Not to his aristocratic world.

Not to him.

He only knew that this past month his voice had held laughter and that somehow he'd found paradise: the kind that came with peace and living again for the sheer pleasure of the day.

Gabriel rubbed the ache in his temples. How could everything be so right between them? When they weren't even on the same side?

Pushing off the wall, he ducked out of the herbal. A flash of gray swept past his legs. Tail swaying in the air, Sarah's cat followed him back to the house.

Gabriel opened the library door and stopped. Stefan stood in front of the window. Berto and two of his men were beside him talking. With a nod, Stefan sent the other men out. Gabriel watched them go, his gaze coming back around to confront Stefan.

"Why are you here?" Gabriel shut the door behind them.

"Doña Betina came to the ship a few days ago," Stefan said.

Crossing his arms, Gabriel leaned against the door.

"She was distraught. I let her stay in your cabin until I could find her another place. Your apartments were already taken."

"*Dios* . . ." Gabriel's jaw clenched.

"Naturally, you weren't thinking when you sent her there." Stefan moved beside the desk. "She's intent on proving your marriage invalid. Spanish doctrine governs who you can take to wife."

"Betina is a bitch." Gabriel picked up the cat as it made a pass between his ankles. "I went to Father Antonio and set in motion proceedings that would ensure my vows to Sarah cannot be undone. Our children will have legal right to claim my name."

When Stefan didn't reply, Gabriel lifted a brow. "You have something to say?"

"I think that you don't know what you're doing anymore."

Gabriel shoved off the door. He set the cat on the back of a chair as he crossed the library. "You didn't spend two days on the road to talk about my love life."

"The governor sent a man to the *Felicity*." Stefan reached inside his coat. "Gossip preceded this," he said, handing Gabriel the missive. "As usual, you are all the talk."

A glance at the wax seal told Gabriel that it was important. Christina's and Cori's voices carried from the front verandah. He resisted looking out the window, where his eyes were drawn. His lips parting on a quiet oath, he slipped a forefinger beneath the seal.

"The governor expects you in Santo Domingo by tomorrow night," Stefan said. "The messenger who delivered this was adamant."

Gabriel scanned the contents. His expression remained placid as he read the words.

"Is it true?" Stefan quietly asked.

Closing his fist around the missive, Gabriel threw it on the desk. "That I killed a priest? Or that I killed the French governor who murdered the priest?"

"Does it matter? Murder is a serious charge." Stefan's gaze fell to the desk. "The *Felicity* can be ready to sail in three days."

"Is that why Berto and the troops were gathered here just now?"

"They are concerned, as well. Witnesses claim you killed both men. France is demanding an inquiry."

"This is no doubt Kendrick's doing."

"There are grumblings coming from the viceroy in Vera Cruz about your failure to appear for your tribunal in Spain. Now with this and the formal complaint Harrison Kendrick lodged against you—"

"What complaint?"

"That you fired on a ship of the English crown. That you are harboring a fugitive who happens to be the sister of a pirate wanted as much by the Spanish as the English. He went to Havana to file his claims properly. Clearly he is taking advantage of Spain's want to develop a cozy diplomatic relationship with England."

"Jesu . . ."

"I am not blind, Don Gabriel." Stefan's chest rose then fell with the quiet frustration in his eyes. "Or as unaffected as you might think by her either."

Hands on his hips, Gabriel turned his head and met Stefan's stare.

"I understand what you see in her, what she does to you inside. But you will grow to resent her for what you lose because of her."

"And what will that be, Stefan?"

"Your peers in Spain will never accept Lady Sarah as your legal wife. Felicity's father is very powerful, and he will do what it takes to protect his granddaughter's name, even if it means raising her himself. You are in a great deal of trouble, Don Gabriel."

His eyes closed. Logic told Gabriel that every word Stefan spoke was right. But logic never battled solitude or loss. Logic didn't renew the body's spirit or nourish a man's soul or mother a little girl. Logic was El Condor making decisions.

But the man who stood before Stefan now was not El Condor.

"You aren't here just to give me this missive, are you?"

"The governor wanted to send his troops. There's a ship waiting to take you to Havana. I was hoping you would run instead."

"Am I charged with anything?"

"Would you run if I told you that you were?"

"Nobody has seen him since Señor Delgato's visit, *señora*," the groomsman told Sarah when she went to the stables with Cori.

Gabriel usually spent this time with Christina. "Stefan was here?" Her voice faded. She would not allow herself to think about the implication of such a visit from Santo Domingo. "Has the mare been found yet?" she quietly asked.

"*Sí, señora.* She was brought back this morning."

Sarah's mouth tightened. "He didn't even tell me, Cori. Not a word," she said later as they left the stables. But then Gabriel hadn't said two words to her since the men came to fix her door. As if she'd been responsible for breaking the glass.

"God's balls, milady," Cori snapped. "The both of you are ridiculously smitten. Profess your undying love to the world and forget all of this ridiculous nonsense."

"We argued." Sarah still couldn't believe it.

"Now isn't that a bloomin' bit a news. Ye actually raised yer voice and someone yelled at ye right back."

"Why should that amuse you, Cori? I don't understand."

"He's the only man in yer life what doesn't coddle ye like a babe. No offense, milady, but ye had us all worried."

Her head ached. "Do *you* think I'm unbalanced, too?"

Cori's foot shoved around dried leaves. "What does it matter what people think anyway, milady, if the two of you are in love?"

"I'm English. Gabriel is Spanish to the core of his heart. He has a daughter. His people expect him to defend Spain, not marry the sister of a sworn enemy."

"His horse wasn't gone," Cori said finally.

Which meant Gabriel had not left her. Not completely.

All around her, frogs and the crickets had long since greeted the moon. Worse, Christina was not in her room when Sarah returned. "Took off in a dither," Jaime told her when she found him on the verandah. "Her papa forgot their riding lessons."

Sarah turned to Cori. "Why didn't you tell me Christina was upset?"

"Seemed to me that you've been in a dither, too, milady."

"Where'd she go?"

"Where she always does when she's upset."

Cori took Sarah past the herbal, following a winding path that meandered to a quiet place surrounded by shade trees, lilac vines, and the subdued sobs of a little girl. Christina sat on a bench in front of her mother's crypt.

Sarah had never known where Felicity was buried. Marble extended from the crypt. The smooth stone was cool beneath her slippered feet. Behind her, Cori left. She was alone with Gabriel's young daughter.

"Papa is leaving," Christina sniffled when Sarah knelt next to the bench. "He'll never be back. Not ever."

Sarah's heart fell like a weight. With a gentle scrape of her fingers, she wiped at Christina's wayward tears. "He is leaving?"

"He's angry with me." Sarah heard the ragged inhale. "I cried when I couldn't go to María's birthday celebration. Doña Betina and Papa argued because of me, and she left. And soon . . . soon he'll send me away, too. I heard Doña Betina talking with María's papa last week. I am to go to Spain. I will never see Papa again. *Ever*."

"Nonsense. If he's sending you back to Spain, it's because he wants the best for you. It's important that you learn to be a lady."

"Why?" The tiny word was belligerent.

"Because your papa is very important."

Sarah could feel Christina's eyes going over her face. "Did you learn to be a lady?" She hiccuped.

"Perhaps I might have, had my father lived."

And as uncertain as Sarah was about mothering another woman's child, Christina's loneliness suddenly reminded Sarah of herself as a young girl. Her father's image attached itself to her now. That and the elusive memory that he, too, had often sailed away.

"You see . . . my father was also important. He was an earl. My brother Talon holds that title now. Or he used to . . ."

"Is he at court?" Christina's voice filled with interest.

"No." Sarah rose off her knees and sat down beside Christina. "He can't go to court. He can't go back to England ever again." She lifted a hand to Christina's damp cheek. "So, you see, going to Spain is like going home for you. You should not take that for granted."

"What is granted?"

Sarah rephrased. "It's an honor for you, *niña*. Only the most important people in all of Spain are ever invited to court."

"My mamma went to court." Christina's tears had faded.

"There, you see? If your mamma went, then it must be fun."

Christina seemed to think about that. "Did you know Mamma?"

Holding Felicity's daughter, Sarah felt a strange kinship to the woman who bore her, and to this secret garden that

Gabriel had created. "No," she said quietly, "but she must have been very special. Your papa loved her very much."

Together they sat in silence. Christina laid her head against her arm. "I don't want Papa to be important."

"*Sí.*" Sarah leaned her cheek against Christina's head. "It's hard to share someone you love with the rest of the world."

Sarah sensed Gabriel's presence before Christina saw him. Her heart seemed to slam. He stood a few feet away, watching them, his impression so strong in Sarah's mind that she could envision him.

Then with a cry, his daughter leaped up, and he was holding her in his arms, apologizing for missing her riding lessons.

The heat rising to her cheeks, Sarah lowered her gaze. This was a private moment between papa and daughter. She reached for her walking stick before remembering it wasn't here. "Stay." Gabriel reached out, stilling her hand. "Please."

Sarah eased back to the bench and let the sound of her racing heart fill the awkward silence that followed. She imagined his eyes went over the crypt, and then, holding Christina, he sat down beside her. "My men told me you were here."

He laid his arm casually across the back of the bench. Sarah heard his cutlass scrape. "There is just enough breeze to keep the mosquitoes away," he said.

"This place is beautiful." Sarah folded her hands in her lap.

The caress of his fingers against her jaw turned her head, and she felt Gabriel's eyes on her face. "Papa planted the flowers," Christina volunteered, her voice muffled against his chest.

He didn't query Sarah about her reasons for being up here. They had never spoken about his famed marriage to Felicity or her death. But they could neither broach the subject nor speak of anything else between them while in Christina's presence.

Gabriel talked of simple things then, like the stars and the half-moon that clung to the sky with the tenacity of a monkey. He pointed out constellations to his eager daughter, his arm gradually closing around Sarah as Christina cheerfully looked for falling stars. His flesh was warm beneath the soft fabric of his sleeve, and for a brief interlude in time, Sarah belonged to this family.

When they all returned to the house, Rosa appeared on the front porch and took a sleeping Christina from her papa's arms. A horse was waiting some yards away. Sensing his eyes on her profile, Sarah stood in anxious silence, his upper arm touching her shoulder. He carried a hat and his stiff gloves in the hand that brushed against her. The doublet he wore framed his presence in stiffened velvet and reached midthigh. He'd changed from the casual attire he usually wore to something more conforming to his rank. The man who stood beside her now bespoke indisputable authority. She absently brushed her skirts.

"I saw you working in the herbal today," he said.

"You were there? Why didn't you say something?"

"The moment seemed . . . too serene. You've done a formidable job restoring the place."

"Does that surprise you?" She wanted to laugh.

"Nothing about you surprises me, *chica*. Not anymore."

Listening to the night sounds, the soft music of chimes, she rubbed a finger over the thick leaves of a plant that draped over the verandah. "I've marked every vat," she said. "That's how I know the differences between the plants. I'll dry and store the herbs down there." Sarah meandered on about how herbs could be used for medicine or cooking because he made no effort to stop her. Talking because she was suddenly, inexplicably afraid.

"Sarah . . ."

She turned slowly, letting him pull her into his arms. Warm citrus touched her senses. "Are you in trouble?" She laid her cheek against his neckcloth. "Is that why Stefan came back here?"

He tipped her chin up. "I've been called to La Habana on official business. A ship is awaiting me in Santo Domingo."

The pillar behind her stopped her from backing away.

He brushed his thumb across her lips in a possessive caress. "I'm not leaving you," he told her softly. "Do you believe that?"

She swore that she would not succumb to a silly fit of

tears; she would not wither and die because Gabriel was leaving the island.

"It's important to me that you believe me," he said.

The vulnerability in his voice lifted her chin. She felt him looking out at the night as if his thoughts were in another place and time, and she knew that he was thinking about Felicity.

"Stefan was with her when she died," he said quietly. "I should have been here. I was out fighting an English brigantine. Playing hero to a cause that was more important to me than my own wife."

Sarah couldn't reply.

"All of my wealth and power had not been enough to save her, and in the end, it was Stefan who held her hand when she'd died. He was the one who buried her because I'd not returned in time to see my own daughter born." He turned. "What good is the world I'm fighting for if I can't protect those I love? I never questioned my responsibility before, and I find myself questioning it now." His deep sense of duty was evident in every nuance, every word he spoke.

Her throat tightened. "I'm not Felicity. And whatever happened, you didn't kill her. You've protected me more than I ever had a right to ask. Don't question your duty because of me. Please."

His hand tilted her chin. "You are crying? Why, Sarah?"

"I fear I have harmed you," she said against her tears.

"How so, *chica*?" Amusement laced his words. "If anyone is to blame for my predicament, it is my sister for not being on Martinique when I came to visit."

Sarah laughed, and some of the tension left her body. "Thank you." That he could joke took some of the weight off her shoulders.

Instead of letting her go, Gabriel's free hand went to the pillar behind her, trapping her between his arm and the drop into the garden. "Our demons are not so different, yours and mine, Sarah." His voice lowered. "Only the means we use to survive."

She wiped her face. "In case you haven't noticed, you're very beloved by your people. I don't even *have* a people."

"I am nothing but a New World Creole who bought respectability with power. You are the closest to heaven I will ever get, *chica*."

The tears came before Sarah could stop them.

"Be my wife, Sarah. No more pretense," he said against her hair. "Stay in my rooms while I'm gone. Be there when I return. I want to know that I am with you. That you are mine."

He stopped her breath and her heart.

But Sarah wanted a future where she wouldn't be an embarrassment to him. Where she could somehow be his equal. Where her children would be accepted and loved, as Felicity's daughter was.

"Gabriel—" Her hands curled into fists. "We—"

"—can, Sarah."

He dipped his head nearer and Sarah felt the touch of his breath against her lips an instant before his mouth came down on hers. The fingers of one hand threaded through her hair, and she heard her name hoarsely whispered as he moved his warm lips to her cheek and down the curve of her neck before resuming the kiss, this time leaving no doubt of his passions. Her resistance died in a groan. She stood on her toes and wrapped her arms around his neck.

Not in her whole life had she ever felt such a powerful drive in a man: a man who demanded so much more from himself than he did others. Gabriel attacked life the same way that he attacked his daughter's simple horseback riding lessons. Grab it and master it. Failure was not an option. A person either conquered or was defeated.

He gave her his courage.

And for the first time in more years than she could remember, Sarah wasn't afraid.

"I've fought for everything in my life," he rasped against her mouth, his moist breath mingling with hers. "I can wage a war that will have you waving your white pantalets in surrender."

His words made her smile and groan at once. "You are so conceited, Gabriel."

"Ah, *chica*." He sucked on her bottom lip. Somehow he no longer held his hat and gloves, and he lifted her in his arms and carried her to his room. "I am so much more than conceited at this moment."

His lips held to their kiss while he removed his cutlass and undressed himself, never letting her go. His hands brushed hers away from her skirt and worked more efficiently, removing the barriers between them. Whispering ungentlemanly words into her ear about all the things he would like to do with her, he didn't undress completely, and she still wore her shift when he took her down to the softness of his bed, laying her there gently. But nothing else about him proved gentle or patient or anywhere near the softness of his words as his mouth encompassed each breast in turn, leaving her shift hot and wet beneath his tongue.

His hands beneath her shift, he straddled her hips, sliding his hand over her and into the damp softness of her sex, filling her with his fingers, then with himself. "*Por Dios.*" He gritted his teeth against her hair, and stopped before he began. "You feel . . . good."

Burying his mouth against her throat, he kissed the wild flutter of her pulse, threaded his fingers in her hair, and began to move, plunging deeper and deeper until she had taken all of him.

She splayed her palms around his corded neck and shoulders, gripping as she joined her strength to his. He was thick and hard sliding inside her, loving her. And when he'd filled her again and again, Sarah didn't care that he'd conquered her so throughly. For she had begun to believe in the rightness of the world.

The rightness of him.

Crying out, she fought for some control of her body, but she had already surrendered too much too soon, and felt the first waves burst over her. He'd braced his palms beside her, remaining poised above her when she had not remained poised at all. She felt his eyes on her face, the subtle quickening of his breath as he watched and felt her climax clench his powerful body. Then his rhythm came faster and faster. His throat rumbled. He filled her mouth with his tongue, kissing her hard. His breath caught on her name, and with his release, he threw his head back, taking her again over the precipice, so deep into his world she clung to his shoulders for life as he spilled hot and deep inside her.

As he rolled onto his back, he took her with him. He wore

no shirt but he still wore his breeches and boots. Cradled against the musculature of his chest, she closed her eyes and listened to his heartbeat slow. The whole week had left her emotionally spent, and with her physical depletion, sleep drifted over her like a mystic cloud. She didn't know how long he held her before she felt him standing beside her again, fully dressed to leave. No longer sleepy, she rose on her elbow and tried to still her pounding heart.

He brushed the hair from her face. "I'll return as soon as I can."

Pulling up to her knees in front of him, she placed her cheek on his chest. "Christina and I will be fine." She ran a finger up the row of buttons that climbed his doublet. "Don't go to Havana worrying about us."

"You are not to leave these grounds." His mouth moved to her ear, where wisps of damp hair had curled. "Berto is here. Stefan is in Santo Domingo with my ship."

He was trusting her with the care of his daughter.

Gently lifting her left hand, he slipped something on her finger. "The ring belonged to my mother," he said against her palm. "It's the only piece of jewelry I have that means anything to me."

Then he covered her mouth with his, kissing her deeply before she could rally from her shock. When she felt the ground level again, she heard the door click shut. Fumbling over the bed, she edged her way to a window and threw the latch. Her heart like an anchor in her stomach, her body still wet and glistening from his touch, she listened as the sound of a horse carried him away.

Chapter Sixteen

"Blimey, milady," Cori's voice whispered, "ye look like a real Spanish doña. Now chin up."

Sarah's chin went up like a soldier at attention. Afternoon sunlight streaked through the palm trees overhead. In the heat, sweat beaded against her spine and she straightened to keep her stays from poking deeper into her flesh. Children's laughter coming from the beach eased the discomfort that knotted her stomach. Most of the children belonged to Gabriel's servants. The breeze carried the scent of hot pork cooking from the pits Berto had dug in the sand.

The Mayfest celebration marked the end of April and brought the village populace down on Gabriel's home like bees to flowers. It was customary for Gabriel to receive the families that worked for him.

This event also afforded her the opportunity to talk to Father Antonio about the tutor for Christina, and he'd sent her a note yesterday telling her that he would introduce her to the young instructor today.

Anxious as Sarah was about venturing into this unfamiliar arena, with Betina gone, Gabriel's absence gave her authority as his wife to handle certain matters. And her first solo steps into the public eye had proved successful. Last week she'd reviewed the month's menu with the housekeeper, helped order new supplies, and handled a disaster in the kitchen. She'd tried hard to live up to expectations, and Father Antonio had reassured her that she was doing what was required of her today by opening up the grounds to Gabriel's house. Her independence, small as it was, granted her a chance to prove herself.

"Why can't I sit in the rocks with Señor Jaime?" Christina fussed.

"Because if I can't, you can't," Cori said, settling the matter with her usual diplomatic flair. "The rocks are too high. You'll fall off the cliff and ruin your pretty dress."

Rosa had collapsed beneath the tree and profusely fanned herself. A swish of robes sounded as Father Antonio approached from the tables. "Doña Sarah . . ." A brisk wind swept over them as he took her hands. "Christina, why aren't you playing?"

At once, Christina clung to Sarah's skirts like a burr. Sarah knelt. "You've wanted to play all day. What's the matter?"

"Go, Christina," Father Antonio urged. "If you decide you do not wish to play with the other children, then you may follow us around."

Gabriel would probably not allow her to run free with the servant's children. At the very least, it would do no harm to allow Christina to mingle with children her age.

"It's true, *niña*. If you tire you may find me."

"*Sí*, Doña Sarah. You promise?"

"I promise, *amor*. Now go have fun."

Giving Sarah a hug, she straightened and ran off. "Go with her, Cori." Sarah stood. "Rosa is in no condition to play."

"Nonsense, *mi hija*," Father Antonio's gravelly voice fell over her. "Christina does not need to be coddled. She used to come to the village often with her aunt. I don't know what has gotten into her."

Sarah traced the pad of her finger over her diamond band. Even after a week of Gabriel's absence, Christina's spark remained dim.

"Milady," Cori whispered, awaiting instruction.

Father Antonio spoke. "Go tell Señor Berto and the others that Christina is on the beach playing." He placed Sarah's hand on his forearm. "But he must remove his weapons first. I will not have him scaring the children to death."

Sarah sensed Cori's hesitancy and knew the reason. She

would not allow Berto and his men to stow their weapons. "Cori, have Berto conceal their weapons as best as they can."

"This place is as near an armed fortress as I have ever seen." Father Antonio clucked as he led her up the path to the yard. "No wonder Christina is not herself."

"Don Gabriel's absence has hurt his daughter."

"He has been gone before. She has never acted this way."

"Perhaps she is getting older and is not so easily bribed by trinkets. That's why I thought it was important that we begin lessons with her. It will put her mind someplace else, where she can learn."

"Don Gabriel will be sending her back to Spain for that. She has been away for too long and has become wild in her ways."

"Christina is not wild," Sarah said, affronted. "She is lonely."

"You think to be her mother then? To fix her heart and that of Don Gabriel? You cannot even see."

"My world is dark, but it's not without love, Father Antonio."

"And you believe love is enough? Then you know Don Gabriel and his family so well?"

Of a sudden, he'd toppled the precarious self-certitude that had boosted her up the last few days. "I think that I do," she answered.

"Don Gabriel has been very generous to the people who live here," he said, his tone more gentle. "He is like my son in many ways, though I would not presume to ever say that to him. I am but a simple man. But that doesn't mean that I'm not protective of him."

Sarah listened to their steps on the soft earth. "Yes, there are people who would harm him."

"Your brothers, for instance." His words startled her. "I fear there is no love lost between your family and El Condor."

No easy reply came forth. "Perhaps there is reason for distrust and hate on both sides, Father Antonio."

"And then there is you." He sighed. "Some have accused you of bewitching Don Gabriel. Yet you are still determined to survive here."

"Survive?" She wanted to laugh. Finally she stopped and

turned slowly to face him. The wind pulled at her skirts. "Do you see this scar?" She traced a slim finger over the long-ago injury that ran from the top of her ear to the back of her head. "When I was first brought to Saint Mary's, no one gave me long to live. They said that I had jumped off a cliff into the sea." Her voice was calm, determined. For she was more of a survivor than any ten people.

"I had no memory of who I was. I ate like an animal. I couldn't speak or dress myself." She folded her hands in front of her. "When I threw food at Father Henri, he merely walked away and let me starve. But he never did anything for me. After a while, I decided that I wanted to bathe because I couldn't stand my own stench." Her hands fidgeted with the tiny buttons on her bodice. "I had to learn my way around the compound if I wanted to go beyond the walls of my room. Speech was harder to master, and it took me a year to string together the simplest of sentences. But over the next five years, I learned to talk again. Gradually most of my memory has returned."

She stopped Father Antonio from replying. "People soon considered me a miracle, and with my hair color, I became something of a holy relic at Saint Mary's. The mind is powerful," she said. "It can heal the body or mend the soul, because I certainly don't possess any extraordinary powers to heal or bewitch people.

"I'm still not used to strangers touching me. I haven't mastered being in a crowd. But the sound of the waves no longer terrifies me. I love the open space beneath the sky and the wind chimes. I've ridden a horse and stood on the deck of my husband's ship. I thought that I would die when Father Henri made me leave sanctuary. But he gave me the greatest gift in my life."

"Doña Sarah—"

She captured his hands as they reached to touch hers. "Gabriel needs me. As does Christina. You ask if I can survive here. I will."

For a long time, Father Antonio was silent. His hands were gentle, as if he tried to reconcile his heart to sudden sympathy. She didn't want his pity and told him so.

"Perhaps it is time that I meet the tutor." She laid her palm on his forearm and they started walking again.

They walked to the house, where she met the young man Father Antonio had brought. She was unsure of the proper questions to ask, but Father Antonio spoke highly of his qualifications. He'd been educated in Vera Cruz. He seemed charming enough, but Sarah wanted a man who could teach Christina her letters and numbers; despite Christina's gender, she would be equally educated as any male child.

Silence met her assertions. "Don Gabriel should not be left out of this decision," Father Antonio finally said.

"Don Gabriel may not be back for a month," she reminded them. Then she smiled graciously. "Perhaps you would care to meet Christina," she offered the man.

Sarah sent a servant to summon Christina. When a half hour passed and Christina didn't appear, Sarah shoved aside her sudden discomfort. "Perhaps we should return to the beach," she suggested.

Father Antonio walked her back to the yard. The area was filled with people. "I don't know what could be taking so long to find Christina. She—"

"Milady." A breathless Jaime ran forward. "We can't find her."

Sarah's stomach dropped. "What do you mean you can't find her? She's with the other children."

"I know. She was," Jaime whispered. "The children are eating now. She's not there."

"Go check the house. Find Rosa."

Berto was suddenly beside her. "Did she go into the water?"

"Don't you dare tell me that! Don't you dare tell me she went into that water by herself!" She stopped abruptly, aware of the futility of panic. Christina could not have disappeared. "You find her. Both of you. She can't have gone far."

But Gabriel's men didn't find her.

Not that day or the next. A search of the surrounding woods and cliffs turned up nothing. No clue, no hint where a little girl might have disappeared. Men dove into the sea, searching the water for any sign of her body. Sarah's terrified assertion that Christina would not leave her father's house drove her to pace in Felicity's garden until Cori forced her back to the house. "Christina would come to this place." She clung to Cori. "Berto must post a guard there."

Then when Rosa turned up missing, Sarah no longer feared that Christina had perished. Berto talked about ransoms, kidnappings, and all the possibilities of why someone might steal Christina. "Rosa did not act alone," he said. "She may not have even been willing."

"Why?" Numbed by grief, Sarah clutched Christina's doll in her lap. "Why would someone take a little girl, Berto? Why?"

"There are a thousand reasons why someone would take Don Gabriel's daughter," he told her.

Her head throbbed painfully. She couldn't breathe. "I shouldn't have made her play. She wanted to stay with me. I sent her away."

"Ye did nothing wrong, milady," Cori said. "Nothing."

But Gabriel had entrusted her with Christina's life. She'd opened the grounds of the house. She'd let his daughter roam free with the other children. Her ignorance had been naught but a boon for the person who did this.

By the end of the week, rain replaced the sunlight that had fallen over the ground in a blanket of warmth, and for the first time since Sarah had become Gabriel's wife, the nightmares began.

Visual pieces of a puzzle—the silent screams, the sound of waves—dreams that ended with Gabriel making love to her in the sand. Good feelings, safe emotions had become tainted with something that she did not understand. Something evil.

"Close your eyes, Sarah. Don't look. Whatever happens, don't open your eyes."

Sarah woke up screaming.

Christina needed her! She must open her eyes!

Berto found Sarah on her knees above the cliffs. He carried her back to her room—Gabriel's room—where Cori was waiting anxiously.

Sarah wanted Gabriel, but she called for her mother, then someone was pressing a pewter cup to her lips, and Sarah tasted laudanum. "Something is wrong with me, Cori," she sobbed, kneading her fists against her temples. She'd fallen asleep fully clothed. "Something terrible. It won't go away. It's tearing my head apart."

Cori held her as if she were a babe in arms, her heartbeat strong against Sarah's ear. "Shh, milady. Ye were havin' a nightmare."

Her head still in Cori's lap, she slipped in and out of sleep.

Cori was wearing a red dress. Sarah's hands clutched the bright taffeta, testing the texture against her palms. Tiny diamonds framed her finger, and Sarah turned her hand. Then her eyes drifted closed, gathering the dream closer to her heart.

When she awoke later Cori still held her. "I've not ever thanked you and Jaime for what you've done for me all these years." Sarah wrapped her arms tighter around her friend. "You don't have to stay here on this island. You should find my brothers."

"All things bein' equal, milady, I like it here," Cori said. "Jaime and me been savin' money."

"You have?"

"After Don Gabriel caught me tryin' to palm some useless emerald off his ship, he told me I could work off my crimes the legitimate way, or he'd cut off my hand."

Sarah sat up and wiped a palm across her wet face.

"That's what they do in some places," Cori confirmed knowingly. "Fer myself, it's a wonder he didn't just lop off my hand right there on the ship, he was so furious. How's a body supposed to know he'd miss a dumb old emerald? Anyway, now I pluck chickens in the kitchen." Her voice rose. "And Jaime Durant can just melt in his breeches before he's earned enough money to marry me!"

"Hah!" Sarah heard Jaime's answer outside her room, where he stood guard beside her door. "I have more than enough already."

"Who says I'd even marry ye anyway, ye overgrown turd," Cori sniffed, and Sarah wrapped her arms around Cori's waist.

She knew that Jaime and Cori were doing everything possible to shelter her from the ongoing search. She felt their fear, as much for Christina as for her. "Will you go to the beach again? Climb the rocks? What if she's fallen?"

"Berto has already been over the rocks, milady," Cori whispered.

"Find her, please. She's just a baby."

But Gabriel's daughter had simply vanished.

As Sarah had almost twelve years ago.

The interior of the church smelled musty and was strangely empty of people so close to mass. Though men continued to comb the woods, Sarah had sent Berto that morning to Santo Domingo to finally give Stefan the terrible news to take to Gabriel. The two men who drove the carriage into the village remained outside with the horses.

Children's laughter, coming from the yard, pulled Sarah to the window. "Doña Sarah." Father Antonio's voice filled the cavernous hall. He took her hands into his. "Where is your *dueña*?" he asked.

"I didn't want to awaken Cori. Your message seemed so urgent. I came as soon as I could dress."

"We can't waste a moment. Follow me." He took her into the chapel and through a narrow door behind the pulpit.

"Father, what have you heard? I must know." Her hands touched the moist stones that curved into a stairwell. "You have to tell me."

"Christina is safe."

The words nearly felled her. Hot tears burned her eyes. Catching back a sob, she worked desperately to compose herself. "How? How did you find her? Where has she been?"

"She's all right. I've seen to that."

Sarah had entered a shallow stone hallway before she realized where she was. Condensation dripped somewhere ahead. "But you cannot have put her down in this awful place." Her feet slowed against his insistent pull. The air smelled stale. "This leads to the cemetery. You said that she was alive. Why are you bringing me here?"

He stopped. "Truly, I am sorry for everything that you've endured at my hands. It was not my choice to see you suffer so."

Sarah was not prepared for those words. Unbelieving, she scraped the heel of her hand over her face.

When Father Antonio spoke again, his voice held regret.

"Until now, you presented a dilemma for us all, *mi hija*. Don Gabriel has not been thinking clearly since he brought you to the island. Because of you, he has ignored the dictums of a king and faces an indictment for sedition. He has killed two men and would start a war with England and France over you."

"Two men?" The words were barely a gasp.

"You didn't know that he is charged with the murder of the French governor on Martinique and a priest?"

"They . . . lie!"

Movement sounded behind her. Heart pounding, every breath clogging her throat, she slid sideways into the arms of a burly man. "He's waitin' in the cemetery," the man's voice said in English.

"Father Antonio," she pleaded, "what have you done?"

"Sarah, if you remain here, I will be forced to turn you over to the Inquisition. Already people have beared witness against you."

She stood paralyzed, barely aware as someone tied her hands. "Gabriel won't let you do this. I am his wife."

"Your priest did not register the marriage before he died. Even if your English father wasn't hanged for a pirate, did you think that you could supplant a royal decree? Don Gabriel is not just any man, *mi hija*. He is El Condor, Spanish aristocracy. His father-in-law is the Duke of Valencia, one of the most powerful sovereignties in Spain. Christina is the man's only grandchild."

Someone started to drag her up narrow stone stairs. *No!* "What have you done to her, Father Antonio? Please . . . you can't—" A rag was stuffed in her mouth. She kicked her legs out only to find them entangled in her skirts. The arm that tightened around her waist nearly cracked her ribs. She tried to suck in air. To breathe.

"On His Grace's order, Doña Betina is bringing Christina to Spain. They will stay with Christina's grandfather until Don Gabriel weds Doña Betina. He knows his responsibility, Sarah. Even as we speak, he is on his way back to Spain. You will not see him again."

Above her on the landing, a stone door grated open, fracturing the shadows with sunlight. Her screams muffled by the gag, Sarah furiously fought the arm that lifted her fighting toward that awful light. A scrape against stone echoed; the step-tap of a walk down the stairs, the sound slowly lifting her gaze.

Time froze.

"Shh, Sarah, child." A gloved hand stole away the single tear that touched her cheek. "I'm taking you home now."

Defeated by the gilded halo of light on darkness, of long-ago memories that softly whispered her mother's name, Sarah let the hands pull her into the light.

"Don Gabriel"—the baritone voice held censure—"your temper is showing. Perhaps you'd best save it for fighting the enemies of Spain and not your family."

Two men held Gabriel's arms. They'd leaped forward at the first sign that Gabriel would tear across the desk and rip the old Duke's throat out. Felicity's father had not changed from the man he'd first met nine years ago when Don Hernández was the *Capitán General* of the *Tierra Firme* treasure fleet, the hard-nosed viceroy who currently ruled New Spain from his seat in Vera Cruz. His uniform gleamed white with the Order of the Golden Fleece on his breast. His Excellency was still arrogant, pious, and a man who put honor and reputation above everything else, including his own life. He was the kind of man Gabriel had once been.

His cutlass long since removed, Gabriel stood before his former father-in-law, aware that a dozen men watched from the back of the room. He lifted his gaze to Betina, who stood behind the older man.

"If something happens to my wife and daughter because of anything you've done, I swear on my life that I will make you regret that you ever knew my name." Her beautiful face visibly paled. "Now tell me again that I'm the man you want in your bed."

"Even if your marriage had been valid, by your own word you've asked to annul your vows." She wagged a delicately gloved finger at the letter she'd stolen from his ship: a letter written months ago and discarded in his desk. "I've done nothing but follow my heart."

"And what thing have I done to you that you would not

know *my* heart?" He shifted his gaze abruptly. "And tell me, Don Hernández, am I a dog who is to be forever commanded by the snap of your fingers?"

Christina's grandfather slammed his hands on the desk. "You have taken what I've given you and thrown it all away!"

"You've given me nothing that I didn't first earn with my own blood and sweat and, too often, the lives of good men!"

"You may arrive in Spain at the helm of your ship, Don Gabriel. Or I will bring you back in chains." He crossed his arms over the buttons on his chest. "The choice is yours. But my granddaughter will not remain in the care of a known seditionist. You will *not* destroy her good name with yours."

"My daughter's future is not up for negotiation."

"You *will* return to Spain and clear the charges lodged by the *Capitán General* against you for desertion of your post. You *will* stand before France's emissary and give your deposition of the events that took place on Martinique during your little escapade there. And you will *then* make a formal apology to Sir Kendrick. Or by Providence, I will raise that child myself and let you rot in a prison of my personal choosing!"

His face expressionless, Gabriel looked at Stefan. "You knew about this?"

Standing next to the picture window that framed Havana's harbor, Stefan wore the blue-and-gold uniform of Gabriel's guard. Behind him, embraced by a flawless dome of blue sky, two fortresses stood guard over the bay where a score of ships bobbed sluggishly at their anchors—including the *Felicity,* which had arrived that morning.

Holding his feathered hat against his side, Stefan met Gabriel's furious gaze. "I don't agree with the methods used to get you here, but I do agree with the principles. His Excellency is correct, Don Gabriel. If you don't return to Spain now, you face arrest."

No one had mentioned Sarah's name. It was as if she didn't exist. He tasted blood in his mouth where he'd bitten down on the words that would have tossed him headfirst into the hold of a ship sailing to Spain. A strange sort of terror had seized him as he realized he could get no word to Sarah. He could not abandon her on Hispaniola.

"Come, Don Gabriel," the duke consoled. His dark mustache turned up: the first sign of a smile Gabriel had seen since he'd arrived. "I have a surprise for you." He lifted his hand, and Gabriel heard the huge doors behind him swing open. "I already spent the morning dining with *mi princesa*. It has been too long since her grandmother and I have seen her. I wish to fix that."

"Papa!"

Christina's voice fell over him in a cold wave.

The men holding him stepped away, and Gabriel turned. His daughter's dark ringlets bounced as she ran with unlady-like haste across the polished floor. Her pink slippers matched the ribbons in her hair and flounces on her new dress. He dropped to one knee, and she ran into his arms. Over the top of her head, he espied Rosa standing nervously beside the door. He also noticed something else that made his heart pause. Ten of his men had entered the room and now stood at attention behind the duke's *soldados*.

"Of course, if you swear on your name that you will not escape, your daughter can travel with you on your ship," Don Hernández said. "It was never my intent to separate the two of you."

Gabriel's leather boots creaked as he stood with his daughter. She'd buried one hand in his cravat. He could feel her heart racing. His anger was a furious thing and exploded inside him. He found Stefan watching him, something alive in his eyes.

Gabriel shifted his eyes to Don Hernández. "You would believe my word when you doubt my honor?" He stepped off the thick carpet onto the hardwood floor. Don Hernández had just made a colossal strategic error in allowing Gabriel to hold Christina. "*Ratón*"—he carefully applied his words to his daughter's temple, his gaze never leaving His Grace's face. "Did you say good-bye to Doña Sarah when you left?"

"No, Papa," she quietly answered, and his gaze darkened on Betina. "I was on the beach playing. Then Doña Betina took me to Señor Delgato and we came here to be with you. She will be very worried, Papa, that I didn't come back."

Gabriel spun on his heel. Behind him, the duke leaped up. His men looked on, unsure, as Gabriel passed.

Christina happily waved. "*Buenos días, mi abuelo.* Grand-papa."

And the order to stop Gabriel from leaving the room did not come. He walked out the huge doors, past the guard, with Rosa running at his side. Either his men were with him or they would stay behind and await the duke's orders.

Stefan joined him. Behind them, his men fanned out. Sounding like soldiers', their steps carried through the enormous hall. *Conquistadores* armor lined the stately corridor. Holding his daughter tightly against him, Gabriel swept past two hundred years of Spain's maritime history painted in murals over the walls. On the last wall, his most famous battle against the English at San Juan de Puerto Rico had been gloriously depicted.

"Where is she?" Gabriel asked before they reached the doors.

"She is not doing well," Stefan replied. "I brought Doña Betina here with your daughter because I guessed that you might be in trouble as well. And because His Excellency's *soldados* have sharp swords. I could not get news to Berto that Christina is safe."

"*Dios . . .*"

He refrained from further discussion in front of Christina. But had Betina appeared before him now, someone would have had to hold him back from throttling the woman for what she'd done to Sarah.

Men dressed formally and awaiting appointments with various state officials stopped to gawk as Gabriel shoved through the main doors and left the enormous whitewashed building. Gilded by afternoon sunlight, a pair of lions guarded either side of the steps.

"You had me worried, Stefan."

"You do realize that Don Hernández will take this personally," Stefan said after they'd reached the *Felicity* and Gabriel had settled his daughter in his cabin with Rosa. He'd torn off his formal jacket down to his white shirt and waistcoat.

His neckcloth caught a sudden gust. "Spain will have to wait." He ordered men to the capstan. "Headsail sheets, Señor Alvarez!"

"If you leave these waters, Don Hernández will declare you a pirate," Stefan warned.

Gabriel leaped the steps to the quarterdeck, where his helmsman awaited his orders. "Are you with me, Stefan?"

The hot land breeze had picked up and mixed with the cooler wind that came off the water. "I have family," Stefan said. "I do not intend to forsake Spain. Even for the gold that you pay me."

Telescope to his eye, Gabriel briskly scanned the shore, then the channel entrance. *Soldados* lined the fortified banks. But Don Hernández would not fire on the ship and risk Christina's life. No, their confrontation would continue another day.

Gabriel lowered the glass and met Stefan's gaze. "I have not forsaken Spain, *mi amigo*. But neither will I bark for any man but the king himself. And even that will wait until I see my wife."

"*Sí.*" Stefan joined him at the helm. "Then we are all with you."

"*Por Dios,* it looks as if someone fought a war here."

Crouched beside Stefan, Gabriel brought the glass to his eyes and scanned the length of his house. His gaze lingered on the shattered door off his verandah. No movement anywhere. Not even smoke from the kitchen. Fear pooled in his stomach.

Bracing an elbow on his knee, he turned to the handful of men who had rowed into the cove with him. Through the trees behind them, he glimpsed the giant masts of his ship anchored off the reefs. His daughter was out there. Overhead, clouds darkened the sky.

"Alvarez, signal the ship that we're here." Gabriel swung his gaze back to Stefan. "We've given the other men enough time to get to the front of the house." Metal hissed as he drew his sword and turned to the remaining men behind him. "Get to the guardhouse. Find out if Berto is still alive."

Cutlass drawn, Gabriel ran the width of his yard. Dead silence greeted him inside the house. Though an effort had been made to clear the rubble, the rooms were in shambles. Shattered porcelain crunched beneath his boots. Chairs were overturned, paintings torn from their anchors on the walls. A fight did not cause this kind of damage.

Adjusting his gaze to the dimness, he stood pressed to the wall near the central hallway. A breeze opened the door he'd just entered and caught the chandelier above the long dining table. Outside, the echo of wind chimes followed. Something brushed his leg. Sarah's cat rubbed against his calves. The tight line on his mouth softened when he saw the animal. Gabriel bent and with one hand lifted the cat to his shoulder.

And froze.

Talon Drake leaned casually against the opposite wall, his pistol pointed at Gabriel's chest. "It's about time you decided to join this little party."

Gabriel's eyes grew cold. Carefully, he set the cat on the table. "Where is my wife?"

Something ugly flashed in those silver eyes. "Put your cutlass on the table."

The years had done little to erase the primal edge from the man's demeanor. Dark hair was swept from his face and pulled back in a queue. A black shirt, breeches, and boots made him no more than a shadow in the twilight enclosing the house. Sarah's oldest brother was as dangerous now as he'd always been.

After Gabriel had done as asked, the gun bobbed toward the hallway. "Now move."

Stefan's voice stopped them both. "I will take the pistol first, Señor Drake, if you don't mind."

The pistol lowered. "And if I did mind?"

Gabriel snatched the pistol from Drake's grip. Easing the hammer back, he asked Stefan about the rest of the men.

"We've rounded up ten of Drake's men. Berto and the others were tied up in the guardhouse. No one was hurt."

Drake merely listened with a bored expression. Gabriel's hands closed into fists. "Only ten?" he asked Stefan. They both knew there should be more. Gabriel looked at Drake. "Where is your ship?"

"These are Spanish waters, Espinosa. Do you think me insane to leave it lying around?"

"If you've hurt anyone here, you will not live long enough to savor your brief victory, small as it is. Where is my wife?"

Drake ignored the question. "Word doesn't travel fast in these realms, or I'd have hunted you down months ago. As it is, I just arrived yesterday. I'm not responsible for what's happened here."

"Where is she?" Gabriel's voice had fallen to a whisper.

"Go into your library and ask a certain Father Antonio. Ask what he did to my sister. Then tell me how fond you are of people who would betray an innocent girl to the likes of Harrison Kendrick."

Disbelief froze him. Backing a horrified step, Gabriel spun on his heel. The library door crashed against the wall. His gaze skimmed a dozen terrified faces before landing on Father Antonio. His brown robes were freshly stained as if he'd been dragged here.

"Is it true?" Gabriel moved into room. "Answer me, Father. Is it?"

A hand on his arm stilled him. He looked down into Cori's frightened eyes, and some of his sanity returned. "A few days ago, we found milady's headrail in the underground passage beneath the church. The tunnel leads to the cemetery. They took Christina, too."

"Shh." he placed a finger on her mouth. "Christina is with me."

Cori burst into tears, and Gabriel wrapped her in his arms. Tough, hard as shale Cori Sheldon: she had always faced misfortune with courage. There was no pleasure in seeing her wilt now, only a horrible recognition of the cause and depth of her terror.

And when his gaze returned to Father Antonio, for the first time in his life, Gabriel wanted to kill a priest. He didn't care that eternal damnation awaited him. There was no worse crime than murdering a holy man. Even if that man had betrayed a young woman to a butcher like Kendrick.

"Why?" he asked Father Antonio.

"The holy tribunal would have come for her anyway," he rasped. "Don Hernández . . . he ordered that she disappear without a scandal. He said that you would forget her once you were in Spain."

Disbelief underscored his fury. "And while he was sucking you into his lies, Kendrick's men were ransacking my house?

For what?" Filled only with the deadly certainty that every breath came with the greatest of control, he swept his gaze across the faces of his servants.

"They came while Berto and most of the men were in the village, Don Gabriel," an old woman he recognized as his housekeeper replied. Her hands trembled in her lap. "They were looking for a Bible."

"Bible? *¡Por Dios!* Kendrick would not be looking for a Bible!"

"Please forgive us." Father Antonio's rheumy eyes were wet with more than fear. "We only did what we thought best for everyone."

"Best for Sarah, old man? You've condemned her to die!" He found Jaime standing next to the window. "Get them out of my house."

Gabriel whirled on his heel. Drake blocked the door. Dark silver eyes went over Gabriel with something close to bafflement. "You're not going after him alone," Drake said flatly.

"*¡Ay de mi!* So help me . . . Get out of my way."

"Normally, I wouldn't let you within a league of me, Espinosa. You're a dangerous bastard. But we need each other."

"I intend to find her and I intend to kill him. He is taking her to Port Royal."

"You have to get to him first. And I know how to do that. Hell, I know better than anyone. I can pilot those waters, but I can't take the *Dark Fury* anywhere near Port Royal."

Gabriel cocked a brow, daring him to make his point.

"With all Spanish signature removed, your ship is a frigate no different than any ten English ships that sail into that place on a daily basis. I'll even add a British union Jack for authenticity."

"Don't disgust me!" Gabriel shoved past him.

"Were you planning to take your daughter to Port Royal with you?"

Gabriel turned slowly.

"You didn't think my men have been sitting on their asses, waiting for you to grace us with your presence? The minute you took most of your men off the ship, mine went on. So, officially, your ship belongs to me anyway, Espinosa."

Gabriel's hands shot out and gripped Drake's shirt, slamming him against the door frame. "You're careless," Drake whispered, "to have left your back door wide open to the likes of me. You're not thinking straight, and I have no intention of letting you get Sarah killed."

Drake's silver eyes were so much like Sarah's, Gabriel felt himself pause, felt his fists loosen. His chest tightened until he could no longer breathe over the burn.

"Christ . . ." Drake whispered. "I know what you're thinking. She's been with Kendrick for over a week. It's tearing me up, too!"

"You don't love her. Not the way I do. You haven't looked into her eyes and seen her soul. You don't know . . ." His hands fell away. "You don't know Kendrick."

"I know him." Drake's words washed over Gabriel. "But we have to do this together. Can I trust your crew to help sail the *Dark Fury* back to New Providence?"

Gabriel looked away. He looked at the ceiling, then at his fisted hands, for all their strength impotent in the face of reality.

"They'll take Cori and your daughter," Drake said. "Marcus is there, with your sister and my family. By the way, Liandra had a little boy."

The breath left Gabriel's lungs. Tears welling in his eyes, he slumped against the wall.

"Cori told me that Sarah is very much in love with you." Drake held out Gabriel's cutlass. Surprise lifted Gabriel's gaze as he took the sword. "Frankly, anyone who can be nice to Sarah's cat can't be a complete asshole. Count yourself lucky I'm letting you live."

Gabriel's gaze fell on Sarah's gray cat sitting beside an overturned chair before narrowing on Drake's retreating back. "The feeling's mutual, *bastardo*," he hissed, and Drake's arm shot up in an obscene gesture before he passed through the doors that led outside.

"Should we untie his men now?" Stefan leaned with his arms crossed against the opposite wall.

"How did he get my cutlass?"

Stefan shrugged. "He took it off the table. After he took the pistol away from me."

"*¡Ay caramba!*" Gabriel slid the cutlass back into its sling.

"You're changing ships. I want you to go with the *Dark Fury* to New Providence. Tell my sister . . . tell her that I will see her soon. And Stefan?" Removing his waistcoat, he stopped his friend from leaving. "Keep my men on the ship when you get there, *sí*?"

Scooping Sarah's cat off the floor, Gabriel wrapped him securely beneath his arm as he followed Drake out of the house.

He would not think about Sarah in Kendrick's hands. He would not think about tomorrow. He would allow nothing in his thoughts.

Nothing . . . was El Condor.

Chapter Seventeen

Harrison Kendrick read the missive. Lifting his gaze, he found the young lieutenant courier still standing at the edge of his desk. Harrison recognized the youthful posture at once: the eagerness to please that grated so much on his nerves. With a certain amount of malicious satisfaction, he knew he'd kept the man waiting, and in the heat of the room, sweat beaded the man's brow.

"Tell Governor White, if he has a question concerning my activities, he can make an appointment to speak to me," Harrison said. "So unless you've come to arrest me for some ill deed, get out."

The man's pretty face paled. He had blond curls tousled from the ride to Harrison's town house. Harrison enjoyed making people pay for their insipid eagerness—as if their acts weren't fraught with motives. He took great pains to teach them quality lessons about life, trust, and all the banal attributes that separated common society from the divine.

But he'd teach no lessons tonight to this eager lieutenant.

Tonight, he thought of Sarah upstairs locked in her room.

People were so inherently stupid and greedy that he'd encountered little trouble in bringing her to Jamaica. But her last escape attempt had somehow reached the ears of the governor. Harrison had not worked his whole life to mishandle his affairs now, not when he was so close to salvation.

Elation briefly touched him, much like the opium that consumed his pain and took away his nightmares. His passion for her was as close to emotion that he'd felt since . . . The thought died.

He was always careful where he let his thoughts travel.

After the lieutenant left, Harrison climbed the stairs to her room and unlocked the door. Sarah lay in bed beneath white lace and moonlight, her hair spread on the pillow. He watched her often when she slept. It was the only time that he completely owned her.

His gaze fell upon the slim hand that lay over her breast. He'd taken Espinosa's ring and thrown it in the sea. A gold band replaced the Spaniard's generosity.

"You have haunted me for almost twelve years, Sarah," Harrison had told her when he'd put the ring on her finger. "The memory of your eyes. Your hair. The child you were. Your innocence. I want . . . I want to go back to the man I was before I walked into your house that day long ago. I was not always as you see me now, Sarah."

But Sarah saw only the monster he was today.

She'd been an innocent on Martinique, easily manipulated, before Espinosa had come along and ruined everything. All of his well-laid plans had been destroyed. Now she'd regained her sight and her memory. If he'd gotten to her first, he might have had a chance. She might have had his.

Deep inside, Harrison understood her danger to him. Between her testimony and the damn Bible Father Henri had kept hidden from him for years, she was the only person alive who could see him hanged. But from the day Harrison had learned that she was alive—alive after all these years—he'd been inexplicably relieved, even exhilarated. He'd loved her always. He couldn't kill her now, any more than he could have years ago.

He only wanted her to love him back. Why couldn't she see that?

Despair fell away from Sarah in slow degrees, dropping into nothingness. Resting her cheek on her hand, she leaned against the window and stared across Port Royal's endless line of red rooftops. The sea was a mirror broken only by the ripple of feeding sharks.

Her eyes slowly focusing, Sarah gripped the cold black metal that barred her window. Absorbed by the play of light that feathered across her hand, she jolted when her gaze fell on her finger.

Since the moment Harrison Kendrick had locked her in his cabin on his ship and put his hands all over her body, Sarah had suffered severe mental exhaustion and the despairing realization that she'd regained her memory and sight at the cost of her peace.

In her naïveté, she'd once believed that all dreams were fraught with sugarcoated endings. She'd believed in the goodness of mankind and her own goodwill. Her arrogance had cost her Christina, her freedom, and her future with Gabriel. It had certainly landed her in Harrison Kendrick's arms.

She'd tried to escape him twice.

The first time she'd leaped out the stern window of his ship when he'd anchored at Port Royal. She couldn't swim in her clothes and had nearly drowned. The second time she'd climbed over the verandah of her bedroom straight into the hands of his guard. Then Kendrick had started drugging her. He'd fed her opium-laced food and drink and boasted to the world that they were a happy couple.

Last night, Sarah had sailed with him from the main island across the harbor. While the lamplighters made their rounds here in Port Royal, she'd taken a fancy carriage to Saint Paul's and married Harrison Kendrick. The banns had been posted two consecutive Sundays.

No one came to stop him.

With only the rector's wife, who lectured her on the duties of a proper bride, and a man suffering from incipient malaria as witnesses, no one cared that she was there against her will or that she'd said naught during the ceremony. Her silence had meant nothing to them, when gold bought everything in Port Royal.

Movement roused Sarah and she turned into the room. Her ivory silk wedding gown no longer lay crumpled on the floor where she'd thrown the dress. Someone had lain it over the settee.

Harrison sat on the edge of a bed that dominated the hot, airless room. Dressed in a closely buttoned silver brocade doublet, he looked as if he'd been there for a while, watching her. A patch covered one brown eye, and part of a scar was hidden by the sable wig that he wore.

"Your maid tells me that you didn't eat at all yesterday or this morning," he said. "Do you intend to starve yourself to death, love?"

Turning her back to him, she let her gaze go to the distant ship moored farthest out in the bay, her tall masts magnificent against a cloudless sky. The ship had not been there last night.

A pall fell over her back. "How do you do that?" Harrison brushed aside the white wrapper she wore, baring her pale shoulder. "How do you turn off the world? Where do you go, Sarah?"

She turned and tried to walk past him.

He blocked her. "Why won't you do as I ask?" His hands held the same plea as they went to her hair, forcing her to look at him. "Have I raped or beaten you? Have I not given you everything? Beautiful clothes, servants, my heart?" He bent his lips over hers.

Sarah turned her face away.

"You're like a shadow, love." His hands moved over her shoulders. "A beautiful, pathetic shadow of a passionate woman."

Her breasts strained against her shift, yielding her modesty to his gaze and then to his loathsome touch. She clenched her fists to keep from tearing his hands away.

He wanted her passion, any kind of passion he could get. She would give him nothing. Not even hate. Perhaps men who warred for a living didn't know of any other way to fight, except to the death. But Sarah had faced death before and would not do so willingly again. In her mind, she told herself that she could endure Kendrick's touch . . . if it meant that she'd live to see Gabriel again.

"You're silent now"—he suckled her throat—"but what about if I put my tongue inside your mouth or touch you in your most private places? Tell me, dearest love." He yanked her face back. "Will you be thinking of him then?"

Hot sunlight beat against her back. "You're so filled with opium, I'll *never* worry that you'll touch me the way he did," she whispered.

"There are other ways I can take my pleasure, Sarah."

"I despise you."

He placed her palm on his chest. "You break my heart, love." Bringing her hand to his mouth, he laid his lips across the band of her white knuckles. His grip tightened. A small cry left her throat as he brought her to her knees in front of him.

"Don't make me hate you," he whispered.

He dropped her hand. Cradling her palm, Sarah sat back on her calves. The muffled step-tap of Harrison's movements lowered her gaze to the bright green carpet. Yellow love knots had been woven into the woolen threads like painted tears.

"The midwife said that you're not with child. At least I won't have his brat to contend with. But then what poetic justice that would have been." He clucked. "His child bearing my name."

Remembering the vulgarity of the midwife's hands, she shuddered. "You can't keep me drugged forever. When I escape, I'll tell the world what you've done . . . what you did to my family."

"And then what, dearest bride?" His words calmly crushed her as if she were no more than a butterfly. "People already think you mad. And the accusations are nothing new in some circles. Even Don Gabriel knew. You haven't heard him talking?"

She snapped her chin up. "You . . . lie." But the sudden emotion in her voice betrayed her.

"I think you're under the impression that your Spaniard is something of a knight, my love. During your acquaintance you should have asked him how many ships he's sent to the bottom of the sea."

"Stop it!"

He tore her hands from her ears. "He and I go back many years. I made much of my fortune and he made his name on information I supplied him about English ships that frequented this port. French, too. My good papa was an emissary to France for many years before he became chief justice here. And, of course, we all know how fond Don Gabriel is of your family. Why not pluck their most precious pearl? A worthy jewel for El Condor, especially after he knew how much I wanted you."

Sarah felt something ignite in her chest. She wouldn't believe it. She . . . wouldn't. Kendrick attempted to manipulate her mind.

"Your maid is bringing up wine and will be here shortly to help finish your toilette. Leave your hair uncovered when you come downstairs for brunch." He hesitated, then pulled her to her feet. "I can't change the past. But here you are. Offering me a chance to redeem myself. To feel something again. I've given you enough time. Tonight, you will join me in my bed as my legal wife."

He smiled eloquently at her disbelief. Despite the scar on his face, he was not ugly, unless one looked into his eye.

Inside he was dead.

When he left the room, Sarah walked to the dresser and slumped onto the chair. The room sweltered in heat. She lifted her head. A looking glass sat atop the frilly white decoration that covered the polished mahogany. Her reflection watched her with a fragile wariness that had begun to awaken her body.

He would kill her.

By killing her spirit, he would kill her soul.

She blinked when her hands touched her reflection.

Regaining her sight wasn't as simple as seeing light again. Nothing felt right inside anymore. In the beginning, she had little perception of depth and distance. Light disoriented her. She'd spent the last weeks attempting to interpret colors and objects that surrounded her. She'd felt as if she were learning to walk again.

And she hated Harrison Kendrick because he'd dared mock her with his benevolence, when he'd done naught but bring her world crashing down around her shoulders.

Again.

Sarah wrenched her hand from the glass and yanked off the ring.

She had only to survive until she could escape, or until her brothers found her. Air filled her lungs. Today was the first morning since she'd been brought to this island prison that she'd awakened with anything close to a clear head. But then she hadn't eaten in two days, and had drank sparingly only the tepid water brought for her baths.

Sarah jerked open the drawers that marched up and down the dresser and searched for the items she'd stolen when the dressmaker had brought her wedding dress for a final fitting. Across the square, the church bell tolled for the morning service.

Pulling out a pair of scissors, Sarah turned her attention back to the glass. Her eyes went to the sheen of white-blond hair that draped her shoulders. Harrison Kendrick had run his filthy fingers through every strand Gabriel had ever touched.

She narrowed her eyes. Once before, she'd tried to escape Kendrick by going over a cliff. The difference now was that she wasn't nine years old. This time she was determined to keep fighting.

Grabbing a handful of hair just below her chin, Sarah raised the scissors, squeezed her eyes shut for a moment, and began to cut. When she'd finished, the last twelve years of her life lay at her feet.

"You look right at home with every cutthroat here, Espinosa," Talon Drake said into the silence that had hovered like a cloud since they'd left the ship. He sat with Espinosa outside a tavern.

Talon had long since lost the ruthless edge that he saw now in the man known as El Condor. Espinosa's eyes looked inky against the shadow of a beard. A black scarf tied in a thin knot at the back of his head covered his dark hair. A leather baldric crossed his doublet and held the heavy cutlass at his side.

No one had bothered them since the little barmaid had brought ale. Most people who passed them on the street were about their morning business. Overhead, the dead heat of the morn slashed at the thatch roof. Down the street, Saint Paul's bell tolled. Richly ornamented with a tall spiral bell tower, the church dominated the busy avenue.

The town had not changed in the two years since Talon had

been here last and nearly died at the gallows. Still a boom-town unrivaled in most of the world, Port Royal boasted more than two thousand buildings jammed together on this narrow sand spit that sat across from the main island. Houses built on pilings driven into the sand reached out into busy Kingston harbor. Because wharfage space was too scarce for them to leave the ship docked without visible loading and unloading of cargo, the Spaniard had moored his ship far enough away that anyone trying to gain unwelcome access would be seen by those who remained aboard.

Stretching out his long legs, Espinosa lounged back in the rickety chair. Clearly, it went against the Spaniard's strict grain to hide out in some offal-ridden watering hole while Talon's men scouted for information about Sarah. Jackboots reached his knees, and he crossed one ankle over the other as he scanned the nearly empty tables around them before bring-ing his gaze back around. He'd skipped the ale completely, and watched as Talon consumed his.

"This is such an intriguing lifestyle." His voice was flat. "I understand how you've enjoyed it for so many years."

Talon sat back. "Before we leave, maybe I'll show you where the infamous Drake family used to live. Or what's left of it. Kendrick burned the place to the ground two years ago."

Something stirred in the man's eyes. He saw the Spaniard shove it aside, but it constantly lurked below the surface. Talon had recognized the emotion in Hispaniola. Vulnerabil-ity in a man of El Condor's repute had caught Talon off guard and, in the end, kept him from making war on a man who clearly loved his young sister.

Talon knew enough from Marcus to understand the choices Espinosa had made in his life. He also knew what a man could become to hide that weakness from the world. But El Condor possessed something else that just might save him in the end. Or kill him.

"You have a heart, Espinosa," Talon said, eyeing him care-fully. "Small as it may be. I never knew that about you. No wonder Marcus respects you, and my sister . . ."

At the thought of Sarah, Talon cradled the pewter mug and

looked away. "Near dusk," he said. "We'll take a skiff across the bay. My men have to be allowed to get into place."

"You've done this before?"

"Aye." Talon's grin was not pleasant. "Getting into Kendrick's house is the easy part," he said, looking across the bay. His eyes fastened on the pillared residence, stark white against a cloudless sky. "Getting out of this harbor, well, that will be your job. Dealing with Kendrick is mine," he whispered. "This is something I should have dealt with long ago. To hell with the consequences."

Lifting his gaze slowly, Gabriel met the gray eyes that had suddenly lost their shroud. "And what are the consequences in killing such a man?" he asked in disgust.

"Do you really want to know?" Drake's brow lifted. "Or is this filler to pass the day away?"

Gabriel's eyes narrowed. "I want to know."

"Kendrick is my wife's half brother. Without going into detail, I will say she's the only person in the world who ever loved the man. Killing him would not have helped my cause."

"Which was?"

"To clear my name. You understand honor, Espinosa. The Drake name is not one that is mentioned in polite circles of society. Kendrick was one of the men who helped destroy that name. My mother was never a traitor to England. My father was never a pirate."

Gabriel said nothing as he listened. An indefinable tremor pulled just beneath the surface as he considered Sarah's oldest brother. They'd spoken little on the ship; now he regretted that they'd spoken at all. Realizing he could do nothing for it now, Gabriel proffered no comment about Drake's father—not when Sarah's life was at stake—and instead let the conversation die. Beside his feet, two yellow mongrels supped on scraps that had been left beneath the tables the night before.

"Kendrick's mine," Drake said, drawing Gabriel's gaze back. "Agreed, Spaniard?"

The church bell stopped tolling. Gabriel squinted against the glare up the busy street, then stood.

Talon pushed aside the ale. "Where are you going?"

"Mass."

"Saint Paul's is not Catholic."

Gabriel crossed himself. "*¡Ay de mi!* God is God. Is he not?"

The sound of voices and laughter drifted up from downstairs. Her hand poised on the banister, Sarah stopped short at the top of the stairway. A crowd had congregated in the drawing room. Gaily dressed in colorful brocades and satins, most were already well into their cups. A glance told her there were few women present. Sarah had oft heard laughter and voices at Harrison's house. Even late at night, carriages had come and gone with parties ending at dawn. It looked as if today was heading toward that boisterous end.

Besieged by a choking helplessness, Sarah turned back, then her gaze fell on the front door.

No guard stood in the entryway.

Reigning in her racing heart, Sarah glided down the staircase on black velvet slippers, her nervous maid following. Spanish mantilla lace covered Sarah's short hair. The headrail had been made for another gown, but she wore it now with the dress Gabriel had had made for her in Hispaniola. The same dress she'd been wearing when Harrison stole her off the island. In defiance, she'd packed it last night. It was a red-and-black satin mantua. Straight sleeves finished with cuffs above the elbow and lace ruffles dipped to her wrist. A decorated stomacher extended over an embroidered and fringed underskirt. Sarah felt every bit the Spanish doña as she paused on the bottom stair.

Ten steps would take her to the front door.

"My dear—" A thin man moved into the entryway and checked her abruptly. He extended his hand in courtly grace. His pale blue gaze went over her speculatively. "Harrison said that you were a beauty. Now I understand why he's been keeping you to himself."

He escorted her to the drawing room, but she stopped in the doorway. The crowd and the noise disconcerted her. Near the window, Harrison's head snapped up. He took in her attire. Alarm briefly skittered through her stomach at the look that grew in his eyes.

"Bloody hell, Sarah," he hissed when he'd reached her.

He'd never so much as raised his voice at her before. Taking her arm, Harrison yanked her stumbling out of the draw-ing room. "What are you doing dressed like some Spanish harlot?"

Over her shoulder, she glimpsed all eyes appraising her. Sarah felt something that she could not explain in their gazes. A shudder went over her. "Who are these people?" She held the stair rail. "Men on the vice-admiralty board and their wives?"

"The admiralty board?" He quietly laughed at her, and she cursed her hands for trembling in front of him. "These are my closest friends. You will treat them accordingly or, by God, you'll answer to me. In front of everyone here if need be." The floor beneath her feet was polished to lustre. Everything around her was so clean, so out of place, with the presence of those people. "Now get upstairs and remove those offensive rags before I rip them off you here and now!"

"Nonsense, Harrison, my boy." An older gent joined them. A monocle went to his eyes as he snaked his gaze over her. "We'll save that for later, shan't we?"

Sarah fully understood the man's remark, and the coarse-ness of his laughter made her draw back. She looked askance at Harrison.

"I want to go back upstairs."

"Hear that, Harrison? Your bride is anxious. Bring her in here. It's about time you let us meet this newest addition to our group."

Terror suddenly struck her cold with panic. She knew with dawning horror that no amount of bravado could make her continue with this farce today. She would not go into that room with those strangers. She would not lie with Harrison Kendrick as his wife!

He could beat her and she'd claw his other eye out—even if they hanged her for the deed.

Sarah ripped her arm from Harrison's grasp, rending her sleeve. "I am *not* his bride! I will never be his bride!"

Harrison wasn't quick enough to grab her.

Without giving a thought that she had nowhere to run, Sarah flew out the door and down the wooden stairs, her dress belling around her legs with her maddened flight. Her only thought was to escape. Instead, she hit a crowd of people gathered in front of the church, knocked against a water cart, and tumbled headlong into the street. The breath left her lungs in a *whoosh*. Perhaps had she not starved herself, she'd have had more strength to fight.

Strong hands enfolded her upper arms and pulled her up. Dazed, she tried to focus. The busy street swam in sickening currents. Men dressed in fine doublets and fancy buckle shoes hurried past her. Down the street, children tossed a ball. Harrison stood half-poised on the bottom step of his town house a few feet away, his eyes widened in shock. Slowly, her hand went to her cropped hair, and she gained a moment of satisfaction to know that she had won some small victory against him before she realized that he wasn't looking at her.

Her back pressed to the chest of the man who held her, she felt capable hands tighten on her arm a moment before he spun her around to face him. Thick lashes framed the ebony fire searching her gaze.

"Chica?" His rasp mingled with disbelief.

Her eyes sprang wide as an almost deathly silence gripped the gathering crowd. Her knees nearly folded.

Gabriel!

Here!

For the barest moment, the seconds froze into a single shared heartbeat.

Her gaze tracing the shaded contours that separated flesh from fantasy, she clutched the loose shirt beneath his sleeveless jerkin. His skin was warm and alive. His heartbeat strong. Black beard stubble darkened the curve of his masculine jaw. He was dangerously handsome, with dark brows and a full mouth that had once borne light from the shadows of her mind and carved her imagination with his kiss.

And he was here!

Here in Port Royal!

"Espinosa." Harrison stepped into the street. "How good to see you again, El Condor," he said loudly with clear purpose.

Sarah tightened her grip on his shirt. A thousand hungry mongrels could not have torn her fingers from him.

Gabriel's eyes lifted from her ashen face and narrowed ominously. "I cannot say that I return the sentiment, you bastard."

"Get your bloody hands off my bride."

The words momentarily betrayed Gabriel's restraint. She felt his muscles bunch beneath her palm.

"Legally wed, Espinosa. Last night. Tell him, love."

Alarm racing over her in suffocating waves, Sarah straightened her slim shoulders, raised her gaze, and looked into Gabriel's face.

"Can you run, Spaniard?" She recognized Talon's low voice and her heart caught anew. Her brother stood out of her line of vision, just behind Gabriel to his right.

No one appeared anxious to interfere.

The circle widened and suddenly opened beside them.

Then she was running. Being pulled by Gabriel as Talon paved the path ahead. Her feet pumped over the street, leaping sidewalks, dodging people. A call went up behind them. Shots were fired. Sarah screamed and stumbled as a ball passed within a hairbreadth of her ear. A horse reared, sending melons rolling over the street. Her skirts dragged against her but somehow she hopped through the melee.

With running steps dogging them, Gabriel tightened his grip and pulled her around the corner of a building into a crowded alley. They tore through lines of clothes, scattering breeches and shirts everywhere. With raised fists, women shouted at them as they passed.

"Can't . . . breathe . . ."

Blackness shadowed the edge of her vision and she stumbled. Talon was beside her then. Barely conscious except of Gabriel's heart beating against her cheek, she was aware that her brother sliced her skirts up to her knees. The laces of her corset followed, and air filled her lungs in huge gulps.

Scattered voices sounded from around the corner. Gabriel lifted her and flung her atop the brick wall that divided the cesspool puddles at her feet from the marketplace. Following behind her, Gabriel and Talon leaped the wall, pulling her along again. They ducked into another alley. Houses and shops were built nearly on top of one another. Gabriel's body pressed hers against the building at her back. Wood dug into her flesh where Talon had cut her bodice to get to her stays. She tried to still her ragged breathing.

Then Gabriel was kissing her, breathing for her, and she

was returning his touch with equal ferocity. She stood on her toes, feeling the weeks melt away in his embrace. God in heaven, but he felt good.

He pulled back. "You can see!"

"*Sí,*" she answered in Spanish, because he'd spoken to her in his tongue. "Not so well, but good enough to see you."

And unexpectedly she laughed, because he was really here!

Staring down at her incredulously, he kissed her again. A black-gloved hand went to her hair. One hand still held his cutlass. "I have been very worried, *chica.*"

He started to say something else when he suddenly tipped her chin sideways. His gaze slowly moving back to hers, his expression closed before her eyes. The laughter died in her throat.

Her hand went to the place on her neck Harrison had marked with his mouth that morning. With the cloak of her hair gone, Sarah suddenly felt exposed inside and out. Shame welled that Gabriel would see that mark on her.

The color fading from her face, nothing could have prepared her for the surge of horror suddenly overwhelming her. The realization that she was not married to Gabriel struck her cold, and without the opium-induced antipathy of the last few weeks, she could no longer hold her hysteria at bay. She'd been so sure of the path in her fight against Harrison, so determined that he'd not claim one ounce of her soul, that she'd managed to lose the one thing that mattered.

Gabriel's mouth moved over her ear. "Tell me it isn't true, *chica.*" His tone was acid. "Tell me you didn't marry that worm. That you didn't—"

Talon turned from where he stood beside the corner of the building. "I understand that you two have much to discuss, but now is not the time." The chase seemed to have faded to another street.

Still looking down at her, Gabriel stepped away.

Sarah found her arms filled with clothes. "I took these from the lines," her brother said, lifting her clouded gaze. "I couldn't take measurements. But they're better than what you're wearing."

Talon's gray eyes were stark in the shadows of the building as his gaze encompassed her with infinite tenderness. Her heart caved beneath the compassion she glimpsed there. Her brother was so much more than the young twenty-something man she remembered as a child who'd forged his destiny on the seas.

He was her family.

Aware of Gabriel watching them, her absolute failure, and the danger surrounding them, she moved into his welcome arms. One hand held a cutlass, but his other arm wrapped her to him. "Are you all right, Sarah?" he asked softly.

"You're really here!"

"Aye. Since this morning." His mouth twisted wryly. "But we have to separate." Talon said the words to her but spoke to Gabriel, who remained unmoving as he watched her. "They'll be looking for two men and a woman. We have a better chance to survive apart."

"Kendrick will eventually find my ship." Dismissing her, Gabriel looked at Talon now. "There's no wind; we can't get out of this bay."

"If they catch us here, you and I will be hanged before dusk, Spaniard."

"You have a strange notion of survival, pirate, with three forts and two batteries staring down at us from our bow to stern."

Talon held Gabriel's gaze. "I'm finished running. Take her." He looked at her. "I'll see you back at the ship."

"No, *amigo*," Gabriel said. "She belongs with you."

Talon snapped around. The tip of Gabriel's cutlass went to his throat, stopping him cold. "I never liked your plan anyway, Drake."

"You don't know this town!"

Gabriel backed him into the alley. "But you know these waters better than I do. If the wind rises, get the ship out in a hurry."

Sarah bounced her gaze between them in disbelief. A black silk scarf framed Talon's face and heightened the predatory stillness in his expression. Sarah was struck by how much his mannerisms resembled Gabriel. Both moved with the solid ease of a hunter, and in her brother's eyes, she read the same unspoken resolve she saw in Gabriel's.

"What are you doing, Gabriel?"

"Sorry, *chica*. This is the way it has to be."

And with the sweep of his foot, he knocked Talon's feet out from beneath him, sending him flat against the litter-strewn ground. Gabriel raised his cutlass in salute. "If you can get out before I return, do so."

His gaze clinging for a heartbeat to hers, Gabriel turned on his heel and walked from the alley.

"Goddamn it, Sarah. I don't need you poking at me!"

"You didn't tell anyone that you'd gotten shot!"

"Do you think that Spaniard would have laid me gently on the ground if I had?"

Sarah tightened the bandage that she'd made from her pet-ticoat. "Don't ask me again to leave you. Because I won't."

She was so scared, she wanted to shake her brother. Finally climbing to her feet, she dusted off her hands. "You need stitches," she announced. "The ball went through the flesh just above your hip. You've lost a lot of blood."

"Aye," he groaned. "That happens a lot when I'm here."

Sarah's gaze swept over the sundry scars that marked his chest and arms. "How have you lived so long?"

She dropped against the wall of the sandstone building where they'd stopped earlier to rest. A green awning shaded the sunbaked ground. Her feet were bare and caked in dirt. She wore a wide-brimmed straw hat and breeches that proba-bly crawled with vermin. Talon had changed as well, and looked more docile in a sleeveless vest and baggy skirt breeches than he had in his black warrior garb. His heavy cut-lass lay between them.

Offering her their last banana, he subsided against the wall next to her. The *Felicity* sat moored near the channel, unmov-ing beneath the hot, merciless sunset. No hint of a breeze swept the water. Down the wharf, militiamen had started searching ships.

"Will he be all right?" she asked.

"That Spaniard can take care of himself. Worry about how we're going to get out of this harbor alive."

"Do you think . . . he'll kill Harrison?"

Talon looked down at her; her hands folded in her lap. She inhaled a ragged breath and straightened.

"What happened, Sarah?" Talon asked after a while. "I got the news that Espinosa killed Father Henri. My house on Martinique has been destroyed. And look at you." He tipped her chin, examining her as if she were a horse on the block. "You can see?"

Sighing, she buried her forehead in the heels of her filthy hands and tried not to think about Gabriel somewhere in the city.

Then she told Talon about her memories. She told him about Gabriel coming to Martinique to see his sister and everything that had followed. Her eyes swam with tears when she spoke about Father Henri. They talked a little more, and Talon told her about Marcus's new son. "Don Gabriel's daughter is with them now," he said.

Talon's hand, brown, long-fingered, and infinitely gentle, covered hers. The security of that touch reminded her of Gabriel. "I thought he was going to Spain," she said. That she might actually be married to Kendrick filled her with sick despair. "I thought . . . did Gabriel ever mention anything about our marriage?"

"The man isn't sociable, Sarah," he said flatly. "If he said twelve words to any Englishman on board, it was to give an order. Frankly, I'm impressed I've been so patient with the bastard."

Sarah narrowed her eyes. "Gabriel is the most wonderful and generous man I know. Perhaps you haven't tried hard enough."

Talon regarded her with raised brows; then, deciding withdrawal the better part of valor, he leaned his head against the building and let the silence draw out between them. A lizard scurried in the sand.

Shading her eyes against the low sunlight, Sarah watched Gabriel's ship and gathered her composure. Aware of the futility of reasoning out anything now, she abandoned the conversation, too. Having visualized Gabriel gone forever from her life, to have him back now lent new purpose to her heart. In her mind, she could take a thousand forced vows; it wouldn't change the one she'd spoken first.

Then her gaze went to the small fishing boats lined up on the beach. Militiamen were coalescing there, walking from man to man, asking questions. "Perhaps you can trade your sword for a boat."

She paused when her gaze caught one of the fishermen pointing in their direction. "Talon?"

"Aye," he said. "I see."

Sarah looked around the corner of the building where people milled in the crowded market. Sentries stood guard everywhere.

Even if Talon could run in his condition, there was no place left to go.

Chapter Eighteen

Harrison stared at the knife in his hand. Candlelight blinked off the edge of the blade. Her hair lay over the polished mahogany, velvet skeins of light that wrapped his numbed senses. He'd long ago dismissed his servants and let the opium embrace him.

Tonight, Sarah would learn that she should never have betrayed him and run away. That she should not have cut her hair and thought to trick him out of the pleasure of ever touching it again.

Wearing only a loose shirt and breeches, Harrison sat at the end of the long dining table. A score of burning candles baked him. The windows and curtains were closed.

The knife slid over his forearm. Twice. Three times.

He would have to kill her now. She gave him no choice, and he despised her for that. His men would catch her and bring her here.

Then he would cut her throat.

Blood snaked down the flesh of his forearm and over his fingers. He'd wanted to feel something. Regret. Anger. Pain.

Anticipation had tricked him earlier. He thought he'd heard noise outside. But not now. He lifted his gaze and knew he'd not been mistaken. Gabriel Espinosa stood framed in the wooden arch of the doorway, pistol in hand, his dark eyes settled with purpose on Harrison's face.

"You are a coward, Kendrick. You hide behind a drug like a child hides behind her mamma's skirts."

"Perhaps we are both cowards. You have your way of facing the world. I have mine. Inside we are the same."

The heavy pistol in Espinosa's hand rose.

Harrison almost flinched. Fingers reached into the cavity of his chest and grabbed his heart, squeezing tight. He could hear the rasp that lodged somewhere in his throat, and he caught the scent of fear.

By God, he was afraid!

Something inside him had escaped. Something he'd tamped down for twelve long years that had locked the man inside and let the monster out.

"You never needed anything to take away the memories, Espinosa? Nothing to guard your dreams while you slept at night?"

Something in the query touched the Spaniard and made him hesitate.

"You can't do it." Harrison nodded to the pistol in Gabriel's hand. "You won't kill me in cold blood. Men of honor are handicapped with a conscience. You should have sent Drake. Murdering Sarah's husband might look a lot like the work of a jealous lover. But then who understands the beast better than I?" Laughing, he sat back in the chair. "Did she tell you about us?" The bloody knife went to the table. "Did she tell you that she'd lain with me?"

His other hand remained out of sight on his thigh. A loaded pistol sat in his lap, where it had been primed all night. With Drake and Espinosa both loose in Port Royal, he'd known one of them would come tonight.

And he'd waited.

Hoping the Spaniard would be the one to die.

Lacking only a golden halo and wings to complete the painting, Gabriel Espinosa looked like a dark angel sent from God. Blaring trumpets hailed his presence; Harrison heard them ringing in his head before he realized the blasted church bells across the square had started again. The man standing before him was an enigmatic son of a bitch, though quite beautiful in a masculine sort of way. He could see why Sarah was attracted to him.

Harrison wrapped his fist around the bone handle of the

pistol. He swung it up. He would kill El Condor. The man had grown soft.

Sarah had ruined him, too.

But Gabriel fired a split second before Harrison.

Gabriel wound his way through the maze of backwater streets to the harbor. As he stood at the water's edge, his gaze went over the glassy onyx surface until he pinpointed his ship lumbering at her anchor. Throwing off his sword, he removed his boots. Carrying those in his baldric, he waded into the sea and started swimming. Impotent rage fueled his arms as they sliced through the glassy surface with ease. Gabriel had hesitated the briefest of seconds back there, long enough to nearly die. He was shaken.

Less than a half hour later, Gabriel reached the ship, barely winded as he scaled the wall of mizzen chains and climbed over the rail to startle the cranky bell watch. Berto hurried from the quarterdeck before Gabriel could be shot as an intruder.

Gabriel cut him off before he could speak. "Has Drake returned?"

His mood was so murderous, Berto was clearly confused as to what had happened and why Gabriel should be back alone.

"I thought he was with you, Don Gabriel."

Gabriel told him the plans had changed and that Sarah had been found. His gaze took in the velvet sky and morass of stars. A breeze touched his face. "*Sí*, this is the first hint of wind we've had all day," Berto agreed in response to the expression on Gabriel's face.

"Have Drake's men made contact yet?"

"No, *Capitán*."

"I'll be in my cabin."

He shoved open the door. Sarah was with Drake, so Gabriel didn't allow himself to worry. At least that was what he told himself.

Tearing the scarf from his head, he tossed it beside his trunk. Hair fell over his eyes. He shoved the strands off his face and walked into the stern gallery. For a long moment he stared out at the open sea. Then he leaned his fists against the thick glass.

Had there ever been a time that he hadn't had any cares? That he hadn't been fighting a war on the sea, in his heart, or his soul? That respect and honor hadn't been a cause that he would die for—or worse, one that he hadn't killed for to achieve? Gabriel turned sick at the thought. Had he sunk to the same sordid depths of a monster like Kendrick?

Suddenly, it was too much effort to think or breathe or question the morality of what he had done tonight. The rage inside would not dissipate. It clenched his chest in agonizing waves.

Slowly, he became aware of the deck moving beneath his feet. The breath of wind had increased outside and wound through the rigging so that the ship leaned slightly to port. He needed to move the *Felicity* before daylight trapped them beneath the guns of Fort Charles.

But he couldn't leave Sarah. Even at the risk to the lives of his men.

He spun back into the room.

Sí, that had been his whole problem since he'd met her. He hadn't behaved rationally. No wonder those who knew him thought him mad. He was a lunatic.

Gabriel had pinpointed the source of his rage earlier and recognized it now for what it was: jealousy, possessiveness, the kind of primitive madness that tore at the fabric of a man's soul. He felt betrayed by her love for her brother and the fact that she'd turned to Drake in that alley rather than him in her need. And most of all he felt dishonored by what Kendrick had done to her.

Gabriel fought the illogic of his emotions. But it didn't matter whether or not the man had held a knife to her throat. He'd touched her, done things to her, and the mere thought of Kendrick's hands on Sarah sent him over the edge, where he floundered helplessly.

And it was that helplessness that had become the fatal flaw in his character. From the very beginning, he'd been seized by his need to protect her, mercilessly driven to conquer her demons as if some instinct for self-preservation drove him. In his mind, saving Sarah had been akin to saving himself. And in that respect, he knew with sudden disgust, he'd been no different than Kendrick.

But clearly, Sarah Drake had never needed anyone to save her. She had survived the past months more intact than he had. While he'd been stone cold with dread, she'd laughed after the chase landed them in that alley. And it galled his pride because he'd lost too damn much to something he didn't understand, when she'd done naught but grow and blossom until she'd become a threat to his very existence.

His eyes narrowed.

At once, Gabriel made the decision to move the ship. But Drake had piloted the *Felicity* into the harbor. Gabriel had no charts. Taking soundings worked, but he had to know of another place to anchor the ship away from Port Royal's cannons. Turning a circle in his room, he searched the shadows, finally halting when his gaze found Sarah's leather sea chest shoved long ago into the corner of his cabin and left on board.

The chest had contained nothing but moldy family relics, and he'd not brought it on shore in Hispaniola. There had never been a need, when he'd never intended that she'd live there for long. But it did hold old sea charts that had once belonged to her father: sea charts that would mark the shoals and landings around Jamaica. Hardly something England would wish to fall into Spain's hands, he thought with savage irony.

Jarring loose the lock, Gabriel flung open the lid.

Maybe it was fate that had prompted him to open the chest: ghosts that beckoned him forward. His hands stilled.

A Bible lay atop the papers inside.

Sarah's family Bible.

They were looking for a Bible, Don Gabriel, his housekeeper had said. *¡Por Dios! Kendrick would not be looking for a Bible!*

Gabriel had seen this book in Martinique and now remembered Father Henri's insistence that Sarah take the Bible. Then he recalled the conversation that he'd walked into at the rectory after the French troops had arrived.

I know Drake keeps it here.

The statement had been brief and spoken in French. Until now, Gabriel had not connected those words to anything that made any sense. Had the man who'd spoken those words that day in Martinique referred to this book?

Golden scrolls rimmed each fragile page, now cracked and worn by age. He'd had this Bible with him the whole time.

Lifting the heavy book, he carried it to his desk where moonlight plundered the shadows. The leather cover was thick in his grasp. Perhaps it was the distaste of touching something so intimately precious to a family that he'd helped to destroy—or maybe it was because Father Henri had intended him to have this book all along—but Gabriel felt a chill go over him.

It was sometime later when voices in the corridor outside the door lifted his head.

Gabriel did not greet Sarah as she helped Talon into the second stern cabin just below the quarterdeck stairs. It was nearly dawn and she was exhausted, ragged, and hungry. After hiding in filthy alleys and two narrow escapes, she'd finally managed to trade Talon's fine cutlass to secure a small boat.

"Is everyone on board now?" she heard Talon ask Berto. Her brother was in worse shape than she.

"No, Captain Drake."

"Christ . . ."

Movement behind Sarah turned her. Gabriel stood in the doorway. His dark liquid gaze held uncertain anger. He wore different clothes from those she'd seen him in that afternoon, but the expensive snowy white shirt with flared sleeves and a silk waistcoat did nothing to tame his strength. His countenance shadowed by black stubble made him look ruthless, the very embodiment of his reputation. She could feel the restraint in his stance, the hostility in his face. "How many of Drake's men are still out?" he asked Berto.

"The whole landing party. No one has returned."

Gabriel was silent as he seemed to assess Talon. "What happened to you?"

Talon's gaze shifted from Berto to Gabriel, who remained like stone. "I stepped in the way of musket fire this afternoon during our escape. Kendrick's men are all over Port Royal. It took us a while to secure a boat."

"You didn't say anything?"

"Would it have mattered?"

Sarah felt insignificant in her breeches and bare feet standing between both men who towered over her. She wanted desperately to go to Gabriel but something in his posture stopped her cold. She needed to get Talon to bed, but he was no more accommodating.

"What are you going to do about my men?" Talon said impatiently, changing the subject back. "Aye, twenty *Englishmen*, Spaniard."

An arched brow confronted Talon's words. "You have a heart, Drake." His voice seemed to smile even as it taunted with self-mockery. "I didn't know that about you." Their gazes held an instant before Gabriel turned back to Berto. "How many men have we on board?"

"Nearly a hundred, *Capitán*. Almost a full crew. We could be out of the harbor before they fired the first cannon shot."

Gabriel looked at Sarah, then back at her brother, his expression unreadable behind the mask that covered his eyes. "We'll give them until dawn and hope the militia in Port Royal are too busy handling drunks to care about us. Business as usual, Berto," he said.

Sarah listened to Berto's heavy footsteps travel up the stairs to the deck. Holding Gabriel's gaze, she felt her heart contract. The harshness in his eyes hid so much vulnerability, she was suddenly afraid to ask the question that lay between them. But Gabriel's presence on this ship told her in more than words that Harrison was dead. His eyes told her other things, too. Blinking back the rush of tears, she was suddenly staring at an empty doorway as he turned and followed Berto on deck.

With shaking hands, Sarah cleaned Talon's wound, thankful that the gash in his side was small. She stitched the taut flesh and left him sleeping. Then dawn came, and the wind died in the heavy heat that arrived with the sunlight. On deck, she heard Gabriel's voice, followed by the deck pump and the footsteps of men as they went about their daily duties. Too exhausted to do anything more than wash her filthy feet, she wanted to cry. It had been her brother's unexpected words that lent some ease to her plight. "Give him time," he'd said. "He'll come around when he's ready to talk." But the past month—the past twenty-four hours—had stretched her nerves. She didn't understand what had happened to Gabriel.

Sarah finally opened the door to his cabin. Sunlight poured through the crystalline windows that stretched the back of a room richly appointed with a desk and thick Turkish carpet. Turning in a slow circle, she absorbed everything as she let her gaze go over the familiar cabin for the first time. Polished mahogany formed the bulkheads, the floor, and archway that separated the sleeping area from the main room. Bookcases stood against the wall to her right. Her hands went at once to the beautiful dolls strewn there and she pressed each to her cheek as if they welcomed her home.

She sat on the edge of the bunk. Gabriel's presence filled her senses. Something bumped her leg, and she cried aloud when her gaze landed on Dog. Gabriel had brought her cat!

She caught Dog in her arms. That was as far as she got before the flood of tears overtook her. She sobbed quietly against his intimate softness. Then, curling into a tight ball, she lay down and wept, letting the years fall away in a river of grief that suddenly seemed to overwhelm after the last month of keeping it all bottled tightly inside. She wept for the little girl she'd been. For a mother and father who'd loved her, and the destruction of something beautiful and sacred. She thought of her years at the mission and her dearest friend who had married Talon. Father Henri had blessed her years with his strength and taught her much about survival.

Finally, her eyes searched the shadows and crevices that stretched beyond this room and deep into her heart. And the whole world suddenly seemed bigger and brighter with windows and doors and beautiful rainbows that beckoned exploration.

She could see! And that counted for a lot.

At last, she fell asleep. When Sarah awakened, a cool breeze stretched across the room. It was dark outside, and a bowl of water sloshed next to a tray of food that sat on the table. The ship was moving at a brisk pace. With the wind in her sails, the *Felicity* canted to starboard, and Sarah rushed to the window to look out.

Port Royal, with its busy streets, sandstone houses, and

memories of Harrison, lay somewhere in the darkness behind her.

At a sound of movement in the room, a flutter started in Sarah's chest. Sensing Gabriel's presence, she scanned the shadows. He leaned against the solid bulkhead, arms folded across his chest. She'd passed him when she'd run into the gallery. Clearly, he'd been there awhile, looking out the windows.

They stood quite still, and she was aware of an odd breathlessness. She couldn't see his face but could feel his eyes on her. "Are you all right?" he finally asked.

Her hands went to the tattered waist of her canvas breeches. "You shouldn't have let me sleep so long."

"Obviously you were in need." He shoved off the wall to stand beside her. "Your brother awoke once when his crew came back on board. We left Port Royal almost five hours ago."

He smelled of citrus. He'd shaved, and her gaze went over the smooth curve of his jaw to touch the blue-black hair that swept his brow. Beside him, she felt unkempt. Her hair was ugly. She dropped her gaze to her toes. "Not much has changed in our favor, has it?" She wiggled her toes. "Since the last time I was on board this ship."

"No, *chica*."

"I'm still in need of attire." She forced herself to laugh.

"You cut your hair."

Her hand went to the blunt thickness that stopped short of her chin. Walking to the table, she snatched up the neatly folded rag lying there and dipped it into the basin. "I need to wash what I'm wearing." She applied the wet cloth to her face and scrubbed her teeth. "Perhaps you wouldn't mind loaning me a shirt."

"What happened, Sarah?"

Her eyes snapped up. "He liked my hair, so I cut it. I'm glad I did, too," she went on, eager to dispel the notion that he should feel sorry for her. "I happen to like it short. It's . . . liberating."

Sarah heard him go to his chest. A moment later one of his costly silk shirts dropped onto the table beside the water bowl.

"I wasn't thinking when I left Hispaniola." He leaned a

shoulder against the archway separating the rooms. "But then I have not been in my right mind since I met you, *chica*. That is obvious to all."

She dropped the rag in the bowl. "What mind is that, Gabriel? The one in your heart or the other one below your belt? Or are you now confusing the two because you don't know what to say to me? You're wondering if another man has been where you've been, and that smacks at your Spanish honor." Something dangerous flashed in his dark eyes, awakening trepidation in her. "And I know that you . . . that you went after Harrison Kendrick because of me. You're hurting as much as I am," she whispered, "and you don't know how to grapple with such rogue emotions in your life."

"I'm taking you to New Providence," he said, ignoring her words. "Christina is awaiting me there." His gaze moved to touch the crumpled bed where she'd slept. "For reasons other than the fact you and I are not married, it's best that I stay away from this room."

As the full breadth of his statement caught her, a stab of pain cut through her so deeply, Sarah thought she might be physically sick.

Everything Father Antonio had told her was true! Their marriage had never been valid.

"You've saved the erring princess, so now you're free to leave? Is that it? Conscience clear?"

His eyes narrowed darkly. "*Por Dios* . . . no."

"You knew our vows might not be legal when you married me on Martinique, didn't you?"

His silence, so barren of emotion, told her he had.

She was trembling. She felt young and foolish, betrayed by him, because he'd known the legalities and she'd been too naïve to understand why he'd given in so easily to Father Henri. "I refuse to believe that you never loved me, Gabriel."

"Jesu . . ." He shoved away from the wall. "Love has little to do with anything in my life."

"Only because you choose to keep it out now."

"I don't *have* a choice!"

"In truth, you never needed an annulment . . . yet you went to Father Antonio. Why?" Dawning understanding laced her rasp and added immeasurably to her sudden determination.

"Because you *wanted* to stay married!" she answered for him, stepping beneath the arch into the main room. "You didn't want to take a chance that the marriage could be dissolved, especially if there were children. Now you're angry because I preferred to salvage my life over my honor."

Gabriel muttered something in disgust and turned to leave.

"Don't you *dare* turn away when I'm talking to you!"

Icy silence slapped her. He turned slowly to face her.

"We have issues that need to be discussed. But first, you will listen to every word I have to say, Gabriel."

Dark fury emanated from his eyes. "What words are those, *chica*?"

Her chest tightened. Her throat closed around her breath, until each furious heartbeat throbbed at the base of her neck. Sarah stopped in front of him, toe to toe, and jabbed an impressive finger at his chest. "I will *not* allow you to walk out of here thinking I'm not good enough for you, Mister Don Gabriel Cristobel de Espinosa y Ramírez, former *Almirante* of New Spain's treasure fleet, the celebrated El Condor, Marqués de Villena, a Knight of Calatrava, and a score of other titles I haven't memorized. All of which the whole world eagerly embraces. Who are you, Gabriel? Really? But a man."

"*Sí*"—he pressed her backward into the room—"I am a man, *chica*. And you have taken that part of me and crushed it in your fist. Do you know what I've gone through because of you? Have you any idea what I feel, knowing . . ."

"Knowing what?"

"You married him, Sarah. He had his hands on you. His dirty, filthy, murdering hands on your body. And you let him *touch* you."

Violence surged from deep inside her. Furious, raw violence. She swung her palm but he caught her wrist before she could land the blow. In a rage, she swung her other hand, but he caught that one, too. His eyes pierced hers in incredulity. But before he could question her fury, she shoved against his grip and the backs of his thighs hit the rim of his desk.

"Father Antonio said you were gone. He took Christina away from me. Then Kendrick came for me. My only thought was to survive any way I could. Do you know how I did that?" She continued to push against him until she stood between his legs. "I kept thinking of you. In my heart, I am married to you, Gabriel. I will always be married to you! So don't you *dare* presume to know what I went through or what I should have done, and never tell me that you are ashamed of me!"

He still held her hands away from her, but it made no difference as she leaned into him, her mouth a whisper against his. "I haven't been with another man except for you. And I won't let you throw away what we had because of your misplaced pride. Not when I love you so much that the very thought of losing you again will surely kill me."

She raised her leg and, climbing onto his lap, edged him flat against the desk until she straddled his hips. He still held her wrists, giving nothing back, yet unable to pull away as she pressed his hands into the cool, smooth wood and mingled her breath with his.

"You're a rock. An arrogant, snobbish rock who defies anyone to find anything soft inside you."

"*¡Ay yi*" His eyes went over her short crop of blond hair that seductively framed her piquant features, then moved to her full mouth. "There is nothing soft about me."

She kissed him.

Inexplicable heat pierced his loins. She shattered his façade. He'd welcomed the inherent fatalism of his plight and character earlier, but now her lips became a brand on his heart, fire in his soul, and he opened his mouth to join his tongue to hers. She was hungry but so was he and he devoured her lips, foraging her mouth, delving still deeper until naught but a savage groan answered her back.

When she pushed away, he let his gaze dip to her wet and swollen lips before rising slowly. "You . . . leave me speechless, *chica*."

Her eyes flashed with energy as she flattened his hands to the desk. He was aware of the way she spilled out of her shirt as she leaned over him. "Why do people call you the Vulture? Are you really as bad as they say you are?"

Kissing him again, she sucked the breath out of any answer he might have given her. Getting loose of his hands, she grabbed both sides of his shirt and pulled the cloth from his tight breeches. Her cool palms roamed the muscled curvature of his chest as if he were a banquet to her fingertips.

"Are you so terrible, Gabriel?"

Wrapping her to him, he sat up. *"Sí, chica."*

He was a bastard and every other perfidious name he could call himself. There was nothing noble or honorable in taking her here on this desk, in this room, anywhere for that matter.

Yet he would have her.

Because he needed her more than he needed to breathe.

Deprived of her for too long, his mouth was hot and greedy on hers. With one arm beneath her shirt, he stripped the cloth over her head. He took the weight of her breasts in his hands, then clasped his hands around her small waist, flicking his tongue over each nipple. She arched her back, offering him more, intensifying the heated rush that shuddered violently through his restraint.

"Am I a pearl then to be plucked?" he heard her rasp, and thought he'd heard wrong. "A worthy jewel for El Condor?"

He pulled back, dazed, and barely clung to the tone in her voice. "What are you talking about?"

"Was I ever your vengeance against my family? Or anyone else?"

His eyes narrowed, impatient with her interrogation.

"Did you know what happened to my mother?"

The tension inside tightened. At once, he stilled. The issues she had spoken of were now upon him. Kendrick had been filling her head, and Gabriel looked into her sleepy silver eyes, knowing that she must have listened to everything, lies and truths. But he didn't see anger in her gaze, only a need to understand what she'd been told. And a willingness to believe whatever he told her.

He raked a palm over her head. *"Sí,* I knew," he answered. She slumped into his lap. "When did you find out?"

"The night Kendrick gave me the poison. It was very amusing for him, feeding me his sins, knowing that I would die before I could get back to you."

"You knew him well? That's why you met with him that night."

"Kendrick is one of the acquaintances in my life that I wish I'd never made. But I did. He fed me information about British transports. Mostly he gave me the names of specific privateer or pirate ships in port. He knew the names of those

I sought. I paid him well for his services. In addition, I agreed not to attack his family's fleet of ships as long as they stayed out of Spanish waters."

"That's how you captured my brothers. You were given a tip?"

"I was waiting when they left Port Royal. Henry Morgan was going to send them back to England. They would have been freed."

"Would that have been so horrible?" she whispered.

"I was twenty years old, Sarah. Full of vengeance that wouldn't let go. Your father helped destroy my home when he joined Henry Morgan's raid in Puerto Bello." He looked into her face, deep into her probing eyes. "He killed my father, Sarah."

She paled. "I . . . I didn't know."

"I was a child when I watched Henry Morgan's men take away my life. Later, I learned the name of almost every captain who sailed with him that day. I learned the names of others involved as well."

"And spent your life hunting them all down. But my brothers never did anything to you."

"They'd been convicted of piracy in your English courts. That was enough for me at the time."

"And now?"

He touched his mouth to the salty curve of her neck. "There are things inside a man that no amount of victory, gold, or fame can ever mask." He raised his face. "Yet—" He could no longer harness the surge of his emotions. "Because of what I've achieved, my daughter will never lack for a place in society. I would die for Spain. She is my heart and my home. It grieves me endlessly to find myself at odds with the tribunal and with the Church. But something has happened inside me. Something that I can't answer."

"Gabriel . . ." Her eyes searched his.

"I have worked for everything I have, Sarah."

She scraped her fingers into his hair and looked at him gravely. "What about your sister?" Her voice quietly broke. "Why hasn't she been excommunicated for marrying Marcus?"

"My sister is not the same."

"Because she is a woman?"

His eyes narrowed on hers. "You really don't know?"

Sarah shook her head.

"Liandra is my half sister," he said. "She . . . was born nine months after Morgan's raid on Puerto Bello. No one knows who her father was."

Sarah's eyes shimmered in moonlight. "Yet you've always accepted her as your sister."

"My mother abandoned her when she was not even Christina's age. I raised her. Of course I would not think any less of her."

Sarah leaned her head on his shoulder. Her quiet tears startled him, and he pulled her away to look into her face. "What's the matter, *chica*?" He wiped at her tears with the side of his hand. "Have I disappointed you again?"

She shook her head. "I think . . ." Cupping his jaw with her hands, she tenderly touched her mouth to his. "I think that I love you very much, Gabriel."

"*Sí, chica.* And I, you," he whispered fiercely, his mouth following the curve of her throat to capture her lips. "I think that this is our biggest problem between us."

He kissed her in a melding of lips and desire. No more words formed. The *Felicity* forged onward through the waves. The wind and darkness became a tempest inside that knew no resistance, only the languid communion of their mouths. A meeting of senses. Her arms went around his neck. He moved his thumbs across her nipples to encase her in his palms. Threading her fingers into his hair, she rose to her knees above him on the desk, forcing his face back to deepen the kiss. Deeper still, potent and hot as his body shuddered for want of her. His waistcoat came loose beneath her hands. The buttons on his shirt were no contest. Only the cravat remained.

Loosening the ties on his breeches, she whispered in his ear. "I would see you unclothed."

"*¡Ay yi!*" he groaned, sliding his hands down her spine and into her breeches over the erotic curve of her bottom. His body absorbed her silken touch, the play of her tongue against his, her hands on his breeches, and as she eased him back against the desk, he let his senses drown him. "You are very bad, *chica*."

"Am I too bold?" Her wet breath quivered over his mouth.

She evaded his hands before he could stop her from wrapping her hands around him. *"Sí,"* he said raggedly, swallowing the primal urge to guide her mouth to where her hands enfolded, "you are much too bold for a woman. Don't . . . stop."

He sat exposed to the breeze and the hot tremble of her hands.

"I wish to know everything about you," she said.

It was the ultimate in surrender he'd ever allowed himself: to be gazed at. The breeze was cool against his face. His blood hummed. All feeling faded to a single carnal throb between his legs.

Then he stood, bringing her to her feet in front of him.

Later he would take her to the bed where they could enjoy a more leisurely pace.

But not now.

He'd been so fearful of touching her. Afraid that she'd been hurt. He'd been cruel to turn away from her for even a moment.

Now all he wanted was to bury himself inside her forever. He dropped with her to the carpet. Poised above her, he moved between her thighs and looked into her beautiful eyes, their silver essence awakening a desperate hunger inside. Then he entered her, felt her living heat close around him, and everything wrong with the world ceased to matter.

Chapter Nineteen

"Christina is safe with your sister?"

"Stefan took her to New Providence on the *Dark Fury*."

With hands propped beneath their heads, Sarah and Gabriel lay facing each other, sharing the predawn darkness in quiet discourse. They'd talked for what seemed like hours, mostly about her eyesight. Sarah didn't tell him that everything wasn't perfect, though when she'd spilled the wine that night at dinner, by the look in his face, he'd guessed.

Dog was blissfully wedged between them on the bunk. Sarah watched Gabriel's fingers stroke the cat's ears, the gentle action so contrary to the hard strength of his hand, to the man who'd made warfare on the high seas an art.

Though he'd said little about how he had ended up back at Hispaniola and not on a ship to Spain as Father Antonio had said, he told her that Talon had been at the house when he'd arrived. "Your brother got to Father Antonio first. Which probably saved the man's life."

Sarah felt the scrutiny of Gabriel's gaze. His warm palm moved to Sarah's shoulder and into her hair. She awaited his anger when he realized all of this had happened because she'd been careless. "I thought myself capable of making the correct decisions," she finally said. "I'd so wanted to do what was right."

"He took advantage of you, Sarah. Of your ignorance of our customs. The Mayfest celebration has not been held at my estate since Felicity's death. Berto should have known that no one should have been allowed onto my property. And he should not have let you leave."

"Please don't punish him. He had no choice."

"Berto is young," was all Gabriel said. But his voice told her that the man would think twice before he ever made such a mistake again.

Distant voices sounded then faded on deck, reminding Sarah that they were not alone. The terror of the past few weeks still clung to her like icy fingers. "He is dead, *chica*," Gabriel whispered against her temple. No regret. No apology. Only the cold promise that Harrison Kendrick would never harm anyone again. She should feel something akin to horror, but could get no further than the memory of her mother. With her eyesight returned and her long hair gone, she had no more armor, and trembled.

"We will never speak of this again." Gabriel's whisper lifted her lashes. Was that how he forgot? "Never again, Sarah."

Her lips opened beneath the force of the utter possession of his mouth. His movement sent Dog scurrying away and he pressed her into the mattress. Warm, rough fingers twined with hers. One knee parting her thighs, he pulled back to look into her eyes, vulnerable beneath the force of his burning gaze. His inky-dark hair fell over his brows. He slid inside her, watching her, guarding her, methodically dominating her every heartbeat. Then his body no longer moved in controlled rhythm. His smoky gaze never relinquishing possession of hers, their ragged breath filled the space between their open mouths. Her heart raced, running wild with the wind and the sea that rushed in cool currents around the ship. The world ceased to be. Except for him. She shuddered and cried out his name. He was still holding her gaze when he came inside her body.

Then he lay beside her, and as the sea blushed with the first hint of dawn, he finally slept. Leaving Sarah to guard his dreams.

Gabriel didn't emerge from his cabin for days except to consult with the ship's pilot and verify their course. Something could be said for the fickle meanderings of the heart. He no longer wore his dignity on his sleeve as if it were some iron cloak to protect him from the world. Sarah had pushed through every wall he'd ever built and walked into the concealed room of his heart to touch his soul. She'd stirred him with her spirit and her hope. And her broken sobbing in Port Royal had torn him in half. He'd been on the quarterdeck when she'd gone to his cabin after nursing her brother, and he'd listened to her helpless sobs, aware that half his crew had listened, too. As angry as he'd been then, he also knew that he loved her beyond reason. Her shuddering tears had stopped by the time he'd gone to the cabin and found her asleep, her arms wrapped around her cat with wrenching tenderness.

Hearing the sound of her laughter now, he turned from his place on the forecastle to look over his shoulder. She stood next to her brother at the rail. One of Drake's men had tamed her hair with a layered cut. The wisps framed her smile and promised much to his hands in the privacy of his room. Aware of the possessive sweep of his gaze, he found his eyes sliding over the curve of her backside. He didn't like her wearing breeches, but neither did he complain when the only other choice of attirè was nothing at all. The fact that a cool silver-eyed glance from her had a way of discouraging others' errant glances amused him and lent him some ease.

"There, Excellency!" Berto said. "Two ships."

Sarah had rarely heard Gabriel's formal title used while on board, and Gabriel felt her eyes go over him.

Then, gripping the ship's rail, she turned to look out at the sea, but it became apparent that she could see nothing wedged between the water and the pewter sky. Moving to stand beside her, Gabriel handed her the glass. Their eyes touched and her gaze beneath her soft lashes smiled before she raised the brass telescope to her eye.

"They are probably from Port Royal," Drake said over Sarah's head. "English navy."

Taking Berto's glass, Gabriel climbed to the quarterdeck to the binnacle to verify the *Felicity*'s course. Having caught the trade winds only that morning, the ship lay over with the wind abeam. He looked at the ugly clouds. A squall moved toward them from the east, and the *Felicity* tilted slightly as the wind shifted.

"They're on a tack for England," Gabriel said, swinging the glass south. The *Felicity* was rising and falling on the waves. "There's another one. Looks like a mass exodus from Port Royal."

Sarah turned the glass toward the quarterdeck.

Gabriel watched her in return. They both lowered their scopes at once.

A gust of wind whipped across the deck and ruffled his hair. A secretive smile touched her lips, and the world soared higher than the masts that stretched over his head. He smiled back, brazenly aware that most of his crew watched the exchange with some dismay. That Drake watched them, too.

And Gabriel checked his mood at the sight of him.

Gabriel disliked the restlessness Drake's presence provoked in him, and the constant on-edge need to jerk Sarah away from him. He didn't understand the source except the years had not allayed the animosity between him and Sarah's eldest brother.

"Put our men on the bell watch tonight, Berto." Gabriel turned.

Berto stood beside the helmsman and they both looked up at him in bewilderment.

"We are a Spanish ship with half an English crew, *sí*?" Gabriel said. "More prudent men than I have lost their ships to pirates."

Aware that Sarah had gone to Drake's cabin to remove his sutures, Gabriel flung himself into his work on the ship.

His discomfort returned after the evening meal he'd shared with Sarah and Drake on deck. "I don't wish to go below yet." Sarah brought out Stefan's chess game and eagerly set up the pieces once the dishes had been cleared off the table. Drake took the bench opposite her. "Talon has been teaching me to play."

Excluded from their circle but unwilling to leave her, Gabriel propped a boot on the bench where Sarah sat. Personally, he'd never cared for contests, but clearly the two Drakes were cast from the same mold. She had a bloodthirsty bent to win. Conscious of a thread of pride, he glanced at Sarah's stern profile. He'd never known that about her before.

"Do they teach Spaniards how to play chess in Seville?" Drake asked, observing his dark mood with a grin.

Up to the challenge, Gabriel straddled the bench where Sarah sat. "He doesn't play." Sarah kissed him on the cheek. "So go gentle, Talon."

Gabriel suddenly wanted to tip her off the bench. His reaction stunned him, considering she'd meant the words as a kindness and not a fact of weakness. "The game belongs to Señor Delgado," he clarified. "*He's* from Seville."

"Aye, you're from near Villena," Drake observed, resetting the pieces across black and gray squares. "In the small kingdom of Valencia to be exact." His eyes smiled. "Where the legendary El Cid held out against the Moors and became a renowned Christian champion, symbol of Spain's struggles, and national hero."

Gabriel's grin was flat. "You know your Spanish history."

"You should be so enlightened, Spaniard. He too, fell just short of sainthood, I do believe."

"Talon," Sarah snapped. "You insult Gabriel."

"But then the anointed ones come from the dead and martyred," Gabriel casually returned. "With your current status in society, you'll be there before I will."

"Gabriel!"

"*¿Qué?*" Gabriel spread his hands in supplication. "What did I say?"

"How many ships *have* you sunk anyway, Gabriel?"

"It is not allowed to kill and tell, sister."

"One black frigate less than I wanted."

Sarah stood. "You are *both* acting like spoiled children."

Gabriel removed himself from the bench, but Sarah snatched away from him. "It's a wonder the two of you found me in Port Royal and didn't kill each other first. I cannot endure this competition between you. Can't I love you both?"

Gabriel narrowed his gaze on her stiff back as she strode across the deck before he rounded his attention on her brother. Though the smile that halted Gabriel reached no further than the tilt of Drake's mouth, Gabriel sensed the man's victory. Jealousy didn't goad Gabriel as much as something far more deceptive and dangerous inside. The rivalry between them stemmed from Gabriel's own misdoubts. Three years Gabriel's senior, Talon Drake was the only man he'd never defeated. Not on the sea, not in prison, and not in Sarah's heart.

From the quarterdeck, Berto said something about the wind direction and Gabriel's gaze shifted to the sky. He suddenly thought about his daughter on New Providence, Spain, and all the reasons he needed to get home. Ordering the ship on a starboard tack, he stalked down the steep stairs to his cabin.

Sarah came awake with a start. She opened her eyes to the darkness. For an instant, she could see nothing. Panic brought her up. Moonlight wavered at the edge of the bunk, and she breathed again. Movement by the window revealed Gabriel had turned and was watching her.

He wore no shirt, only a pair of black breeches. Framed by a moonbeam, his strength showed in the corded arms and shoulders that tapered down into his ribs. A sprinkling of hair disappeared below his waistband. He held a wineglass. Shadows hid his face.

Sarah's heart ached. Even as she felt the proof of his lovemaking still damp between her legs, she sensed that he was not a part of her. He was pulling away. Sarah had listened to Talon snarl only yesterday that Gabriel was an arrogant tyrant with the instincts of a jackal. She knew that they had a past, but she'd not been prepared for the depth of their aversion to each other or that somehow she might be the tinder igniting the fire in this long-standing rift.

"Why do you enjoy antagonizing my brother?" she'd asked Gabriel last night before he'd erased the question from her lips and taken her to bed. No more words. Just the finality of his possession.

"What are you afraid of?" she asked now, and by his subtle response knew that he heard her.

She realized that Gabriel's restlessness had been what had awakened her.

"Go back to sleep, Sarah. Everything is all right."

She wouldn't let his volatile unpredictability frighten her

into retreating. Tucking the sheet over her breasts, she went to stand beside him, and caught her breath when she looked outside. Reverence laced her expression as she surveyed this Neptunian world of glistening darkness. "'Tis truly beautiful, Gabriel."

She leaned forward to press her palms to the window, but in the shadows, she misjudged the distance and missed.

Gabriel was there to catch her hand and kept her from falling. Dark lashes framed his inky eyes. Eyes that touched her gently even if nothing else about him was tame. He led her hand to the glass.

"The moon is full tonight," he said.

Closing her eyes, she didn't let him pull away. "Have you ever stood on the deck of your ship and just breathed in the moonlight?"

"My men would think I'd lost my mind." His voice was flat.

"Then it matters to you what people think?" she asked, turning.

"It matters that my men respect me. I can't go around breathing in moonlight or it will seriously ruin my reputation."

Sensing his amusement, she stiffened. "It must be a burden to maintain the distance that you do, Gabriel." The ship canted slightly and she caught her hand on his arm. She didn't have the physical adeptness that Gabriel had, and it suddenly annoyed her that he should not appreciate his gifts more. "Don't you ever get lonely up there in the clouds? Perhaps that house you once wanted to build for me, you should build for yourself. How can you even abide by your own standards? I certainly can't."

His brow lifted.

"You judge people too harshly."

Anger flashed in his eyes. "Is that why you never ate with me in the dining room? Because you thought I would judge you?"

"It's only that . . . I've always wanted to make you proud. But the obstacles were never mine to hurdle. They were your expectations of the world. You set us all up to fail. I don't want Talon to be your excuse for walking away from me."

"*Por Dios.* You're impossible, Sarah." His voice flattened with exasperation. But his body relaxed. "Have I told you that yet?"

Draping her arms around his neck, she fed him a long and luxurious kiss. "There are many forms of blindness, Gabriel. Sometimes seeing means looking with your heart. There is no such thing as impossible."

For her statement, she received a hooded glance.

"We're all scared." Her hand cupped his bristly jaw to keep him from turning away. "I want my family to know you the way I do."

"I think—his corded arms went around her—"some things are better kept private, *sí?*"

"This has not been easy for Talon either."

"I hope not."

"Are you this confrontational with Marcus, too?" She shook him. "We're family, Gabriel. All of us. Including Christina."

"And I promise not to kill either of your brothers."

She raised her palms. "Oh Lord, grant me more miracles, please!"

His mouth quirked and she was aware that she had just won something momentous here. He pressed his lips to her ear. "Very well. No hitting or cutting him up into little pieces and feeding him to the sharks either."

Sarah suddenly laughed. "He said the same thing about you yesterday. Except he was more generous about which parts he'd spare. Especially since I love you."

Gabriel frowned, and she leaned into his arms. "I'd say that just about makes you friends."

"Enlighten me."

A solid *thunk* dropped Talon's gaze to the table.

He was in his cabin bent over a glass of wine when Gabriel entered. The lanthorn secured in the wall cast a sallow glow over the leather casing of the Bible. Surprise briefly registering in Drake's expression, he sat back against the bulkhead.

"Indeed?" Silver eyes flashed. As brother to brother? Pirate hunter to pirate? You want to know my excuse?"

"Don't stretch my goodwill, Drake. I'm not being benevolent. You should never have been brought to trial for piracy, but that didn't mean I would have been any more generous with your life."

"Wine?" Drake offered, reaching beneath the table and presenting Gabriel with his finest bottle of Madeira. "From your personal stores. Had I known you'd make a nocturnal visit, I'd have stolen another glass."

With a ghost of a smile, Gabriel eased onto the bench across from Drake. "You're too kind . . . my lord."

Drake flipped open the front cover of the Bible. Inside the satin casing were letters of marque for Talon Drake and his father, both of whom had been convicted of piracy. An unclaimed pardon issued by King William sat atop a map and an order signed by Harrison Kendrick to seize the Drake family and every servant.

"Sarah told me that Father Henri had given her the Bible," Talon said quietly. "I've been in a quandary deciding how I was going to get back into your house on Hispaniola and finish Kendrick's search."

Observing his former nemesis, Gabriel finally took a swig from the bottle. "I've been in a quandary myself." He crossed his ankles. "The book has been here on board this ship the whole time."

"Does your sudden capitulation have something to do with my sister, or your sense of conscience? Did you decide that you'd made an error twelve years ago when you let Kendrick hand us over to you?"

Gabriel's hands went around the bottle of Madeira as he contemplated the truth of that last observation. "How long have you had those papers in your possession?"

"They came to me unexpectedly about two years ago."

"Father Henri must have known that if Kendrick found that book, no one would ever be able to prove anything against him. And as long as Kendrick had Sarah as hostage, he would never worry about you again."

Talon leaned his head back. There was tenseness in the movement.

"Your family is innocent," Gabriel said.

"It's not as simple as walking into the court and presenting evidence, or I'd have done that long ago. The English officer who was going to testify on my behalf in England disappeared before he could do so. He was taking the *Dark Fury* back when you seized the ship last year.

Gabriel's gaze traced the golden spirals on the Bible. *Sí,* that incident had been the beginning of his troubles . . . and the downfall of his whole life. Last year Gabriel had captured the *Dark Fury* but lost it to Marcus. He'd lost his sister to the pirate as well. But he'd never murdered any officers on that ship.

"Does Sarah know the truth about what happened to her family?" Gabriel asked.

"We've talked."

Gabriel nodded toward the pardon. "Why didn't you take that?"

"I received the pardon too late. Kendrick had held on to it. Too much was at stake for him to allow anyone in my family to go free."

Then Drake told Gabriel the story, beginning with Henry Morgan's raid on Puerto Bello twenty-two years before, a raid Gabriel knew well enough. "My father had been one of his captains," Drake said. "Some of the gold taken out disappeared before it ever made it to Port Royal. Speculation laid the suspicion on one of Morgan's captains. The clime was right for intrigue, and when it comes to gold, most people will believe anything." Talon flicked a finger at the map. "My life was destroyed for this. A coastal sea chart of the waters and shoals surrounding Puerto Bello."

"But the map doesn't explain the charges of treason lodged against you."

"My mother was Spanish," Drake said. "She'd been excommunicated when she married my father. Returning to Spain was forbidden to her after that. But she was still Spanish and was never truly accepted in English society either. So we never lived in England. Unfortunately, the political clime in Jamaica wasn't so kind to those of Spanish blood either, considering our constant state of war. When this map surfaced, trumped-up charges were brought against my mother for spying. The chief justice at the time confiscated the letters of marque my father and I both carried, then claimed never to have issued them. I wasn't there that day the soldiers came to the house. But Marcus was . . . and Sarah." Talon sat back, crossing his arms. "All my father had to do was tell the secrets of the map and they would drop the charges of treason. Since there were no secrets, he could tell nothing. The rest as they say is history."

"How many people are left alive to bear witness against you?"

"You took care of the last one in Port Royal." Drake closed the Bible. "Answer me this, Espinosa. How is it someone like you was so well acquainted with Kendrick?"

"Kendrick was in my pocket before you even knew who he was. I won't go into detail as to why I put him there, but he had his uses."

"And it didn't go against your Spanish honor?"

Drake held out his empty glass and Gabriel sloshed wine over the rim. "There is no honor in war." He swigged from the bottle. "Only in winning."

Drake met Gabriel's dark gaze. "I was not prepared for the woman Sarah has become since she met you," he suddenly said. "She'd always been so fragile. But only yesterday, she threatened to stitch my lips shut if I continued to interfere between you two."

Gabriel slumped back. That Sarah would defend him so staunchly to her brother cracked the last vestige of uncertainty. "*Sí*, she can be very forceful."

"Your marriage to her is legal, Espinosa," Drake said as if he only just resigned himself to that fact. "Before I learned that you were in Hispaniola, I went to Martinique. Father Henri had registered everything properly with the bishop. It looks as if he had you picked for her husband before you took your vows." At Gabriel's disbelief, Drake crossed his arms, clearly misinterpreting Gabriel's response. "You didn't think I'd have allowed you near my sister if you weren't married, did you?"

Gabriel sat with his back against the bulkhead and let his eyes close. Silence stretched between them then and gradually melted away until there was naught but the sounds of the ship around them.

"That's good to hear, Drake." Then he turned his head and

for a long time said nothing. "You will never have peace until your name is cleared," he finally said.

Drake leaned forward and rested an elbow on the table. "Treason isn't a crime to skip around," he said, his gaze on the Bible. "Neither Marcus nor I can ever go back to Port Royal, and I wouldn't get within a league of English shores to state my case before the admiralty beard." Their eyes met across the table. "I have a family, and frankly, I'm just too damn sentimental about their safety. I won't gamble their lives. Or anyone else's."

For Gabriel, to whom honor meant everything, the statement was a profound contradiction to all that he believed. "I think . . . I would never give up."

"And what of you, Espinosa? Proud, stoic, ruthlessly honest. For all of your duty to king and country, Father Antonio was very precise about the poor state of your current affairs. Is it true that you've been ordered to Spain? Maybe to marry a certain Spanish doña?"

Something savage in the reality of that statement, something physical that tore through him at the thought that nothing at all had really changed. He started to ask if Father Antonio also told Drake that Gabriel could lose his daughter.

"*Sí.*" He dangled a fist ever one knee. "My former father-in-law has authorized my arrest. It appears that my decisions of late have been what one might call imprudent. I have been . . . summoned."

"Who is your father-in-law?"

"Don Hernández y Diego Garcia, Duke of Valencia, Viceroy of New Spain, and diplomat to the court of King Charles." He waved an impatient hand. "I give you my esteemed relative by marriage."

Drake looked impressed. Then realizing the import of Gabriel's statement, he straightened. "Christ . . . you're not jesting. What are you planning to do?"

With a slow exhale, Gabriel lifted his gaze to the slanted ceiling barely inches from his head. A watermark drew a thin ragged circle across the timber. "I have a daughter, Drake. Everything I am is Spain. How does a man tear out his soul to save his heart? And still have something left so that he can live with himself?"

"How do you live with yourself if you do either, Spaniard?"

Swinging from a sense of frustration to indelible yearning, Gabriel suddenly considered what it would take to be a part of Sarah's family and her English world, but vanquished the thought before it took root. Not only would the task be impossible considering who he was, he would never jeopardize his daughter's future in such a manner.

And therein lay the core of his problems. The pith of his existence summed up in one thought, one sentence; the reality that would swallow his future. The status and security he'd sacrificed his life to attain would be the very bane that defeated him in the end.

But whatever vulnerability had surged through him crashed to a stumbling halt in the path of that thought. His disgust was at himself for not having had the moral courage to fight for Sarah sooner: when he'd known the state of his affairs was in question. Sarah belonged to him. His life was his own. No government or church would take that away.

Dawn was a pale blur on the horizon when Gabriel returned to his cabin a long time later. Half-drunk, he shut the door. No lanthorn marked his path as he walked to the bunk. Sarah sat against the wall, her arms wrapped around her knees. They looked at each other in the shadows and said nothing. She wore her clothes.

"Is it true?" she asked.

So she'd been at Drake's door, listening. But for how long?

Scattered moonlight defined the gentle rise and fall of her chest beneath the soft cambric cloth of her shirt. She had given him back so much of the life that he'd lost when Felicity died.

And he smiled.

Sí . . . he actually smiled, the simple act unprecedented as warmth rushed through him.

He loved her.

He loved her more than the sea, more than the very air he breathed.

It hadn't always been so for him. Lust, sympathy, and duty to protect her had driven him relentlessly in the beginning.

Then somewhere, perhaps in the rectory with Father Henri
when she'd refused to marry him, he had become aware of the
kind of monster the world perceived him to be. Never once
doubting that she wasn't good enough to be the bride of Don
Gabriel Cristobel de Espinosa y Ramírez, she'd made him
feel as if the honor and privilege of marrying a Drake were all
his—poor, blind Sarah Drake, who'd rapidly shown him that
she was neither.

Had Sarah been any other kind of woman but the bright
existential force that blew through his life like a hurricane,
something of his old character might still be left standing to
defend the choice he was about to make. She was no coward
to trust so unerringly in a future that ached to crush her softness. He would be no less than her equal.

"Is it *true*?" Sarah demanded.

Finally, she saw something cross his expression. "I will return to Spain." His voice was flat. But his eyes were fire. "I
have been gone too long. And they have become too much
like tyrants, *sí*?"

"Will you marry Doña Betina? Are you under arrest because you came after me—"

"No." Then she watched as he grinned, shocked that he
was not afraid. "And yes."

Sarah stood. The distant sky outside was restless with
thunder.

Her fingers curled into a fist. Part of her wanted to vent her
outrage. But she couldn't. Not when she understood his position better than she wanted to, when fear kicked her so ruthlessly. He had protected her and loved her for so long, even
when he'd tried to tell her long ago that he couldn't stay married to her. Now he would go back to Spain to fight this war
without her.

"Don't go, Gabriel."

His mouth moved against her hair and pressed against her
temple.

"I should have followed my instinct in Port Royal and kept
away from you," she said in a desperate whisper, reluctant to
yield.

He buried his hands in her hair. "*Sí*, you could have tried."

"What about Christina?"

He pulled back just before he kissed her. "She will stay with you until I return."

"Perhaps we could all live on a deserted island." She tried to alleviate the knot in her throat. His lips were hot on her neck. "Is there such a place left? We could build a house in the trees like the monkeys. Forget the world."

Gabriel cupped her chin. "I'd make a poor monkey, *chica*."

Then, breathing in the sound of his name, his mouth descended on hers, and Sarah ceased to be afraid anymore.

Later he told her what Talon had said about their marriage. Much later even than that, they stood on the balcony outside the room and watched the distant storm clouds diminish.

And all the while, Gabriel kept the *Felicity* sailing with only half her canvas spread, in little hurry to reach New Providence.

So that when he finally arrived, he'd missed Don Hernández by three days.

And his daughter was gone.

Chapter Twenty

Still wearing breeches and one of Gabriel's silk shirts, Sarah sat alone on the wooden stairs beneath the veranda overhang. Built high on a stone foundation, Marcus's house dominated the inland forest that surrounded the secluded beach. The residence was a testament to the determination and skill of the man who'd forged a new life out of the land.

She had yet to see Marcus. He'd been across the island last night when they'd arrived.

Today rain surrounded Sarah. Sheets of crystalline glass fell in cooling torrents over the terraced gardens and the dirt road that led away from the house, past the fields into town. Magnificent palms fringed the distant alcove from which Sarah watched the *Felicity* twist against her moorings. *Dark Fury*'s stately masts tipped through the treetops farther away.

Gabriel's voice carried from the house. A house remarkably empty, as servants fled, but not so far that they couldn't listen to every word Gabriel said to his sister and to Stefan. He spoke so volubly in Spanish that Sarah couldn't catch the words that spilled out the open window. Last night Gabriel's wrath had been restrained by the sheer will of a man who knew the dangers of emotions. Today he was the father who must now deal with the loss of his child. Sarah heard in him the man so many people feared: dark, dangerous, and defiant to the point of self-destruction. She also heard what nobody else did: he was terribly frightened. Not only for his daughter, who had been spirited away and would now be used as a pawn to control him, but for *her* as well. He knew, as she did, that when he left this island, he'd not return as her husband or the man he'd become during their time together.

Don Hernández had arrived at Marcus's home four days ago. Cori had told her that Christina had not been afraid, that Don Hernández had been overtly adoring of his granddaughter.

That Christina seemed to reciprocate the affection did not ease the fact that she'd been kidnapped, or that Liandra had been endangered. With three warships guarding the bay, the implied threat of violence had left no doubt that Don Hernández would not hesitate in resorting to brutality should he have been denied his granddaughter.

Gabriel would have gone after the tyrant last night had it not been for the fact that the *Felicity* was not equipped for the voyage to Spain. *Dark Fury* was. But Talon had stopped him cold.

"And what will you do if you catch them?" her brother had asked.

Liandra had been the only person able to penetrate the stone fortress that had suddenly become Gabriel's heart.

Sarah didn't know how to ease his plight, especially when her own panic had suppressed her emotional insight. She only knew that she'd inadvertently been the root of the volatile forces that had upended his life. If not for her presence, he would have returned to Spain long ago. Nor had she fully appreciated Gabriel's dilemma. Sarah had naïvely believed that in time love could surmount all political and economic boundaries that separated them. That surviving adversity would merely be a matter of enduring. Hadn't her own past taught her that much?

But a higher echelon of rules governed men of Gabriel's station. And if such a man deviated from the mores, he was systematically annihilated, whittled away to a nub of his former self. Spain had effectively cut Gabriel off at the knees, demonstrating even to El Condor that Spain's majesty held dominion over all her subjects and no man was immune to her laws, her courts, or her Church. If he didn't yield now, Sarah was sure that he would simply be made to vanish.

Last night she'd found refuge with Cori. Cori, her spritely, flame-haired, mother-of-all-reasoning friend, who had dared to lecture her for running away. And she'd been right.

Sarah wept through panic and self-pity, gathered her strength, and resolved to stand with Gabriel. She would not perish when he left her. Already she'd decided to find a way to carry on Father Henri's work. Life would continue as it always had.

Leaving Cori asleep, come dawn, Sarah had walked back to the house to await Gabriel, when she heard him already inside. Then the clouds had opened. Inhaling a ragged breath, Sarah huddled on the porch stairs beneath the overhang to await his exit. The turquoise waters, dimpled now by rain, drew her gaze.

Talon suddenly appeared beside her. Sarah turned to meet his concerned gaze. "He went looking for you last night," he said.

Her brother had changed his attire. A white silk shirt fluttered in the wind. Buff breeches and a sleeveless jerkin added a hint of respectability to his dark appearance. She suddenly felt in need of a hot bath. "I have no clothes." She flicked at the breeches she wore.

"I'm sure something can be found here. Regan isn't that much taller than you."

Regan was his wife and, at one time, Sarah's dearest friend. She hadn't even spoken to Regan since they'd arrived. In the house, Gabriel's voice had quieted, and Sarah vaguely wondered if poor Stefan had survived the tongue-lashing. "I was remiss last night by leaving everyone," she said. "But I had no desire to socialize."

"Our daughter kept her up all last night," Talon said. "Regan's still abed or would be out here now to see you."

"What about your home on Martinique?" Sarah looked at her brother in earnest. "Are you never going back there? Have I ruined your chances there as well?"

"What happened in Martinique wasn't your fault, Sarah."

"Perhaps not directly. But if I hadn't been such a coward in the first place, I would have come here with you and the last six months would never have happened. Father Henri would still be alive. . . ."

Talon walked down the steps; then turning, braced a foot

on the step below where she sat. He looked her directly in the eyes. "You were never responsible for what happened to any of us, in the past or on Martinique. But you can lay the sins at your feet, Sarah, if that will make you feel better. Just don't do it in front of me. I have no stomach for it." He swept past her up the stairs.

Before Sarah could reply, the sound of a fast-running horse came up the road, and a dark-haired man, soaked to the flesh, rounded the corner of the yard in a spray of mud. Reining in the horse, he leaped out of the saddle before anyone reached him to take the horse.

Blood drummed in her ears as she came to her feet, the man approaching at a run looked too much like Talon not to be Marcus. Almost the same height and breadth of shoulder as Talon. His face was more angular, perhaps because his teeth were set in a clench. His wet hair, plastered now to his head, curled at his nape. A shadow as dark as his eyelashes rimmed his jaw. He looked about as respectable as a pirate and certainly as lethal as he swept past her up the stairs toward Talon.

"Hell, Talon! I came as soon as I received—" His voice stopped. His back went straight, and he spun around.

Sarah watched his expression bounce from confused disbelief as his gaze raked her rumpled form to astonishment when he looked into her eyes. His feet carried him down a step. "Sarah?" For a full second, it seemed the earth had halted its rotation. "You can see?" His voice was a whisper. "When?"

Talon's hand touched him on the shoulder. "It's a long story."

Marcus scooped her up, and suddenly he was whirling her in a circle. They were in the rain surrounded by pansies and trellised scarlet runners. "Look at you! Look at your hair!"

Tasting the clouds and the sky, Sarah wrapped her arms around her brother's neck and started laughing with him. She needed to laugh. She needed to grab on to the belief that something wonderful could survive the darkness that had descended over her life. "You look nothing like I remember, Marcus Drake. You're handsome!"

He laughed. "And you, my silver-haired angel, look like a pixie doll." He lowered her to the wet ground. "A wet one to be sure. Why are you dressed like—?" He suddenly came to a halt.

Sarah brushed the hair and rain from her eyes and blinked. Gabriel and Liandra stood on the porch, watching them. Liandra's eyes, as they went over Marcus, were the turquoise color of the sea. Painted by her mixed heritage of English and Spanish blood, she was a portrait of refinement as she stood beside her brother.

Gabriel's hand rested at his waist just above the hilt of his cutlass. Polished boots reached his knees. The hem of his black velvet jerkin opened over his breeches. Looking very much the Spanish aristocrat, he stood with a certain arrogance. Sarah was again reminded how much separated her world from his. With the rain beating against her head and shoulders, she grew utterly still.

Marcus stepped away from her. "What the hell have you done to her, Espinosa? She looks like a field-worker. Couldn't you afford a decent gown?"

"Marcus!" Still standing in the rain, Sarah was suddenly aware that her wet clothes clung to every feminine curve of her body.

"Good morning, *chica*." Gabriel's gaze wrapped around hers. "I missed you last night." Whatever fury she'd heard in Gabriel's voice earlier remained in check as he shifted his gaze to survey her brother. "Good to see you again, Marcus." Sarcasm laced the words.

"Son of a bitch!" Marcus would have launched at Gabriel had Talon not been there to stop him.

"You're out of line, Marcus."

"The hell I am. That bastard put my wife and son in danger. They could have been killed because no one bothered to warn us that we'd have the whole of Spain down our throats! Your wife and daughter are here as well, Talon."

Gabriel didn't reply. But his hand tightened over the hilt of his cutlass. Liandra rushed down the stairs to fling herself into Marcus's arms. Talking gently against his cheek, she held him tightly, and for an instant as rain began to lessen, Marcus closed his eyes, before snapping them open again to impale the granitelike figure standing alone on the porch.

"Do you know where I've been for the past two days?" he

growled. "In Nassau reassuring the officials that I have not in-advertently started a war with Spain. We don't have anywhere else to go, Espinosa. Not in this whole damn world. I won't have you destroy what we've built here. Not when I've spent too many years of my life as a fugitive . . . Where is my son?" he suddenly asked Liandra.

"He is upstairs. Come." Liandra took his hand. A hand that trembled with emotion, Sarah realized as she watched them begin to leave.

Marcus hesitated. Turning to her, he cupped her cheek. "I'm sorry, Sarah," he said quietly.

Then together he and Liandra walked out of the rain, past Gabriel who still hadn't moved, and into the house.

"I can't atone for my brother." Talon moved to the stairs. "I understand too much how he feels. But I am sorry about your daughter."

Gabriel's gaze locked with her brother's. Then as if something went over him, his expression became less stiff, more vulnerable perhaps, as the harsh, impenetrable mask of El Condor fell away. He nodded. Talon walked past him into the house, and Sarah was left looking at Gabriel.

"Your brother is correct," he said after a moment, his voice strangely awkward. "You need new attire."

Sarah looked down at herself, her pale cheeks flushing. "At least they are clean now."

When her response elicited no reply, she lifted her gaze and found herself caught in his tender regard. "I shouldn't have left you last night," she said.

"I was an ass. Not very good company either."

Then he stepped down off the porch and into her arms.

Indistinguishable from the shadows, Gabriel moved quietly into the house. A half-moon waned just above the tall treetops. Clouds skittered across the sky, marking the approaching storm. He'd waited two days for the wind to blow, but the decision that drove him now had naught to do with the weather.

A scrape of flint followed as Gabriel lit the candle he carried before he set it carefully in the sconce beside the door. Outside, bushes slapped against the house. The noise covered his steps across the study, past bookcases to the desk. Moonlight slanted through the razor-thin opening in the drapes. He knew where to go because he'd seen Talon place the Bible here. He knelt beside the leather armchair and stretched his hand deep into the bottom shelf of the desk. Laying the Bible on the floor, he found and removed the papers inside.

Gabriel possessed no illusion about his life or his future once he left this island.

If he went to Spain, eventually the conquering hero would be mercifully forgiven his misdeeds. After all, what other Spaniard in ten years had accomplished what he had in the name of king and country? He'd return to his daughter, wed Betina . . . and be forever exiled to the sea.

In some way, he understood the politics of his world, and had become tolerant if not indifferent to its customs and expectations. But he'd taken no more from his country than he'd given back tenfold. And in that piece of insight, Gabriel found the reflection of a man the years had helped mold. Relentless, determined, and loyal to the people of Spain. A man who had willingly sacrificed everyone that he'd ever loved in the pursuit of some nameless honor.

He had no want to return to the sea. No desire to fight any more battles, save the one deepest in his heart.

Sarah was the daughter of a hanged pirate wrongly condemned for treason. But Father Henri had put into Gabriel's hands the means to free her.

A cool draft swirled around his calves. The sconce on the wall fluttered. Without lingering another moment, Gabriel shoved the papers in the canvas bag he carried, then placed the Bible back.

He opened the door to peer into the hallway. The hall smelled of beeswax, lemon oil, and a fresh coat of blue paint. Light spilled over the slatted floor. His eyes were on the stairs before he stepped out of the room and saw Liandra standing against the wall.

They looked at each other. Her gaze dropped to the canvas bag tucked beneath his arm before rising again to narrow on his face. "You are leaving?" She crossed her arms. "Without saying good-bye?"

"Sí. They would only stop me." The door closed with a

click behind him. "Especially since it is their ship that I am stealing."

"You're not worried that I'll stop you?"

Gabriel's gaze went over her face. "You know that what I'm doing is the right thing."

Tears filled her beautiful eyes. "Why? You risk your life."

"Once long ago bad things happened to a young boy. That boy carried the shame of someone else's crimes against him his whole life. By conquering Spain's foes, he was trying to conquer his own and doing a poor job at it, until he met someone . . . someone who taught him that nothing in life is truly impossible, including forgetting the unforgivable. If I could repay what I once took away from her, I would do so with my life."

"You think that you are responsible for her family?"

"No. But I am responsible for what happened afterward and for the choices her brothers have had to make in the years since."

"What about Christina?" Liandra's whisper broke. "You leave her to Don Hernández."

"Don Hernández is many things, but he loves Felicity's daughter with his whole being. He might use her to manipulate me"—Gabriel grinned, confident now of his course— "but he will not harm her. And he will learn soon enough that I'll not go down to my knees because he or any man chooses to threaten me."

"If something should happen to you, I will lose you both. I will never see Christina again."

Slim arms suddenly enfolded him and his sister pressed against him. Her cool temple lay against his chin. "I never did ask if you are happy here," he said against her brow.

"Marcus is a wonderful husband."

He smoothed her hair and smiled down at her. "That is very good for him, *querida*."

"You have seen our son?" Her tears were gone now.

"*Sí*, many times these past few days."

"Do you like our house?"

"Your pirate husband has impressed me."

"The *Dark Fury* is no longer a ship of war. Marcus has used it to carry cargo. We've earned enough to buy more land.

His crew settled here. The governor is more lenient than most
when it comes to accepting men of . . . questionable character.
They need settlers here to establish an English colony."

"It is inevitable, I suppose. The English will try to take
over the world."

Her palm cupped his cheek. "Talon and Marcus will not
appreciate that you are going to steal the *Dark Fury*. But it
will make an impressive trophy to present England. I wish I
could be there when you sail her up the Thames."

Upstairs, a door closed. Gabriel met her eyes. She clung to
him. He kissed her one final time before turning on his heel to
let himself out the main door. The yard was empty. The distant beach was deserted. He knew a longboat would be awaiting him a mile down the alcove. Stefan had amassed the
needed crew. Loyalty to the Drakes and a fortune in gold from
him had secured the *Dark Fury* for the needed trek to London.
For the last time, he sought the shadow of his own ship bobbing in the swells. He'd left Sarah asleep there.

Casting his gaze to the sky, he finally set out in a trot, following the freshwater stream past the cooking house. Lush
green vegetation grew on either side of the bank. He continued into the woods until he reached the white sand of the
beach.

"Espinosa!"

Gabriel stepped abruptly beneath the shadows of twin
palms. Marcus appeared just over the bank. He was unarmed
but it made no difference. As Marcus passed the place where
Gabriel hid, he stepped out.

"You wanted to speak to me?" His cutlass stopped Marcus
from turning.

"Christ, Espinosa . . . I saw you leaving the house."

"And that's a crime?"

"I wanted to talk to you. About the other day . . . about losing my temper," his sister's husband said in the ensuing silence. "I wanted you to know that Christina means a lot to all
of us."

"Apology accepted, Drake." Gabriel's cutlass kept Marcus
from turning. "Unfortunately, your benevolence cannot at this
moment be reciprocated. And for *that*, I apologize."

Marcus stiffened. "We've danced these steps before, Espinosa."

"*Sí.*"Gabriel laughed softly, sheathing his cutlass. "And as I recall, *mi amigo*, it ended the same way."

Marcus turned, and Gabriel hit him.

Chapter Twenty-one

A moonless sky stretched across the river Thames, an endless blanket of gloom, as the *Felicity* rode the breath of wind into the heart of London. Late September had brought a chill to the desolate wharves filled now with roaming whores and pickpockets who scattered like discordant shadows in the enveloping mists of dawn.

Sarah stood with a heavy blanket wrapped around her shoulders, watching the city grow in the pearlescent light of a distant day. A stench rose from the water, and she wrinkled her nose, burying her chin deeper into the woolen blanket that had become her cloak during the arduous fifty-two-day Atlantic crossing. In the earliest hours before dawn, the *Felicity* had passed Gravesend on her way to Greenwich. A jumble of wharves, wooden cranes, and timber yards greeted her scrutiny. Beyond the wharves were narrow streets lined with houses. Farther upriver, the main port of London was centered on Custom House Quay. There, arriving ships were moored three and four deep, creating a forest of masts and sails as far as the river bend. Three bodies, tarred and caged, swung from gibbets on the shores of Wapping, a veritable example of maritime law.

Talon's voice carried from the quarterdeck as he spoke to the helm. Heart racing for her brother, she turned to better gauge the tangle of emotions she sensed in his voice, and found herself in his gaze. Then she saw the expression leave his face as he looked ahead of her. Sarah swung around. Her hand went to her chest.

Gabriel had made it to England!

Silhouetted against the approaching day, *Dark Fury* bobbed at her anchor chains. Her tall, stark masts stood apart from the timber of swaying ships, lonely in her grandeur as she languished like an abandoned mistress. Sarah stared at the thirty-four-gun frigate, her infamous black sails furled tightly against the huge masts. Even in bondage, the ship's presence could not be ignored. Her heart pounded as her gaze searched for any hint of the man who had sailed her into the very bastion of English dominion.

Nothing moved on the decks.

Nothing.

Almost four months had passed since she'd last seen Gabriel. Four aching months of not knowing, and now a bitter sense of triumph unfurled in her heart. It had taken a furious Talon five weeks to supply the *Felicity* for the long haul to England. Marcus had remained behind with Regan and Liandra. Without preamble or need to seek permission, Sarah had taken Cori and boarded the *Felicity*. Neither one of her brothers would have allowed her to make the trek, except she was their only witness to crimes that Harrison Kendrick had committed against their family. She would not stand idly by while her husband and brothers fought this battle without her. Armed with pride for Gabriel and the prevailing sense that justice always won, Sarah had crossed the Atlantic with Talon. Although hurricane season made traveling hazardous, they'd endured remarkably good weather.

Sarah reached outside the warmth of her blanket to tent a hand over her eyes and longingly searched the *Dark Fury*. "She's been impounded," Talon said from beside her. His voice held no emotion, a sure harbinger that something dreadful had occurred here.

Then she looked at her brother, his handsome profile stern in the dawning of this beautiful day, and felt a sudden despair. "You must not go ashore," she whispered. She didn't know why Gabriel would have been arrested. England was not at war with Spain. She didn't know if he had failed in his quest.

But it was suddenly very important that she not let Talon risk his life as well.

"He is El Condor, Sarah," her brother said, as if reading the panic in her eyes. "There is not a naval officer or government official in England who doesn't know who he is."

"But he sailed with a legal commission. He cannot be arrested for piracy."

"Hell, Sarah . . . he can be executed for being Catholic. And he damn well knew that before sailing here!"

"Don't leave this ship," she bid. "We'll send someone else ashore to fetch news—"

He placed a gloved finger against her lips. "Whatever he started will be finished . . . one way or another. Your stubborn husband intended to go before the Lord High Admiral himself."

A sudden order came from near the stern to heave the ship to and lay by for boarding. "Customs," Talon said, then he kissed Sarah and told her to get below to the cabin.

But within the walls of the cabin, Sarah found herself prey to her fear. Less than an hour later, a tap on the door awakened Cori. Sarah threw the bolt.

Holding a hat beneath his arm, Talon stood in the doorway. Dressed in a black velvet coat with wide buttoned cuffs and a sapphire waistcoat beneath, he gave a lopsided grin that matched his carelessly tied stark white cravat. Only the tall black boots were out of style with the formal attire.

Cori whistled softly. "Blimey, Cap. You and that Spaniard know how to fill a jacket right proper. Respectability suits you."

"Thank you, Cori. It's been a long time since I've worn anything . . . civil."

"Where is *Dark Fury*'s crew?" Sarah asked.

"They were taken to Marshalsea prison and held for almost a month. There was no evidence against them and since most had voluntarily surrendered, they were acquitted."

"Most?"

"Seven were tried at Old Bailey's. Three were hanged. Seems they were deserters from various naval crews. It doesn't take but one witness to condemn a man these days."

Sarah's knees started to buckle. She'd seen what remained of the men hanging from gibbets for the tide to consume.

"Milady." Cori's hands braced her. "Sit down."

"No . . ." She straightened and, looking her brother in the eye, asked, "Where is Gabriel? Tell me, Talon," she whispered when he didn't speak. "What did you find out?"

"They took him off the *Dark Fury* in chains. That's all I know. He wasn't taken to Marshalsea or Newgate like the others." The tips of his roughened fingers lifted her chin. "If they come for you in the next few days, it will be to testify. I can't guarantee your safety. But whatever has happened, we have not yet been clapped in chains. That is a good sign."

After he left, Sarah ran to the stern and pressed against the window. She watched the uniformed men who had boarded take Talon away.

During the following days a growing crowd gathered on the planked walk at the docks. Their raucous voices grew as their numbers increased. Shutting the window coverings, Sarah ate her meals in the darkness with Cori, and when terror threatened to overtake her, she laid her hand on her belly, on the child that grew inside her. And waited. Watched as the sun set over the city for a third day.

A pounding on the door roused Sarah from sleep. She sat at the desk, her cheek cradled against her arm. "Milady?" Cori shook her. Sarah wiped a hand across her eyes. "Look who came aboard!"

Looking past Cori, Sarah's gaze stopped abruptly on Stefan and Berto, who stood near the door. She surged to her feet, and heedless of the display, ran into Stefan's arms. Then she kissed Berto on the cheek. "You're alive! We didn't know."

Their hair was in need of a pair of shears and their clothes had not been cleaned for weeks. In the face of her excitement, they looked ashamed, and Sarah drew back.

"We are hungry, Doña Sarah," Stefan said. "And very glad to see this ship. But Don Gabriel will not like that you have come here."

Sarah instructed Cori to bring a meal. "Where is he, Sefan? What has happened?"

"None of us were prepared for what happened when we arrived, Don Gabriel most of all. He expected that he would take full responsibility when the authorities came on board. In Spain, it is the *capitán* who bears the punishment for the crew. Most of the crew have found their way home. Others are on the docks waiting to come on board here to leave. Some are trying to get to Spain."

"Your brother, he's been taken to the Lord Chancellor," Berto said as they sat on the bench beneath the window. "That is why a crowd has gathered outside. They know who you are. They know that El Condor's wife is out here and they've been trying to get a glimpse."

"It was the same when the *Dark Fury* arrived, and they took Don Gabriel off in chains." Stefan snorted. "These fickle *ingleses* cheer for a man who outmaneuvered the king's every vessel to sail down the throat of fortified stronghold, only to gather eagerly as they now await his execution on Tower Hill."

Sarah's heartbeat stopped. *"What?"*

"I am sorry, Doña Sarah." Stefan's eyes sheened with moisture. "They have him at the Tower. They say only the highest-ranked prisoners are kept there. The place is a fortress."

"Why?" Sarah whispered. "Why has he been condemned?"

"He's been charged with Harrison Kendrick's murder, despite all of it being circumstantial, considering there is no body and no witnesses left alive who actually saw him commit the deed."

Sarah shook her head. "What are you talking about?"

"Nine hours after we left Port Royal on June seventh, an earthquake struck and wiped out the city." Berto sat back. "They say less than ten acres survived the quake. The city is in ruins, sunk into the sea. Those who got away came to England on the few ships that survived the tidal waves."

Sarah remembered the mass exodus of ships they'd seen and felt a momentary stab of horror for what they'd endured.

"Some who arrived here before us claimed to have heard that Kendrick had been killed and that El Condor had been in Port Royal."

"What did Gabriel say in his defense?"

"He did not lie, Doña Sarah."

No, her Spanish husband had too much honor to lie even if it meant saving his life. Unwilling to bear the grisly picture of Gabriel's neck on the block, Sarah went to stand beside the window. Her eyes were gritty. She blinked away blinding tears. She was suddenly tired. So completely exhausted. "If the powers here wish to murder El Condor, it will not be for Harrison Kendrick's death. I must find a way to get to Talon."

"The high court convened yesterday. I know where they are holding your brother."

Sarah's heart jolted. "Then Talon has not been cleared either."

"Since this ship has not been impounded, it is very probable that with Don Gabriel's earlier testimony, your brother is safe."

Stefan's confidence was not proved unfounded, and three days later Sarah received the summons she'd been waiting for—nay, that she'd been praying to receive. Wearing a gown of the finest white linen, she met the soldiers who had been dispatched to take her to Westminster. Wedged between the red-coated guards, she threaded her way through the crowd gathered on the docks, their whispers as she passed swirling through her head like bees to a hive.

Flanked by guards on horseback, her carriage rattled over cobblestones of Cheapside, past the royal exchange, with the square keep of the Tower just ahead. The coach clattered beneath the iron and wood portal into the infamous Tower grounds. Behind her, the gate closed on Cori and the others who had followed from the ship. She would be taken by barge to stand before the high court of admiralty, a civil law court closely identified with the king's prerogative and the rim of England's jurisprudence domain.

Morning mists framed the distant spires of Westminster Abby. All around her an early autumn had painted the trees brown, a lifeless parody against the backdrop of such extravagant beauty. Two lines of fortifications with twelve inner towers girdled White Tower. A moat, fed by the Thames, surrounded the outer wall. Men garbed in colorful uniforms guarded the gateway through which she passed. Such majesty was in complete disparity to the barbaric spectacle that would take place on Tower Hill if she could not find a way to free Gabriel.

Aided by a kindly hand, Sarah was helped from the carriage and guided to the place where a barge awaited.

And then she saw him.

"Gabriel!"

Wearing a pair of black breeches, boots, and a rumpled white silk shirt, Gabriel stood at his full height as he turned at the sound of his name from his place on the barge. Chains secured his wrists and ankles. His hair had grown unruly and had to be restrained by a leather thong, emphasizing his unshaven face. His dark eyes widened in surprise when they stopped on her, then narrowed with torment. He cast his gaze around as if to see who might have heard her cry.

Realizing what she'd done, Sarah stepped back into the shadows of the carriage. But it was too late. The soldiers guarding the barge hastily separated them. She did not see Gabriel again until she entered the High Lord's chamber.

Talon stood on one side of the crowded room and Gabriel, still in chains, stood on the other. A casement window opened to the river. A crowd had gathered on the benches at the back of the room.

Sarah was called to a black wooden stall, where a bewigged man ushered her inside. Unsure in whose defense she spoke, she faced the front of the room, standing. Her palms damp, she clasped them at her side. One man sat on a wooden bench, flanked by two equally authoritative figures wearing black wigs and robes. Her testimony was long. She'd never before spoken in public. Heart racing, she calmly began her story as they requested from the day the soldiers had come to her house. She told of witnessing her mother's murder and what it did to her life until Gabriel had come to Martinique. Her voice never faltered during the grueling hours that followed, her calm never abated. A mist had appeared in her eyes when she spoke of her kidnapping and subsequent rescue. And once, asked to describe Harrison Kendrick, she flung her gaze around the room, afraid that he might still be alive! But he wasn't, and they'd merely wanted to confirm that she spoke of the same man whom they all knew: a man who had outwardly been a pillar of English society, a man whom they could not reconcile with the image painted by so many these past weeks.

Then her testimony was over.

Sarah glanced at Talon to ask him what would happen next, and as a guard escorted her to the back of the room, her gaze swung to Gabriel. His smile, hinting at so much more than pride, touched her with sudden splendor.

Other testimony followed, and with dismay, Sarah listened to the condemning words of English captains who had felt the bite of El Condor's guns. It was Gabriel who was on trial for his life here.

Gabriel!

He'd earned both the respect and enmity of the British navy. Outside, the crowd gathered in the street for a chance to glimpse the Vulture. Yet, even in chains, Gabriel had not surrendered to British authority. It showed in his bearing and his pride. He was El Condor to the core of his being.

The myth.

But to her, he was only Gabriel. Father to Christina and father to her child. An honorable man who had boldly come to England to right a wrong perpetuated against her family.

But when the chief high justice raised his voice and asked if Gabriel would swear to the Act of Supremacy, Sarah knew to the depths of her soul that her husband would no more renounce his faith than he would his country. She knew before the gavel fell and the justice announced that he would be taken to Tower Hill and executed for high treason that nothing could save him.

Sarah stood. Pain seared her breast. Talon had turned, and she knew he was trying to reach her through the crowd. She didn't belong in this place or this country. These were not her people.

"Is betraying his faith and his country any less of an offense than murder?" she cried, shocking the noisy court into silence. Her long flowing sleeves covered her clenched fists. "You cannot condemn him for murder. You cannot condemn him for crimes on the seas, or you would have to condemn your own captains as well! So you condemn him because he will not renounce his *faith*?"

"Stop, Sarah!" Gabriel's forceful command spun her around.

Sunlight from the window gleamed on his icy black hair and defined the shadow of his body beneath the white shirt. Sarah flew past the guards into his arms, pinning his chained hands between them. "I won't let you die. I won't!"

He pulled her into his arms and pressed her face against his shirt. "Stop!" he rasped against her hair. "Do you understand?"

"You can't die . . ." she sobbed into his shirt. "You can't!"

"You will leave on the morrow, Sarah," he whispered into her hair. "I beg of you to do so. I want you out of this city. Swear to me, Sarah . . . please. Your brother is free. Go with him."

"Who . . . who will take you home, Gabriel?" she whispered.

"*Por Dios,* Sarah . . ."

She clung to him as he buried his cheek against her shoulder, and she felt in his proud, corded grip the desperate restraint not to weep. Taking her face between his chained hands, he kissed her lips.

He wore no cravat, and the scar on one side of his neck was visible. On Martinique when he'd been unconscious, she'd touched the scar and the pulse it protected beneath. But what would protect his pulse when he laid his neck against the block . . .

She screamed when the guards tore her away and Gabriel was taken from the room. There was a sudden rush as Talon pulled her from the court into an adjoining chamber and slammed the door.

Her chest heaving in panic and fury, she spun on her brother. In the darkness and muted silence of the room, they both glared at each other. "Not a word," he hissed. "Not a single goddamn word, Sarah. Or you'll find yourself beside your husband tomorrow."

"How can you stand there?" she rasped. "Knowing what he did for you? We have men on the *Felicity*—"

"Sarah," he warned again. "You will be forgiven once for your outburst considering your emotional and physical state. But I won't be able to save you if you speak another word."

"You didn't come back to the ship, Talon. Why not?"

Suddenly he smiled. "Do you think I've been sitting around doing nothing this past week?"

"You knew this trial would end this way?" she accused in horror.

"He had to be cleared of murder, and you did that for him."

"I don't understand," she whispered.

"Come." He took her into his arms. "You will soon enough."

The carriage stopped near nightfall in an isolated hamlet off the river Thames. Gabriel stood at the doorway to the dilapidated chapel rectory as a guard knelt and released the chains on his ankles. The air smelled musty and stale, as if death lingered in the walls of this place. Disgust twisted his gut. That or fear. He'd faced his own mortality so often in the past that to do so now with anything less than courage shattered the last vestiges of his own image that he'd held like a shield over his heart. Perhaps it was more than shame that violated the sanctity inside. It was a lifetime of good-byes that he didn't say and a world of sunrises that he would never see again. It was never seeing Sarah or his daughter or Liandra again.

Strangely, the chains on his wrists followed his ankle chains to the floor, and he rubbed his palms over the bruises. He'd never been given last rites before. He wondered vaguely if the English church had such a ritual.

The guard reached around Gabriel and opened the heavy wooden portal. Gabriel stepped inside and came to an abrupt stop. Behind him the door closed. Don Hernández stood in the center of the room. Gabriel couldn't have been more surprised had the man been the Holy Virgin. They stood staring at each other. The window slats were drawn. Candles fluttered in brass sconces on the walls. The smell of wax permeated the shadows.

"You have come so far to watch me die, Don Hernández?"

"It's a wonder I am here at all. You left me in La Habana cooling my heels and unable to face my own men for your defiance."

"You tried to kidnap my daughter and ruin my marriage. You *did* kidnap my daughter—"

"*Sí,*" the man sighed with all the grace of a bull. "Now I see why my daughter was so in love with you. You are impossible," Don Hernández continued as he sat in one of the two leather chairs that encompassed the table. A black goatee framed the man's mouth. Brown eyes looked over his nose as he leaned back in the chair and crossed his arms. "I cannot have Christina's father executed for an English heretic. Can I? I had to know," he finally said. "I had to know the kind of man you were, where your loyalties were."

Gabriel shook his head in sudden confusion. "My loyalties?" he whispered in disbelief. "My loyalties have always been with Spain."

"Had you renounced your faith or your king, I would not be here," Don Hernández said. "And tomorrow you would go to the block."

Overtaken by sudden rage, Gabriel took a step forward.

"*¡Ay yi!* You have a bad temper, Don Gabriel. If you kill me, then you will not hear what I have to say."

"*Bastardo.* You had no right to play with my life up there in that court. No right to play with Sarah's life."

"What happened in that courtroom was no act. There is something very noble about a man who sails down the throat of an enemy and risks his life to repay a debt. The romance of it all is as dangerous as you are on the deck of your ship. England is currently at war with the Netherlands and wishes to preserve whatever peace can be found with Spain and France," he said. "Executing you will not be the way to achieve that. But neither can they allow your image to stand in people's minds. You are very beloved, Don Gabriel. The men who sailed with me here, who once served you, are proof of that. But the government here also wants you out of the way."

Gabriel could no longer stand and dropped into the chair across from Don Hernández. "What are you saying?"

"I have not become a leader of our people because I am hotheaded," Don Hernández snapped petulantly. "Clearly, you will never be a diplomat. And your brilliant military career is ruined beyond repair." He leaned forward on his elbows. "Lest you think that you are suddenly free, allow me to clarify that before you walk out of here, there are certain conditions that you will agree to meet."

Gabriel braced for the inevitable. He looked away, unwilling to allow Don Hernández to see his eyes. Unwilling to look at the man while being told that his marriage would be annulled. Unwilling to be bullied and threatened, even now. Yet willing to agree to almost anything to keep his head from the block.

"Your peerage has been attained by His Catholic Majesty," Don Hernández said over Gabriel's thoughts. "There is nothing I can do for that, and even if I could, I would not. You may be the father of my granddaughter, but I am also a soldier and a diplomat and I know that you have not answered charges of sedition or other accusations that have been brought against you."

Gabriel understood this, so said nothing as his gaze found solace in the scars that marked the table.

"As of now you have been stripped of your lands in Spain just to pay the reparation to free you today. I have tried to hold what I could for Christina's sake. In addition, I have made an oath to the *inglés* king William that you will never raise arms again against England. In so doing, I have made an arrangement. Rather than see you returned to Spain and brought to trial all over again, I have something else to offer that I think benefits us all."

Gabriel looked up when Don Hernández withdrew a packet from inside his burgundy vest. "Call this a belated wedding gift, if you will, for you and the former Lady Sarah Drake. I was sitting in the judge's antechamber and heard everything that she said. I also heard her commit treason when she begged her brother to raise arms against the crown to free you." He chuckled. "I would have tried to meet this exemplary bride of yours, but I was not there for social reasons and you were not yet free. Word of your arrest reached Spain weeks ago and I have been here trying to keep that head of yours attached to your shoulders."

Gabriel dropped his gaze to the parchment. With both palms, he spread the vellum over the table. His hands shook.

"It's a land grant for you and those who choose to follow. Sixty thousand acres in New Spain, north of the Rio Bravo, on the banks of the Nueces. We have a rich settlement in Coahuila, but the king wishes to establish a presence further north in Tejas. Currently there are only a handful of missions. We need settlers, families to raise cattle and crops, and there are a hundred fifty men out there willing to follow you for a piece of that grant."

Lifting his gaze, Gabriel stared in shock at Don Hernández.

"It will not be an easy life for you or your bride, but it will be a new start. If you are strong, your children and their children will shape the New World and make it a powerful force for any other country to reckon with."

"What about Christina?" Gabriel's voice was a rasp.

"You will send her to live with us in Spain, perhaps during the summer months. And she will stay with us while you are building your home. One day she will marry as her mother did, and I can only pray to Providence that she will be as much trouble to you as Felicity was to me." Don Hernández's solemn brown eyes narrowed. "Despite what you think, I've never regretted my daughter's choice in a husband. You are a good man, Don Gabriel. I would choose no other for the job that you have been asked to do."

Outside the door, voices drew Gabriel's gaze. He closed his eyes. But something awakened his pulse, and edging out of the chair, he struggled to stand. "I will take your bargain, Don Hernández."

"That is good," he laughed. "Because your wife and daughter are outside that door right now, waiting for you. I don't know how much longer the guards can hold them back."

The parchment in Gabriel's hand suddenly trembled. Then he strode across the room and threw open the door. Most of the people he knew were gathered in the small chapel. People who had become his heart. Only Liandra, Marcus, and Talon's wife, who had helped secret his way to England by aiding him to find a crew to sail the *Dark Fury*, were missing. But he would see them soon.

Before he could blink, a small body slammed into his legs. "Papa!" Christina squealed, and he lifted his daughter close. "Look, Papa"—she held up her finger for examination—"I got a scrape."

Gabriel rubbed his cheek over the wound. "It is not so big, *ratón,* for such a brave girl."

His gaze found Sarah.

Tears burned at the back of his throat. Never had Gabriel loved her more than the moment in that courtroom when she'd stood before them all and vowed before man and God to save him.

Sarah Drake *had* saved him.

As surely as he breathed, she had put the air in his lungs.

One day he would thank Father Henri, the man who had given him the blessings in his life. He took three steps until he was toe to toe with his wife. A smile, one that promised so much more than the future, touched her silver eyes.

He shifted his gaze to Talon. "You are free . . . Lord Sunderland," he said, and something went through Drake's eyes as he held Gabriel's gaze. "What will you do?"

"I'll be returning to England with my family," Talon said. "Knowing Marcus, he will go with you to see this new land where you are headed. Aye, he will probably expect you to let him build the whole town, considering you owe him for the bruise on his jaw."

Still holding Christina, Gabriel returned his full attention to his beautiful wife. His hand traveled over Sarah's face and into her hair, the strength in her gaze holding him.

"Blimey, Spaniard." Cori sniffed. "Are ye goin' to stare her to death or kiss her?"

"Take me home, Gabriel," she whispered as his lips crushed hers.

Home.

Home to a place called Texas.

And with Sarah and Christina wrapped in his arms, Gabriel Espinosa, the man once known as the Vulture, stepped out of the darkness and forever into the sunlight.

Seduction Romance

Prepare to be seduced...by the sexy
new romance series from Jove!

Brand-new, full-length, one-night-stand-alone
novels featuring the most seductive heroes in the
history of love...

A HINT OF HEATHER
Rebecca Hagan Lee   0-515-12905-4

A ROGUE'S PLEASURE
Hope Tarr   0-515-12951-8

MY LORD PIRATE
Laura Renken   0-515-12984-4

HERO FOR HIRE
Sheridon Smythe   0-515-13055-9

TO ORDER CALL:

1-800-788-6262

(Ad # B107)

Irish Eyes

From the fiery passion of the Middle Ages, to the
magical charm of Celtic legends, to the timeless allure
of modern Ireland, these brand-new romances will surely
steal your heart away.

❑ **Irish Hope** by Donna Fletcher   0-515-13043-5

❑ **The Irish Devil** by Donna Fletcher   0-515-12749-3

❑ **To Marry an Irish Rogue** by Lisa Hendrix   0-515-12786-8

❑ **Daughter of Ireland** by Sonja Massie   0-515-12835-X

❑ **Irish Moonlight** by Kate Freiman   0-515-12927-5

❑ **Love's Labyrinth** by Anne Kelleher   0-515-12973-9

❑ **Rose in the Mist** by Ana Seymour   0-515-13254-3

❑ **The Irish Bride** by Lynn Bailey   0-515-13014-1

❑ **The Black Swan** by Ana Seymour   0-515-12973-9

❑ **The Highwayman** by Anne Kelleher   0-515-13114-8

TO ORDER CALL:

1-800-788-6262

(Ad #B104)